When Snow Fell

Barbara Kastelin

D1514067

Matador
9 Priory Business Park,
Wistow Road, Kibworth Beauchamp,
Leicestershire. LE8 0RX
Tel: 0116 279 2299
Email: books@troubador.co.uk
Web: www.troubador.co.uk/matador
Twitter: @matadorbooks

ISBN 978 1788037 051

British Library Cataloguing in Publication Data.
A catalogue record for this book is available from the British Library.

Printed and bound by CPI Group (UK) Ltd, Croydon, CR0 4YY
Typeset in 11pt Aldine401 BT by Troubador Publishing Ltd, Leicester, UK

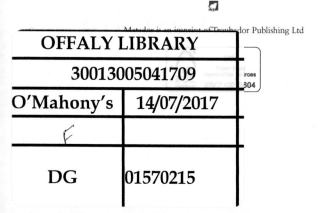

Matador is an imprint of Troubador Publishing Ltd

For Isabelle and Florence

CHAPTER ONE

December 1966

"We are desecrating her." Anna holding one side and Fydo the other, they gently lifted the Ikon from its hook. On the wall above the mantelpiece, the bejewelled Virgin of Kazan had left her mark.

"It's rotten, I agree." Fydo's pallid face, surrounded by tousled hair, looked older than his forty-two years. He was still in his bathrobe.

Together they lay the Ikon on the spread motoring rug and Fydo folded in the edges. They carried the valuable burden from the music room into the vestibule. Anna's mother watched them from the foot of the staircase, her features hard. At that moment the letter-box clattered open and mail slithered into the wire basket, but Valentina did not move. Usually, Anna thought, her mother would have timed the young postman and grabbed the letters before they had settled in the basket. But, immobile now, Mother watched her and Fydo instead.

The swing-door to the back-quarters opened, and their Russian nanny, 'Njanja' Durov, walked towards them, her solid shoes clapping on the marble floor. She unlocked the oak door with practised movements and opened it for them. Her face was tear-streaked.

"It cannot be. It cannot be," she wept and drew a cross over the rug in blessing, as Anna and Fydo carried it out of the house.

Under the portico, Anna hesitated. "I can't do this without my sister."

"Antonina had to do an errand for me in Oxford." Valentina brushed her off. "This has to be gone through today."

"If only there were another way," Anna insisted. "The Virgin has blessed Podzhin Hall all these years. Perhaps if you and Antonina and I got jobs…"

Valentina had come to the door. She laughed through her nose. "My dear child, you have no idea how much it costs to keep up the Hall."

Anna sighed deeply.

"Don't make this worse than it is. Go now. Go."

Anna said nothing more. Mother was the main cause of all this, because she was incapable of curbing her expensive tastes.

They carried the Ikon across the gravel to the black Bentley Continental, and Anna shuddered as they lay the treasure into the open boot.

On the steps stood Valentina and Njanja, and up in Countess Olga's bedroom the curtains were pulled apart, but Anna did not see her grandmother's face. Viscount Sasha's room was hermetically sealed with thick festoon curtains. *And my twin sister is absent on such an important day!*

Fydo closed the boot. He did not wish his niece luck but squeezed her arm in comfort or protest.

Anna sat in the car and turned the key. Thank God, the engine started first time. Slowly she drove around the oval pond on crunchy gravel and away towards the gate, and she thought of a hearse bearing off the dearest member of the family. Ponderously she turned the heavy car through the bends in the village and accelerated gingerly into the straight stretch beyond. It was a cloud-laden December morning, and the verge was candied still with frost.

There was a pinking in the engine. *What if Smelly Ben gave out now?* Mother had originally nicknamed the Bentley for its strong leather smell, and as if to live up to its name the smell had not diminished but increased over the years. There were more than a hundred and thirty thousand miles on the clock. Nowadays, it was normally driven only by the gardener, and Fydo used it occasionally. Under his touch however, Smelly Ben tended to develop ailments. "Not today, please," Anna begged silently.

She asked herself why Grandmother had chosen her to deliver the precious Ikon to the auctioneers. Logically, it should have been Mother, but she would almost certainly have brought Russian émigré hysteria to the delicate task. Anna would have preferred to share the task with her more self-assured twin, Antonina. *Had Antonina been excluded because the close-knit family considered her not dedicated enough to them?* It was true that Antonina was constantly talking about leaving, about going to America.

The winged silver B on the bonnet dutifully followed the bends in the Oxfordshire lane. Anna had chosen the long way to the A40, which was more picturesque, where the hoar-frost looked like snow – like Russia.

In Chislehampton, Lady Mortimer was just coming out of her garden gate in a black mink coat and hat, with the red setter. Recognising the car and Anna, she stopped, stooped, and gave a little wave. For a moment Anna thought Her Ladyship had come out in homage to this final journey, but then chased the ridiculous idea from her mind. Margaret could not possibly know what was in the boot of the car. It could even be argued that it was partly because of Margaret, Mother's closest friend, that the Ikon was now in the car.

Since Anna could remember, her mother had only had two English friends, total opposites. One was the rather formal well-to-do Lady Mortimer, wife of a senior diplomat. When she was given black mink by Sir Hugh, a few weeks later Valentina too had bought a fur coat. Every time Valentina went for a luncheon with Margaret, she needed a new expensive outfit and came back imitating English mannerisms. As a result the tension with Grandmother would grow, and they argued about money and Mother banged doors.

The opposite of Margaret was Paul, Valentina's lover whom Grandmother called her "fiancé". Paul was an artist, a painter, and Anna would have approved of him, had he not totally ignored Valentina's twin daughters. Influenced by Paul, dark-eyed and tan-skinned Mother would wear her black hair swinging and dress as if she had come from a Mediterranean jumble sale. She drank too much vodka and gibbered about art, and tension grew with Grandmother, and they argued about decency and Mother banged doors.

Mother somehow never seemed to be in balance and her behaviour could not be relied upon. Anna and

Antonina were always on nervous alert that Mother would be aggressive or, worse, embarrass them all. Maybe Fydo had been right in suggesting that Countess Olga and Viscount Sasha had forgotten to pack the soul of three-year-old Valentina when they fled from the revolution in St Petersburg.

Typically overblown and insensitive, Mother had suggested commissioning Paul to paint a replacement for the Ikon.

"A replacement! Oh Mummy!"

Anna felt increasingly annoyed with herself. *Why had she not just said "no" to Grandmother?* Confident Antonina would have. Last night Anna had spent much time awake amidst cold and crumpled bedsheets, battling with the demons of her insecurity which went back to her birth. The family had all prepared for a much desired baby who had appeared and been named Antonina, when another head had emerged. *They must have said, "And what's that – an extra baby?"*

Around one in the morning, she had sneaked into Antonina's room to share her anxieties, but her sister was fast asleep as if uncaring. It was not just the selling of the Ikon: Anna felt that with this loss, their existence would be precarious; they would be easy targets for misfortune – even though the money problem would be solved.

At Great Milton, Anna joined the A40 where the Bentley was swallowed up by the London-bound traffic.

*

The big city was busy with pre-Christmas shoppers. As Anna reached the West End, wadded snowflakes broke loose from the stony sky and fell into Bond Street. She switched on the windscreen wipers and recovered a fan-shaped view of the crowds on the pavement. There was nowhere to park. The Bentley advanced slowly in bumps and starts, and Anna thoughtfully sucked her lower lip.

Today she resented the Christmas tumult around her. So close to her goal, she was assailed by a bout of claustrophobia and felt like bursting free of the car and the cramped city, but she could do neither. On the first floor window-ledges of Frost & Reed, silver tinsel wavered. Shoppers emerged from Bloomfield Place muffled in woollen winter coats, hats and scarves, bent against the driving cotton snow. Now her hands were moist in their gloves. She rolled down the window. Crude air streamed in. The rhythmic tambourine beat of Salvation Army carols made it unbearably Christmas. At the kerb was a solid line of cars. She was forced to drive past Sotheby's for the second time.

In the auctioneers they were waiting for her. A reserve price of nearly a million pounds had already been negotiated by Sotheby's with a representative of the Smithsonian Institute in Washington. In fact, they had suggested sending their own packers out to Hatley today, but to have let strangers wrench the Virgin from Podzhin Hall would have been unbearable.

This time round, half a car's length was free in front of Sotheby's. Anna turned Ben's bonnet into the space. The car's protruding rear forced the traffic to veer. She was shaking now from stress. She calculated the distance to the double glass doors of the auctioneers, the short steps where the Russian Imperial treasure might be at risk.

6

Anna got out and unlocked the boot. Puffed snow-crystals were eagerly absorbed by the tweed of her three-quarter-length coat. A security guard on a stool near a radiator inside watched her. She reached into the boot and carefully lifted out the wrapped Virgin. Cars hooted next to her. She felt as if she were committing sacrilege, exposing the Ikon to such mundane noises.

Trying to balance the heavy treasure with one hand and close the boot lid with the other, she slipped on the wet road. Involuntarily she reached out to steady herself, and the Ikon evaded her grip. To her helpless horror she saw it crash against the rim of the boot and the bumper, before hitting the road at her feet. Anna stood rigid for a moment, and then bent and scooped up the packet. She gathered the Virgin into her arms as though it were a hurt child. "I'm sorry. I'm so sorry," she mumbled into the roughness of the motoring rug. When she looked up, she saw that the guard had risen from his stool, still watching her. Disoriented by the shock she staggered to the door, which he opened for her. She gave the man a swift guilty glance.

The lobby smelled of lemon polish, an artificial world of treasures.

With a sigh, she put her precious burden on a console table at the foot of the stairs.

The receptionist replaced the receiver. "It is Miss Anna Brodsky, isn't it? Mr Charles is on his way down."

Anna dared to lift a flap of the rug. The Virgin's gold halo was bent, and rubies, champagne diamonds and pearls scuttled loose over the sweet face of the Christ-child. The Prince of Pozharsky's insignia on the gold-encrusted frame had lost a corner. Anna gasped. The knock against the car and the crash onto the road had broken the Virgin of Kazan. Anna's boots seemed to melt into the thick carpet. Hastily she covered up her crime.

Mr Charles glided down the carpeted stairs, the long jacket of his wide-lapelled herringbone suit adorned with a white handkerchief in the breast pocket. His well-combed hair was lustrous in the flattering lighting.

"Miss Brodsky, you should have…" He made a silent gesture of finger-snapping as if to flick annoyance away. A second Sotheby's salesman, modelled on Mr Charles, appeared.

"Please let us take care of her."

"No!" Anna felt a blush creep over her face.

"Our client is waiting upstairs." Mr Charles made it sound like a conspiracy.

"Sorry." Anna shook her damp hair, daring to face them. "I have changed my mind."

Both men smiled. "Perhaps we can discuss this in a more suitable place."

Anna took hold of the Ikon again. "The Brodskys are not going to sell after all."

There was an inelegant pause.

"Believe me, Miss Brodsky, these feelings are not uncommon when parting with a substantial heirloom."

Anna lifted the Ikon and headed for the door. The security man's hand hesitated on the brass knob, a questioning frown on his face.

"A misunderstanding," said Anna.

The two men rushed after her. "How can you go back on an agreed sale, Miss Brodsky?"

"Miss Brodsky, let us discuss this matter calmly now that you have come…"

"No, I am sorry, terribly sorry." Anna looked down at her parcel. The doorman shrugged his shoulders and pulled open the door.

"Miss Brodsky, please." Both men stepped onto the busy pavement after her, as Anna walked towards Ben.

"We would very much like you to come to a pre-auction drinks party tonight." Mr Charles pulled an embossed invitation from his jacket pocket, hesitated, then laid it on the wrapped Ikon. "It would make things easier. The buyer will be there. These things can't be rushed, we understand. My compliments to the countess." His voice quivered from either cold or irritation. Anna lodged the Ikon in the boot and shut it; then she pulled the parking ticket from beneath the windscreen wiper and got into the car. The two Sotheby's salesmen still stood in the road. The snow was now falling with conviction.

★

"Explain, my dear man." Mr Snell from the Smithsonian pulled his mouth into a grimace.

Mr Charles rubbed his hands to warm them. "We at Sotheby's do not use pressure sales techniques; we don't need to."

"May I remind you that this is not your average artwork changing hands? This is the Russian Mona Lisa."

"We are only too glad to negotiate further with the family on your behalf. However, if they refuse, there is nothing more we can do."

9

"It is of the utmost importance that the Virgin of Kazan be sold by the Brodskys."

"As I said, I regret their change of heart, but we cannot consider pressuring a client."

"Kid-glove handling will lose you important sales, and eventually your reputation."

"Kid-glove handling *is* our reputation."

★

It was past seven o'clock when Anna entered Sotheby's again. She had not dared return to Podzhin Hall, nor had she had the courage to inspect the damage caused to the Ikon. In her misery she had driven around London, gone to the deserted zoo to have her red nose stared at by huddled and frozen monkeys, burnt her fingers on roasted chestnuts, and been momentarily distracted by the glittering window displays of Harrods. All the time though, she had been wrestling with her conscience for having broken the heirloom on which the Brodsky family's future depended. There was time pressure; she had heard Grandmother say that time was running out, that in two years their funds would be exhausted and their financial situation drastic. They would lose Podzhin Hall, the only home left to them. And she, Anna, had just shattered their only way out of this predicament.

Perhaps some expert jeweller and goldsmith could do some repairs, but by how much had it been devalued?

Anna, in her inability to assimilate the consequences of her vandalism, sought solace in the thought that, after all, the Ikon was of greater emotional value to the family than to the world, and that even maimed it would still comfort them. *Did that not stand good as an excuse for not selling?*

She would attend the drinks invitation to give the buyer and Sotheby's a convincing explanation for the rash decision she had taken.

★

The cupola showroom upstairs was the perfect setting for the slow-motion cocktail party already under way. Anna, still gagging with guilt and still in the worn woollen two-piece suit, felt like a blemish on the varnished sheen of the occasion. Other women wore low-cut, wide-skirted cocktail dresses puffed out by petticoats. Their high heels drilled into the carpet. Some sported hats with mock veils and others had their hair piled in elaborate curls fastened by satin bows. None of these women had just condemned their whole family to ruin. Anna tentatively stepped forward. Immediately Mr Charles appeared at her side, and she did her best to convey aloofness.

"A drink, Miss Brodsky?"

She looked helplessly around. He removed a high-stemmed glass of champagne from a passing silver tray and, smiling at her, drew her to a corner of the room.

"I would like to introduce you to Mr Snell, a Byzantine specialist from the Smithsonian Institute. Mr Snell, Miss Brodsky." With a dry laugh he added, "I'll leave you to it."

Mr Snell's strong face searched Anna's. His bushy eyebrows rose. "Well?"

He has power, she thought. He was in his early forties, his dark hair as straight and coarse as a brushed horse's mane, the eyes hooded under equally coarse brows expressing a primitive animal-like attentiveness, rather than intelligence. Her fragile self-control wavered. "Selling our Ikon feels somehow wrong," she managed to say.

"There is no place more suitable for the Virgin than the Smithsonian Institute in Washington, where all can enjoy her." The smile did not suit his face and he spoke with a leaden mid-European accent.

Anna tried again. "You see, the Virgin's face resembles my grandmother's or rather the other way round." She coughed on the champagne bubbles.

"Is that so?"

Anna wished she was older than her twenty-three years. "It would be unfair really to sell it."

"There seems nothing unfair about the price negotiated so far."

"No, of course not. I mean some things do not have a price."

"If I understand correctly, your grandmother is against the sale." His heavy-lidded eyes scrutinised her.

"Something like that." Anna noticed his pointed leather shoes. *How did his toes fit in them, and how was she going to get out of this disaster?*

"I urge you to put it to your family and ask them to reconsider, since you have been chosen as their ambassadress, a charming choice I confess."

Anna gulped more of the champagne. *If only Antonina were at her side.*

12

"What do you do in life, may I ask, apart from acting on behalf of your family?"

"I am a post-graduate student of Russian history at Oxford."

"We seem to have a lot in common. I ask you in the name of the history of Russian art to get your family to agree to this sale."

Anna's palate felt dry from the wine.

"The Virgin is only a copy," she said in desperation. *Oh Christ, if Grandmother could hear her now!*

"That is for the experts to decide, but if you think so, the parting should be easier." He took a slow step backwards to appreciate the whole of her better. "I hope to be hearing from your family through Sotheby's soon." His eyes travelled up and down what showed of her in the heavy two-piece suit.

He has an evil power, she decided and burped. "Excuse me, I don't feel well." With a brusque movement she forced her half-drunk glass into his hand, turned and fled through the New Room.

CHAPTER TWO

January 1967

Snow had fallen all night.

Upstairs, from her bedroom Anna saw the park white. She strained to push open her window, and it creaked in the stiff frame. It was windless, and on the sill lay a coat of snow so fine as to be lifted by her hot breath. It was beautiful.

Out there in the whiteness, Cahill stomped towards the stables to feed Rasputin, Mother's horse, and his boots left clear tracks in the untouched perfection. Cloudy breath belched from his mouth.

This morning, for the first time, her thoughts were taken away completely from the injured Ikon and the confession she had had to make to Grandmother. Enough. It had spoiled Christmas.

It had been snowing too when she drove back from London with the Ikon, sneaked into Countess Olga's bedroom, wordlessly laid the wrapped Virgin onto Grandmother's bed and looked up to meet her stare, distorted in the guessing of what could have gone wrong. Lifting the corner of the rug, Grandmother had let out a terrible gasp. Anna had sat down at the foot of the four-poster bed, hugging herself in her cold wet coat, while tears boiled over onto her cheeks.

Njanja had come in at that moment with tea and set the tray down on the French guéridon table, but Grandmother had hidden the Ikon under the silk quilt and said nothing to Anna apart from, "My poor child." Anna had hugged herself tighter.

Now over the fireplace the space was still empty. Anna would never dare to mention the subject to Grandmother. She had to wait in anxiety until Olga decided to bring it out into the open. The others still did not know what had happened, believing that Anna had performed her task successfully, and their ignorance made her guilt all the more oppressive.

She needed them, she knew. She could feel the presence of her twin in the room at the other end of the landing, being pleased about the snow. She could imagine Grandmother, edged forward on a chair, pushing aside the curtain to see some decent snow at last.

Tomorrow, Hilary term would start in Oxford, and amongst student friends again her inadequacy and guilt could be buried for a few weeks.

The door opened, and a draught came with it. "Did you see? Isn't it fab?" Antonina appeared. "Thick snow like that is rare in England. Let's have breakfast and then make a snowman."

"Before you know, it's all sludge."

"Come on, Anna, cheer up." Antonina's arm went around her twin sister, who busied herself with pulling the window shut in its swollen frame. "It's your last day before the bus-commutes to the grindstone of wisdom in Oxford. And I might be leaving soon."

Anna twisted free of the sisterly arm and hooked the brass latch into its holder.

"Let's go downstairs. Grandmother will be in a good mood."

At the breakfast table, the empty place setting showed that Countess Olga had already eaten and was in the music room working at the bureau. Fydo in a T-shirt and sarong, wrap-knotted at the waist, was eating untoasted wholemeal bread whilst reading Kahlil Gibran.

"Butter?" Antonina held out the glass dish.

He shook his head.

"We're going to make a snowman. Eat faster, Anna."

"Oh really? Are snowmen still made?"

Njanja walked in with scrambled eggs under a silver dome. On the bellboard across the vestibule, the bell corresponding to Valentina's bedroom jangled.

"Oolong," Fydo muttered, his mouth full of dry bread.

"I know. I know." Durov put the dish on the linen-covered sideboard as she did every morning, whether scrambles were wanted or not. It was a ritual, a testimony that plenty was still available to them. Njanja never required such fussing for herself but she had a soft heart and could weep. Anna had seen the china-blue eyes shed tears. Faithful Durov with her patient presence and her skill was the steady eternal light before the picture of their homesickness: a small reassuring flame, whose flickering shadows caressed them.

Njanja left the room, feet tapping on the echoing floor of the vestibule and then fading through the swing-door, to make Oolong tea and bring it up to Valentina.

In the boot room Antonina opened the cupboard and threw out Wellington boots. Anna stepped into a pair and started to clump to the back door.

"You're wearing two left ones, you dodo."

Anna looked down at her feet. "That's because I have two left feet."

"Weehee!" Antonina shouted, running out of the house. Around her neck was a blue and white scarf to match her gloves and she pulled the fur hat down to cover her ears. Anna wore the same accessories but the scarf and gloves were red and white. They always received sets.

"Let's build him right here so that we can see him from the house," suggested Antonina.

"Let's make him face the house."

"When Uncle Sasha looks out of his window, he'll think Moscow has sent a statue of Lenin for the park!"

"That's not funny, Sis." Anna picked up some snow, patted it quickly, and tossed it.

In the throw the snow separated and splattered over Antonina's face. She pulled off her hat and shook the snow off the fur. "Why does snow always get down the neck?"

"Because." A new snowball landed on Antonina. They raced toward the statue of Artemis, panting, spitting with laughter, their steps clumsy in boots. There they started with a large snowball and rolled it laboriously back over unsoiled snow to make it grow.

"I reckon it's trunky enough." With an effort they both gave the snow-boulder one more roll and let it settle.

"Look, like Christmas tree bells." Antonina held up her hands and from the wool fibres on her gloves ice-clots dangled.

Christmas, thought Anna. This year they had only had a small tree in the dining room, not the usual large one in the vestibule. Uncle Sasha had been unwell, and Grandmother had gone to Baroness Aksakova on Christmas Day.

"What are you dreaming about, Sis? We've got to make a head."

Again they started rolling snow for a head. Just as they lifted it onto the shoulders it was struck by a well-formed snowball. Valentina was up at the round window, and she was busily scraping more snow from its curved ledge.

"Watch out." The twins ducked. The snow exploded on Antonina's shoulder.

"Come down, Mum, and help us."

The bull's eye window closed and Valentina gave a wave.

"With this snow it is easier to believe the family stories from St Petersburg, isn't it? It's the Brodskys' natural setting."

"I like troika sleighs," Anna said.

"Shortly before they fled, the family owned an open-drive limousine; I've seen a picture of it."

"Now Mother wants her own, immensely expensive Jaguar, did you know that, Antonina?"

"I guess with the million from the Ikon we can afford it."

"That's just it. I doubt whether we can. It's very worrying."

"We don't really know about their finances. Olga and Sasha are secretive about it. All I know is that we've managed all these years despite Mum's expensive tastes."

"What's this about Mum's expensive tastes?" Valentina asked, and the girls looked up from patting a neck to join head to trunk.

"You've come to help – great!"

Energetically, Valentina patted fresh snow to the top of the head. "Hair, he needs to have a mop of hair." Mother was wonderful when she was in a playful mood. Anna smoothed the face, and Valentina started rolling another ball.

"A nose?"

"Genitals."

"So predictable." Antonina gathered snow and tossed it at her mother.

"You wait!" Valentina was about to hurl the shaped snow at her daughter but, screaming, Antonina ran away, and Valentina chased her, the snow in her upheld hand. Antonina stumbled rather from laughter than the boots, and fell headlong into the snow. Valentina caught up with her and rubbed the snow into her face. Both were panting and Anna lobbed snowballs after them. Today she felt happy.

★

Countess Olga had gone to the music room early to work on their finances. Crisply dressed, fresh and scented, she sat writing figures on a sheet of paper.

It was time that she told the rest of the family a lie about the Ikon. She rested her pen and rose to walk to

19

the French windows. It was indeed a perfect winter's day.

Outside, the twins and their mother threw snowballs at each other, their voices vociferous, their cheeks painted red. Olga felt the smile on her face fade and her fingers tightened on the chintz curtain: the ghost of someone else, shouting across snow, hastening towards them as they stood under the snow-laden porch of the house in St Petersburg. It was the messenger with the devastating news that had shocked the Empire: "Grand Duke Yerivanski has been executed."

Executed! Her father killed in prison, murdered in the uproar of 1905. She was eighteen years old only and had repeated the messenger's words to herself, whispered them, and eddies of snow had blackened her view as if the whole of the porch-load had fallen on her: she had fainted into the arms of her mother.

"Grandmother! Grandmother! Come and see the snowman we made."

Olga pressed the bell-button next to the fireplace. On the mantelpiece was a vase with precocious roses. Sasha had ordered them for her in a tender-hearted gesture. The inbred and glasshouse-reared flowers were starting to unfurl their petals. They were devoid of scent and certainly did not hide the stained and empty wall space.

"Durov, my coat and shawl. I want to go and see the snowman."

★

The breath of Valentina and the twins mingled milky white, as they finalised the snow figure.

"It's so easy to have fun, and it doesn't cost anything," Anna said. Antonina patted the effigy's shoulders, giving her twin an exasperated look.

"Ah, your extravagant mother."

"I just meant that it doesn't have to be expensive to be... to be enjoyable."

"There you go again, criticising me." Valentina dusted her gloves. "You and your sister are just afraid of being left destitute. How I choose to spend my money is none of your business. Why are you so concerned, Anna? I thought you were a socialist."

Anna sighed, and Antonina shook her head.

"I just thought that the capital won't last forever, and that we should be careful."

"Shut up." Turning away from blushing Anna, Valentina started to smack snow at the snowman.

Antonina, idly sucking at the ice-clumps on her gloves, suddenly bent down and threw snow at Anna. "Let's have fun then if it's so cheap."

Anna did not react. "I'll go and get a carrot and coal for his face."

"Bring a hat," Antonina called after her.

"Anna bores everyone with her ideas of socialism," complained Valentina.

"It's the student influence at Oxford. She thinks it wrong for a few people to have everything and everyone else nothing."

"When you get down to the nitty-gritty in politics, it is only striving for more that works for people, anywhere, anytime. Oxford is full of students from good families. She could befriend the son of Margaret, but no – she joins the Progressive Society."

"The Mortimers," Antonina enunciated slowly. "Mother, do you fancy Sir Hugh?"

"What sort of a question is that? No, I don't. I fancy their elegance, their style. If we were still in Russia, I would have a life like theirs: invitations to embassies, balls, the Queen's garden party. But I am deprived of all that in England."

"But you like Paul, and he's English."

Valentina did not respond.

"Will Paul marry you eventually?"

"Paul is the only man I can bear, because he is like a Russian; he is art for me." Valentina looked at her daughter. "My darling, if only I could offer you a Russian man, strong yet sensitive. They can grab a woman with poetry. It is an accomplishment they learned from the hussars and lancers and the poet-gypsies: the perfect mixture."

"Anna too, when it really comes down to it, is dreaming of a Russian man. Mother, it's all the stories we heard from you and Olga."

"Yes, but Anna's dream is a *kolkhoz* peasant."

Antonina let that go. Valentina's gloved fist punched buttonholes into the snowman's belly. "I get so frustrated trying to live in England. Fur and feathers don't mix."

"And you are mink, and the Englishmen are lame ducks," Antonina joked.

Valentina guffawed.

Anna returned with the items she had collected in the house. She smiled timidly, seeing Valentina and

Antonina laughing. Perhaps during her absence the mood had changed.

"Here," she said.

"Let me!" Valentina aimed for the middle of the face and then twisted in the carrot.

Antonina and Anna simultaneously fitted the eyes.

The three stood away from the symbolic man they had shaped. "He squints," observed Antonina.

"It's because Anna brought a stubby limp carrot."

"It was the only one I could find."

Valentina shook her head and jammed the hat Anna had brought onto the snow head. "So touchy always."

From the French windows emerged Olga wrapped in cloak and shawl. In galoshes, gingerly she tested her way along the others' footprints.

"Three generations of Brodsky women and a melting snowman," announced Antonina grandly.

"His straw hat is most unfashionable for the season," declared Olga.

The girls puffed with laughter.

"Here." Olga advanced and pulled off her scarf. She tossed the hat away and wrapped the snow-head in her scarf, knotting it under the chin. "Better."

"This isn't a *babushka*, Grandmother; it's an English snowman."

"I have an idea." Anna ran back to the house.

"How's Sasha?" Valentina asked her mother. "He hasn't come down for his breakfast."

"It's too raw outside for him – the chest." Olga patted her own.

23

"I wonder how dash-daring the viscount was in the service of the Czar if every time it snowed, he stayed in bed."

"I forbid you to mock Sasha. Do you hear me? It's tasteless and lacks breeding."

Antonina saw Mother's jaw tense, but luckily she made no reply.

Anna came running back with a felt hat and an umbrella.

"Open it and stick it into his shoulder."

"No, no. English umbrellas stay furled, always furled."

Antonina laughed with her mother. Anna remained thoughtful.

★

Later that day Fydo was leaning against the door of the laundry room as if to discourage anyone from entering. The only reason for him to be down there was to launder his peculiar clothes and hand-dyed wraps. Njanja refused to wash them with anything else, as their colours ran.

Anna, heading for the basement boiler room to meet her twin, caught sight of Fydo and tried to sneak past him without getting entangled with some of his 'wisdom'.

"You consider yourself lesser, and it pains me."

Anna hated herself for being affected by his words. It was just what she was feeling after their horseplay in the snow.

"They had not known about you, and you have let this prevent yourself from unfolding."

Anna looked up at her uncle, waiting, in case he would clarify or say more obscure things.

"They were taken aback when, four minutes later, your head appeared. *Another Antonina,* they were about to exclaim, but stopped at *An…* and you have suffered ever since."

"Were you there at our birth?"

"Having given it thought, I must reassure you that you have not been disadvantaged. Once they had pronounced you a beginning, they treasured you without an end."

"What exactly are you saying?"

"*An* is the start of Antonina, *na* is the end of Antonina. You are wrapped around your sister, and she is your core."

Anna clearly had to work this out for herself. "Thank you, Fydo," she said and pushed past him. She found the boiler room empty.

CHAPTER THREE

April 1967

"Durov!"

Anna heard the frustrated call from her grandmother's bedroom. They were all so busy today; perhaps Njanja had not heard. *Should she step in?* Anna wondered, and bent to peek through the keyhole.

She could make out Olga pulling the bell-rope again. The countess was reclining on her collection of pillows and glaring at the roof of her four-poster bed. *Was that because on top of it was the broken Ikon, where Olga had asked Anna to slide it, or because today was Grandmother's eightieth birthday and nobody seemed to care?*

"*Chert poberi!*"

The old lady was cursing now. Anna dared to open the door. "Morning, Grandmother."

The hand, mottled with liverspots, gripped the angora bolero more tightly around the shoulders. "Finally."

Anna shut the door, enclosing herself in the stuffy rose-scented air of the room.

"In my home – my real home – Durov would have rushed in at the first tinkle of my summons and curtsied in a starched apron, OEB embroidered over the left knee, a butterfly bow at the back. None of that anymore. Durov is old and slow."

Anna approached the bed.

"If only my dear husband Ivan had not forced me to leave our lovely house on Vasilyevsky Island for that ghastly Red Cross train out of St Petersburg. Nothing since then has been the same, and Ivan has now been dead for more than ten years. At least Sasha still remembers Czarist Russia."

"But you have lived in England now for nearly fifty years."

"Time is irrelevant. Vivid memories of glamorous days fill the empty years of exile. Look out of the window and, down in the park, you can see what's left of the graves. Sasha's wife, the elegant Tatyana, and Ivan, my handsome husband: dust now, but it was they who shared those times with me."

Anna made no attempt to go to the window. Antonina and she used to play on the graves.

"Had it not been for Podzhin Hall, that generous gift…" Olga sighed. "Tell me what would have happened if the Brodsky family had not had a foreign property to flee to!"

Anna could not tell, but knew that Olga was assailed with what they call an identity crisis. If one reached eighty, that was probably unavoidable.

"Yesteryear, I was radiant and beautiful." Olga reached for her silver hand-mirror to check the side of her face, patting her cheek with the other hand. "At least my aristocratic bone structure has held up. And of course there are still my eyes – malachite, I was told, and mesmerising."

"You have beautiful eyes, Grandmother," confirmed Anna and sniggered, head down.

"What's funny?"

"Nothing; it's just that I was thinking of Little Red Riding Hood." It was safe to say because Anna knew Olga had no idea who that was.

"For my age, my hair is still good too and I hold my posture."

"It really is and, yes, you do," agreed Anna.

"You see, my dear, my body has refused to give in. I will get it back – not my youth, but all the rest: the money, the glamour, the lovely clothes. You cannot imagine how many blushing men have bent over my be-gloved hand." Olga smiled at herself in the looking glass and frowned. "I seem to have a withered mouth."

"Not really."

"Don't lie. My mouth resembles a walnut, doesn't it? The family takes up so much of my time that I can't keep up with the exercises my mother taught me." Slowly and distinctly, her lips unnaturally deformed, she enunciated, "Lila, lala, lola…"

"We should perhaps start getting dressed."

"… lula. Lila…"

Anna interrupted. "All this talking about golden old Russian times. History has moved on. There is a new Russia grown from it."

"How dare you?"

Anna regretted having upset the old lady. Since the disaster trip to Sotheby's, their relationship had been strained. Mercifully, Grandmother was protecting her by not telling the rest of the family the truth. Anna feared the moment when Olga would have to approach that subject.

"I see you looking up at the roof of my bed."

Anna immediately looked elsewhere.

"I am still debating with myself what to do," Olga started slowly. "There are few possibilities. The only viable one is to suggest that Sotheby's think the Ikon might be a copy. This deception would undermine the confidence of Sasha, Fydo and Antonina. Knowing Valentina, she will be stubborn in her belief that the Virgin is genuine."

"I am so sorry for what I have done."

"Despite our financial pressures, I am somewhat relieved that we have not lost the heirloom, for the moment at least."

Anna adjusted the collar around her neck. To honour the occasion, she wore an orange dress with a wide lace collar and a short puffy skirt, instead of her usual spartan style. But with the savage pageboy haircut she had recently inflicted on herself, probably in penance, she resembled an ill-chosen Romeo.

"Don't just stand there, dear Anna. Help me get dressed."

Anna twitched. "Which dress do you want to put on for the special day?"

"You remembered then."

"Oh, Grandmother." Anna rushed up to the bed and gave her grandmother a loose hug. "It has just not started yet, so I haven't said anything."

"What weather have we got today? The blue of an uninspired English spring day, or the enigmatic emerald of the Neva once the ice has melted?"

Anna walked to the window. "Definitely English."

"In which case I want to wear the hydrangea taffeta."

Anna pulled the substantial dress from the wardrobe.

"You know, my child, I wore this gown for the last dinner at the Winter Palace. Of course, it wants long gloves."

A head appeared at the door. "Can you launch the battleship, Anna?" Valentina asked.

"We're fine, Mummy; we're under control."

Anna saw that Valentina's brief appearance had brought added tension to Olga's mood.

"One of these days, that daughter of mine will succeed in killing me." There was glee and pride for Valentina in that remark, and Olga went on, "My unruly daughter reminds me of my old self. From the moment of her birth, she has symbolised for me a past passion."

With gauche movements Anna helped her grandmother get ready. It was eleven o'clock and the family birthday party was about to begin.

*

Antonina stood, feet apart, head forward, and brushed through her long chestnut hair one hundred times. A map of the world stretched across the wall of her bedroom, with a scattering of coloured pinheads, most of them pricked into North America: places she dreamed of seeing.

She straightened up and tossed her head back. There was giddiness, and then the hair settled. It was dreaming of foreign places that had made her choose geography for university, but it had disappointed her with all its statistics. After a conversation with the college tutor, who had praised Anna's academic brain and dedication, Antonina had switched to psychology which had turned out not to interest her either. Last week she had turned down a year's extension and thus walked away from a degree.

In a sage-green mini dress with flared sleeves, she bolted down the stairs and along the back passage towards the kitchen. *Strange*, she thought, *that she was so little affected by her decision to give up university*.

Antonina had named the blue-painted kitchen *Aladdin's cave*. Amidst its amassed clutter, Njanja conjured up meals for the Brodskys' table. Today was an exception because Valentina with the help of Antonina was to cook the birthday meal.

At the long kitchen table sat Fydo, playing absent-mindedly with the vinegar and oil set, pulling each bottle out and letting it drop back into its tight metal holder.

Unfamiliar with what was kept where, Valentina rifled through the condiments. "Pepper – what has she done with the pepper?"

Antonina searched the ultramarine shelves which reached to the ceiling. Like coral growth, knick-knacks had multiplied on them over years. The porcelain cow creamer, with a bent tail handle and open mouth regurgitating cream, had been her childhood favourite.

An untidy wad of newspaper margins was pricked on a nail. On the top one was written a slanting shopping list in Russian script.

"I wish she'd learn to write in English." Valentina, in an ample gypsy skirt and a low-cut white blouse which had escaped from it, swished past.

Antonina unhooked the semi-cylindrical nutmeg grater and prised open the little lid to enjoy the aroma.

"Don't just finger things. Fetch the honey."

The jar was kept in the larder, and when Antonina closed its door, the wooden cross above the picture of a saint clapped against the wood.

At the Aga, Antonina knelt to peek into the oven.

"Checking is not going to get that duck roasted any faster." Valentina clamped the Napoleon brandy bottle between her thighs amongst the floral skirt, and with a *cloop* the cork popped out. She sampled the brandy, tilting the bottle to her carmine-painted mouth.

Fydo sat slumped on the bench, childishly scooping honey from the jar with his thumb.

"Read me that recipe again," ordered Valentina.

Antonina bent over the open cookbook, and glossy hair slid slowly over her ears to curtain her face, while her eyes followed the greasy stains. "For the sauce, mix the butter with the flour to make a paste. Add the apricot jam and honey and gently heat, stirring until well blended. Then add the brandy."

"How ghastly," commented Fydo.

"Who asked you? And leave that honey alone." Valentina jerked the jar away from him and started pouring its elastic contents into a copper pan on the stove.

"I'm going, if I'm not wanted."

"Good idea." Valentina spooned jam into the pan.

The kitchen door opened and Njanja appeared followed by Sasha in his scarlet and gold regimental tunic, medals pinned to the chest. It brought out some remnants of military bearing in him. His handlebar moustaches, now grey, still twirled expansively over red-veined cheeks. "Can I be of assistance?"

"Get the wine, the 1917 Mouton de Rothschild."

Sasha disappeared on this honourable mission, and Fydo slunk out of the kitchen behind his father.

"Have we planned to make the *Always*?" Antonina asked with some panic.

Njanja took place mats from a drawer. "Durov made already."

"What are the *Always*? Enlighten me," Valentina wanted to know.

"The Kolomensky pastels they always ate in St Petersburg."

"Those bloody things." Valentina sampled the brandy again. "Hmm, so far that's the only reasonable ingredient in this apricot slosh." She drank some more. "Antonina, check whether the ice is ready."

In the refrigerator sat a large jar of Beluga caviar on a crystal dish. The ice in the freezer compartment would be crushed as a bed for the dish.

"We need paprika," declared Valentina.

Antonina watched her mother shake a generous measure of brick-red powder into the pan. "Paprika with honey? Grandmother hates paprika."

"Oh, what a lot of fuss over a boring birthday! Let's

pep it up." Valentina reached for the brandy bottle.

At moments like this Antonina wished her mother would behave less eccentrically. Black smoke curled from the edges of the oven door. She said nothing and began to cut dainty zigzag shapes into lemon rinds, wondering how her twin was getting on with Olga.

★

In the dining room Njanja walked around the oval dining table. On the right side of each starched linen placemat she deposited a heavy silver knife from the bunch she held in a napkin.

The antique statue in a niche of the wall was bathed in peach by the sun pouring through the windows. The rays, diffused by the glass, highlighted the crackled gilt fissures on the frames of old etchings. In the centre of the table two silver cockerels with fanned tail-feathers bracketed the freesia and iris bouquet sent to Olga by her friend, Baroness Aksakova.

Pedantically Njanja walked around the table dispensing silver.

★

In the park Fydo sat daydreaming at the feet of the statue of Artemis. Casually he caught and stroked blades of grass between his toes, absorbed in the physical sensation. He dwelt on the fact that everyone called him Fydo: a dog's name. He should have lived up somehow to his real name – Fyodor Alexandreich Brodsky – married perhaps, continued the line since there were no other male heirs. Today was his aunt's eightieth birthday; time flew away from him.

Suddenly a dark cloud passed across the sun. He felt as if a forefather had put a hand on his shoulder. The shadow crept further and the grass lost its lustre. The honey-coloured stone of Podzhin Hall turned dun. This change in light seemed brutal to Fydo's sensitive nature. More clouds crowded in, bulging, rolling. A threat lay upon the park. In the stable Rasputin whinnied. Fydo dropped his head into his hands. There was too much confusion in his life, too many shadows keeping him from the light.

*

The door to the music room opened; the family hushed. Antonina gave Anna a conspiratorial smile. Rustles preceded the formidable appearance. Countess Olga was framed by the door. Her hand cupped the curl on her forehead in her habitual tic. The ample taffeta dress, gathered at the bosom in tight folds, played light and shade and fell to the points of her shoes.

Her head held high, she wore an expression of condescending dignity, rendered theatrical by the over-applied rouge on her faltering cheeks. A tight row of pearls with an elaborate clasp seemed to hold her loose neck together. An ostrich feather, yellowed by time and stuck in her chignon, testified to the occasion.

Sasha advanced towards his sister-in-law, emotions battling on his face. He let his lips browse across her cheek in a brotherly kiss. Valentina stuck a Sobranie cigarette into a holder and lit it. "Act One," she said, exhaling.

Anna moved closer to her sister for reassurance, and Antonina asked, "Are you ready? We're going back to Petersburg today."

Fydo was absent.

"Happy Birthday," said Sasha in a shaky voice, ushering Olga into a seat.

"Many happy returns." Valentina puffed out smoke.

"Champagne everyone?" Sasha twisted the bottle deeper into the ice-bucket before uncorking it.

Anna detached herself from her sister's side and put a wrapped present unadroitly into her grandmother's lap. Olga laid her hand protectively on the small gift and looked expectantly at Anna's mother.

Valentina's nose rose up as smoke emerged from it. "My gift, in fact the big present from all of us, unfortunately has not arrived yet. It ought to be here by now." Her chin pointed to the naked space above the fireplace. For a moment they all contemplated the light patch on the wall left by the Ikon: the ominous absence, an empty space reproaching them for their weakness, emphasising the danger of their predicament.

"How long are Sotheby's going to take over valuing our Ikon?" asked Sasha.

Anna's eyes were enlarged and fixed on her grandmother.

Olga was dismayed that the empty space would probably not be filled today as Valentina had promised. "As I told you before, the sixteenth century jewel is unique, even as a copy. Each of the dozens of pearls, diamonds and rubies needs to be assessed separately. It will take months."

"Hasn't that already been done?"

"And we sit here and have nothing decent to assuage the sacrifice of parting with it." Sasha could not contain his affront. He seemed the most genuinely pained, especially as Olga had taken the decision to sell the Virgin without consulting him.

"I told you," Valentina reacted. "A replacement is ordered. Works of art can't be rushed. A gifted artist needs his time."

Olga let the corners of her mouth drop cynically. "You couldn't get it ready for my birthday, could you? Despite all your attentions to the gifted artist." The sarcasm crackled in her voice.

Valentina squashed the cigarette stub viciously into the ashtray.

"Where is Fydo?" Anna interposed.

"Our crown jewel to be sold, and the decision taken without asking me." Sasha clung to his outrage.

Antonina joined her twin near the French windows. An oppressive atmosphere, familiar to them all, had grown in the room. "Ah, here he comes."

Fydo came in from the garden, his face preoccupied. "Oh," he said and stopped. He wore no shoes.

Sasha straightened his frail body out of its stoop, in reaction to the additional annoyance of his son. "Who do you think you are, arriving at your aunt's birthday without shoes?"

"The feel of the earth on which we tread brings us back to our basic natures."

37

Sasha curled his fingers around the crystal stem of the glass. "It is unhygienic and rude."

"There's nothing wrong with my feet." Fydo attempted to lift and display one of them to the view of everyone.

"Feelings can pass through feet." Anna took Fydo's side.

"Shut up, Anna. This is a party for Olga."

Sasha twisted the champagne bottle in the silver cooler, while Fydo padded up to his aunt, reciting, "Life is a rough uncertain wave. The splendour of youth is a transient bloom. Fortune is imagination's whim…"

"Idiot," hissed his father.

"No, Confucius." Fydo gave Olga a small box on which was written *Chinese Puzzles*. "Happy Birthday."

Olga smiled at her nephew indulgently.

"That's from me." Antonina proffered her present. "It's a book on America." She divulged the contents of the gold-wrapped gift. "And I think it's super."

"Thank you, my dear. Thank you all." Olga looked around at them with disappointment.

"More champagne?" With unsteady hands, Sasha refilled their glasses.

Njanja, in a black dress and the old embroidered apron, came in. "For zr countess birthday. Eighty year is zr long time. May zr countess remain as beautiful…" Her words failed. She knelt at Olga's feet and gave her a present in white tissue paper. Olga put her hand on the servant's shoulder.

"Have some champers, Njanja," suggested Valentina.

"Is lunch ready?" asked Sasha.

From Njanja's offering emerged a pair of hand-knitted foot-warmers with taffeta ribbons.

"Is zr nothing much," remonstrated Njanja, leaving the room to serve the caviar.

Antonina opened the folding doors, and Sasha held out his crooked arm to Olga who gave him a grateful glance. Slowly the younger generation proceeded behind the matriarch, Countess Brodsky, and Viscount Sasha, into the festive dining room. Valentina pinched Fydo in the buttock.

★

Olga, seated at the head of the table, watched her faithful servant remove the remnants of the charred duck. The old claret in its bottles layered with dust had unfortunately over-matured into a thick sweet liqueur.

The countess observed in turn her descendants who were celebrating her birthday.

Valentina threw her head back and belly-laughed, showing the fillings in her teeth. One of her horn hairpins had fallen out; the dark hair tumbled messily down her back. She had stuck a camellia behind her ear. "Labour Party? Wilson?" she railed. "You've got to be joking. He's losing fast against the dockers."

"That should not be of concern to a family whose prerogative it is not to soil their hands with work," countered Fydo, the muddle-headed nephew, his face shadowed by the lamp behind him.

"Why do you get so heated up about something you can't change?" asked Antonina, the twin with a mind of her own.

"We can and must; we're all part of England now." A dear Anna remark.

"Sometimes I wonder whether we are."

"You're a proper British subject – birth, citizenship, the lot."

"For taxes we are particularly welcome," grumbled Sasha.

"Anyway, the Conservatives have just won control of the GLC and that's a turn for the better," contributed Antonina who read the newspapers. *Too much knowledge about a man's world never served a woman well*, Olga thought. As for the girl's determination to go to the New World, it showed lack of dedication and respect to the family.

"Joining the Common Market could strengthen Britain," said Anna.

"Rubbish." Her mother cut her down.

Tears started into Anna's eyes. Antonina got up and came over to her twin. "It's not a serious debate," Olga heard her soothe.

"That's the trouble in this family: political consequences are just played with." Anna flared up.

Antonina changed the subject by complimenting Anna. "You decided to be colourful today."

"It's all wrong on me, this orange dress with that collar. And I shouldn't have had my hair cut short."

"Well, that is a bit of a pity. But at least now people can tell us apart."

Olga studied the twins, two young women with the same features. While Anna had turned inward, scholarly, to protect her blend of innocence and concealed chaste passion, Antonina was determinedly independent, driven to assert her own individuality. Yes, they were different, not so much by the length of hair but by what they thought and said.

"The British are too insular and chauvinistic to join up with France," Sasha continued the conversation.

As he spoke, Olga experienced a sensation of remoteness, something that had been happening more frequently. Sasha's voice came from a distance. The rest of the family were distorted in an opaque fog. Was this her mind preparing for death perhaps?

Sasha looked old and worn out despite his festive uniform. The intense colour on his cheeks gave away his high blood pressure. She saw him raise his swollen knobbly hand to hide a yawn; this was a sign of lack of oxygen. Her old Sasha of style and dash was suffocating. How close they had been all their lives! Their fondness had not been tarnished, even grown after she had married his brother, Ivan.

The family's means to live and dine like this were running thin. It was impossible to hang onto an illusion; they were sliding towards penury.

"Olga, dearest sister-in-law." Sasha extended his hand across the table and took hers prisoner under his. "I can't believe that you are *vosyem'desyat*, eighty today."

The discussion of Britain continued. Valentina, sitting next to Fydo, was imitating the Queen, while her hand disappeared under the table, no doubt to play capricious physical games on her cousin. She had an intoxicating effect on men, not because of her beauty even now at the start of her fifties, but because of her concentration on her victim. Playing with Fydo would have to do for this birthday party which obviously bored her.

Olga sat up straight. They may see her as a relic but there was vigour and strength left in her still. She pinged on her crystal glass with a silver spoon. "Dear Brodskys, I want you to remember on my birthday that the failing British Government does not concern us. We were the ruling class once and still ought to be."

"To rule, you need influence and money."

"Indeed, Sasha. Influence comes naturally with money. Therefore we need our money back."

"In Russia now, comrades, all is shared equally."

"Is that so, Anna? As long as there are Russians, there will be those born with pedigree, the *dvorianstvo*, and the peasants."

"Olga, what are you trying to say?" asked Sasha.

"I mean that the Brodskys are going to demand the Russian state compensate us for what they took in the Revolution."

"Fat chance, Mother."

"Dearest Olga, do you think they might?"

"They will have to be brought to do so."

"Didn't we destroy all the bonds, making paper aeroplanes and shooting them at the pond from the upstairs window?"

"Fear not." Sasha sounded reassuring. "There are many of them left."

"We clogged the pond, and when Baroness Aksakova arrived…" Anna recalled, "… gallant Grandfather Ivan offered to carry her to the door, despite her weighing a ton."

"Ivan lodged a property claim with the Foreign Office and sent it to Buckingham Palace before he died," explained Olga.

"And?"

"They must still have it on their files."

"Do they play paper aeroplanes from the Buckingham Palace balcony?"

"Antonina, would you be serious for a moment?"

"But how can we go about getting anything back?"

"I could go to Russia and talk to someone with influence," said Anna into her half-eaten pudding.

"Hello, Comrade Chairman of the Politburo. I am the Brodsky offspring – you know, the ones you amused yourself with by stretching their necks. Give me back my money."

"Stop it, Mummy. Let Grandmother talk."

"I was thinking of approaching the Russian Embassy in London. I have heard from the baroness that some émigrés have done that."

Olga looked at the faces around the table, waiting for a reaction. Antonina smiled first. "What a splendid idea!"

"Do you really think it might work?" Sasha gazed at Olga with astonishment, spoilt by a yawn.

"They stole it from us," she said and cupped the curl across her forehead.

"You are amazing," commented Valentina quite seriously. "With the million or more from the Ikon and the compensation – imagine!" Her eyes flashed.

"Imagine, all those bonds in my desk." Sasha sat there, seeing visions. "We wouldn't need to sell the Ikon then."

"What do you think, Anna?" asked Antonina.

Anna blushed slightly. "The money the Brodskys invested, along with the rest of the aristocracy, has long since been distributed justly amongst the people."

"On a military note, Russia is spending billions of roubles on weapons, rather than distributing to the people."

"Many of the bonds are signed by the Czar himself." Sasha's gaze was far away.

"Anna, wouldn't it be wonderful to get it back?" Antonina leaned towards her sister.

"Yes, of course it would."

There was silence. Njanja came in with the *Always* on a porcelain cake stand.

"Grandmother, you had a marvellous idea."

"Soviet swine, here we come!" shouted Valentina. "Let's celebrate!"

Olga crumpled up her napkin and laid it on her uneaten pudding.

They all rose.

*

The park lawn was flecked by alternating sun and shade. Behind chintz curtains in the music room the Brodskys drank vodka neat and ate Kolomensky pastels, the *Always*. Russian songs blared from the record-player. The family had contaminated each other with the anticipation of recovering their Russian fortune. Valentina was ablaze at the thought of vast riches soon to be theirs again. Sasha's cheeks became an unhealthy crimson as he drank and

44

shouted, "Long live Olga Brodsky! Long live the new Russian Government!"

"Union of Soviet Socialist Republics, Uncle," corrected Anna.

"Sounds revolting," said Sasha.

"What do you expect after a revolution?"

Fydo, visibly loosening up, tapped his father jocularly on the back. "My dear *tovarich* Brodsky."

"Don't be rude – Viscount, if you please. Cheers!" Sasha toasted the music room in general.

"Off to Siberia with you, Comrade."

"Stop it, Fydo." Valentina smacked her cousin on his backside. She whirled around the room, her wide skirt slapping furniture, her hair trailing after her. Antonina reached into the inset bookshelf and handed her mother the tambourine.

Ochi Chernye…

Antonina started to dance with Anna whose face was eager, her lips parted in the glow of acceptance into this warm cradle.

"Oh, how I shall miss you all if I ever get to America!" shouted Antonina.

"Don't go," pleaded Anna with serious eyes. "Please don't go."

"I'll write and I'll be back."

The door opened and revealed Cahill, the Irish gardener-handyman. He was carrying an imposing platter with a substantial choice of cheeses.

Valentina danced by him, shaking the tambourine in his face. "We're past cheese. Feed it to my stallion, Rasputin," she shouted.

"Yes, ma'am." He disappeared.

"Come and dance with me, my beloved Fydo." Valentina grabbed her cousin and pulled him into the centre of the room.

Ochi Chernye…

Out of breath, Sasha plunged into the armchair next to Olga's, who sat cooling her face with a Chinese fan and looking over it at the frolicking family.

"Tell me we'll get the money back. Tell me, tell me." Sasha burped.

"I am uplifted by this decision. There is now something to fight for, something to live for, and not just a future but, even better, a revival of the past." She fluttered the fan.

"Last week, our lawyer spoke to me about our finances and gave me a ghastly headache. He would kiss you if he heard you."

"It would be wiser to talk about this tomorrow."

Sasha, undeterred, continued, "What was so humiliating to hear was: *Having studied your financial situation, dear man, I am afraid I do not come with happy tidings – your family is facing disaster.*" Sasha raised his arm with a legal finger-wagging.

"You told me. And he is right of course, more than you know. And here we all are drinking and some prancing around. Now, only an act of daring and courage can save Podzhin Hall and keep the remainder of the family drinking and dancing. I am eighty today and the matriarch, and in the name of the Brodskys I have to succeed. Count Ivan, grandson of the Duke Alexander Brodsky, would have expected no less of me."

Sasha rose from his seat unsteadily. "Long live Count Ivan."

"Long dead Count Ivan, buried in the garden." Valentina with ruched-up skirt and petticoats displaying her stockinged legs, waltzed past her uncle who started marching about in toxic inebriation from the combination of alcohol and his pills.

"You should have seen Nikolai II in the uniform of Colonel-in-Chief of the Scots Greys and the Czarevitch Alexei, four years old and already as straight as a birch, awaiting the arrival of Edward VII," he enthused.

Anna changed the record on the gramophone.

"Down with the red terror!" yelled Valentina, pirouetting and making the lamps shake.

"Those were the days." Sasha swayed and opened a new bottle of vodka.

"They must have been. Bang goes the Czar in Ekaterinburg," contributed Fydo, no more sober than his father.

Sasha sternly eyed his son who was busy trying to grab Valentina's kicking legs.

★

In dark silence Antonina padded from her west-facing bedroom with its square bay window along the first floor landing to the east-facing bedroom with an identical bay window. It had been explained to the twins that the further apart, the fewer nightly whisperings there would be.

Without knocking, Antonina entered Anna's bedroom to find her sister sitting in her pyjamas sideways on the bed. "I knew you would come now," she said without looking up.

"Are you drunk?"

"No. Are you?"

Antonina shook her head. "Grandmother didn't really get good gifts, did she?"

"We can't afford Fabergé any longer."

"Actually, then they were just fancy trinkets."

"Remember the Fabergé egg Mother gave us for our tenth birthday which she thought was our twelfth? When we fought over it, she suggested we simply halve it."

"We could not have known at ten that we also split the fertilised egg in her womb."

Anna stroked along Antonina's long hair down over her shoulders.

"Yours will grow back. Anyway, don't you think that Grandmother was in great shape tonight? At eighty, it's impressive."

"I'm not so sure. She is hiding a lot."

"Come on, Anna. The great pompous entrance, the trailing dress, the dishevelled plume on her head…"

"That's her theatrical side."

"That's her only side. That's all she's ever been taught to do."

"You and your psychology studies. You might have stayed with geography. Grandmother has insight and wisdom."

"If that were so, why doesn't she use any of it on herself? The grand old Russia time is long gone, and anyway I didn't enjoy psychology. I have no idea what I want to do. I think I'm going to do a secretarial course; that seems to be of some use at least."

"All those choices you have for schooling. Imagine we never went to any school, did not know what a lesson was or a teacher or homework or textbooks. For Olga, it was all about coming out, receptions, tea parties, chaperoned outings in troikas, and clothes fittings."

"But from newspapers she could get an idea of what is going on. She can read."

"I watched her the other day reading *The Telegraph* and then throwing the paper down on the table complaining, *Threats of a national railstrike, just like in Russia*. Of course, that is exactly what did happen."

"I'm too tired to discuss this now. I hope you don't mind." Antonina got off the bed and walked to the door. "Sleep well my *bliznyets* – twin," she said softly and was gone.

CHAPTER FOUR

Twenty-five miles west of Moscow are the forests of
Nikolina Gora. Even in April it is still winter; the nights
are frosty, and when the sun filters obliquely onto the
birch trees, their flanks are so white and silvery that it
hurts the eye. In their shadows, patches of snow persist.
Here, influential Muscovites have dachas: wood-built
houses nestling amidst the forest, houses decorated in
the hunting lodge style.

Pavel Miliukov was sitting in his wicker wheelchair
on the glassed-in verandah with a rug over his lap. He
was now seventy-four and officially retired. However as
a Party member of the highest circles, he was still able
to remain active from a distance and to influence crucial
decisions in the Kremlin. That influence was carving a
successful career in the Party for his only son, Georgi.

Through Georgi, who came to visit him often, Pavel
could keep his old contacts in the KGB, the Ministry of
Foreign Affairs, and the Central Committee. The Party
knew about this and approved. His successful political
career had been based not just on psychology, patience
and clever manoeuvring, but also on a conscientious

sweeping of the ground behind him, the ground on which denunciations would otherwise have had a chance to germinate and grow. Pavel came to be judged as solid, dependable and single-minded, yet there was more to him. Pavel believed every man should endeavour to achieve something individual, even if it was only the modest attempt to grow the largest cabbage in the allotment.

The fact that no-one else but Georgi ever visited did not bother the old man; he had a lot to think about still. Pavel reached out for his crossword book but not the pencil. Between the pages was the card he always used as a bookmark. On it was printed Lenin's wisdom: *Give us the child for eight years and it will be a bolshevik forever.*

In 1917 Pavel had been a poor farm boy suffering the social injustice of Czarist society, both in spirit and physically in the form of a sabre slice from a drunken tempestuous aristocrat on a horse. Pavel drew his finger down the side of his face: the scar-arc on his chin could be felt as an embossed sickle.

When the wound was fresh, Pavel had joined the bolsheviks and from there begun his steep ascent in his career, propelled by a vision of a country in which there was no place for sword-wielding aristocrats. He had not been alone. Many came from the farm-middens to seize the chance they were offered – the chance to be more, to reach more.

"Lenin was a genius," he said out loud.

An orange cat slinked onto the verandah.

"Coming for a chat about Lenin, are you?"

The cat jumped up onto the window ledge and weaved its body in and out amongst the potted plants.

It pretended to be interested in a blooming cactus. Pavel laughed. "I know your games, Koshka. You want my attention. You want me to tell you stories that are secret."

The cat padded all the way to the end of the ledge, narrowed its shoulder blades and jumped to the floor with a soft plop, where it settled near his feet and close to the heater.

"All right then. The last time we talked, I told you about the aristocracy in St Petersburg, the royal family in their polished boots and expensive clothes from exclusive shops catering for their fancies. You should have seen the women covered in jewellery and plumes, driving in carriages from expensive apartments to receptions and balls – yes, balls.

"Today, I will tell you a story of what happened one evening. I was walking in front of the Winter Palace, and it was ablaze with electric lights. Behind the tall bowed-top windows, I saw silhouettes moving, dancing, frolicking. Those marionettes were not proper Russians; they were not even real exploiters: they were a blemish on Russia's existence. They had it all. And if they felt an itch to own more, they made sure they helped each other to get more. None of them appreciated any of it.

"I came to walk close behind a gentleman in black tails who dropped his gold lighter after lighting his cigarette. I bent and picked it up, wiped it on my jerkin and held it out him. He waved it away. It had touched dirt; it had become beneath him.

"Do you know what, Koshka? I flung the lighter way out into the Neva. I so would have loved to have a swing at that aristocratic bastard. I wasn't the only one feeling like that. The Revolution had already embarked on destroying this elite, on erasing such injustice. Many aristocrats were killed, but not enough. Some fled to other countries, taking with them valuable things belonging to Mother Russia.

"And now…" Pavel lowered his voice and bent his body closer to the rolled-up feline at his feet, "… I still plan to have a swing at them. Too old now, you think I am. That is so. But I have groomed someone secretly to do it for me. It is not Georgi; he needs a safe career because he has a wife and a child. The one I have trained to become a model communist is called Vasily Voronov, and he does not know what I plan for him to do to prove Lenin's theory – how to make a bolshevik forever. Nobody knows except you, Koshka, and me. And I only tell you, because you love Lenin."

Pavel reached out for the packet of cigarettes on the trolley. Behind the glazed door inside the house moved the private carer tidying the room. She was a big woman, sturdy. A messy tangle of grey hair crowned her fleshy face. She wore a white uniform and her bosom sank close to the elasticated belt.

Guiltily Pavel put the packet of cigarettes down again. She would tell him off. For him the times of shapely gracious women were over. The carer's bosom was a solid brick balustrade, which crushed his ears when she helped him out of the chair. All his needs were on the creaky trolley now, rolling along with him.

He checked again and the carer had moved out of sight. He shook a cigarette from the packet and, with a shaking hand, rubbed the matchhead against the strip.

He had to do it three times. The broken matches fell to the floor but finally he succeeded and sucked avidly at the tobacco.

The carer came out onto the verandah. The cat, without unrolling, started to flick its tail.

"I can see what you're doing. And if you think I can't, I still can smell it."

"It warms me."

"Since when do cigarettes warm a mouth?"

"Look out there. It is still winter. When I was a young country lad, I skated on ponds like a winged devil over frozen water."

"I'm sure you did."

"The high-born landowners banned us farmhands from skating."

"I'm sure they did."

She picked the cigarette out of his mouth and went with it inside the house.

The smoke dissipated and the cat's tail stopped tapping.

"I didn't meet enough good-looking women in my life, but that side of things can't be put right now. And you don't care, do you? My son, Georgi, has a wife, but I wouldn't wish her on me. One who will not have a wife is Vasily Voronov. I'll make sure of that. Humping would distract him from becoming a Hero Socialist."

The nurse returned, and the cat unrolled and stood up.

"It's unhygienic." She picked up the animal and carried it, pendulous from her grip, to the verandah's outside door. "After tea, it will be time for your exercises," she said, dusting her hands, her pale-lashed eyes fixed on him.

CHAPTER FIVE

The morning after her birthday Olga rested in a suffering pose on her bed.

"Heartburn," she winced. The charred duck in sweet devil's sauce had jolted her aged stomach; the family had done the rest.

Anna twitched and wriggled on the dressing table stool, chewing on a pen.

"Write!" ordered Olga, who had composed a series of letters to the Russian Embassy during the tormented night.

Anna pulled the pen from between her teeth.

"Your Excellency comma, in the name of an old and illustrious Imperial family I address myself to you…"

Anna wrote, shoulders rounded.

"… you have unlawfully expropriated… Oh poppycock! … stolen from the Brodsky family. It lies in your honour to recognise this, and in your much vaunted integrity to return our expropriated fortune."

Anna ventured, "Grandmother, don't you think that perhaps it wasn't quite like that?"

"What a stupid remark, my darling. That is exactly how it was." Olga dictated the rest of the letter. "Make it from Countess Olga Ekaterina Yerivanski-Brodsky."

"But Great-Grandfather Yerivanski was legally executed for civil crimes."

"Is that what those ignoramuses teach you at Oxford? The grand duke was simply murdered," stated Olga and popped two pills into her mouth. "After *expropriated fortune* add *and compensate us for all our lost family heirlooms*."

Anna lingered.

"Get on with it child, and bring it to me for signing."

Anna glanced at her grandmother's four-poster bed, the painted roof depicting a sparsely clad youth strumming a mandolin with an anaemic hand, a smile of beatitude on his pastel-pink face, all of it floating in a blue sky with odd white clouds. Of the ill-fated Ikon above it, nothing could be seen. Anna averted her eyes. "Yes, Grandmother."

As an afterthought, Olga added, "Tell your mother to come and see me."

"Mummy has gone to London to see Paul."

Olga clasped her hands on her knotted stomach. "She would. Then get me Antonina."

"My sister?"

"How many twins are there?"

Anna tried an unsuccessful smile and left the room, stumbling slightly over the edge of the carpet.

★

"I hope you don't mind me resting on my bed. I feel indisposed."

56

"That's okay. What do you want?" asked Antonina, who had been summoned.

"I want you to stop being so brusque and curt. It is not becoming."

"Sor-ree," said Antonina, in a singsong voice, and plumped down onto the tapestry bergère.

"You have turned your back on a university degree and now trumpet your desire to travel to America. How are you planning to realise this? Have you connections there? Does anyone want you there?"

"Not really."

"That's what I thought. Headstrong as you are, and despite me not grasping why you would want to leave the family for such a barbaric country, I nevertheless believe that the least harm would be done if I helped you get there, and obviously back."

"Do you know anyone there?"

"I do, indeed. Her name is Irina Potresov. We were introduced – I mean, she was introduced to me – at a social event in the Winter Palace. She is a mere baronetess, always contradicting everyone, a rather irritating, corpulent woman who wore white for the event. White being reserved for the princess; everyone with breeding knew that. That just shows you why she ended up in New York."

"How long is it since you had contact with this presumably eighty-year-old, possibly not-alive-any-longer, baronetess?"

"We write to each other at Easter, but it has been a while. She had bad hair quality but wore elaborate build-ups, as if nobody noticed."

"None of this is helping me."

"Oh, but she has a son. Let me think… He is someone in the navy."

"In the navy in New York?"

"I presume it will not harm writing to Irina and suggesting she hosts you during your little visit."

"It's not going to be a short visit. Never mind about that. Thank you for your help, Olga."

"*Grandmother* to you, insolent girl!"

*

The train from Oxford rattled into London. By the time Valentina made it to Tottenham Court Road, offices were closing for lunch. Tightly packed masses of humans were conveyor-belted on escalators in the belly of London's Underground system. Slowly Valentina ascended and, in the neon light, the blank faces descending beside her appeared worn and lifeless.

"Cannon fodder," she muttered and emerged at the top where she yielded her ticket. Stepping into the street she was immediately animated by the electricity of spring in the air. The yearly revival of nature intensified Valentina's thirst for pleasure-seeking. Or was it a reaction to the British temperance, the self-restraint of people about her, even after shedding the confinement of their winter clothes?

Years before, she had married a perfect example of the mediocre middle class. His pedantic manners, resting on assumed superiority, had driven Valentina to bursts of frenzy during which she provoked destructive rows with him. He had called her sexually under-inhibited; she threw his frigidity into his face and had several inconclusive, miserable affairs. Had he been able to recognise his limits and open his arms to her, calling her sexy, pulling her to him, there could have been a chance for the marriage. When instead of one baby she gave birth to twins, he had eyed her as if that too was one of her exaggerations. By the time the girls were two years old, neither he nor she could bear the strain of the relationship any longer. He had asked his bank for a transfer to South America, and Valentina had let him go and never mentioned him again.

He is probably still there, she thought walking along Starkeley Street. Into his place had stepped, eventually, an artist, a painter ten years her junior. Paul was anything but a conformist; he was volatile and his temper was unpredictable and sometimes violent. The Brodskys never considered him more than a fad in Valentina's life even though the relationship had now lasted for fourteen years. She had never brought him to Podzhin Hall. She believed that she kept him by playing the older, rich and elegant woman, and by carefully controlling his incoherent rage and humiliation at not being accepted by her family.

At the end of the street, in a fashionable artists' enclave in Soho, was a narrow passage bordered by small blind houses. A chained bicycle leaned against a lamppost coated by so many layers of paint that the original ornate base was just a shapeless blob. She stepped over discarded boxes and other rubbish and opened a small door. Leading up were wooden stairs littered with take-away food wrappings and beer-cans. Valentina trod on an empty cigarette carton which deflated with a *pflot* under her Italian leather boot; the artist had obviously not managed to give up smoking.

In the studio at the top, in a lived-in and mature chaos, Paul was being creative. He lay on a sofa-bed covered by a collection of rugs and patchwork quilts and stared up at the large skylight. Valentina's Van Cleef & Arpels perfume made only a little headway against the sour stench of stale cigarettes and bodily exudations.

"I see you're at work," she greeted him, the exotic appeal of the room overcoming her natural revulsion.

Canvas propped up canvas, dust covered; some leaned against a broken chair, some against the seamstress model embellished by turquoise nipples. On the easel was a painting, more than half of its surface covered in sepia, the rest hinting at something organic. Uncleaned paintbrushes of all sizes, like quills, were stuck into a chamber pot from which the newly crowned Queen Elizabeth and Prince Philip smiled regally under glaze. The palette, a ratatouille of oil-paints, had been carelessly thrown onto the gritty floor.

"Spring challenges my creativity."

"How would you know it is spring?"

"I saw a dead sparrow in the gutter this morning."

"Oh yes, and you diagnose death from over-mating?" Valentina removed her astrakhan toque and hung it on a rusty nail driven into a ceiling beam. She pushed a mildewed sweater from a crate and sat down.

Paul levered himself up languidly, his vivid red hair giving a false impression of activity. "How was the Czarina's birthday party?"

"You dare to ask! You made a complete fool of me."

"But I wasn't there."

"The painting, the commissioned life-size portrait of Olga for our mantelpiece in the music room. Does that mean anything to you?"

"Oh that."

"Yes, that. Months ago I gave you three hundred pounds, and photographs of her and the Ikon for the portrait's background. It had to be ready for the party. Last month, you said it was coming on fine and you'd deliver it as a surprise."

He shrugged his shoulders.

"I had a premonition when you wouldn't let me see it. Where are the canvas and the frame we chose, and for which incidentally I paid you separately?"

"In the fireplace. It was a bloody cold winter, you must admit."

"When are you going to paint it?"

"Soon."

"On Saint Give-Me-Hope Day?"

"No, Saint Francis of the Asses. I need to see the Ikon – touch it – to paint it. The old bitch, no problem; she's under my skin. It's you in thirty years' time." Paul rolled himself off the bed. Empty beer-cans clattered to the floor. "Sit for me."

"Now?"

"In five minutes it'll be too late, the moment lost to the past. Take all those Knightsbridge togs off."

Valentina grinned. The excitement of exposing herself, of modelling for this rough talent at her age and with her breeding, was irresistible; she started to strip.

"Lie on the bed; prop yourself up on your elbows and spread your legs. Come on, I need a woman's sex to reveal the futility of Man's search for bliss."

His creative enthusiasm often swept her into believing that she was the inspiration of his art. As she lay back on the bed she felt the coarse quilt against her pampered baby-oiled buttocks. Her nipples grew.

Paul picked out a large paintbrush. "I am going to take that power between your legs and transpose it into pseudo-abstract." The brush made generous movements on the canvas. "Have to paint this over my *Velocity*. Can't afford a new canvas."

Valentina felt the discomfort of her position, and her elbows sank into the mattress.

"Jerk that pure gift; devour mankind with its power."

The pubic hair bristled on her mound of Venus as she was aroused by his tempestuous translation of coarseness into art.

"Great." He set his feet wide apart; jutted his pelvis forward. "I feel it. The basic earthly dream superimposed on speed," he mumbled with one brush between his teeth, while he painted with rapid strokes with a second, short wide one. He eyed the crude sight Valentina exposed to him. He paused, frowned. He tore the large brush from his mouth and dropped the other. "Imagine you own the world by the merits of your sex, and kinetic energy will flow into my work."

Valentina hesitated but kept up her pose. "This is uncomfortable."

"Art is uncomfortable."

He painted with zest and his eyes were wild. A vibrancy flowed from him, an intensity that had spellbound Valentina since their meeting at an art exhibition. His paintings always reminded her of that first thrill.

Almost despite herself Valentina responded to his urging. He had done it again: aroused her voluptuous hunger for fulfilment. Her breathing accelerated as her right hand crept between her thighs. Paul switched brushes rapidly. She arched her back and the mattress creaked. In front of the canvas Paul trembled with the intensity of capture and reproduction. Suddenly Valentina had her orgasm and howled. She sank back, realising that the satisfaction of her body had been not just a sacrifice to art but a physical phenomenon to be preserved on canvas for ever.

Paul stopped painting and gazed into space. "What time is it?" he asked nonchalantly.

"Eh? Ten past seven." She was still panting.

"You're really loaded now, aren't you?"

Valentina got up. "What do you mean?"

"One million for the Imperial Virgin."

"Who told you?"

"You did, pussy-cat."

"Don't be so vulgar."

"Look who's vulgar."

Valentina covered herself. He came over to her, his face menacingly close, and she saw his stained teeth. He grabbed her shoulders and started shaking her, red flames surrounding his head. "We can't marry. We can't live together. I'm not good enough for you," he mocked.

He's got my post-coital depression, flashed through her mind. "Stop it."

He did not let go and climbed onto the bed. "I'm good enough to be paid to paint that old cow of a countess."

"Cut it out, Paul," she said with force.

"And whose baby did you abort?"

She averted her eyes. They had gone through that so many times.

"Whose? Mine!"

"Ours," she corrected, as she always did. "Please, Paul."

"*Please, Paul.* You probably had it murdered because it would have had my hair."

"Let's not."

"No, let's not. Fourteen years I tried to satisfy you; fourteen bloody years you satisfied yourself more. A child conceived and gotten rid of."

"You know it would not have worked, the way we live, least of all for the baby."

"Valentina, marry me or I'll go mad. You must have the dough from Sotheby's by now."

She knew he had got over his anger and was feeling sorry for himself. She smiled. "Let's think about it, Paul," she said.

"I have thought about it, believe you me. Thought and thought, nights and days, freezing, hungry and untalented."

"Hold it. You're a fantastic artist and you know it."

"I'm a piss-artist thrice over. I'm pissed with beer; I'm pissed off with the way we carry on, and critics piss on my work."

She hugged him. He let himself go limp. She felt his sobs against her chest. She stroked his unruly hair. "It's not as easy as all that. There are the twins to be considered."

"You wouldn't know *consideration* if it punched you in your pretty nose," he sniffled.

Valentina knew that the storm was safely over again. "Why don't we go to Marcelle's exhibition?" she suggested. She was not really interested in the daubings of Marcelle Silver, Paul's next door neighbour, but hoped the party would bring him out of himself.

"I could do with some free booze," he agreed.

★

In Nikolina Gora, Georgi walked straight into the dacha, tossed his fur hat onto the table, forked through his greasy hair, then took a bottle of vodka from his coat pocket.

"What?" asked Pavel from his wheelchair. "We're not greeting an old comrade, nor the old cat?"

"There have been developments."

"Open that bottle; get glasses. The carer has gone to the village. We're alone."

"You'll like what I have come to say."

"Then say it."

They toasted first. "*Nazdroviye.*" Then they chucked the clear liquid down their open throats.

"Our embassy in London keeps a watch on the auction houses. They learned that an émigré family were offering Sotheby's an ikon of the Virgin of Kazan, and

65

sent in an agent pretending to be from the Smithsonian Institute."

"Which family?"

"The problem is that they withdrew from the sale almost immediately. It is not a case any longer."

"Fuck it," exploded Pavel. "It's the Brodskys who have the bejewelled Ikon. They must need the money. That's what is bringing them to their knees – has to be." The scar on his chin began to quiver, and he put a finger on it. "I'll tell you what happened: someone else made a better offer."

"Maybe that's the case."

"Maybe? You have a fish on the hook at last and you throw the fishing rod into the pond and walk away?"

"The embassy don't seem to be giving this priority."

"No priority! Descendants of Grand Duke Yerivanski no priority! You've got to arrange to follow each of the Brodsky family members, where they go, who they talk to. Cultivate them. We cannot miss the chance of getting the Ikon back to Russia."

"I guess from your reaction that I will have to put forward a certain groomed peasant for this job."

"I detect in you some resentment."

"As far as I am concerned, the Czar and his family were shot, emotions buried. Our interest in émigrés has to serve the modern Soviet Union. All we can hope for is to get Russian treasures back and to plant in the new generation of émigrés a wish to return to their roots. They will find a communist democratic country ready to forgive them their past with generosity."

"A rather narrow view."

"The Soviet Union is looking forward, not back. We are reaching out, and the world will be stunned by Russian advances, in science, sport and industry."

Pavel grabbed the bottle by its neck and poured them new drinks. "Sure, we're beating the others in space, but out there is a mass of émigrés who still poison our image and flaunt our stolen treasures. They multiply with offspring. Old accounts are still not settled."

"Maybe."

"Old things give directions for new things. Start the process of getting Vasily Voronov sent to our embassy in London."

"Sure, Father." Georgi pushed the chair back, put his large hands on the table and rose to stand.

The men froze at a noise behind them.

"The carer," whispered Pavel. "Quick! Hide the bottle in the sofa."

CHAPTER SIX

At the start of May, one of the letters clattering into the letter-basket bore a stamp from the USA. Njanja peered at it long and hard. Valentina had missed the postal delivery; she was spending more time these days in the stable.

When Njanja brought the letter into the music room where Olga was discussing papers with Sasha, she could not restrain herself from commenting meaningfully, "Is from America."

"But not for you." Olga took the envelope and sliced it across its top with the silver knife Sasha had passed her. She unfolded the letter and read, turned the page and read, folded the paper and put it back into the envelope. "Irina," she said with a little heave.

"And what does Potresov write?"

Olga took her reading glasses off. "She is still alive and kicking. And living with her son, Travis – what kind of name is that? – and his family on a small island close to New York. Travis is with the coast guard. They welcome Antonina to their home at any time."

"She will be pleased."

"Nobody else will be, especially not Anna."

"What do you think the son is doing for the coast guard in New York?"

"You're the military man. I presume on the small island there is a lighthouse, or something, and Travis is guarding the coast from it."

"Olga, we can't just send Antonina so far away to someone we don't know anything about."

"All I know is that Irina is a snob, and Travis might have inherited it. But the girl is dead set to go. What can we do?"

"I had rather hoped we would get an answer from the Russian Embassy today. Now that would have pleased me."

"Be patient."

★

"I can't *wait* to tell Anna about this." Antonina, arms outstretched, twirled under the chandelier in the vestibule. "America – here I come!"

There was the squeak of a bicycle brake outside, then silence. Finally, the door was pushed open.

"Anna! I'm going to America!"

"Are you?"

"Come on; be happy for me."

"What's that racket in the hall?" Sasha asked from the music room.

The twins gave each other *that look* and sneaked off to the boiler room, their hideout.

"Grandmother got an answer from that old baronetess in New York. She and her son invite me to stay with them as long as I wish."

"How can you be so excited about travelling across treacherous seas to sit with an old White Russian woman, telling you the same stories as you hear in this house?"

"I'll have more freedom. They don't know me there."

"I wish I knew how to keep you back. I remain, alone, just me – everywhere just me."

"We're twenty-three years old. Get that. Mum is giving me money for America. You have the same rights. Move out into lodgings for this last year at Oxford. Go in the summer; say you need to install yourself before term starts."

"Do you know that we have grown up together every day of our lives? Remember when we were cast as Lottie and Lisa in the school play, and I got chickenpox?"

"I do. Mum painted spots on me too so the play would go on, because she fancied the teacher."

"And the time when you switched with me in the changing room at the swimming pool so that I got my swimming certificate," Anna added carefully.

"Because you can't put your head under water."

"And…" they said simultaneously.

"You were going to bring up Peregrine."

"Yes, Peregrine McGilligan who invited us together to the May ball to show off."

"And then we only ever danced with each other."

"What really annoyed him was our photograph on the front page the next day while he was edited off the picture."

"Oh, and do you remember that Oliver who was so mean to you? He had it coming."

"Ollie brought me to the station, and I waved out of the carriage as it pulled out."

"And when he came out of the station with that smirk on his face, I stepped in his way with: *So pleased to see me gone?*"

"He got a surprise."

"No, Anna. He screamed like demented and ran away."

"And now this perfect togetherness will be broken by you going away."

"You mean mutual dependence."

"A perfectly satisfactory relationship."

"That's actually rather pathetic. We're not Siamese twins."

You're the core and I am wrapped around you, thought Anna.

"I'll need a visa because I plan to stay there more than three months, and they want me to bring a chest X-ray." Antonina changed the subject.

"What? Not a picture of you topless?" Anna forced herself to be more cheerful.

"Anna, come with me to the consulate to get some feel of America."

"Because it's you. Let me know when you are going."

★

"I swear." Antonina stood before the solemn American consul who showed her the pink of his palm. Behind him hung a framed copy of the Constitution, and a large Stars and Stripes flag topped with a carved

71

eagle leaned in the corner of the office. Antonina, her hand also raised, swore not to possess a criminal record, to abide by American law, and not to seek work in the USA, and her voice choked on tears of patriotic pride for a country she did not yet know.

At the reception desk she picked up her passport with the visa sticker, Blue Cross and Blue Shield medical forms, a wad of general information and her chest X-ray in a large brown envelope to prove she did not have tuberculosis.

"The consul called me *Miss Bradsky* in there."

"Well *Bradsky*, what's next?"

"Next, I invite my twin for a sandwich and Coca Cola although it's not quite as hip as a burger they eat in diners."

When the twins were seated in the coffee shop, and people had finished staring at them, they ordered. Antonina did her best to jolly her sister along but Anna could only pick disconsolately at her cheese and tomato sandwich. Finally Antonina, feeling her sister's pain, suggested, "Let's go home."

★

From the bus-stop in Hatley the twins walked home. It was evening and the light was fading fast. They took the shortcut across the field to avoid the wide curve in the road out of the village. The grass was tussocky, the little-trodden pathway overgrown. When they came out onto asphalt again, they were only a few yards from the corner in the wall of Podzhin Hall's park. They flanked the wall. As children, they had dragged their hands along the bricks, their eyes closed as they felt the corroded porous, sleek polished, or moss-bearded ones.

"Before I leave," Antonina said, "I thought to take some secretarial lessons."

"How many will you have time for?"

"No more than two. Enough to distinguish a sewing machine from a typewriter. I'm not supposed to get a job there anyway."

"You could always help the lighthouse keeper on the island!"

"Have you thought that this Travis might have a dashing son about our age? He would have some Russian blood from his Irina grandmother."

"You will write to me, promise?"

"Every detail."

The girls passed under the branches of a birch tree, reaching over the wall and dropping its catkins like yellow caterpillars at their feet. Further along drooped a crab-apple tree in bloom. However, in the evening hour the wall, the sky, even the tree in bridal array, had discoloured.

A male figure was walking towards them, drowned to a shadow beside the wall, but they recognised Fydo's gait. He was wearing a long beige raincoat flapping at the back of his legs, the collar turned up, and a hat was pulled low over his eyes. He slowed, reached up to an overhanging branch and made it nod. The apple blossom snowed down on him. The gesture had the self-absorption so typical of him. He shambled on and before them he stopped, becoming aware of their presence.

"I got my visa today. Do you want to see?" Antonina searched for her passport in the straw basket hanging by long rush plaits over her shoulder. She licked her finger and flicked the stiff pages of the passport, and then prised the pages open so that he could see the blue, red and green sticker. *Non-immigrant, Classification B-2*.

"I had to swear before the American flag that I would respect the country and abide by its constitution. My hosts live in magic New York, just as I wanted. New York, Fydo, New York!"

"I don't know," he said with maddening calm, and looked at her strangely, as though he too held vistas of magic places, but could see them without having to go there. "Life isn't just about conquering things."

"Aren't you pleased for me?"

"They have large Buddhist societies there."

"Ah, Fydo. That's not interesting."

"The largest Hare Krishna Consciousness sect in the world."

She put her passport away. "Where are you going so late?"

"To Oxford."

"What for?"

"There is a meeting I have to go to."

"Hare Krishnas?"

"Bless you in America," he said.

"I'm not going for three weeks."

He walked on a little way, turned and lifted his hand as if to bless her again.

Antonina shook her head. "He is definitely getting weirder."

Where the wall started to curve towards the entrance, they followed it. Cahill had already closed one of the iron gates, and one by one the twins slipped through the narrowing gap as he pushed shut the other. The metal doors joined with a rattle and the impact made them sway. The large key from the gardener's pocket crunched in the lock. Cahill walked away. It was seven thirty and the family inside, and nobody was expected. Fydo would obviously stay in Oxford for the night.

CHAPTER SEVEN

The letter Olga had dictated to Anna reached the Soviet Embassy in London. The receptionist refrained from opening it because it was marked *Personal* and passed it to the registry clerk. He slipped it into the pigeonhole of the first secretary. The first secretary opened the letter and, having read it, decided it should be handled by the counsellor who, having consulted the ambassador, took action. The outcome was a memo sent to Moscow by diplomatic bag on an Aeroflot flight.

Memo PSPE/09/248/67

To the Chairman
Sub-Committee on Policy towards Emigrés (SPE)
of the Party Committee for Foreign Affairs.
From the Embassy of the Union of Soviet Socialist Republics
Kensington Palace Gardens, London

THE IKON OF THE VIRGIN OF KAZAN

BACKGROUND

Following the issue of Central Committee document 084/64 (To Recover Soviet Treasures from Emigré Communities), the embassy established contacts among the major auction houses.

In 1966 Sotheby's in London were approached by the family Brodsky, offering to sell the Ikon titled above. An SPE agent attempted to buy it, but the Brodskys withdrew in December of that year, suggesting their picture was only a copy.

NEW DEVELOPMENTS

A letter from 'Countess' Olga Brodsky has been received by the embassy, requesting compensation from the Supreme Soviet for the loss of property the family claim to have sustained at the Triumph of the Revolution.

ANALYSIS

There is no question of *compensating* the family Brodsky for wealth which they had stolen from the masses. Clearly however they are in need of money, and our archives indicate that the Brodsky Ikon is the original.

Why will the family Brodsky not sell? It may be that the object's sentimental value remains for the moment greater than their need for money. It may be that they have discovered our interest in the item and declined to sell on anti-Soviet grounds. We are in no position to discover the truth but their letter to the embassy provides us perhaps with a chance to put ourselves in that position.

Past experience shows that the creation of an effective relationship with an unknown émigré family is most rare, especially as we are unwilling to meet their demands, but we understand SPE has a trained candidate for such cases.

PROPOSAL

THAT such individual be posted to fill the position of second secretary (Social Structures) at the Soviet Embassy, London and, once he is in place, the embassy invite Count Brodsky to a reception.

THAT, the candidate having established the true motivation and political attitude of the family Brodsky and the location of the Ikon, this section will make a proposal for further action to SPE based on these findings.

Oleg Turchin
Counsellor (Political).

Georgi Miliukov, thanks to his father's help, was Chairman of the Sub-Committee on Policy towards Emigrés. He now held the three-page memo in both his hands. It was weighty with meaningfulness because it offered the prospect of the successful culmination of a life's work – his father's.

Even now at his advanced age Pavel was still passionate about the aristocrats who had saved their pelts by fleeing abroad and taking valuables with them. There was justification for it particularly in the case of the Brodskys and the bejewelled Lady of Kazan, but with Father there was more to it than just that, much more.

Georgi leaned back in his seat and asked himself again about his father's personal interest in the Ukrainian farm-boy he had made it his goal to shape into an exemplary communist. Everyone knew what Lenin had said about taking eight years to turn a boy into a Bolshevik; it was a point of dogma but it did not explain Father's irrational passion. That was linked somehow to what had happened to him before and during the Revolution. The Party liked people to work according to principles; hidden, personal motivations risked conflict with duty. It was a danger and made Georgi shiver with discomfort. This was the sort of ground his father had taught him to sweep behind him.

He needed to know more.

★

"Is the cat dead?"

"I'm your father's carer, not a vet."

"Of course not." Georgi approached the sofa. Stroking the elongated ginger cat, he declared the animal still warm. He bent to the cat's mouth. "Reeks of alcohol."

"So, the cat is drunk. Not surprising. Here is the bottle of vodka which miraculously fell from an aeroplane just after your last visit, and in there…" she pointed with the empty bottle to the bedroom door, "… is your father on his bed, as drunk as the cat."

Georgi knocked on the wood. There was no answer, and he went in and closed the door behind him.

"Father?"

"I dreamed I was back in the Ukraine, watching Vasily in the horse race I organised with the district pioneer leaders. You should have seen the violence of the rainstorm that day. The farm horses and young lads had to jump over fences in the mud."

"Father?"

"Oh. It's you, is it?"

"Yes, it is me, and you and the cat are both drunk and blabber dangerously. I think you'd better have some strong tea and then tell me some things I need to know."

Pavel started to roll himself off the bed into the wheelchair. Georgi helped him first to the toilet, and then put a mug of strong tea into his hand. The cat was no longer on the sofa by the time Georgi wheeled his father out of the dacha into pale sunshine. He took him all the way to the white birch trees.

"That's far enough," said Pavel.

"Are you sure there are no microphones fixed to these trunks?"

"No known device can survive temperatures of minus twenty degrees Celsius."

"You know a lot."

"That's why I own a dacha after all these years of service and why they envy me."

Georgi lit two cigarettes and passed one to his father; then he leaned against a birch and puffed out smoke through his nose, watching it trail away, his head slightly tilted back.

"Show me the document," Pavel said calmly, holding his anticipation in check.

The son handed the memo over to his father. "The Brodskys have raised their ugly heads again, this time to ask for compensation for the money they had to leave behind when they buggered off."

"Excellent," was Pavel's sharply enunciated reaction. "Now we have a lever, finally."

"They might just be playing games to taunt us."

"No." Pavel shook his head. "Oh, no. I know the type. Time has come for a showdown. Getting our man on the job is essential." Pavel smiled knowingly.

"Father, you sound unnervingly personal about all this."

"Do I?"

"Then you'd better tell me about your protégé, Vasily Voronov. From the start right to the end. I need to sweep behind me ahead."

"Son, I guess the time has come for me to tell you."

"About time, and all of it."

"I first saw Vasily Voronov as a young boy in a muddy farmyard," Pavel started. "He balanced across planking to the fenced enclosure, containing a shaggy, dirty sheep. Rising onto his toes, he reached over the tall stinging nettles to stroke the animal's head. His dark hair with sun on it resembled black lacquer."

"Lenin's *child*."

"The first time I interfered in his life was the horse race I dreamed about. One of the boys got killed in the race, trampled by the horse after a jump. Vasily won despite his old, cave-backed mare, despite the shitty conditions. When I gave out the prizes in the schoolhouse, the dead boy got first prize for his dedication and his wish to see the Kremlin. Vasily received the second, a medallion of Lenin. *Are you pleased*? I asked him, and I will always remember the pleasant way in which he responded, *It is an honour*. That was when I noticed that his eyes… damn it, his eyes were the brown of beaver fur."

"Do you know how unprofessional you sound? And I'm sorry my eyes aren't brown."

"Georgi, you don't have to be jealous. What I put Vasily through physically, I would never have imposed on you. I nearly killed him in the ravines of the Urals, when he was a Komsomol fledgling. He was chosen to battle through an ice-cold torrent with a heavy rope on his shoulder, for the team to build a hanging bridge across the chasm. I was watching from an old lookout post built by the partisans in the Revolution. It was…"

"That part you told me once in Moscow. Tell me about how you pushed him along in his political career."

"I got him into the International Relations Institute when he was nineteen years old. I reckoned that it was time to make sure his thinking was moulded to suit his trained body. I went to check several times. In the language laboratory, repeating English phrases on a tape-recorder, his mouth was distorted by the effort of producing the right sounds. He had no idea who the man was, prowling between the desks, stopping at his and flicking some pages of his textbook, while he kept repeating with the others. There was sweat on his brow.

"After graduating, Vasily was accepted in the Party. I let him find his feet on his own. I didn't want, at that early stage, to arouse any suspicions of my involvement with him. Unaided, he did quite well and earned some respect. Encouraged, I intervened and pushed him through the Party's hierarchy upwards and towards the areas of interest to me, by prodding and manipulating the right people."

"That, at least, you did for me too."

"See, no jealousy is called for. It was a proud moment for me when I received the list of new job allocations and saw the name *Vasily Voronov* on the Foreign Observation Reports Group. The first taste of what lay beyond the Soviet Union would be fed to him. Things were coming together and going my way. He didn't disappoint me; unwavering and dependable, he analysed correctly, and condensed properly the reports sent in by the Soviet members on missions abroad. All that achievement, starting with a muck-covered farm-boy. And listen to this... but give me first another cigarette."

Georgi lit two again and with pointed fingers pushed one of them between his father's dry lips.

Mechanical-sounding high-pitched screeches made Pavel glance up. "Swallows! Spring! I made it through another winter."

"Father, you were telling me about Vasily..."

"He was moved to the Foreign Visits Group and trailed around with foreign delegations, in a suit provided by the Party's official supplies, looking so dapper. I had a photograph of him but destroyed it for security reasons. He was interpreting for groups of foreigners in front of the Kremlin, smiling and being the perfect young Soviet official. That was something."

"I bet."

"A KGB phone-tap on the hotel revealed one of Vasily's American visitors saying, *He's helpful, young and sociable. He could be a candidate for defection.* Ha, not a chance!" Pavel laughed out loud. "And it was the same with female approaches. Good-looking and charming, of course he got the attention of women, but those he had affairs with were the kind of females who do not remonstrate. Such a man does not marry, but devotes his passion to work."

"Thanks for not doing the same to me, and letting me marry."

"Everyone wants grandchildren. Anyway, in 1959, I got Vasily the experience of interpreting during the British Prime Minister Macmillan's visit to Moscow."

"You must have torn a limb off getting that for him."

"He had deserved it after years of bureaucratic excellence, report-writing, watching, uncovering and denouncing, apart from making tourists happy. And then, as you know, they retired me."

"And since then you have pursued your project through me. I have helped you without asking questions but now, in order to protect myself, I need to know what is behind your little hobby."

Pavel coughed, fumbled for his handkerchief in his trouser pocket under the rug and, holding it against his mouth, coughed renewedly.

"Stop that trick. I am not falling for it."

Pavel cleared his throat. "What the bloody hell is a hobby?"

CHAPTER EIGHT

Olga paced around her bedroom, her malachite eyes darkened by a sullen mood. Antonina in a miniskirt and tall boots had just left the room after offering profuse wishes for her grandmother's well-being. The young woman's pretty face had been set in concern, not entirely able to conceal her excitement and the spice of the unknown awaiting her.

Once Fydo had driven Antonina away to the airport, then the house and the park would become quieter and a shade sadder; her laughter would be missed. Olga shook her head, then cupped the curl. It was incomprehensible that any person should choose to go to a new country, suffer the uprooting and discomfort by their own choice, and all that to end up in the lap of Irina Potresov.

Olga felt the arthritic ache in her joints and heard Antonina shout "Bye, Uncle Sasha" from the landing gallery and "Keep your spirits up" before rumbling down the stairs.

"Wrong touch," Olga mumbled in a burst of irritation. The young generation had the wrong approach, thinking they were inventing values, being offered novel excitements they were entitled to. How recognisable all of those values were to Olga, and how she regretted the contemporary failure to cultivate the art of seduction. Women's skirts had risen above the knees to disclose no more than fleshy thighs, quelling the desires that spring from imagination: the most effective aphrodisiac.

With Antonina gone abroad, there would remain Anna, probably feeling the loss of her twin like an amputation. On her own Anna would be half of an entity, not brave enough to seek integrality or alter her unpractical ideas. Honest and pure, Anna had been drawn to socialism at university. Misguided, the girl thought she had discovered the merits of the peasantry. Olga snorted shortly. Worse, Anna had stayed with the idea when most others had gone on to practise something else. Anna was a dear child: too sensitive and not sufficiently self-assured to make the step to adulthood by rebelling against her mother – but then it was given to few to have the courage to rebel against Valentina, a fifty-year-old woman with long flowing hair belying her ripe age; a mother behaving as her daughters should, punishing others for her own neuroses.

What purpose did it serve to talk to either of her granddaughters? They did not listen, engrossed in their own new things, one of them going all the way across the Atlantic Ocean. In 1917 some of those fleeing Russia had also gone to the Americas. At least Antonina would be staying with one of those who embodied the glorious old times.

The occasion which came to Olga's mind was a party given by Princess Cherkanicha in the Winter Palace. The

Czar and the Empress were already exiled to Tsarskoye Selo. Irina, on the arm of her husband, had suggested that in order to honour the absent it was their duty not to falter but celebrate their allegiance to them. There had been a feel of desperate elegance, heart-in-mouth conversations about mundane matters. Oddly now, Olga's mind chose to recall Irina's fashionable Dior perfume but in her memory the scent became rancid as it brought back the hideous way in which the party had terminated. Irina too was alive to remember that event.

She should have told Antonina something of this. Olga left her bedroom and stepped onto the landing gallery but it was obvious that the girl had left, was gone.

*

Anna stood in the empty forecourt where an uninvolved fountain glugged. The dreaded moment had been imminent and then it had happened, and now the Bentley had driven away. Her twin had chosen to move on in life by leaving Anna behind, for an indefinite period of time with an uncertain outcome. She, Anna, had had to wish her twin luck in the new world and wave goodbye; had restrained the urge to beg *Don't forget me, Bliznyets*.

Anna had to remain contented by her sister's promise to write regularly. She crept past the kitchen as she and Antonina had used to on their way to their hideout. There came no sound from Njanja. Going down the backstairs, she put both hands to her violently beating heart and slipped into the boiler room where no-one ever went. The *boiler beast* took up most of the room, its funnel reaching up to the ceiling and through it. Anna pulled one of the two stools from under the narrow rough-hewn pine table and sat down. There was a faint sound: the familiar creaking of floorboards in the music room above her. On shelves were the same old stained rags, some tools and a candle-stump in its holder next to a box of matches.

Anna pulled open the drawer of the table. It was empty, dusty in corners, but at the back she felt the roundness of a pencil stump. Once she had clawed it out, hot tears gathered. They were children who had only just mastered writing, when they had laboriously composed a list of the objectionable words:

EITHER
ONE OF THEM
EITHER ONE
THE OTHER ONE.

With grown-up hindsight it was clear they had done that out of resentment at not meriting individuality in the eyes of those who were supposed to love them, each in their own way.

Once the list was long, they had devised ruses to confuse and punish the adults. Anna had a chipped tooth so both kept their lips closed. The birthmark on Antonina's upper arm was drawn on Anna's. *Oh, it wasn't me...*

*

Still in her bedroom, Olga checked her face in the silver hand-mirror; these upheavals were bad for her complexion. She saw Valentina, down in the park, walk away from the house in breeches, her crop whipping against her riding boots. Olga decided that, with one of the twins flown, there was now time to concentrate on Valentina, and shortly afterwards walked purposefully under her parasol away from the Hall towards the stables.

Despite the radiance of the day, the park lay in tense stillness. The elm's coarse-toothed leaves hung motionless. Olga had decided to tell Valentina the truth about the Ikon's fate; bring her daughter down to earth and curb her extravagances. Why should her daughter not carry at least some of the responsibilities? It would clear the air to argue with her.

Before the stable stood Rasputin, saddled and bridled. Despite the martingale, the animal threw its head forcefully and kicked up dirt with its hooves. Olga walked a safe circle around the wild-eyed stallion, closed her parasol and pushed open the stable door.

From behind the stacked hay in a corner came laughter, the excited melodious sound of her daughter at her worst. Momentarily blinded by the sudden dark, Olga only distinguished shapes by degree as she crept along the wall on tip-toe until she saw Valentina and the groom. They stood in profile and Valentina slashed and twisted as the man restrained her with both hands on her hips. The riding coat was half-brushed off one of her shoulders and its flapping coat-tails lit up red suddenly in the one filtering ray of light.

"Let me go. Don't be stupid." Valentina frisked about, and the jacket caught the light again. The groom grabbed her harder and tried to pull her towards him.

"You're just a tease, aren't you?" His voice was insistent.

"Let me go, I say."

"One kiss. You promised."

Obviously he did let go of Valentina for she scudded across the stable shouting, "Gotcha!"

"I'll get you one of these days," threatened the groom, standing outfoxed.

A loose plank creaked under Olga's shoe and she hastened outside into the sunshine where Rasputin snorted impatiently and attempted to yank the hook from the wall.

"Mother." Valentina emerged from the stable, readjusting her jacket. "What are you doing here?"

"We have serious problems. There is no way for you to ignore it and go on playing childish games."

Valentina's cheeks were flushed; her eyes shone liquid.

Olga thought, *she looks just like I used to*. "There is something you ought to know concerning the Ikon. Get decent and meet me in the music room at once."

The groom appeared at the door, his face sheepish in embarrassment. He was stuffing his checked shirt back into his trouser waistband.

"Forgive me, Countess. I'm most awfully sorry, but it wasn't my fault. It was your daughter…"

"Stop snivelling!" Olga's contempt had brought colour to her own cheeks. The muslin collar rose and fell on her chest.

"I mean…"

Olga opened her parasol and turned to walk back to the house.

I know who else Valentina takes after. What shall I do with her? Olga wondered, bygone passion mingled with dismay. As she passed the statue of Artemis, she heard hooves pounding the ground and turned round. The dark horse pranced, then reared. Valentina's spurs dug deep into his belly. Rasputin bolted across the park, leapt over the family graves and headed towards the gate and the open fields beyond. Valentina's long-tailed dark hair fluttered on her shoulders. Olga puffed with outrage; her daughter was riding the stallion like a cossack chased by demons.

★

"For the last time, Miss, it will be now only twenty minutes before we land at J F Kennedy Airport," the TWA stewardess in the pillbox hat and with a tired voice said to Antonina in seat 10B.

"Just tell me one more thing. Is it difficult to land such a heavy aeroplane?"

"I'm not a pilot."

"But you fly all the time. What's that strange noise?"

"It's the landing gear deploying. I told you about the retraction into the fuselage just after we took off. All is fine, trust me. The crew will have to sit down. We're not far from landing."

On safe ground, pushing the luggage trolley heaped with two Vuitton suitcases and a round beauty case on top, Antonina proceeded through the customs channel to emerge in the arrival hall. At first she was taken aback by its size, the jumble of lights, people and noise. Leaning against a barrier were people waiting for passengers from the flight. Antonina traipsed past them. None of them held up a sign with her name, nor did anyone shout it out. *What if nobody was here for her? All she had was an address. Please someone.*

She had nearly reached the end of the pick-up line. All around was greeting, hooing and haaing, and hugging. No-one had come for her.

"Miss Antonina Brodsky?"

"That's me. Definitely me." Antonina was relieved to have been met but had not expected a young man with hair cut like a bathbrush, up and straight at the top. He wore blue jeans and a jean jacket, obviously a denim fan. Antonina wore a Burberry trenchcoat, newly bought against the Northern American climate; Olga had insisted, and Valentina had selected during the mother-and-daughter shopping expedition. "I didn't expect James Dean to meet me."

"Heh, heh, heh," laughed the bathbrush man. "Do you want a gum?"

"Who are you?"

"Didn't Gran write? I'm her grandson, Ricky. She sent me to fetch you and bring you home."

"That's good of you."

"She still pushes people around. We just had her eightieth birthday – a nightmare."

"From the frying pan into the fire," said Antonina.

"Is that English?"

"That's international, I come to think."

The youth took off, walking fast in white tennis shoes, and she struggled to keep up, having to dodge luggage and people. Whoever he was, he surely had not been brought up as a gentleman.

In the carpark he held open the back of the Chevrolet for her to swing in the heavy suitcases. Then he sat at the steering wheel while she struggled out of her coat and opened her own door, to sit down and lay the coat over her knees.

"Ready?" he asked and drove off.

"I'm in New York," she said flight-drunk. "How amazing!"

"You're only in Idlewild, just coming into Queens."

Rows of buildings sped past her dizzied eyes, everything different from what she had ever seen. Ricky had switched on the car radio blasting out music.

"Do you have Elvis in England?"

"We do have Elvis, and some see elves," she joked.

"He's funky."

"His voice is like chocolate mousseline. *Yaint nuttin butta hounddag, cran all the time*." She imitated Elvis.

Eventually the car stopped.

"Are we there?"

"We're in the Battery. We've got to get onto the ferry."

"Governor's Island you live on. Of course. I forgot."

The tyres rattled over the welts onto the flat of the ferry. She got out of the car to look back.

"You wanna gum? Awkward is my speciality."

She waited for him to say more.

"Don't you know Charlie Brown?"

She stood rooted, her flitting hair held away from her face to watch with incredulity the perfect Manhattan skyline: the outline of the Chrysler Building, the piled-together building blocks of apartments and offices, an unreal metropolis just starting to light up with millions of lights against a darkening evening sky, shrouded in brown summer-heat pollution.

The crossing was short, and soon the Chevvy bumped off the ferry and she was on Governor's Island. Men in uniform stood at the port, saluting. A flagpole displayed the Stars and Stripes which two soldiers were just about to lower. A soldier stood ready with a gleaming bugle, the light of pride reflected on his face.

After a short drive in silence the teddy boy behind the steering wheel stopped in front of a substantial house, the same as those either side of it. They were surrounded by neatly cut grass, no flowerbeds and no marked boundaries but a cluster of hickory trees at a distance behind them.

At the front door stood an old woman. She had blond corkscrew curls with lace ribbons woven into them. From the jacket of her stiff gold suit burst forth an opulently frilled blouse. Her neck was circled by a wide black choker with an oval brooch under her slack chin. The stick she was leaning on had a silver saddle-shaped top.

"Come to me," she proclaimed with a guttural Russian accent. "Welcome home." Irina opened both her arms, the stick dangling from one. "I couldn't wait for you to arrive, have been standing here for ages. We have so much to catch up on." Antonina was ushered into the house.

"Ricky, bring our guest's luggage to her room," Irina ordered back over her shoulder.

"Old goat," Antonina thought she heard.

"He is not polite. There is a lot of work to be done on him."

In the drawing room, which Irina called the *lounge*, Antonina sank onto a flower-print frilly covered sofa. It was all quite different from Podzhin Hall. The fireplace was obviously unfinished, still showing raw bricks. Over it hung a framed photograph of the Grand Canyon. Irina fetched a platter from the adjoining dining room table and walked in with it, holding it high like a trophy. "Kolomensky pastels I made for you," she announced proudly.

Always, the *Always*.

"I must make sure that you will not miss your grandmother and Sasha. Now, tell me all about the countess. You know, we were such good friends. Olga always complimented me on my dress sense; she admired my style and taste. Of course, she turned herself out well, with all the money there was, but somehow it was always just a hint too brash. When we were invited to the charity ball at…"

"Gran, Antonina is fast asleep."

CHAPTER NINE

In the university library Anna worked on finalising her essay. *Social attitudes amongst Russian workers are comparable to those of Western blue-collar workers; there is the same camaraderie. But the Soviet way is for the labourers themselves to propose objectives which they meet and take pride in exceeding. The Five Year Plan is a welcome challenge for the Motherland. Communists are the New Class; their economic privileges are due to the bureaucratic monopoly they hold.*

Anna bit the end of her pen. At the tables of the library sat a few students deep in books. One of them, a Titian-haired young man, was also studying Russian history. She had fancied him from afar for a while until he invited her for a coffee. "I read your piece in the student paper," he had begun aggressively. "Stalin's propaganda overkill undermined the ideological fervour. Behind the façade of communism and its vaunted Five Year Plans, lies rotting doubt. Even high Party officials are cynical about the whole system and mock it in private."

"As a Brodsky…" She had tried to counter his callousness.

"Before the October Revolution, you, *Countess* Anna, and a peasant in Siberia had a lot in common – neither of you thought you had anything to lose. It's in the middle it didn't work – still doesn't."

Anna never talked to him again, nor to anyone else on her course. Now term was about to finish, and the long summer holiday start – weeks and weeks without Antonina. Anna decided to search for rented accommodation as her twin had suggested.

★

She lugged the trunk down the staircase behind her. It was filled with a few of her belongings, mostly books at the bottom and some clothes on top. As the case landed on each new tread, a dull thud echoed in the vestibule and she winced. She hoped not to make a big thing out of this.

Sasha came out of his bedroom and watched her for a while in silence. "Is that for the poor?" he asked.

She went on descending with the heavy trunk behind her.

"Why are you standing in the draught without your cardigan, my dear brother-in-law? You'll catch a cold."

Oh no, thought Anna, *not Grandmother as well*.

At that moment Valentina came through the front door in a windswept swagger-coat. She had obviously been out with Lady Mortimer and been driven back by the Foreign Office car. There was this air about her: the hair piled neatly, a hat and gloves. She shook out the umbrella, aimed and cast it accurately into the elephant-foot stand. Then she pulled the hat from her head, groaned and looked up.

Anna stood caught on the staircase.

"What are you doing, Anna, and why is Smelly Ben in front of the house?"

"Remember, Mummy? Today, I'm moving some things into the vicarage."

"What vicarage?" Sasha twirled his moustache.

"Anna has decided to rent a room closer to Oxford."

"This is beyond all comprehension," said Olga. "I hoped you had succeeded in changing her mind."

"Ha!" Valentina laughed, concentrating on her precise movements as she plucked off a glove. "She is pig-headed." The second glove was pulled off. The pair of limp hands were lodged behind the brass newel ball at the bottom of the railings.

"Darling Anna," Olga started, obviously cross because Anna too was leaving Podzhin Hall. "Sasha and I have tried to guide you, but you do not make it easy for us."

"Anna has these strange ideas about poor people," said Valentina, unbuttoning her coat.

"Order her to stay," said Sasha up at the landing rail.

"And why can Antonina set off to America, and you just accept it? Why don't you try to understand me for a change?"

"How can we understand you, when you behave in such an extraordinary way, dear?"

"Grandmother, Antonina thought it a good idea for me to get more experience. I simply want to live with ordinary people. I will be back most weekends. That's all."

"Don't let her go, Olga. I know about ordinary people; they are rebellious peasants," Sasha declared.

"You treat me like a stupid child. It's always Antonina who is allowed to do what she wants: Antonina the clever one, the more beautiful one. You've never tried to understand me – never."

"We cannot let this child go out there without protection." Sasha turned and walked back to his room.

"We would not be standing here now, if the mother of the child did not spend her nights in artistic circles in dubious parts of London." Olga gazed haughtily down into the vestibule.

Valentina took off her coat to reveal a new peach deux-pièces, bordered in black velvet. "And how much time did you spend with me when I was a child? You have no right to dispense morality from up there. You chucked me into that émigrés' boarding school as soon as you could."

"Valentina, I think we should finish this conversation."

"And when I came home for holidays, you had a headache," Valentina shouted up the stairs.

Anna stood there wishing she had decided to go without books or clothes.

"I said, the conversation is finished."

This mercifully silenced Valentina. On the stairs stood Anna, not daring to drag the trunk further down towards the stout front door.

"I insist she takes this with her." Uncle Sasha appeared on the landing again and the light from the bull's eye window behind him revealed a revolver in his hand.

"Carrying fire-arms is illegal in England," said Valentina.

"That is why there are so many strikes. Shoot the rebels, we were told; there's no other way."

Olga walked slowly over to her brother-in-law and coaxed his outstretched hand back against his chest. "Put it back. You might need it still."

He nodded. "I know. I don't understand anymore," he said, as Olga led him back to his room and closed the door.

"You always create problems," Valentina said to Anna with anger. "You could have been a little more diplomatic."

Anna did not remonstrate; did not point out that in all this she had hardly said anything. Valentina came up the stairs to help her daughter carry the trunk down the last steps and then they slid it with a grating noise over the marble floor.

Outside Cahill took over.

"Take care of yourself, darling," said Valentina, once Anna sat in the car.

"I am sorry I have angered you all."

"Olga is simply upset that you want to leave Podzhin Hall too."

"Bye, Mummy."

The Bentley drove off.

But it was true, thought Anna. It was always Antonina who in the end could get away with things.

★

Njanja Durov wore a wax bib-apron and, as she drew soapy circles on the pine table with her scourer, the white foam turned grimy grey. Afterwards she wiped the table-top, rinsing the rag repeatedly.

The old nanny was proud of her kitchen. Last winter Countess Olga had handed down an old Afghan carpet now lying before the Aga and the sink. It prevented the flagstone floor from crawling into the marrow of elderly bones but it also added to the kitchen's dark richness. Njanja twisted the rag under the tap a last time.

Through the window she watched Cahill put the Bentley into the garage. His gingery blond hair played in the temperamental May wind, which carried barbed rain. The sky had suddenly darkened. Raindrops dashed against the glass. She saw him run towards the tradesman's entrance, his hand sheltering his face. It was nearly dark enough to put on the lamp but she did not. Electricity was expensive.

She heard him rumble up the backstairs; they each had a room above the kitchen and scullery. She lifted off the stiff apron and hung it next to the refrigerator. With her puffed red hands she stroked over the drying table top. The pine grain showed clear in the honey colour. It smelled of drenched sawdust and sour apples. From the refrigerator she took a blue polka-dotted ceramic jug with a chipped handle. She put it on the table together with the sugar bowl. Cahill thundered down the stairs again into the scullery to change his shoes. She insisted that he wore his slippers in the kitchen. The flagstones were hard to clean.

She took down the metal prong hanging above the cooker and dragged the cast-iron ring across the stove. With a clear clatter it settled snugly over the coke hole.

She poured a little water from the kettle into the royal blue teapot to warm it and set it on the hot-plate.

Cahill came in. "Any tea going?" He rubbed his hands. "No boasting about spring yet." His combed-down hair shone tangerine. Another shower of rain crashed against the window. In the Aga the fire crackled.

He took his usual seat on the bench alongside the table. "What was all this weeping and moaning that nobody understands her? Miss Anna kept it up all the way to Brampton." Cahill took off his jacket and reached back to hang it on a knob on the dresser base. He opened the buttons on his sleeves and started to roll them back displaying gingery hair on a muscled forearm.

Njanja put saucers and cups on the table. "Where does Miss Anna stay?" She sat down on her special high-backed chair and pulled the embroidered Russian muslin apron into her lap. It was threadbare and needed constant repairing. Njanja tried to thread the white cotton through the needle's eye.

"It's a dank vicarage in a small village. The vicar's wife was about as chummy as a Dublin lawyer."

"Poor Miss Anna."

He saw her squint in concentration.

"You can't see a thing."

Her hands sank down. She shook her head with impatience, and the opal droplet earrings dangled on her ear-lobes. They had been a gift from the countess for Njanja's twentieth birthday. He had never seen her without them.

"Is no light. You do it, and I make zr tea."

With a cloth from the guard-rail she lifted the kettle to pour boiling water over the tea-leaves in the warmed pot. He sat, both elbows propped on the table, the tip of his tongue out as he tried to fit the licked and twisted cotton through the eye. "Got it." He pulled the thread through and then pricked the needle into the table close to her chair.

She flopped the woven mat on the table and put the teapot down. Picking up the needle, she complained, "Dirty finger made it brown."

"Sewing is for womenfolk."

"Anna always make needles ready for me. Now zr Anna gone."

"There is one mouth less to feed," he said and poured milk into the cups.

"Zr Anna gone," she repeated and absent-mindedly pinned the needle into the black dress over her left breast. "I hope she will find zr nice young man." She poured the tea, holding the lid as if it were a baby's bonnet.

"Difficult," he muttered, shovelling sugar into his tea. "The twins got no tits and are all brainy."

Njanja put down the pot. "No criticising zr twins, not in my kitchen."

"It's the way their mother fills their heads about Russian men; the way she wants them to behave schizzy Russian, like her." He put down his cup. "Sorry," he added, seeing Njanja's face.

"Zr Russian men are fetching. Ah."

"Oh ho ho, you knew many of them back in the old country?"

"At Revolution, I was zr seventeen, but officers handsome."

"What's a Russian man got that we haven't? Do they have two, or something?"

Durov rattled off in Russian, angry creases between her eyebrows. He did not need a translation. He sat there nursing his hot cup and watched her over the rim. Against the grey light of the rainy window her snow-white hair, plaited and rolled over her head, looked like an ermine crown. Her skin was dry and powdery but her blue eyes were alive.

He sucked his tea, his eyes on her. Small and old but upright still, she governed this warm cavern – a little old Russian woman in a black dress with black ribbed stockings, sturdy lace-up shoes and fancy earrings which were out of place.

"The Brodsky twins will probably never marry," he said and put his empty cup down.

"Stupid talk," she hissed, recognising his mood. They knew each other well; they ate at this table together every day but she sat at the head while he was on the flank further down. As she had explained once, in Russia an outside man would never have eaten with the nanny.

What he had come to learn about her and respect in her he had pieced together over time.

Durov had suffered a revolution, lost her home and motherland. For her employers, she had sacrificed herself in Podzhin Hall through the Second World War with its shortages and coupons, baking sagging ersatz cakes; patching and struggling through the hand-to-mouth days.

Once, after getting tipsy, she admitted to Cahill that at thirty-nine, a butcher in Hatley had caught her eye. He had a lame leg from polio and apologised for not having been drafted, which had nothing to do with being able or not. He was a man and he was generous with meat.

Tragically the one bomb dropped over the area at the very end of the war had landed on the butcher's house and Durov's romance was gone.

Cahill's eyes showed fondness. She had remained single, dedicating all she had to the family she adored.

A new salvo burst against the window. Cahill groaned. "I've got to do that Rasputin brute before dinner."

"Is zr good horse."

He stroked over his hair which was springy again; had paled back to barley corn. "He hates me. All horses hate me. They try to bite me with their long yellow teeth, staring at me with them blood-veined marble eyes."

She shrugged her shoulders and picked up the cups and saucers from the table. "You shout at zr horse, make nervous."

Cahill sulked. He was in charge of the stallion on the odd days when the youth from the village whom Miss Valentina called "the groom" did not come out to Podzhin Hall.

"I'll be off then," he grumbled, picking his jacket from the knob, but Njanja had her back turned as she scraped carrots at the sink for dinner. He saw the earrings swing as her arms worked.

CHAPTER TEN

Vasily Voronov was proud to be a socialist. Calling himself a faultless communist would have been bragging.

In the windowless office he had requested, because views distracted the brain with colours and shapes, he steeled himself to be sent abroad on a mission to London.

It had all started with a man with a red scar the shape of a sickle on his chin – the patron-comrade who had schooled and trained him with an iron fist. Thanks to that attention Vasily had been accepted in the Party with its opportunities.

He had made it into Foreign Visits Group without once having to reach out for guidance. The benefactor had long ago retreated into shadow yet somehow, when Vasily was preferred over another or got praise, he always assumed that the tough philanthropist was still behind it.

He was entrusted with meeting foreigners. During a debriefing session he learned that an American was recorded saying that he should be approached for defection. Vasily was shocked at first and then angry. *How could the concept of defection from Mother Russia be mentioned in the same breath as his name?*

It was then also that the Party probed his opinion on relationships with women. He was prepared for this question; it was easy to answer. Women undermined his régime of strict obedience and tough physical training. What he aimed to achieve was ascetic purity in mind as in body.

It had been more difficult for him in private to arrive at this response. He avoided married couples as they had given in to behaviour that was ignoble, often even grotesque. He almost had to force himself to obligatory physical intimacy in order to rate as a healthy male.

During the last few months he had gone through the process of preparation to be posted abroad. He had attended a multitude of lectures on the Rules of Behaviour of Soviet Citizens held in a closed section he had not known existed, guarded by KGB men. Eventually he had passed the last test and signed his oath of obedience: to respect prohibitions, be vigilant against provocations, heed hostile surroundings, and to watch out for the cunning manoeuvres of the British Special Services.

The British people, he now knew, had largely accepted the achievements of the power apparatus Stalin had created for the people. They admired the fact that everyone in the Soviet Union had access to education and political direction. Abroad, Vasily's duty would be to further the respect for Soviet policy and to prepare the British for their own eventual revolution.

The past week he had sprinted from departments to sections, handing in his internal passport and Party card; he was now 'in transit'.

107

Vasily's last lecture was behind him. He felt filled with knowledge as he walked down the corridor on the twelfth floor of the Foreign Ministry, east of Smolenskaya Square. On a thick milk-glassed door was the simple number three. He knocked. It was two o'clock on the wood-framed clock down the hall.

"Enter."

Much could still go wrong – a veto come from the Central Committee, intervention by senior KGB officers. Perhaps the chairman of the sub-committee had received a report on Vasily's misbehaviour at a criticism session in the ninth grade in Obodovka.

He entered the office of a Party god. However, no ostentation showed in Room No 3; only a large desk and some functional chairs.

"Comrade Voronov." Georgi Miliukov put the receiver into its cradle and scrutinised Vasily who, upright and unblinking, dark hair cropped short, six feet tall and tightly muscled, managed to show no sign of unease.

Miliukov smiled slightly. "You're joining the elite, Comrade Voronov." The smile hardened as he picked out a brown folder and opened it. Irrational guilt flamed through Vasily. The chairman's eyes glanced over the text, then he turned a page and read on.

Through the window Vasily saw the traffic pass, way below on Smolensky Boulevard. Soviet citizens without a chance of seeing the world hurried along in a bland Muscovite sun: comrades who had pledged their loyalty to the Party just as he had. At eleven years old as a Pioneer in front of propped-up cardboard posters of Soviet leaders he had promised to wear the red scarf clean and bright as a symbol of allegiance.

Miliukov tore Vasily from his contemplations. "The Party and government place a big trust in you by sending you to the front line in the struggle for the final victory of communism."

Vasily knew that on leaving the building he would be given the external passport which was his way out of the Soviet Union. Still things could go wrong after that: the airport control stop him; the final check at the ticket desk discover something to make him ineligible. Changes of mind had even occurred in foreign airports where, instead of Soviet colleagues whisking the arrival from the terminal, people had been put speedily back onto Aeroflot, destination Moscow, without explanation.

"Privileged," Miliukov puffed out. The telephone rang, and a short conversation took place. "You can pick up your passport in Office 13."

"Thank you," said Vasily and felt the strong presence at his side of his benefactor with the scar.

Back on the ground floor with his passport in his pocket he stepped into the reception office to sign the exit form. A plump comrade-typist was hacking slowly on her machine. A pencil-sharpener was clamped to the side of the desk and he knew that it was the only one on the floor. He had worked in offices long enough to know that there was only one on each floor. No matter how deep one pushed the pencil in nor how fast one turned the handle, the pencil came out either blunt or chafed. At worst a piece of lead fell out instantly. The typist turned the book towards him. Vasily signed his name and put down the time of day. It was said that consumer goods in the West were vastly superior to those of Russia. He gave the typist a charming smile.

At Smolenskaya he took the Metro, changed at Kiyevskaya, and got off at Paveletskaya. The sun warmed his face as he walked along backstreets. He approached the gloomy block of flats from the back, crossing the narrow court intended for the tenants' children. No grass was planted and no children played. Two women leaned against the wall, chatting. Two by two he ascended the steps in the unlit staircase.

This was Vasily's most important social call before he left Moscow. He recognised the captive smell of onions and cabbage, the vibrant feel of human presence in a grey warren in which he had spent so many years during his studies at the University and the Institute: the years of cold, hunger, suffering and sacrifice; but also the years of soldering his best friendships. A woman with a bundle of washed sheets passed him. Vasily squeezed against the wall. He knew that she was headed for the cellar to hang them up where they would take forever to dry and where one risked them being stolen. There was not enough room in the crowded flats to dry washing.

How many times had he descended these stairs to turn ration cards into bread? How often had he returned crestfallen for the queue had been discharged, supplies exhausted? He had used the time wasted in queues to study while listening with half an ear to the whispered local gossip. It was vital to hear what was going on and his aunt did not have a radio.

On the fifth floor he tapped three times at the door.

It opened immediately for she knew her nephew was coming. She peered shortly up and down the staircase, then pulled him inside. Yelena was still reticent and wary of everyone.

Wordlessly she clasped him in her arms, and Vasily was aware that she smelled like his mother to whom he could not say goodbye for she had died two years ago in Obodovka.

"Vasilyotchka!" Over her shoulder he smiled when he saw the same old rug on the floor, the tilting bookshelf.

"Are you really going abroad?" She held him in front of her and looked at him.

"I am leaving tomorrow."

"With an aeroplane?"

Vasily nodded. Nothing had changed in that one-bedroom flat where, despite her age and her husband's death, she was allowed to remain. She now shared it with another widow from the annex block.

"I must be going soon to scrub the tax offices on Leningradsky Prospekt, but there is time to heat up some borscht."

"Auntie Yelena, I will be fed."

Vasily had slept on a couch in the recess of that kitchen right behind the door. Now the couch was gone, the two women slept in the bedroom and a pot-bellied refrigerator stood in its place: a gift from Vasily once he had begun to receive his huge salary from the Party. At first she had not used the fridge; only cleaned it and covered it with her best cloth.

Now Yelena opened the refrigerator door. "I have butter," she tempted him.

"I must rush. There are still things to do," which was not quite true but Vasily wanted to have time for himself after the hectic days of preparation.

"A drink then?"

He agreed, and she brought a narrow vodka bottle and placed it on the table. They sat down.

It was around this very table that Vasily had drunk vodka with student friends during the war and talked about America and jazz, while the German threat to Moscow grew. Leningrad was encircled by Hitler's armies; Moscow predicted to be under siege next. Despite the hunger, the cold, the greyness in their lives, they felt committed to Russia, committed to Stalin; they were happy communists. That was more than twenty years ago.

"So, tomorrow you leave with an aeroplane to London." Yelena gaped at him in disbelief.

He removed the passport from his pocket and showed it to her. She wiped her hands carefully on her apron before touching the soft green leather booklet. She did not open it. "A foreign passport. It will be dangerous."

"What would you like me to bring you back from England?"

"You should have gone and said goodbye to your father."

"There was no time to travel all the way to the Ukraine. We have written to each other."

"How is he?"

"Getting on. He says willpower keeps him going."

"He must be proud of you; he always wanted you to know languages. He always pushed you on."

"He wrote something strange like *You can't keep a thoroughbred from the trough*. His handwriting has deteriorated. I will see him when I come back."

"Will they let you come back?"

"Auntie, I will stay a Soviet citizen, and the embassy in which I will work is sort of a clump of Russian land transported to England, on which Russians work for the Soviet Union."

She did not understand.

"What shall I bring you back?" he asked again.

She looked down, then up at him and he recognised the flecks which had been in his mother's eyes.

"Vasily, I would like you to photograph the Queen of England for me."

"I shall do so when I meet her. But in case I don't..."

"Don't take risks."

"If she won't let me photograph her, what else would you like?"

"I would like a pair of soft leather gloves like the ones I saw the other day in the window of GUM emporium, a pair so smooth, so elegant."

Vasily looked at her knobbly hands resting on the table.

"What colour?"

"What colour, *durak*? The colour they come in."

"I'll choose the finest I can find in all of England."

She finished her drink, and he left some and felt suddenly sad. She put the little glass he had drunk from onto the shelf to preserve until he returned, as was the Russian custom.

CHAPTER ELEVEN

The air of May was benign. Anna in a short-sleeved blouse was cycling from Oxford to Brampton. She cruised into the village to the sound of bells, rounded the village green and its pond, and close to the church squeezed the brake-handles to reduce her speed. The mellow change-ringing embraced the whole of the village. Even the ducks nestled under the willow tree, leaving the water calm to mirror the yellow eel-shaped vesper clouds. The pub's black dog lay asleep on its side, uninvolved. Anna felt a strong belonging to this village.

Wheeling the bicycle into the vicarage garden, she noticed a smoke-curl rise from one of the Victorian chimneys showing her that the vicar's wife was cooking.

Anna had rented the annex to the vicarage, consisting of a living-cum-bedroom, a small kitchen and a cheaply added shower-room. The only surface to study on was a wooden ironing-board set up on its lowest notch.

She and her course tutor had just reviewed her thesis: *The impact of industrious, organised and politically guided Russians on society.* His concern about her display of *extreme ideas* had been raised yet again between them.

She did not see it that way. All her life she had been exposed to the bygone values of Imperial Russia. The natural reaction to this had to be a belief in something one could grasp, something one could stand on – that was the soil. Russian politics were about agriculture and peasants, and their lifestyle: working and praising the noble land. Therefore to live in humble surroundings, in a rural village on the border of Ot Moor, feeling the annual rhythm of the seasons, was precisely the right thing for her. To be able to snuggle in its heart exceeded her dreams. The fact that entrance to her living quarters could only be gained via the vicarage kitchen, she considered a bonus.

She opened the outer door and went inside. "Good evening," she said.

The vicar's wife was busy at her stove. At the table with its oranges-and-lemons print waxcloth sat the vicar, gaunt and bitter, his half-moon glasses fixed on the *Oxford Diocese Gazette*.

"Ev'ning," he grunted briefly over the rim of the paper.

Anna had lived here for two weeks now but still wondered whether they liked her. She had done her best to be amiable; to make it clear to them that she was one of them. Tonight, receiving no greeting from the vicar's wife, Anna decided to renew her efforts.

"What a lovely spring evening!"

"Hmm."

"Everything is in bloom, and the peasants' hope will rise anew."

"..."

"I know I belong here; it's a good feeling." Anna sucked her lower lip. "So, I'll be off studying then." She felt a familiar impulse to shake them into an awareness of their surroundings, their value. The bout passed and she went through to her lodgings.

In her room dominated by a carpet with large maroon roses, she glanced at the cross-stitched picture over her bed. *Let Jesus into your home.* She shrugged on a brown cardigan, tilted her head and with her brush pulled energetic strokes through her short dark hair until it puffed with static electricity, the way Olga had taught the twins.

Country people needed coaxing into showing their withheld emotions. *Someone had to unlock them, help them to exteriorise*, she thought, sitting on the candlewick bedcover and pulling tangled hair from the brush. Later she would try again.

Later was when the pealing from the church tower dwindled away. One after another the chimes died and each was curiously missed. One thin bell called the full chorus before it too fell silent. For a moment Anna's ears sang as if the chiming still went on but the village lay hushed. The silence brought a stronger awareness of the musty smell of the vicarage, somewhat clammy and sour.

She decided to go for something to eat at the pub which was now open. In the Lamb and Flag at a corner table in the public bar she sipped at her half-pint of draught beer and ate scampi-in-a-basket.

The regulars stood around the bar in sweaters, grubby trousers and country shoes. She could never distinguish one from another. They reached out their rough hands from time to time to take swigs from their tankards; then they wiped the foam from their lips with their sleeves. Anna strained to hear their conversation. None of them ever said more than a sentence. It sounded like a secret language for it made no sense to her but seemed satisfactorily invigorating to them. "Ah ya," were key words, then another swig, another wipe. At the billiard table a lanky one was bending over, the pole resting on the back of his gristly hand. He closed one eye. *Tzwang*, a ball shot across the green felt and collided with another one, which rushed down a hole with a hollow rumble.

The landlord leant at the bar, chin in one hand. The door opened and a short man came in. His trunky legs were in jeans. Encrusted dirt garnished his calves. His feet stood in black rubber boots with straps. He wore several layers of sweaters one over the other to judge by what emerged around his dirty neck. The outer knitwear was moss-green and had seen rough times. He established himself at the bar in a spot which seemed to be reserved for him. The landlord unglued his elbow and drew a pint. The dark curly hair of the man was matted and greasy, and his unruly beard suggested a prolonged hatred of soap and razor. Fleetingly he passed over Anna with his dark eyes; then he squared his back solidly against her.

She knew that they knew about her, talked about her, and she wondered what they said and when. A compact unity around the bar was formed; the short man was integrated. Anna watched, fascinated but again with

117

frustration. *If only they knew how well she understood them, could help them have a better communication, become more fulfilled. There was so much she could give them.*

Having finished her meal, she had no more reason to sit there, stare and listen. She left the pub giving the group of men her most charming smile which she laced with feelings of camaraderie. Clearly they were taken aback for none reciprocated. The short man stared with positive loathing at her. *He needs my help most*, decided Anna. *Washed, combed and dressed in nice clothes, he would certainly gain a lot in self-esteem.*

*

The conversation stopped the moment Anna stepped into the vicarage kitchen. The vicar's wife had finished cooking and was sitting at the table knitting.

"Hello again!" Anna took breath. "Perhaps you can tell me who the short dark man in the pub is. He has a beard and wears a green sweater and boots with straps."

The vicar glanced at his wife.

"That could be Ron," she ventured and yanked at her ball of wool. "Why do you want to know, my dear?" It was said in a tone Anna interpreted as disapproving.

Anna traced along the design on the tablecloth. "He struck me as different from the others."

"Ah, that must be Ned Worship then." The vicar's wife turned her knitting and started a new row.

"Who is he?" Anna dared to ask. "He seemed troubled."

"Troubled, our Ned?"

The vicar's wife pointed at her husband with the knitting needle. "Perhaps it's because his mother has to have one of those bolts put into her hip."

"What does he do?" insisted Anna since she felt encouraged by the couple talking to each other in her presence.

"The Worships are a farming family."

"I heard he's writing more of his poetry. Maybe, he'll send us one for the parish magazine again."

"Poetry!" exclaimed Anna. "That's why he looked troubled. How marvellous!"

Anna, aware that she had let herself go, felt the couple's eyes on her.

"All in all, he's rather grubby, I think," said the wife of the vicar.

"What's the farm called?"

"South Field Farm, down that way." The vicar pointed towards the sink.

"Is she having her hip done in the Radcliffe, you reckon?" The wife turned to her husband.

Anna left the kitchen, leaving the two in conversation.

A troubled farmer with the heart of a poet. Baratynsky: the sad reflections of eternity, the insurmountable laws of existence. Great seeds lodged in a simple chest.

Anna had to find out more about the farmer-poet.

At least now she had something to write to Antonina about. Her sister's last letter had not mentioned Anna leaving home; she had only written about herself. Anna took out the thin airmail letter and read it for the umpteenth time.

… it feels as if I've been here for ages. You should see me in faded bell-bottomed jeans, a cotton shirt knotted at the waist. I'm wearing my hair open, parted in the middle, a pair of huge sunglasses stuck on top. Ricky is showing me all the groovy sights of New York.

Yesterday, he took me to a demo in front of the UN. That's a demonstration. There was a large crowd of young people, all sorts of folk. It was against drafting young men into the Vietnam War. We carried flowers and stopped all the traffic. The cops watched, arms crossed, truncheons on their belts. We handed them flowers with the message make love, not war, *and they grinned. It all went without incident. And then, read this, right in front of the UN building on 42nd Street, Peter, Paul and Mary were singing.* The Cruel War is Raging, *and other songs. It started to rain, but everyone stayed, and they kept singing – a fantastic atmosphere.*

Loudspeakers started to howl, asking us to go home and to walk, not to run. Abolish reality, *many shouted. Ricky was great. Sadly, he is packing to leave for Princeton University summer course. He is doing sociology. There won't be any fun left without him. Keeping Irina company is no joy, and Travis, her son, is hardly ever home.*

I miss you a lot.

The OTHER ONE.

P.S. In the crowd walking away from the event, I was sure I saw you. Me, with your tilting of head, your profile, our colour of hair but yours cut short. You kept checking the red light waiting for the green man to cross the road.

"If you knew how much I miss you," Anna said into the darkening room as evening had come. Despite the distance between them the telepathic link still worked. Antonina had seen her wait at the curb, prevented from moving on until the green man appeared and allowed her to cross to the other side – a man wearing a green sweater?

Ungenerously Anna was relieved to read that the young American had to go back to Princeton and that Irina was a pain in the neck. Wouldn't that prompt Antonina to come home sooner? For hours Anna had fretted that Ricky would become Antonina's boyfriend, then quickly her beloved. In her fear she had imagined the two of them on the steps of a New England chapel, her twin in a white dress and she, Anna, in a tailored suit on a short visit for the wedding only.

What had probably happened was that Antonina, in that country of rock'n'roll, had made love to Ricky. With such an experience of a man's way in bed: the warming up to sex – foreplay, they called it – the actual act and then the feelings after; and how to cope with all that, Antonina was now way ahead of Anna. This could easily put a separation between them. It would probably show on Antonina when she returned. Anna had to do something to catch up with her twin.

*

The following evening as she approached South Field Farm, the rooks in the crown of the oak tree were still boisterous. It sounded as if there were too many rooks and not enough nests. Underneath in the meadow were the dark outlines of cows, standing dumbfounded. Anna's hand trembled.

She knocked the rusty ring against the wood of the cottage door. A dog started to bark. Jerking and swaying, a tractor rumbled down the road, the two headlights picking up details in the asphalt. Nervously Anna looked over her shoulder. The jolted farmer in a cap with a visor checked her out. The dog still barked. She regretted having come.

She was wearing a longline jacket, all-round pleated skirt in white linen and a pale blue satin blouse. In her short hair was an Alice band.

The dog changed tune. The blouse stuck to Anna's armpit. Someone fiddled with the lock. Her heart was throbbing. The rooks croaked.

The cottage door opened a crack offering a slice of light. In it a dishevelled head appeared. Dark eyes the colour of onyx peered at her.

"Hello," came from Anna louder than she would have ideally liked.

"What do you want?"

"Talk to you about yourself, poetry, Tolstoy, Pushkin and the sad and beautiful things in life…"

"Shut up!"

"Sorry?"

"The dog."

"Ah, I see. Can I come in, please?"

"No."

"I won't take much of your time, I promise."

The dark eyes travelled up and down her white ensemble; the fleshy mouth curled. "I'm busy."

The same tractor as before rolled along the road coming from the other direction. The driver in his high seat stared at Anna.

"In the name of poetry, let me in for a few moments or I'll scream." Anna, animated, had dropped out of her rehearsed role.

The onyx eyes contained a dangerous glint. The door opened a little wider.

Anna pushed through. A shaggy grey dog with a caked pelt sniffed at her stockings. He stank of manure.

The farmer-poet stood away from Anna, his back safely against the front parlour.

"You have a dog. That's nice. He needs a bath."

"He'd shrink."

In the intimacy of the narrow corridor she looked at her green man more closely. He was a head shorter than she. His feet were bare, his toenails black. She smiled at him. Having come so far, she was not going to give in to the urge to turn and run away.

"Is that the kitchen?" She made a move further into the hall.

"No." He shook his head.

"Ah, a typical country kitchen."

Ned pushed himself into the room past her and sat proprietorially on a spindleback chair. The garden visible through the window was a grown-over mess leading into a field. The grey dog followed the spirals of the hearth rug in circles before lying down, eyes secured on his master. A frail bookshelf was heaped with books. Their owner, sitting taut with both his hands gripping the armrests of his chair, was watching Anna's every move.

"Books – I knew I was right!" She pointed to the shelf. "By the way, I am Anna Brodsky. You do not have to be impressed; we're not as important as we used to be in St Petersburg."

A wry smile garnished the farmer's mouth.

"I'm doing an MA in Russian history at Oxford and I love people who understand the earth and poetry. As you must know, the two go hand in hand. What's your name?"

"Ned."

"Very nice."

"No, it isn't."

After that, an unwholesome silence ensued, broken only by the dog who lifted his head and emitted a strange barking sneeze. A clock somewhere chimed and she realised that she would have to leave it at that.

Despite the rapid way in which he ushered her back to the house door which he held open for her, she still managed to say, "You'd be surprised how much we have in common" and "Let's meet again and talk about your writing."

Ned remained in the corridor, like a troll in the crevice of a rock.

"Take care," she said, and her heels clicked on the stone steps outside.

The door was banged shut. The rooks were still arguing in the oak trees.

CHAPTER TWELVE

On Governor's Island it was lunchtime. Antonina sat on a rock near the sea and fed stale bread and left-over *Always* to the seagulls fighting for it in the choppy waters. Offshore, a brown motorboat fought through the waves and beyond was the faint outline of the Statue of Liberty. The place she had found was ideal because it was in a sheltered cove and rendered her invisible from the land, yet she could see down the coast for a bit. The island was less than a kilometre across and it took less than an hour to walk around it. It seemed to Antonina that the boat out there had stopped and, now stationary, pitched violently to and fro. *What if it capsized, and the two men aboard fell in?* She stood up and peered out to sea.

It was clear she was not the only one to see the boat because three coast guards appeared on the shore further along and raised their rifles towards it. Were they so bored or drunk that they shot at passing vessels rather than offer maritime safety? The motorboat took off and the guards went away.

This little incident was the only excitement for her since Ricky had left a week ago for Princeton with his trunk and his guitar.

My country 'tis of thee, sweet land of liberty – not so sweet: America for Antonina had turned out to be imprisonment on this coast guard base. Twice a day the flag was saluted, the cannon fired, with everyone having to remain motionless for thirty seconds: an old tradition. Two thousand men lived in barracks onshore, either in training or working in administration in Admiral's House, or on leave which was worst of all. There were only about forty-five women on the island: some wives, daughters and mothers, two elderly primary teachers, and one single female under twenty-five – herself, constantly being approached with curiosity and checked lust.

Whenever she sat in the sun in front of the kitchen they appeared in their sailor uniforms, or in the black coats of officers with two rows of gold buttons, the white cap clamped under the arm. "Do you need assistance, ma'am? Is our information that you are from England correct, ma'am? May we have permission to approach, ma'am, to formally invite you to the Mess, ma'am?"

Antonina had complained to Irina about this and suggested that, with some help from Travis perhaps, there might be a typing job in Admiral's House, a uniform for her to wear for protection.

Irina was outraged by the mere thought and enjoyed every minute of it. She had taken to ordering evening wear for Antonina with the help of the Sears catalogue. Antonina had to fetch the large cardboard boxes and return them to the postal service in the barracks. She did not want the dresses.

And then Irina remembered another White Russian from St Petersburg, now in New Jersey: one who definitely had a good-looking unmarried grandson, Count Aleksinsky. From the photograph, the man was short and fat with the complexion of an unhappy alcoholic.

More *Always* were made and an imaginary wedding planned in the brain of the lonely old Russian under her blond screw-curl wig: the Russian Orthodox Cathedral; Antonina in an embroidered Empress dress, a diamond crown on her head; a regal reception in the ballroom of the Plaza Hotel, with the Brodskys, the Tarnovskys, the Tolstoys...

A wave crashed against Antonina's rock. She crumpled up the paper bag and brushed breadcrumbs off her clothes. The seagulls flew elsewhere as she walked back to the house.

It had emerged that Travis was a Lieutenant Commander, a lawyer with the US Coast Guard. When he came home, which was not often, he wore his uniform, and Antonina felt his discomfort in a house where his wife had died of cancer: a Coast Guard property which went with the job. It was a convenient arrangement as he needed to pay for his son's expensive education and provide a secure shelter for his old White Russian mother. The combination of all this did not leave a happy atmosphere in the house, especially not now without Ricky and his Charlie Brown wisdom, security-blanket-trailing Linus. *Of all the Charlie Browns in the world, you're the Charlie Browniest.*

Besides enjoying this philosophy disguised as childishness, Antonina had taken to making herself peanut butter and jelly sandwiches and listening to

Elvis Presley records in Ricky's bedroom. He was an undemonstrative, thoroughly kind, young man, alas too young for her, and had left her his record-player on loan until he was settled in at Princeton. This was an act of generosity only a former sophomore could appreciate.

However, that *until* was something positive for him, not for her. She saw herself turning into an unwelcome guest; indeed, she could by now already be regarded as a squatter here. It filled her with anger and a sense of betrayal, but it was her own fault, and living with unhappy people as she did, the disappointment in herself was the only personal aspect she had in common with them.

Antonina sat cross-legged on the carpet, her skirt tucked in under her ankles and her hair draped over her shoulders. Outside it was drizzling insipidly. Leaning back against the broad side of the sofa, she read the *Herald Tribune* in search of a way out of her predicament. Upstairs Irina was having her two-hour nap. Through the open window, Antonina could hear the thump of the military band practising on the parade ground. On the dining room table lay an open cardboard box from Sears, in which was an organdie debutante dress for her to try on.

A chill seized her, and a hollow vault seemed to open around her. In it floated Anna's eyes, wide and vacant, while her twin's warm breath was on her face and she felt a hand crawl along her neck under her hair for a desperate hug. Antonina struggled to sit up higher against the sofa to gain control over the chimera.

It evaporated as suddenly as it had appeared. Antonina felt drained and a solitary helplessness remained. "Anna, I hope you're managing better than me."

Irina, snoring upstairs, was assuming that Olga had sent her here as a present: a companion who would gratefully listen to the old Petersburg stories, one who would assume the role of a granddaughter.

Antonina had to get away and she was not ready to go back home – hell, she hadn't done anything, been anywhere, yet. California was the place where young Americans dreamed of going; Ricky had told her that hippies lived there. In the *ads* section of the newspaper were flights to San Francisco. For that she would have to ask Olga for more money, and back home they would not understand why she wanted to go to California.

★

Saturday morning at breakfast, she found Travis in his bathrobe in the kitchen, toasting waffles. Before Irina had a chance to overwhelm the conversation, Antonina announced that she had to go to San Francisco. "Cheaply," she added. "Very cheaply."

"It's three thousand miles away."

"There seems to be a Greyhound bus service, ninety-nine dollars for ninety-nine days, I saw in the paper."

"It would take weeks."

"I could hitchhike, some of it."

"In most states there are laws against it."

"My dearest Antonina," cooed Irina, "it's Ricky who has put these ideas in your head, isn't it?"

Antonina nearly choked with impatience. "I have to get there. I can't just give in and go home."

129

Travis noticed her frantic tone and guessed at her panic. He poured maple syrup over two waffles resembling toy mattresses and offered her the plate. "I happen to know that the church organises trips across the States for foreign students."

"The Coptic Pope in his mitre behind the wheel of a tourist bus?"

"No, Mamushka. It's organised by the Catholic church – Father Bernard in fact, whom you know."

"I only have to know him because I have no way to visit the Orthodox Cathedral in New York. You keep telling me that Eastern Orthodox belief is compatibly catholicose, but it is not the same, not the same at all."

As Antonina had feared, Irina prattled on about religious subjects while her son went upstairs to change.

Coming down dressed to the nines in his parade uniform, he promised that he would get in touch with Father Bernard.

"There is no hurry, Turskopolk, my dearest, no hurry at all," Irina shouted after her son, and Antonina understood why he called himself Travis.

CHAPTER THIRTEEN

Whitsun had passed and it was the month of June. Sasha woke and knew at once that it was early again. Each morning for the last year night had cheated him of a few minutes: a curse inflicted by old age which no sedative had the power to remedy, nor exhaustion to eradicate. Rather than toss and turn in a bed that had become an instrument of torture, he got up and put on his silk monogrammed dressing gown. He encased his blue-veined, deathly pale feet in fur-lined pantoufles and crept down the stairs, holding tightly onto the metal banister. The vestibule lay sombre; the immense chandelier from Murano with dropping crystal prisms and strings of petrified tears hung dull. Silence shrouded the house.

Sasha pushed open the door to the music room. The smell of yesterday's conversation and Valentina's cigarettes lingered. The furniture stood dark against the ash panels. He drew the chintz curtains aside and carefully unlatched the French windows to push the doors outward.

A tremolant pre-dawn bird sounded vigorously from a bush. Ground-hugging daisies, determined to exist despite Cahill's mowing, studded the dark formal lawn, like stars in a clear firmament. Bland misty vapour rose in nebulous shapes before Sasha. They fled from him over a dew-drenched park, sucking more shapes to join them from between hedges and borders, distorting into tailed floating ghosts towards the graves, towards the wood.

He turned and went back inside. He switched on the tasselled silk-shaded lamp and stood in the middle of the lit room, exorcised of ghosts as the park had been cleared before his eyes. The day would grow, take shape, outline reality, and Sasha still heard the lawyer's worrying words about the reality of their finances.

Olga, his courageous sister-in-law by three years his senior and so much stronger, had always had astuteness as well as beauty. Her decision to ask for compensation had already borne most encouraging fruit.

Sasha rolled open the desk lid and took out the invitation card to read it again.

The Embassy of the Union of Soviet Socialist Republics requests the pleasure of the company of Count and Countess Ivan Brodsky.

They did not know that Count Ivan was dead nor that he, Viscount, was living at Podzhin Hall. Sasha tapped the invitation against the manicured nail of his left thumb. Olga had already decided not to enlighten the Soviets about the changes in the family "to spare him pain", as she had put it. He hated to have to be spared pain but knew that he was not up to the strain of a luncheon party.

After a shouting match in Olga's bedroom, from which Njanja later brought down potsherds in a pail,

Valentina had won agreement that she should replace Ivan and accompany Olga to the embassy luncheon.

Declared too weak to attend the lunch there were still important affairs Sasha was able to take care of. He removed a thick folder from the desk drawer and sat down.

With punctiliousness he examined each bond and every share. Once he had drawn up a list of them, he checked it and added up the amounts. The shares in the *Société Metallurgique of Dnieprovienne* and the *Trans-Siberian Railway* bonds alone were in the range of thirty-five million roubles. He calculated and concentrated, then put down his fountain pen to stare at the enormous figure. There were also the two thick bundles of bank notes. He flicked through the large decorative paper money and his thoughts trailed. Those notes were the ones he had stuffed into his coat pocket in haste before they set off for the train station in St Petersburg in January 1918, the day he could never forget. Haste is what he remembered, and chaotic images etched deeply by fear into his memory. They had packed many cases. However, once arrived at the station, it became clear that saving their skin had priority. His brother Ivan and he had fought to get the family into a carriage. Before there was any opportunity to load more than two trunks, the over-crowded train started to roll. Sasha remembered leaning out of the wagon window to see the servant guarding the pile of crates and the two Great Danes, Sasha's dogs, sitting obedient as Sasha had ordered them to do. Even now in nightmares he sometimes saw the dogs sitting still on the platform, loyal to the order of the only one whom they obeyed, waiting. Sasha wiped his eyes and turned his mind to more positive thoughts.

If the Russians paid back half of the enormous amount in front of him, or a tenth even – then all could be repaired. He could think of Great Danes again; no, that he would never do. Converted, half the figure meant something like two million pounds. Podzhin Hall would be safe and he could return to the style of life which was becoming to him.

With shaking fingers Sasha lit one of Valentina's Sobranie cigarettes. The inhaled smoke contracted his lungs, and his fingertips tingled. A wave of guilt rushed through him as the strong Sobranie worked through his veins. *If Olga saw him smoking before breakfast had even started in the kitchen!* He pouted his lips and a perfect ring extruded from his mouth and travelled upwards, distorting into an oval before fizzing out.

"Shit!"

Sasha jumped at the coarse voice coming from the French windows. He squashed his cigarette hurriedly in the ashtray and covered it. Then he faced the intruder.

"This has to be Podzhin Hall."

"I beg your pardon?"

"I don't dispense pardons."

"How dare you break into houses at this early hour?"

"The window was open."

Sasha tried to hide his shaking by twirling the tips of his moustache but he did not succeed, so he hid his hand behind his back and adopted a pose as impressive as his dressing gown allowed. "Are you a burglar?"

"Are you destroying incriminating documents?" retorted the intruder.

Sasha looked blank.

"Burglars usually remove goods from houses. They don't bring them."

Sasha did not think the individual facing him could in any way bring anything beneficial to Podzhin Hall. An ill-treated mop of flaming red hair covered his head, his ears and most of his neck. A smell of smouldering surrounded him. Sasha's eyes dared to travel down over a cotton shirt splattered with what appeared to be dried toothpaste. The long legs stood apart in cream trousers which bell-bottomed out over canvas shoes into which holes had been carved to give the big toes a chance to stretch.

"Who are you?" Sasha tried to bellow.

"Try Dr Livingstone."

The intruder's muddy-coloured eyes looked straight at Sasha, then around the room. The smell of burning around him had intensified.

"Posh!" The stranger approached the fireplace. Sasha got up slowly and moved towards the bell-button. Surely Durov or Cahill were up by now.

The gingertop framed the space above the mantelpiece with his hand, as if he intended to photograph it. "Spot on."

Sasha pointed his finger to the button.

"Why don't you burn your bonds in the fireplace?"

Sasha twisted round. The bundle of *Trans-Siberian Railway* bonds were on fire. A large dark hole had burnt in the middle and little flames were eating their way further out. The cigarette! He dashed to the desk and stamped out the fire with his rocking blotter. His heart leaped in his chest.

"Dash it." He was in the clutches of an onslaught of irrational fury. "Man!" He spun to face the objectionable creature. "State your name and business, or I'll call the police."

Paul grinned. "Take it easy, Grandpop. I brought the painting as a surprise."

Sasha sank back on a chair. "Painting. What painting?"

"The work of art your inspired family commissioned for the countess's birthday."

The attitude of Paul unnerved Sasha deeply. He remembered now. Anger against Valentina who had instigated this move to replace the Ikon flamed up in him. The anger, paired with the shock and the cigarette on his empty stomach, made his head spin. He gulped for air.

Paul turned and went outside, to return carrying a square parcel wrapped in paint-splattered newspaper.

"Olga's portrait," whispered Sasha, over his tantrum.

"Better than that, Pop. The Virgin Emblem branded onto immortality." Paul carried the ungainly parcel to the mantelpiece and started to unravel it. Overcome by faintness Sasha watched, his arms pendant, hands trembling.

"Ta-da!" Paul lifted out the canvas and propped it on the mantelpiece.

Sasha squinted, then stared. An unintelligible sound escaped his congested chest.

Nonchalantly, one arm draping the mantelpiece slab, Paul posed in front of his work of art. "You can't ask for more, now can you?"

There was a long silence inside the music room while, in the park outside, the birds shrilly announced a new day.

On the canvas were overlaid brush-strokes of oil in flesh colours, apparently a naked prostrate female, legs spread, painted from a point of perspective at bed level. The detailed reproduction of the Prince of Pozharsky insignia, copied from a photograph of the Ikon, lodged incongruously in the middle of the modern painting.

CHAPTER FOURTEEN

On the third Wednesday in July the Bentley approached the front portal of the Soviet Embassy in Kensington Palace Gardens. Countess Olga sat rigidly upright on the back seat, conveying an impression of superiority over Valentina who was chain-smoking next to her. All morning had been spent in a slanging match between mother and daughter on what the other could not possibly wear for the lunch at the embassy. Finally leaving in haste, Smelly Ben played up and had to be driven at slow speed, for the catch on the bonnet had come loose and threatened at any time to open like the jaws of a large black animal. Now they were late.

An embassy guard stepped towards the car door before Cahill could oblige. Valentina, closer to the pavement, alighted first. She gave her mother a triumphant smile. Regally Olga remained seated until the gardener, kitted out with one of Sasha's old uniforms, helped her out on her side.

The white embassy mansion was distinguished and blended well into elegant Kensington.

"Trust the Commies to get the best," muttered Valentina.

Inside, the carpet of the hall was a burgundy red. Above the stairs hung a framed picture of Leonid Brezhnev. Discreet red ribbons were entwined in the staircase railings. Apart from this, the décor was devoid of pomp; indeed the only furnishing was a mobile coat-rail. Valentina was disappointed; she had heard so many stories from Sasha of gold-encrusted ushers and liveried footmen that they had been firmly embedded in her imagination. Instead, a well-dressed man with a touch of silver at his temples came up to them, while a dumpy woman in a white apron relieved them of their summer wraps.

Next to the stern tufty-eyebrowed portrait of Brezhnev lingered a dour individual whose function was obvious from the way he eyed the door and the removal of coats.

"I am Rozhkov, the first secretary," said the distinguishedly greying man with calm reserve.

Olga handed him a faded visiting card: *Count and Countess Ivan Mikhailevich Brodsky, Director, Imperial Bank, St Petersburg.*

The first secretary read it carefully, then scrutinised the two women, one in a purple cocktail dress and pill-box hat, the other in black silk with a tight pearl choker, as if they had been removed temporarily from a glass case for dusting.

"Please follow me."

Olga remained, her right hand raised limply. Rozhkov smiled indulgently and proceeded towards an open double door.

Cocktails were to be served in a reception room furnished with the old-fashioned gilt ornateness of

France. The same red decorations were wound around pictures close to the plaster mould of the coving.

"Tasteless," said Olga, standing undecided at the door, Valentina behind her.

The ambassador strode towards them. "My dear…" he hesitated, "… Brodskaya."

"Countess," insisted Olga, proffering her hand again. The ambassador's eyes were impenetrably cold. In those bottomless depths whirled many immediate assessments of people whose hands he had shaken. He made his judgement and bent over Olga's hand without touching it.

"Countess," he whispered, just audibly. Olga smiled over the balding patch on the top of his head. A waiter offered them white wine unsuccessfully.

"Let me introduce you," said the ambassador and led the two women into the room.

"My wife."

Her Ladyship reminded Olga of a well-fed Russian peasant in an outmoded frock and thick stockings.

"We are very pleased you could come," she said in good English.

"*U vas yest shampanskoye*?" asked Olga.

A flicker of panic showed in Her Ladyship's eyes. "Of course. Champagne for these ladies," she ordered from the passing waiter.

"May I introduce you to Mrs Rozhkov? You have already met her husband, the first secretary."

"How do you do?"

"This is Mr and Mrs Ne Win from the Burmese Embassy."

"How do you do?"

"And this is Vasily Voronov, recently arrived at our embassy."

Olga stopped and asked the handsome forty-year-old man, "Tell me Mr Voronov, what is the meaning of all these red ribbons?"

Vasily avoided the aggressive eyes of Valentina which troubled him. "I am sorry?"

"Those gaudy garlands?"

"This year, we are celebrating the fiftieth anniversary of the Glorious Revolution." He looked up and quickly down again, met by two outraged stares.

"Young man," said Olga, "you held your history book upside down at school."

Flutes of champagne were handed to the ladies. On Valentina's face a greedy interest in Vasily was clearly visible. "What do you do in the embassy?"

Vasily hesitated and finally replied nonchalantly, "Like all diplomats, I serve the interests of my country abroad."

"For a communist, you're quite dishy."

"I beg your pardon?"

Valentina laughed out loud. "You're probably only a commie because Russia gives you no other choice."

Vasily genuinely did not seem to understand her. "Sorry," he repeated. It was obvious he yearned to escape from these women, but could not for he had his back against a sofa.

Olga's mouth was slightly pursed. "How nice to meet an elegant Russian." She nodded in Vasily's direction.

"Cheers," proposed Valentina, holding her glass precariously near Vasily's nose. "We used to drink excellent sparkling wines from Georgia."

"We still grow many worthy vines in the Georgian region."

"I am talking about before your – how did you call the massacre? – glorious revolution."

Valentina challenged Vasily. "Do we frighten you?"

He was saved by the distraction of a door opening. "I believe lunch is served."

The table in the next room was set in the British fashion. No embroidered tablecloth, no ornate silver; just mats on a polished rosewood table. Vasily was seated opposite Valentina. Olga was to the right of the short and swarthy Burmese diplomat. Her Ladyship was at one end of the table. She smiled uninterruptedly as if she had left her brain back home in Moscow. The ambassador was seated at the other end. Chilled cucumber soup was served.

"Have you ever been to Rangoon?" Mr Ne Win bent towards Olga.

"No."

"It is wonderful in the winter, which of course we do not have."

"Where is Rangoon?"

The man set to spooning his soup.

"To friendship amongst all peoples," toasted the ambassador. His diction was flawless.

The luncheon wine was Mukuzani from Georgia, and Olga smiled appeased. Her Ladyship led the conversation to sightseeing in London. She had visited Hampton Court and the Tower of London. The first secretary talked to the Burmese lady.

Olga leaned forward. "The Alexander Palace was far superior to any Hampton Court," she countered.

"But of course, it was where they held the Czar prisoner."

The ambassador cleared his throat. "You have been to Kew Gardens as well, haven't you, dear?"

"Oh yes," smiled his wife. "It is really very pleasant." Her end of the table fell to discussing the gardens.

"Tell me U Ne Win, how is the Secretary General of the United Nations?"

The small dark face gleamed. "We are of course proud that a Burmese statesman was chosen for such an honour."

"Where exactly is this Burma?" Olga cupped her curl.

Valentina was unusually quiet. She did not listen to the conversations; her eyes were fastened on Vasily who seemed to choke on the smooth cool soup.

"Mr Voronov – or should I say *Comrade*? – are you having fun in London?" she asked him at last.

"London is a remarkable city."

"And you will feel little of its pulse. Compared with what Moscow nowadays offers, London is probably Nirvana."

Vasily, his face pale, focused on her across the table. He was lost for words, lost for guidance.

"Don't worry," Valentina said soothingly. "If you now spout propaganda for what Moscow has to offer, you'll diminish the value of London. And that won't do, seeing as you've just been sent here."

Vasily seemed to deflate in his seat.

"Do you still have relations in the Soviet Union?" the first secretary asked Olga bravely.

"All shot or hung long ago," she retorted before being beset again by Ne Win trying to explain exactly where Rangoon was.

"I think you are mistaken; we do not execute people for political offences."

"You used to."

"At the Bloody Tower, to which Her Ladyship referred earlier, the British executed many people. This is history and past. We now live a better life of understanding."

"Really? Commemorating your fiftieth anniversary with red ribbons? Today is the seventeenth of July; does that mean anything to you, Mr Voronov?" Olga turned her attention down the table.

Vasily frowned. "I believe not," he said cautiously, aware that he was being led towards a new trap.

"Czar Nikolai II was assassinated today forty-nine years ago in Ekaterinburg."

Shocked, Vasily shot a glance at the ambassador who had led his conversation into admiring the good work of the United Nations.

"You know, my dear Mrs Brodsky, in Rangoon we also have…"

"I am sorry but I am not interested."

Mr Ne Win turned his back on Olga as far as could still be considered acceptable.

"Now of course, with the roses in full bloom, Kew is a picture."

Stuffed breast of lamb, cauliflower and new potatoes were served.

"Tell me the truth, Mr Voronov," started Valentina. "Do we look like aristocratic monsters to you?"

"The English are accomplished gardeners, don't you think, Mrs Brodskaya?"

Olga, her eyes fixed on Vasily for his reply, ignored Her Ladyship's effort.

"The important thing in the study of history, I believe, is to remember that in every great cause, there are uncontrolled, perhaps sometimes unfortunate, side-effects," Vasily finally answered.

"We take it you know why we have been asked for lunch today," said Olga.

"Indeed."

"Do you agree that you owe us some of what you took?"

"Excuse me for a moment, please." Vasily got up and left the table, to disappear through the door. Valentina shrugged her shoulders and attacked the lamb.

The ambassador stubbornly confined himself to the United Nations. "… a neutral theatre where the community of nations can gather."

The conversation was stilted. The majority around the table were Soviet diplomats as if to ensure control. The Burmese was very defensive and his wife not much of a conversationalist judging from the way Rozhkov sturdily ate.

When a mousse in individual glass bowls was served, Vasily returned. Finally they got up and were offered coffee in the same room as they had had cocktails.

Olga turned over an empty cup. "Limoges," she read, holding it at a distance from her eyes. "We always ate off French porcelain in Russia."

The ambassador placed himself next to her on the sofa. To his other side sat Valentina. Opposite them Vasily had pulled up a chair. Madame Ne Win and Mrs Rozhkov were turning the pages of a book on Kew Gardens which Her Ladyship had brought. The Burmese tried to talk to Rozhkov.

Liqueurs were offered from a trolley. Olga declined with thanks. Valentina chose vodka. Vasily glanced at her and followed her lead.

"*Nazdroviye,*" she exclaimed and swallowed the contents of the small glass. Vasily contemplated his glass, nodded and drained it.

"That's better," said Valentina. "Again!"

Vasily excused himself and left the room.

The ambassador raised his eyebrows. "Your daughter has a strong stomach. I guess it is a sign of good health."

"My daughter and I are very honoured at having been treated so well today," said Olga civilly. "You see, it reminds us of home a little."

"How interesting you consider Russia your home after so many years as a privileged foreigner."

"All our privileges had to be left back in St Petersburg," said Olga dryly.

Vasily returned and sat down again.

"We have naturally informed Moscow of your request for compensation."

"The Kremlin?"

"I believe so."

"Is St Basil's still the same silly collection of red-shelled onions?"

The ambassador laughed. "It was when I saw it last. We take every care to maintain our historic buildings.

Russia is still rich in valuable artworks despite the fact that so much has unfortunately found its way abroad."

"We own the Virgin of Kazan." Valentina tapped her chest.

"How very fortunate for you."

Vasily crossed his legs.

Valentina added, "I am afraid we are in the process of selling it to a rich American due, let's say, to the lack of the privileges you consider we enjoy."

Vasily re-crossed his legs.

Pretending to search for a handkerchief in her purse, Olga gave Valentina a nudge in the ribs. "I am afraid my daughter is not entirely familiar with the present whereabouts of our heirloom."

"You are still in possession of the Ikon, I take it then?"

"Of course. She is absolutely magnificent. It is true that the Americans are showing great interest in her, but I am afraid I would not part with her without being duly recompensed and assured of her fate."

Valentina gave her mother a puzzled glance and accepted a third vodka from the trolley. The others declined.

"You see, my granddaughter Antonina is currently in America." Olga cupped her curl. "She has taken the Ikon with her to assess a would-be purchaser."

Without seeking a pretext Valentina kicked her mother's shin. Vasily glanced at the ambassador shortly.

"We are careful with our Virgin, believe me," Olga continued. "It is all we have left from home."

"Naturally," said Vasily, who had not said anything since his return.

"I believe that the hoarding of precious artworks from Europe appeases the American nation for having not much history of their own," said the ambassador.

Valentina turned to Vasily. "My grandfather was the Grand Duke Alexander Yerivanski. Doesn't that make you feel awkward?"

Vasily got up.

"Don't always excuse yourself," whispered Valentina. Vasily paled and sat down again. "Where do you come from?"

"From the Ukraine – a small village."

"Pretty?"

"Very charming."

"See, we share a motherland," she said. "One can never change one's origins."

"To the benefit of this origin, one can change mentality, habits, opinions."

Valentina laughed. "Not the Brodskys!"

He smiled a little crisply. The ambassador rose. Unmistakably, the lunch party had come to its end.

At the door Mr Ne Win said to Olga, "It was most interesting to talk about Rangoon with you."

The ambassador bent over Olga's hand. "I am delighted to have made this first contact with you. Your letter will receive serious consideration and you will be hearing from us formally in due course."

"*Spasibo*," she said.

"You're welcome," he answered in English.

"See you again I hope," said Valentina to Vasily, who did not hear for his back was turned in retreat.

The first secretary showed them out and made sure they were safely tucked into their car.

"I've got an atrocious headache."

"Comrade Voronov." Counsellor Turchin shook his head. "I hear you were introduced to the target of your operation at lunch today and that you walked out on two occasions."

"I apologise," Vasily sighed. "Their manners were so brutal; their approach so direct. How shall I put it?" He searched for the proper word. "Bearlike." There was exasperation in his voice.

"Frightening, perhaps?"

"Yes, one could put it that way."

"Now, my dear Vasily, you have met two examples of the misguided victims of feudalism, against whom you have been trained to work."

Vasily nodded. He felt like a vessel filled with instructions, text books, a reconstructed drawing of the face of an Ikon to chase, but he could not get a grip of the whole picture of what Moscow had sent him to do in London.

"Perhaps you should consider it an honourable coincidence that in the fiftieth year since our revolution, you have been entrusted with a task directed against those who escaped."

Vasily started to feel a little better.

"Comrade Voronov, you have been chosen by the Party with a special word from Chairman Georgi Miliukov. Bears should not frighten you. There used to be many wild ones in the Taiga, which were cornered and driven from their hides. From so close, I agree, they appear frightening. Surely, as a child you saw tamed bears dancing with rings in their noses."

"Yes, I did."

"They can be tamed and taught to dance. Then they seem far less vicious, perhaps only monstrous caricatures. However, remember that you are not dealing here with the average Western enemy. The Brodskys are Russian émigrés. The Soviet Union did not force them to abandon their country, yet they blame us for their unhappy flight. The loss of homeland, the degrading effect of Western capitalism and their own feudal backgrounds have combined to make them the most complicated subjects of study. It is made all the more difficult for us by their need to see us as the devils who caused this reversal in their fortunes. All the Brodskys and other émigrés desire is to return to being bears in Russia. Let them think they can and let the Brodskys lead other bears. Promise them the woods of Russia again, and their peers will follow. It's up to you, comrade, to lead the first by the nose-ring. We will pretend to consider repaying them. Growing to trust us, they will give us back the Ikon. The Party is convinced that this ridiculous symbol wields extraordinary influence over the émigrés."

"But they are enemies of the State."

"We must appear to be flexible."

Vasily rubbed over his tired forehead.

"Furthermore, we had better inform Moscow of the strong possibility that the Ikon is with Antonina Brodsky in America and ask for instructions. It would be most unfortunate if they did sell to the Americans, or discovered that there is no Mr Snell at the Smithsonian.

Remember, some tamed bears did starve, but there is no record of a starved bear-tamer: he can always eat the bear!"

This time Vasily smiled genuinely.

★

The first telexed report on Vasily Voronov, fresh in from London and decoded, lay on Georgi Miliukov's desk.

Moscow was suffering under a heatwave. The chairman wished he could open the window for the fan in his office was inadequate. Rolling up his shirt sleeves, he settled to read London's missive.

Count Ivan Brodsky had died twelve years ago. Georgi's father would be sorry to have lost him. Countess Olga was described as full of vigour and capacity but she was eighty years old; there was not much time left with her. The offspring Valentina had accompanied the countess to the lunch in lieu of her late father. She was said to have shown provocative behaviour towards Vasily. *Valentina could turn into a major challenge for him*, thought Georgi, *as Vasily will be asked to develop the contact with her.*

"Good," he said, in the same manner as his father did. There seemed wisdom in the use of the simple word.

Bearlike was how Voronov had described the two Brodsky women. Georgi was aware how much his father would have revelled in handling Vasily himself, leading him gently into the demoralisation of those émigré traitors. Thanks to his father's groundwork, Georgi would be able to closely follow the frivolous game-plans

151

of these pawns with a clarity denied to others in the Party.

Of course it could be a problem if the Ikon were indeed in America, a concern Turchin had raised. Georgi would have to warn the agent Snell, following Antonina Brodsky in New York, that she might have the Ikon with her.

The Ikon was the Party's primary objective, and his father's private ambition – the snaring of the Brodskys – was a secret his father would hate to be revealed.

On the subject of sweeping the ground, Georgi was appeased that the transfer abroad of Vasily Voronov had gone smoothly. No-one had given the slightest hint of disquiet about the choice of man. Just to be on the safe side Georgi had requested Turchin's personal file. He now flicked through the folder marked *Secret and Confidential*. There was nothing convincingly incriminating against Turchin; if he should encounter any opposition, rumours against Turchin would have to be built up and spread – the ground brushed behind the decision to send Voronov to London. Georgi lodged the file in the bottom drawer of his desk and locked it.

The electric fan stopped whirring. Georgi cursed. It was too hot today to travel out to the dacha and tell his father about Voronov's first encounter in London. Georgi would wait for the next report from the embassy.

The phone rang. It was maintenance to tell him that no other fan was available. Georgi sighed and hung up.

CHAPTER FIFTEEN

A poster for the June village fête was nailed to the trunk of the chestnut tree. On Brampton's most important day of the year, the sun shone with confidence and chairs and tables were set up in the vicarage garden. Morris dancers in costume chatted animatedly, while above them paper flags and balloons played in the breeze.

Next to the metal beer keg in the kitchen leaned Pisa towers of cardboard cups. The vicar wore his dark suit which Anna had seen being rejuvenated with black ink painted over threadbare patches. The dog-collar seemed to push his chin out.

The first arrivals stood around on the lawn in their Sunday best. Anna watched from her kitchenette window.

Flustered, the vicar's wife rushed in and out of the kitchen. The dancers discussed the quality of the lawn, expertly patting the ground here and there while sipping lemonade. A disturbing crackle came from the cedar tree; there would be a loudspeaker this year. Clinging to the arm of the benevolently smiling vicar, the eldest in the village was escorted to a deck chair and settled. Still the sun shone. Children chased each other amongst the cluster of adults while a dog lifted his leg against a stall.

Anna, in a beige chemisier dress, her washed hair shining like chestnuts, stepped over the lintel and mingled in the garden. And then she perceived him: Ned, near the cedar tree trunk with a young woman close next to him. Anna expected of herself to behave as if nothing had ever happened between her and Ned. Reassuringly he had not dressed up for his companion; he was in his green sweater but had changed his boots for leather shoes. The young woman with him laughed. Anna settled her belt down over her hips and rallied her courage.

"Ah, hello Ned." The two came face to face. Ned looked out of sorts today. He seemed particularly interested in the two musicians tuning their instruments. Anna, determined to stand her ground, paid attention to the young woman whose face was common and bore a certain resemblance to Ned's coarse features. "May I have the pleasure of being introduced?"

The young woman glanced at Ned for help. His chin shooting shortly at Anna, he said, "This is the village madam," and to Anna, "Me sister."

"Wonderful. What's her name?"

"Trish. Excuse us." Ned turned away from her, pulling Trish after him.

A first encounter in public, mused Anna, *with the bonus of meeting his sister*. Pleased with this progress, Anna started to browse through the items for sale, but the grocer's wife seemed to dislike her standing in front of the books without purchasing. Anna smiled defensively and ended up buying a book on modern economics in German. She had meant to buy a different book but there must have been a misunderstanding. Never mind; it was all for a good cause. The cardboard-tasting lemonade slowly flattened Anna's positive mood. She pretended not to search for Ned but Trish's flowery frock stood out. Anna let them exist in their own ways to observe them only out of the corner of her eyes.

The dance began. The Morris dancers moved in an effeminate way, hopping lightly on the much-discussed grass. The fiddler and the flautist played out of tune. The bells on the dancers' feet tinkled. The village was gratified and proud. The old woman in the garden chair had dozed off.

Despite herself, inch by inch Anna wedged herself closer to where Ned leaned his back against the trunk of the famous vicarage cedar again, because Trish had moved away. Gaily the dancers knocked their wooden batons together.

Anna felt nervous excitement growing in her because of their proximity to each other. Ned's dog came up to her. "You remember me then." She bent down to him.

"Shush." The grocer's wife turned to glare at her. Anna shrank back.

Close by, Ned chewed on a grass stalk only playing at absorption with the spectacle. Anna felt his aura strongly. The dog left her side to continue prowling amongst the tables. The Morrismen bowed; the village applauded. The musicians bowed; the villagers clapped harder.

"And now, ladies and gentlemen of Brampton, we have a special..." The vicar was interrupted. The technician fiddled with the microphone to adjust it to the vicar's height. The loud distorted voice of the man of the church rang through the garden. "... we have a special treat for you all. Our village poet is going to read us some of his work."

Anna blushed. With a bump of his buttock Ned disengaged himself from the tree and strutted towards the microphone. He extracted a folded sheet of paper from his trouser pocket. Anna made a move closer to Trish. "You must be proud of your brother."

"Ned's all right."

"Do you help on the farm?"

"No, I'm a nurse."

"Laudable. Where do you work?"

"I'm on the dole."

"How sad, with qualifications and..."

The technician had lowered the microphone two feet. Ned cleared his throat.

The poet's feet pawed the grass. "My first poem is about..." He stopped and held still. "Well, you'll hear anyway." In the direct sun his sweater had turned the tint of peatbog. He read,

> Beneath this clumpy earth there lies
> A lady born with dark blue eyes.
> > Her skin was warm and milky;
> > The earlobes plump and silky.
> You'd never find a girl more fetching,
> Beyond the skill of any etching.
> > Alas her beauty is forgotten
> > And now her flesh is rotten.

Ned scratched his hair. Amplified, it sounded like sandpapering a rough surface. There was silence amongst the villagers. Anna felt unwanted tears fill her eyes.

The vicar stooped. "Of course, we want to hear more of Ned's poetic talent, don't we?"

Isolated affirmative cries were heard.

"Okay, one more." Ned smirked self-consciously. "It's dopey:

> *Green is the meadow and blue is the sky.*
> *Now the grass quivers, and the waves sigh.*
> *All the men shiver, deprived of their fix;*
> *At the pub down the lane, it's only six.*
> *Brown is the mudpile and white is the sky;*
> *Still the waves quiver and meadows sigh.*
> *Men yawn at the killing of time till seven,*
> *When the starlings fly east and the men are in heaven.*

Ned turned to go, stuffing the paper back into his pocket, and people moved about again; their embarrassment was over. A majority of paper cups now contained beer while the shadow of the square belfry grew steadily over them.

"Our Sunday School children are now going to sing for us," announced the vicar.

★

The face of Brampton's church clock shone in the spotlight the village had purchased with the proceeds of last year's fête. It was late, and on the empty lamp-lit High Street Anna's shoes clacked loudly, the noise fading

157

up garden paths toward the houses. The small stirring of fear grew rapidly into excitement; this was the beginning of Anna's own adventure. At that moment a familiar tidal wave of emotions overwhelmed her: Antonina's presence felt so tangible next to her, behind her, all around her; her twin's body exuding breath on Anna's face for a second. And then it was gone, leaving behind a cold disappointment, some fleeting image she was unable to capture or duplicate. *Did that very sensation occur to Antonina at the same time?* Anna asked herself, and a furry cat gave her a halogen stare before slipping through a hedge.

When Ned's cottage came into view, Anna rallied herself to confront the facts for her own protection. Of course it was a shame that Ned was short and so rough, but the excuse was the misunderstood artist in him – the sort of man Mother might be interested in, perhaps another Paul? Mother actually loved Paul if she were honest with herself; the painter possessed the inspired qualities of a Russian male.

Anna too had Russian blood in her veins, and Ned's impact on her had clearly demonstrated this. Perhaps with an attachment to Ned, she would grow closer to Mother who would draw her in and respect her personality. And she, Anna, would grow back her hair to swing it about. Everything would become easier, and Antonina would not come back to find the same clumsy old OTHER.

Anna knocked at the cottage door.

"Who's there?" A body leaned from the upper window.

"It's me – Anna. Let me in, Ned."

For the second time the cottage door was opened and she stepped in. The farmer was in green flannel pyjamas and a woollen dressing gown. The rope cord was tight over his belly.

"Can't you leave people in peace?"

"Ned." Emotions made it difficult for Anna to speak. "Ned," she quivered.

Ned eyed her unsympathetically.

"I had to come, simply had to. Don't you understand?"

"No I don't, and it's me bedtime."

"Ned, you are talented. Artists need to express themselves to others outside their art."

"What the deuce?" Dark eyes scrutinised hers.

"Poetry weds men and nature in a familiar tie. It also makes men aware of their union with one another in origin and destiny." She sniffled. "You are special and gifted."

"And you've got a cold – go home."

"I couldn't, not any more, now that I have heard your poetry."

The farmer pulled the cord tighter. It made his body appear stockier.

"Can you not sense it, Ned?"

"Yeah, you stink of some kind of perfume."

"Sense, Ned. Refinement of understanding between us."

"Oh, not that."

"Please talk to me. It is very special and destined, I know."

"I'm destined to hit the sack and I don't want people around here to know I'm with a wanton woman in me own house."

159

"Please."

"What do you want from me?"

"What do I want?" Anna stroked over her hot head. "Communication, growth through the exchange of thoughts." She looked at the securely tied belt.

"Is that all?"

"It's limitless what we can discover from each other."

"Hold it. I'm a farmer. You're a lady tart who's trying to bring me trouble. So you'd better leave." His voice rang out harsh, and he turned to walk away. She put her arms round him from behind, laying her cheek down on his shoulder blade. He shook her off, turned round and held her at bay with spread fingers. "If I need a rucksack, I'll buy meself one."

"You're a poet. A poet! And I am not letting this opportunity go."

He brushed her imprint from his shoulders as one does dandruff.

"Don't push me away. I can give you inspiration," she pleaded.

"Holy Cow, that's all I need. A grovelling Madam Broderick."

They eyed each other in the light of the unshaded lightbulb. He wrapped his arms around himself.

"I think I could be in love with you," she said.

"Push off!"

CHAPTER SIXTEEN

Dawn edged stealthily over the skylight, and Valentina gradually emerged from another of her recurring nightmares about her infancy in Russia. She had lived in St Petersburg only three short years but some images, possibly memories, haunted her. Frequently she dreamed of a man's pale face bending over her, closer and closer, his eyes like firelamps. His jaw falls open to show teeth dotted with gold. *Konfetka*, and again, *Konfetka*. She is lifted up to be smothered in kisses.

As the dream faded, her relief was tempered by a sense of regret at the loss of some past affection. *Konfetka*, she knew, meant *sweetie*.

Now the morning was rising and the smell of oil paint mingled with turpentine. She lifted herself onto her elbows. Next to her lay Paul. He was awake, put out most probably because she had woken him with her thrashing. His face was rough with stubble, and grooves were dryly drawn around his eyes.

"Since you woke us, go and make coffee." He yawned langorously.

Naked, she crossed to the kitchen corner of the studio: a grimy two-burner cooker, kettle, and sink so small that it was impossible to get the kettle under the tap unless one twisted it at just the right angle.

Sensing Paul's scrutiny on her, she turned, vulnerable, her arms hanging.

"You look your age today," he said.

She crouched and opened the cupboard. Rummaging through tins and jars, she picked out the Nescafé and then changed her mind.

"The twins have left home, both of them." She went to her clothes, heaped next to her Jourdan shoes with the little glue-stiff ribbon-bows. As she pulled the bottle of vodka from her carrier bag, she felt her breasts touch a fold above her belly, warm, soft, and alarming. She twisted the cap off the bottle and tilted the clear liquid to drink. As she righted the bottle, the contents sloshed, settled, and she wiped her mouth with her forearm.

"You want some?" She held out the bottle to him.

He pulled himself up and leaned the back of his head against the grease spot on the wall but said nothing.

"What are you gawking at?"

"Toulouse-Lautrec. The old drunken slut."

She tilted the bottle again, and the potent undiluted liquid burned her throat.

"Small wonder they left, with a mother like that."

"They don't care about me. I suppose for them I'm now old and decrepit. They were my babies."

"Fancy that! I always thought they had to baby you."

"They were precious and beautiful, not too Russian but, thank God, not completely English."

162

"I see. We're pushing the boat out today for a drinking weeping session."

"I had to protect them from their Russian blood. I took it all on myself."

"By acting drunk, vile – ridiculous? Couldn't their English father have protected them better?"

She drank from the bottle. "Russian blood is a curse," she added. "One drop of it is heavier than ten of another kind. It was hell to bring up the girls alone."

"Oh, for Heaven's sake. Don't start mourning the father of the twins. Not now. For years I had to nod; agree with you that he was a boring banker with no dick to his name."

"The other day at the Russian Embassy, I was introduced to a Russian diplomat called Vasily." Valentina changed tactics.

Paul suddenly rolled and jumped out of bed. His crumpled shirt reached to the middle of his thighs. The back of his hair was messily caked and flat from the wall. He forced the kettle under the tap.

"A fetching man. I was compelled to reach out to him but touched an automaton. Bolshevism, communism and the Party have castrated him. I felt like hitting him, hitting him hard because he had become that way."

The gushing of water drummed inside the kettle. "*We* could have had children if you weren't so neurotic. Schizophrenic is the word. One minute you eat me up with lust and needs, and the next I am an oil-blotch in your classy, racy life – no better for you than that diplomat."

"Russian blood is a curse," she repeated stubbornly and took another swig; liquid ran down her chin.

"Why haven't you tried to conform?"

"Like you?"

"Look at us. We drink, fight and abuse each other – parallels that meet at vanishing point." The spoon clinked against the mug as he poured boiling water over the coffee powder.

"But still, I stuck to the norm. When I gave birth to twins, the English mothers in the ward approved of me. Olga offered them peppered vodka and Russian pancakes, and Viscount Sasha gave a speech about Imperial glory. My husband was sure my family's behaviour was certifiable. So after two years trying to be English, I gave up, walked out and went back home to the comforting armpit-smelling Podzhin Hall. End of story. Pathetic, really. *Nazdroviye!*" She proffered the bottle.

"Fascinating, the way you put it today," he commented. "Artistic."

"Artistic," she repeated, and the word came out slightly slurred. It was the only word amid the burden of relics around her, in her, with true meaning, one which made her feel less homeless.

She tottered about, the bottle swinging in her hand like a felled game-bird. Missing twice, she grabbed a black shawl hanging on a nail driven into the ceiling beam – hers, which she had left there once and forgotten, like the skin of a mood she had been in on arriving and shed when she left, unmissed. She swung the shawl around her shoulders and spilled some vodka in the swift movement. In the direct beam of light under the skylight, she struck a pose and saw her visual impact on Paul: a glittery-eyed slightly drunk and completely naked, mature woman, standing among dusty smelly clutter and tossing back her head, dragging the long dark hair with silver streaks she refused to notice back over her finely chiselled shoulder, heavy, dark and exotic.

"Fuck my brain." Paul put the mug down and reached for his sketch-pad. "You've got what made them great: Dalí, Lautrec, Picasso." His chalk scratched on the rough paper.

She changed her weight, put her right foot forward for a safer balance, and a shadow fell along her body. Her glassy eyes shone feverish.

"Goya," mumbled Paul still sketching on his pad. One side of the shawl slowly slipped off her shoulder. He tried to draw again, gave a sigh then threw the charcoal into the mess on the rickety table against the wall. "I can't catch you today. I can't live up to what I see." He threw the pad from him. "What makes it so impossible to pin you down?"

"Guess!" she snarled and reached down to the bottle.

"Don't bend that body. Don't break the mood." His hands framed her. "Stay."

She sidled up to the nippled seamstress model. "Hi, gorgeous," circling the stuffed shoulders with a sisterly arm. "Has he done it to you lately? Sorry, I forgot; someone screwed a stand into you. You're luckier than most."

Paul gave up. Valentina was hopelessly sloshed. "The twins will be back," he said soothingly and prised the bottle from her grip.

"It'll be too late to fix things between us. I'll be too old – and dead inside, just like Vasily."

"Achievements are relative. Life and art are measured by input. I suppose you count as a good mother. Valentina, damn you, sober up. I love you. Don't always fight me. Can't you see what you mean to me?"

"Proportion and vitality."

"I'd do anything for you, and you know that."

"Yeah, sneaking into Podzhin Hall at night to bring your sublime masterpiece; freakish and perverted, my open cunt is now hanging in place of the Ikon, and they loathe it with passion."

"They don't understand it, trust me."

"I only trust vodka." She felt as if she were rising and falling, and the skylight danced in capricious patterns, a little like on a swing in a garden on Nevsky Prospekt.

"Valentina, pull yourself together. Christ, it's nine o'clock in the morning!"

★

Pursuing his main occupation as second secretary, Vasily Voronov spent an hour discussing the British trade union movement with a professor at the London School of Economics. The academic was a member of the Communist Party of Great Britain but Vasily seemed to be talking to a lapdog in a soft swivel chair. The comrade professor was a disgrace to the cause.

When Vasily brought up the urgent need to recruit revolutionary leaders, to train them to infiltrate the most influential institutions, the professor shook his head.

"Let us not be simplistic, please, Voronov. Let Britain experience its revolution peacefully, inevitably. All we need here is to develop our bargaining power." He smiled. "After all, Britain's balance of payments is in the red, and strikes are on the increase."

"Yes, but what about gaining ruling power, the only way to acquire control of the country?"

"Dear Voronov, after all, we have a socialist government ruling in Westminster. Right? Step by step, we're going in the right direction."

Through clenched teeth Vasily exclaimed, "How about the abolition of the Royal Family, the dismissal of the House of Lords, the closure of public schools?" There were more reactionary symbols Vasily could have named.

The professor locked his fingers together, turned out the palms and strained the joints with a cracking noise. "Britain cannot yet do without some trappings of feudal society."

Shocked by these words, Vasily moved forward on his chair. He saw the silver-framed photograph of a blonde broad woman in her forties and two teenage children. The picture was taken in front of a large suburban house.

The professor followed Vasily's gaze. "My wife and children."

At the end of their rag-tag conversation which reached no satisfactory conclusion, Vasily sighed and rose. His eyes travelled along shelves well stocked with books interrupted by silver trophies on wooden stands.

The professor swivelled in his chair. He snorted proudly through his nose. "Tennis," he said. "I won those for tennis."

Two hours later, in the debriefing session, Turchin interrupted Vasily's heated words. "Have you kept to the textbook Party line too vigorously?"

De-routed by the question, Vasily was at a loss. In Moscow such direct questions were never asked. Turchin, Vasily thought, had been living in London for three years – slacking, perhaps.

"In some cases you have to take stiff material and bend it to fit."

Vasily felt confused as to what to say. In the Moscow rule book it was forbidden to bend one's principles to suit the occasion.

"The professor owns a large house, a Rover 2000, and admitted to playing tennis."

"They all play tennis or cricket."

"Pardon?"

"It's a ball-game played on the village common ground. The *gentlemen* used to play the proletariat, but now it's all mixed up."

Vasily reprimanded himself for not having argued more intelligently while Turchin escorted him slowly to the door of the safe speech room, a hand on his shoulder.

"The best we can hope for is to bowl out the lords of the manors by building strong communist teams."

"It's not a game!" Vasily twisted away under the patronising hand.

"The British take life with amusement but they never joke about games."

To Vasily it was all hazy in crucial places. Rover, tennis trophies: the words became senseless to him. What was clear in his head was what he had been taught. The only way was sticking to the rules which some people seemed to have forgotten. If necessary he would have to bring the erring ones back to the measuring stick, even if it meant denouncing someone. There was one pencilled in on his list already.

★

At the end of the working day, in the official minibus taking the single employees of the embassy back to the block of bedsit flats, Vasily still pondered on the attitude of the so-called *British communists* he had met so far. Those who did not play tennis or cricket, watched birds.

No wonder the gentry in the times of the Czars were defeated. They *watched* birds instead of raising them as food for the starving peasants. In Ekaterinburg in 1918 crows had circled over the communal grave.

"You left your coat," the Soviet driver shouted to Vasily when the group was deposited at the building's entrance and the door-security man took them into charge, unchaining the door for them, letting them in, checking one by one as they walked through.

Vasily went back to the bus and took the raincoat from the driver. He grinned apologetically. They had been instructed to dress like the British who kitted themselves out for battle with rain at all times. Physically fit, in the mild weather Vasily kept forgetting his raincoat.

In his small bedsit in the capitalist city Vasily watched

from his hermetically sealed window as, four storeys below him, cars snailed around a roundabout like cogs in a wheel. London's squandering enemies of the working class were driving home to their large houses in the suburbs, their flabby pampered wives, and today he had learned that the country's communist leaders were amongst them.

It was communist steel forged in the furnace of exploitation that was needed in Britain, not cotton-padded socialists.

In the miniature kitchenette Vasily put the kettle on the gas-ring. He sat down on the two-seater sofa. On a narrow table with one chair were his weekly bottle of Stolichnaya vodka and a packet of Russian cigarettes imported for embassy employees: the taste and smell of home. The rough cover of the upholstery grated in his nape as he relaxed his head and contemplated the red fire extinguisher fixed to the wall next to his bed. It ought to have been lodged somewhere in the kitchenette. He thought the same thing every evening. A cupboard with a narrow mirror completed the furnishings.

There was the slamming of a door and footsteps in the staircase. The apartment block seemed to be built of cardboard. It was Thursday. Tomorrow was rubbish collection day; he'd better not forget to put out the bag which would be checked by the maintenance team.

Vasily was drawn back to the window to contemplate the busy traffic in the sombre evening. Pearly lights drove south and west, and his forehead felt cool against the glass as he watched the display of a decaying society.

A stringent whistling sound made his body jerk.

Nerves, mere nerves. It was that confounded kettle with the whistling nozzle. He turned off the gas and lifted the kettle from the stove. Trains snailing through the Urals whistled not unlike it.

His youth in the Urals: *how fit he had been then!* A physical training room was offered in the basement of the embassy. He would have to put his name down. He touched his belly. It felt too soft.

Vasily poured the hot water over the soup powder. Lumps floated on top and when he tried to submerge them, they evaded the spoon. He carried the cup back to the window, his only diversion. Now the traffic was distorted in a light drizzle. Night had fallen, and in the distance above Chelsea the sky was painted an uncertain, artificially tinted yellow while the wailing of an ambulance penetrated even the reinforced window. He saw the spasmodic blue flashes work themselves through the dense traffic, exploding in the eye like flash-bulbs, while he sipped the lumpy soup. He saw the ambulance stop and turn, flickering the façade of a building and plunging it back into night. A fire? A crime? He turned his back to the display. At the sink he poured his soup into the outlet. *A waste*, he thought guiltily.

He twisted the top of the vodka bottle and poured some into his rinsed mug. Sipping, and feeling the heat line his stomach, he sat slowly down on his bed, then reclined and gazed at the brilliantly red extinguisher. At least that was red still, he thought.

CHAPTER SEVENTEEN

It was arranged for the priest to come to Governor's Island for tea that afternoon. Travis had proved to be an understanding American. He had not brushed Antonina aside as a tiresome young woman who would just go away, but had taken the trouble to speak to Father Bernard about the church-run cultural trip for students.

More than that, Travis trusted her not to change her mind and was taking time off work specifically to help her get what she wanted. The kindly Catholic priest and muddled but Orthodox Irina, determined to hang onto Antonina, could not be left to themselves.

By lunchtime Antonina knew from the atlas she had found in the house just how many more states there were between New York and the Pacific Ocean than she had been aware of. Irina moped around the house, her wig askew. She sighed meaningfully, playing hard-done-by. She complained of a headache and sent Antonina to the pharmacy for pills.

Antonina forced herself not to be affected by the emptiness of the old lady, hollowed by lost love; the helplessness of an old Russian in a foreign country was familiar. *Would she be strong enough to keep her vision clear once the priest was here? She did not bear responsibility for the sanity of Irina; she had to keep that in mind.*

At precisely three o'clock Father Bernard, accompanied by Travis, was in the hallway.

Antonina rushed out to greet them. "How swell that you're both here!"

Travis shook his head at her fondly.

Irina with measured steps descended the stairs while Travis guided the priest into the lounge. He was in full black cassock, a cross dangling from his waistband, probably to please Irina.

"So, here we have our foreign adventuress." Father Bernard opened the conversation once the tray with tea and the *Always* was in place on the coffee table and Irina had stopped fussing with the pleats of her dress.

Travis bestowed an encouraging wink on Antonina and explained that she was the granddaughter of a White Russian friend of his mother, who was visiting and desperate to see more of America.

"An awful lot more!" Antonina came to life. "I want to get a feel for the country, live the freedom of it and have adventures."

Father Bernard turned to Antonina. "God bless you, my child, and prevent you from foolishness. There are many bad things in America, even though you do see our country through rose-coloured spectacles. But it so happens that the Good Lord arranges things, even when we think we could do it better ourselves. We have gathered a group of four students for a trip to the West Coast and back, leaving in ten days' time. It's a cultural exchange we offer to young visitors twice a year. Father Larry will drive and guide, and the Catholic Centre's car is available."

"Is there a tiny place left for a fifth in the car please, Father?"

"Where there is a will, there is a way, but I have to warn you that Father Larry is not the youngest. A good soul but…"

"We'll see," Irina interfered. "I believe that I owe it to Olga to ask her permission before Antonina goes anywhere."

"I'm not a child."

"I tried to reach Podzhin Hall on the telephone about noon," Irina admitted. "But nobody answered. Now I'm asking myself, how well is Olga training her domestics?"

"Who did you call, Mamushka?" asked Travis.

"Countess Brodsky, who has my solemn promise to chaperone her precious granddaughter. I cannot just let her go on an irresponsible drive to a wild existence in California. In fact, I ordered the telephone service to keep trying to reach Podzhin Hall for me."

"Dearest Baronetess, the young want to go out there and find out what there is. We mustn't hold them back. Try to remember: you were young once."

"Father Bernard, I remember with exactitude. I did as my parents told me to. They arranged my marriage, and I was grateful to them. I did not even complain about their choice, when my husband started to gamble our money away. Luckily, he was a handsome man. Oh, the days when men were stylish! He wore a gold monocle, you know, his perfumed hair slicked back."

"Oh dear" escaped Father Bernard, and Antonina hid a grin behind the embroidered napkin.

"There is little good left out there," she went on. "Hippies, women in trousers, no manners any more, like my grandson Ricky. And I presume these foreign students will sleep in tents, male and female alike, like wildebeests."

"The students will stay at Catholic Centres or in host families."

"Are there any Russian Orthodox families?"

"In fact, there is a St Nikolas community in Fletcher, Virginia. They have a church."

"Thank God for that." Irina cupped her fake corkscrew curl, and Antonina hiccupped in shock.

The telephone rang in the hallway. Antonina jumped up. "I'll get it."

"No, I'll get it." Travis stood up.

"I have ordered the call. It's for me to take it."

"Perhaps you should let me…" Father Bernard looked innocently from one to the other.

"Yes," Travis spun to him. "That's actually a good idea. Go, go."

He obviously reached it in time, because they heard his voice but could not discern what he was saying. After a while the priest returned, smiled and took his seat.

"Tell us."

"Oh, it was a call for me. One of those begging calls we're getting. I always inform the centre of my whereabouts in case of an emergency. In fact," Father Bernard leaned forward to pick up his teacup which Antonina had refilled "… the one just now was from an excited woman with a strong accent. These people repeatedly try to make the church believe in their destitute state. She was adamant that a relative, presumably her sole support, has just had a heart attack. We do not fall for this one anymore. We ignore it."

"That's a shame." Irina sounded put out. "I had hoped to speak to the countess."

★

That evening in her frilly visitors' bedroom Antonina wrote a letter to Anna on thin blue airmail paper, enthusing about her forthcoming adventurous trip across North America to San Francisco and its hippies.

The second, shorter letter she wrote was addressed to Ricky in Princeton. It started with the Peanuts' *Good Grief! I'm gonna become a hippie in Frisco! You can have your record-player back.*

The days that followed dragged, with a tearful Irina clinging to Antonina and being extremely demanding. To soothe her Antonina read her Baba Yaga stories from old books and watched American soaps for hours every morning. She was also cajoled into describing Olga's jewellery in fine detail. When the departure drew closer, Irina decided to take *her granddaughter* Antonina to Saks, Manhattan to purchase suitable clothes for the trip. This had *all over again* written on it, and it hurt to spend good money on quality clothes which were totally unsuitable but which, in the eager shopper's mind, were a necessity.

A few days later a package arrived in the Mess, addressed to Antonina. She found a black rigid carrying-box the size of an attaché case. Inside was an autoharp with hand-painted flowers decorating the wood beneath the many strings. It came with a handbook, a finger gadget for strumming, and music sheets: *Simple Songs for a Beginner*, with the key numbers indicated. *Good luck to a soon-to-be hippety-hoppety hippie. Ricky.*

CHAPTER EIGHTEEN

Anna felt frisky. Unable to concentrate on studying, she decided to pay Ned a surprise visit. Such a move would surely advance their budding relationship.

She was greeted with, "Not you again." Steeled against something of the kind, she succeeded nevertheless in wrangling herself into the cottage.

"Can't you see that your writing is a continuum of the primitive style of John Clare, the Suffolk poet?"

"Sure. I was just writing to the Prime Minister to ask for a new milk subsidy, when you barged in."

"Nothing to do with what I am trying to say."

"No, of course not. You can be all high-falutin', you selfish bitch, while some of us have a living to make."

"You're always finding an excuse to squirm out of communication or any start to a friendship between us, pinning shortcomings on me."

"And boo to you too."

Anna was left sitting alone in his kitchen with the dog whose ears flapped as he scratched manically behind his head with his hind leg, an awkward manoeuvre to observe. She pulled a book from the rickety bookshelf.

The door was flung open. "Don't touch anything!"

Both hands up, she waved sorry.

"Look. You can't just come here. People will talk. This is a village."

"There's only your dog."

"That's not a dog. It's me sister in disguise."

"People talk, no matter what. They gleefully distort nice and normal things."

"I don't want you here."

"You do. You have just not admitted it to yourself."

"What bloody choice am I given?"

"Ned," she said with warmth.

"I am forty-one and have lived in peace all these years. Suddenly, I'm set upon by a tenacious aristocratic tart." He pulled his hand from scratching his mop of hair and inspected the fingernails. "Fleas."

"Have you written any poetry lately, Ned?"

"No time."

"You must make time."

"Cow udders don't wait."

"The world can't wait."

His artificially loud laughter of bitter mirth filled the kitchen. The desire to hug him was powerful. Instead of Ned, she stroked the dog's wiry back which reactivated the fleas. The animal bit madly into his flank and his teeth clicked. Anna pulled her hand away. "I'll only leave if you read me some of your writing."

"And why should I?"

"Because you want me to go."

He eyed her for a moment and then fetched his exercise book. "Promise?"

"Cross my heart."

Without opening the notebook he started,

> *"The pussy cat shat*
> *on the famous mat.*
> *And splat! – a 35 calibre."*

Ned peered with exaggerated expectancy at Anna.

She slowly rose from the worn sofa, but then with a sudden leap jumped at him and tore the notebook from his hand. His defensive reaction was too slow. Returning to her seat, she read from a random page.

> *"There is this flea that bothers me,*
> *I rub my back against the tree…"*

Vibrating with constraint, he could not bring himself to tear the book from her hands, so he slapped her instead. She turned away but then read the last line,

> *"… now I'm bitten on the knee."*

In frustration he spat at her. With the heel of her hand she wiped the spittle from her chin and gave him back his exercise book.

He clasped it to him and then slipped it under the flat cushion on the spindleback chair before sitting down on it.

His neurotic physical aggression had excited her. "So much passion."

"Oh, please." His voice was a derisive hiss.

"Forgive me. I don't know what comes over me when I am with you."

"You're overblown. It's not Shelley or Keats. I'm just putting together rhymes for fun."

"Writing poetry isn't like carpentry. It comes from some wealth inside someone."

"Compared to you who has wealth outside."

"This conversation is stupid. So let's change it to something meaningful: feelings," she dared say, but quickly added, "love. Am I shocking you?"

"You've come up with that before. It's nowt but dirty sex you're after, with just about anyone."

"There is a connection between us which you choose to ignore." She groaned in frustration and wound her arms around her knees. Putting her forehead down on them, muffled, she said, "I'm trying *so* hard for something I know is right."

"Too bloody hard. I don't dislike you. For a posh, you ain't half bad."

She looked up with an impish smile.

"I need a drink." Ned went to the understair cupboard and fetched a bottle of ginger beer. He tilted it to his mouth for quite a while before putting it back. A clock chimed somewhere.

"Let's sit together on the rug," she suggested. "Did you know that Lenin wrote poetry? And quite earthbound ones too." This time she took hold of his hand and pulled him with her down to sit in front of the ash-dusted fireplace. "With you I don't feel inhibited."

"Surely you can find some other bloke."

She was touched that his rejections of her were weakening. Challenging his eyes onto hers, she pushed the top button of her blouse through the buttonhole.

"Your mother in her mansion would *love* to see you right now."

She unbuttoned her blouse and pushed the cotton material off her shoulders to expose her flesh-coloured lace bra. "Take your shirt off." He did not move. "It's you that's scared. How come? You're twice my age, or almost."

"Shut up." Ned's anger showed. "Shut up, will you?"

"It's no good losing your temper."

"I haven't."

"Then take off your shirt."

Slowly he worked the buttons and then took the shirt off to reveal a manly chest with tufts of black hair. While he was concentrating on that, she had wriggled her skirt and slip off her hips and worked both down over her outstretched legs.

When he saw her in panties, he turned to his dog, "There's nothing for it, eh? We've got no choice." The dog's tail beat the rug with intermittent thumps.

She crawled closer to him and attempted to kiss him but he bent away, lifting his elbow to protect his face. "Get off me. You've got the stench of a decomposing rat in your mouth."

Anna smiled intimately. With a sudden swift movement, she unhooked her bra and pulled it away from her upper body.

He glanced at her breasts. "Don't take your skin off as well."

"Relax. Remove your jeans." Anna extended her arms above her playfully. "Liberate yourself." The stretched breasts had diminished to slight mounds with hardened nipples.

"Don't do that; you'll frighten me dog."

"Trousers off."

"You're some kind of kinky sex maniac, aren't you?"

"Have you never been intimate with a woman?"

"Me? You must be joking." With unsteady fingers he unbuckled his belt. And she reached over to help and was amazed at herself.

"I can undo me trousers all by meself. Me mum taught me when I was three." Ned lifted his quatch-buttock to remove the stiff jeans. He put them next to the dog who sniffed them animatedly.

To Anna's disappointment Ned wore beige longjohns. The reinforced crotch piece was stained yellow.

He lowered his eyes to inspect the part of the underwear she was concentrating on. From his expression he seemed to be seeing his longjohns for the first time, and struggled back into his jeans and buckled the belt. "Out of me house!" he shouted in a shrill voice, once he was standing.

Anna was shaken.

"Seize her, old boy. Bite!" The dog rose, his teeth jutted forward; the gums showed. He growled and snarled at Anna's legs. On all fours, she grabbed her blouse, skirt and slip, and hurriedly dressed, hopping on alternate feet while the teeth snapped close to her ankles.

"Out!" shouted Ned, his cruel eyes focused on her.

"But Ned…" Anna fled through the corridor. The cottage door banged shut. She straightened out her clothes, keeping her bra balled in her fist. Mortified, she walked back to the vicarage.

★

By the time Anna stood in front of the vicarage kitchen door, her thoughts had fermented. She pushed the door and stopped dead: at the round kitchen table sat Valentina. For a moment Anna had the sensation of a mirage, induced by the emotional stress Ned had put her through.

"Don't stand there gaping, darling. Come in."

Anna faced the unnatural trio in the room. The vicar sat next to Valentina, and his wife was sorting a heap of washing from the basket.

"Cotton socks," said Valentina, as the vicar's wife rolled long, grey socks into each other.

Anna looked shamefaced as though she were responsible for her mother's words.

"You know," said Valentina and put her hand on the vicar's arm, "I am familiar with country life."

He sat nodding.

"I participate in the local hunt. In fact, in a week's time is Lady Beaufort's charity fox hunt, and I'm invited. My diplomatic connections, you see…"

The vicar still nodded.

"Mummy, what are you doing here?" Anna was the only one to call Valentina *Mummy*. Valentina hated it, especially in the presence of outsiders, but it was hard to abolish that childhood habit, because Anna thought that the baby-word could protect her from her mother's fiery temper.

Valentina started to get up and said, smiling sinisterly down to the vicar, "Only faith in God helps in times of crisis."

Anna had never heard such words from her mother; never seen her wear such a facial expression before. "Mummy, is something wrong?"

The vicar looked up at Valentina and shortly put his hand on the soft furred sleeve. "One can but pray and hope."

"Mother!"

"I haven't slept a wink all night." Valentina sighed deeply. "Oh, these family worries!"

"Family is the best life offers us," said the vicar, getting up himself.

"Family worries? Mother, talk to me!"

"Let's go into your private quarters," said Valentina.

Quickly Anna glanced back at the vicar's wife who mouthed, silently and mockingly, *private quarters.*

Anna led her mother into her dull room and quickly slipped the bra into the narrow chest of drawers. Valentina's eyes fell on the cross-stitched picture above the bed. "How can you live in a hovel like this?" she asked, twisting her astrakhan hat around her finger. "The vicar's socks stink of sour communion wine."

"What was all that about praying?"

"Oh." Valentina lifted the bedspread and tested the springy horsehair mattress with her hand.

Anna objected strongly to her mother's presence and lack of reverence in the small sanctum.

Valentina detached her eyes from the testimonies of country life around her to focus on her daughter. "Sasha's had a coronary."

"A what?"

"For an Oxford graduate, you are singularly ignorant. He is in hospital. He has suffered a heart attack."

"Oh no!" Anna felt rocked by guilt; then she reasoned that her visit to Ned could not possibly have had anything to do with Uncle Sasha's condition.

185

"The family has to get together. You'd better come to Podzhin Hall with me right away."

"Does Antonina know about Sasha? Is she coming home?"

"I gather Olga tried to call America but the connection was bad. Some Catholic priest answered the phone and spoke about Antonina making a pilgrimage to Saint Francis. When Olga tried to tell him about Sasha, he changed his tone and said not to bother them again, and hung up."

"That can't be right."

"Search me. Perhaps Irina is on her deathbed, and the priest is with them giving her the last rites."

"Unlikely."

"I do remember this Irina. She came for tea in St Petersburg and brought yucky Mont Blanc marron glacé paste, brown worms with cream. I was scolded for spitting them out. Ah yes, and there was a little boy, her son. He was always in a sailor suit."

CHAPTER NINETEEN

At two o'clock Valentina led her mother into the Beaumont ward, ignoring the notice *Visiting Hours 4-6 pm*. The others followed, a small sombre party between two rows of hospital beds on either side of a large ward the colour of unripe tomato. Iron rails like toy train tracks ran on the ceiling around the beds, curtains pulled aside. As Olga entered beside her daughter, human illness stared at them from each bed. The old lady's face was set in disgust. The patient in bed B coughed wheezingly and expulsed phlegm into a bowl. Olga stiffened on her daughter's arm. "Don't tell me Sasha is here."

Anna tiptoed after them, unable to conceal the anxiety in her voice. "He'll be perfectly well looked after, Grandmother. It's the National Health Service."

Fydo came last with a carrier bag from Fortnum & Mason containing Malaga grapes. For once he wore a suit.

Valentina gave a stiff and bleak grin to a young black man sitting in a bed, holding a portable radio to his ear, his eyes blank from monotonous days in that sunless fever-spent ward. The golden autumn days following Harvest Festival were translated in here by bland walls, limp curtains.

Olga's eyes shied away from the feathery granules under the beds and the dust hanging like spores in the indirect light of the high windows. The patients seemed bodiless, two-dimensional, carelessly slipped between the sheets. The Brodskys passed patients who did not move, lay sleeping. *Unconscious?*

Valentina stopped at patient H. In a narrow bed covered by a thin taupe-coloured blanket lay a gaunt spectre resembling Sasha.

"What kind of an idea is this?" exploded Olga, her voice trembling with indignation.

Sasha tried to slide further down under his blanket.

"Just look where they put the viscount!"

Several patients who had been dozing and nursing their ailments sat up. The black man started to get out of his bed, his swollen feet trying to catch his slippers.

"We do have visiting rules, you know," snapped a nurse walking by, a napkin over the bedpan.

"There is dust under that bed." Olga pointed her gloved hand. She spun to Valentina. "How could you let him come here? We're not destitute, and only two days ago we were received by the Ambassador of all the Russias."

"Hush, Mother."

"I will not hush. Do something to get Sasha into a private room this very minute."

Olga sat down on the metal chair next to Sasha's bed as if all strength had left her limbs.

"It is free to all." Anna tried to point out the positive side of the situation. "And a remarkable social achievement of Great Britain."

"Anna, if only you knew how nauseous your words are in my ears. Half a century ago, Russian proletarian voices spoke of *social achievements*. It has the makings of a horror story. It is what we left behind in Russia: lack of privacy, crowding and filth." Olga exhaled audibly.

Anna regretted voicing her ideas so directly. She focused anxiously on her grandmother, hoping to be enveloped again with warmth, but instead Olga turned away, tucking her finely gloved hands into the folds of the grenadine dress.

Valentina at her shoulder glanced narrow-eyed around the ward with a slightly sneering mouth, her expression mirroring Olga's distress. "We count for nothing in here, just like in that train."

Olga twisted up to behold her daughter. "What did you say?"

"You know."

"*I* do know but how can *you*? You were a toddler."

Of Sasha's face only the pale tip of a nose was visible. Fydo unwrapped the grapes and pressed the call-button. Anna leant over Sasha. "Hello, Uncle. You're looking great."

"Anna," he mumbled, "promise me something. Get rid of the horrible painting in the music room while I am here. I hate it."

"You mustn't worry about that now."

"'Ere mate, are they for real?" Sasha's bed-neighbour craned his neck from his pillow.

"Valentina, get Sasha's doctor." Olga's voice was dulled, oppressed with sadness.

The black man had made it to the foot of Sasha's bed, ogling each of them with gross and ill-concealed interest.

"Go back to your bed," snapped Valentina. Slowly, with regret, he turned to shuffle away in his tartan slippers.

Anna was itching from self-consciousness caused by the display the family created. She kept reassuring Uncle Sasha who lay helpless on his pillow, his pampered moustache bent and neglected, that all would be fine, just fine. The words of reassurance she whispered to him were largely addressed to herself and her own anguish. It seemed urgent to improve the situation but there was nothing to be done.

Her family was dear to her, essential in fact, but so traumatised as to be unable to function. In a histrionic way Mother and Grandmother, faced by the possible loss of Sasha, were reaching out to each other; it showed from the way Valentina's hand gripped on Olga's shoulder. Anna was left out and she felt the immense isolation of jealousy. *No*, she thought. She was reading too much into what was simply her upset over Sasha's illness and the absence of her twin. And there was Ned too, who had hurt her and maimed her personal pride.

"Valentina, get the doctor will you?" Olga asked again.

Valentina walked off in search of the physician. The West Indian still lingered, undecided whether to go back to his bed or come closer again in order to watch the old man with the exotic long-tailed moustache and his amazing family.

"Olga," whispered Sasha.

"My dear Sasha, I shall not leave this chair until you are moved to a clean and decent place."

Sasha's eyes had panic in them. "They are all very nice to me here, really. The man in the bed behind you has a ruptured spleen."

Anna contemplated a humorous description of all this to Antonina later but her heart was not entirely in the thought.

"This is Sasha's doctor, Mother."

Olga swung her head swiftly and found herself staring into the bright and shiny face of an Indian. A tightly wound turban crowned his head. She recoiled.

"I am Dr Srikkanth."

The other patients silently watched the group around bed H.

"Can't you see Viscount Brodsky does not belong here?" Olga's eyes shone in the liquid of tears.

Dr Srikkanth appeared totally unmoved. "Viscount Brodsky has been very lucky, ma'am. We should get the results back soon to see how much heart tissue has been lost. If it is as we expect, he should be released in a week's time."

"A week in here! Doctor, this is impossible for us." Olga clasped her hands in horror at the thought.

"He needs expert attention."

"We'll get a private nurse and take him home right away."

"I would not advise it."

Now Olga saw that the doctor wore a bracelet on his wrist. She frowned.

Anna started to shake out Sasha's pillows and straighten his covers. "I know a nurse who could start right away," she piped, delighted to find a way to contribute.

"Anna, get that nurse for tomorrow night."

"Yes, Grandmother."

"What sort is she?"

"She is straightforward English and has a very gifted brother…"

"Never mind her brother." Olga turned back to Dr Srikkanth. "We will come and fetch the viscount tomorrow evening."

"It is against my advice, but he is your relative and if you take the responsibility for his release, that is fine with me. I shall make sure the staff sister gives you the necessary instructions and medicines. Good day." With bouncy strides the doctor left the ward. His purple turban had added a cheerful touch to the worn green.

The patient in the bed next to Sasha sat up again. "They're taking you away, mate. They want you under the ground, poor blighter."

"If you say one more foul thing, I will give you a shaking, ruptured spleen or not," Valentina threatened the man.

The matron marched towards them on thick rubber soles from the end of the ward. "What is going on here?"

"Stuffed arses," mumbled the bed-neighbour and turned away from the Brodskys.

"May I remind you that this is a hospital?" Matron was caustic.

"Tomorrow you come home," declared Olga to Sasha and stood up.

"Will I be well enough?"

"Anna has organised a private nurse for you." She bent over her brother-in-law and stroked his head.

A hospital volunteer entered carrying a flower arrangement in a basket and put it down on Sasha's metal side-table. Wordlessly, she walked away again. The arrangement stood out in the ward.

Olga picked up the little envelope. *With many wishes for a speedy recovery from Vasily Voronov, Second Secretary, Soviet Embassy.*

"How splendid!" exclaimed Olga, and some colour came back into her pale cheeks. "They must be considering paying us back. Njanja said they telephoned."

"I just wish you hadn't told them that rot about the Ikon being in America with Antonina," complained Valentina.

"While you were busy mesmerising Mr Voronov, I noticed how peculiarly interested the ambassador was in the Ikon. Just a little white lie." Olga cupped her curl.

The family made ready to leave. Anna planted a quick kiss on Sasha's brow and joined the others.

"See you, Pop," said Fydo. "We'll get you out of this hole in no time."

Sasha grabbed his son's sleeve. "I like it here," he whispered.

When the Brodskys emerged from the hospital, slowly, in silence, walking over painted *Emergency and Ambulances*, they sought their stodgy Bentley. As Fydo drove haphazardly out of the carpark, shadows of the avenue of trees lay across the road, so clear-cut that they seemed carved in relief. It was as if dark figures known to them were felled one by one across their path. Olga leaned back in the smelly leather and closed her eyes.

CHAPTER TWENTY

Anna stepped over the dog in Ned's cottage in her haste. "Fydo, I mean Fyodor, drove me back to Brampton early this morning."

"Don't they have road accidents anymore?" Ned had obviously not worked out the ambiguities in their relationship.

"My reason for coming is important." She was eager to capture his interest before he started to battle against her presence. It was imperative that she succeeded with him today, for she had spoken up rather presumptuously at the hospital.

Around Ned's neck showed a check shirtcollar which she had not seen before. Perhaps she was beginning to have an effect on him.

"You see, my Uncle Sasha suffered a heart attack."

"I hope it's hereditary."

"Ned, just listen, please," she begged.

"Oh shit! There's someone at me door," he hissed, and she heard the front door rattle.

"In here." Ned opened the understair cupboard and pushed the bewildered Anna into it, her bag after her, then closed the wood-batten door and fastened its latch.

Crouched in the dark cramped space, she heard voices.

"Hello, Sis."

"Dad sent me about the tractor. The bleedin' rotavator's jammed again."

"I bet you've tried to unblock it without revving the motor first."

"We haven't, I swear."

One narrow light-slice from a warped wood panel helped Anna position her feet next to a plastic bucket.

"I greased the damn thing a week ago."

"Well, you didn't do a good job then, did you?"

"I'd better come over."

Anna felt giddy and disoriented. The conversation outside had stopped; her heartbeat boomed. A definite thud indicated that Trish and Ned had left the cottage. Claustrophobic panic seized her. She pushed her shoulder against the door; beat her fists against unyielding Victorian pine, then slumped onto the rim of the bucket. Ned would just fix that tractor, get rid of his sister, and come back to release her. Of course there would be enough air for a long time; her biology teacher had been adamant that mice enclosed in a jar could survive for days. She arched her back but banged her head against a step of the rising staircase.

The clock chimed twice and no more. The silence beyond felt impenetrable. There was a game they used to play as children at Podzhin Hall. The guesser had a scarf tied over the eyes. *What is that?* Once, Fydo had placed a toad from the pond on Antonina's palm. When the animal flexed its legs, Antonina had guessed right and screamed wildly.

Anna picked an object from the shelf next to her shoulder. "Metal," she said. Teeth could be felt, a messy woolly substance caught between them. An animal comb, perhaps for a lamb. It could not be the dog's because he was never groomed.

She fingered another item: definitely a jar with a lid. She unscrewed the top and smelled something pungent. And then she remembered that her bag was with her. In it was Antonina's last letter. With her glasses on her nose, Anna held it out to the light strip and was able to make out the words she pretty much knew by heart already.

Dear Anna,

I have to be honest with you. So far, going to America has not really worked out. Anyone can look at photographs of the Chrysler and the UN buildings while eating Always. Yes, you read right.

Irina's son understands my disappointment and is fixing it for me to join a foreign students' cultural trip to San Francisco and back, but it's organised by the Catholic church. Still, I can't wait. Imagine when I shall be in Texas, I will be as far from you as St Petersburg is from Podzhin Hall. And that's only halfway to California. A drive of thousands of miles, taking weeks.

Of course, I will think of you and be wondering what you are doing. Hopefully you are having fun in your village.

I'll write to you and everyone again before I leave. After that, it might be more difficult but I'll try.

Big hug,

The OTHER ONE.

Anna put the letter away. Was the air getting scarce or was she just imagining it? The light was fading; the sky must have become overcast.

The family, she thought. *I promised a nurse for tonight. What is keeping Ned so long?*

She started to count to keep busy and to maintain some track of time.

"… 297, 298, 299, 300."

A dull pain throbbed at the back of her skull and she became aware that she would need to go to the bathroom soon. She rose stooped and sighed deeply, reminding herself that she mustn't use up excessive air.

"Ned, please Ned, come back; I implore you. 1, 2, 3…"

She felt around desperately for a sharp object with which to break down the door. In so doing, she brushed the open jar from the shelf into the bucket she had sat on. It released a revolting smell. She sat down again to block the stench.

"… 214, 215, 216."

The bucket rim burnt into her thighs. Her nape ached from keeping the head bent. The vile smell in the confined space made her wretch. Anna started to sob. "You nasty ugly country clod."

★

"Why the hell are you still in there?"

Anna tumbled out of the cupboard and sank onto the spindleback chair.

"Yech, you crapped in my cubbyhole."

"No. I only dropped a jar of something from a shelf." She made an immense effort not to cry.

"Disgusting!" Ned opened the window wide. "Clean that up."

She went and seized the bucket. Ned pinched his nose while she approached the kitchen sink.

"Not in there, you dirty slut. Loo, where it should have been in the first place."

She stood helpless, dumbstruck by his bland cruelty.

"Upstairs."

Once she found the bathroom in which socks and underclothes were strewn on the curling mildewed lino, she picked out the jar: it was liquidised rose fertiliser. She poured it into the discoloured toilet to flush it away. With her elbow she held back the mouldy shower-curtain and rinsed the bucket in the bath; a grime ring indicated the level to which Ned filled his bathtub.

Sasha, the family! I have to go through this.

Down in the kitchen she put the pail back in the cupboard. "You must have had a lot of trouble with the tractor."

"What would you know?"

"I came to offer Trish a job at Podzhin Hall as private nurse to my Uncle Sasha," she said with some self-assurance.

He scrutinised her face. She knew she was not attractive after crying.

"The family will pay her well. She will have her own room and…"

"Me sis is too good for that."

"Uncle will be released from hospital tonight. He needs expert nursing. He's very sick. Podzhin Hall is nice, I assure you." Anna's eyes pleaded with the glinting dark ones.

"Trish would have to clean out the cupboards you upper-class people crap into."

Anna ignored him. "She'd be paid fifty pounds a week, with full board."

Ned whistled. The dog trotted to him, searching his master's face eagerly.

"Can we send Trish there, you reckon?" Ned asked the dog, who licked his hand. Ned turned to Anna. "Me sis got no fancy uniform."

"Allowance for uniform will be extra," she said on her own initiative.

"When?"

"Tonight. My mother is driving up. If Trish could be ready by then, it would…"

"She's got no posh suitcase."

"That can be put on the uniform bill." She started to feel hot.

He took his time before saying disdainfully, "I'll send her to the vicarage at six o'clock."

"Really? That makes up for a lot of things, I guess."

The episode of her confinement lay behind her. She approached him as one does a potentially hostile creature. When his shoulders did not rise and he did not flinch, she dared to put her right arm up, her hand

on his shoulder close to his nape, and gave him almost
a hug.

"You stink of shit," he muttered more amiably.

"Thank you," she exclaimed. "Thank you so much."
Light-footed, she jogged away from the cottage.

★

It was half-past six and on the Aga bubbled supper. Trish
put her suitcase on the flagstones.

"What do you want?" asked Cahill of the mannish
young woman with short brown hair teased high around
her head, and small eyes close together underlined in
kohl. Her narrow lips were glossed candy-pink. She
wore a mint-green coat on which the gold buttons hung
limp, and the hem of a skirt underneath showed uneven.
Her feet were in a pair of imitation-crocodile sling-back
shoes. She looked blowsy.

"I'm the private nurse."

"Crikey. Who talked you into that?"

"I've just signed a contract for three months to nurse
the viscount."

"How much are they paying you?" Cahill asked, and
Njanja stopped riddling the ash at the Aga.

"Fifty pounds a week and full board in the main
house, upstairs."

"*Chert voz'mi!*"

"Who is she?"

"She is Vera Durov, and I am Cahill, the only
Irishman in England who doesn't drink."

"Great," said Trish and pulled a pink gossamer scarf out

201

of the neck of her coat. "Tomorrow, some uniforms should arrive for me from Oxford. Now, show me to my room."

Cahill saw Njanja on her carpet in front of the stove, small, in black and at a loss. "I am also the family's undertaker," he said in a querulous tone. "The one who silences mouths by shovelling earth into them."

Trish looked around her at the shelves, the collections of objects, and her mouth was pursed. The painted lips were the only red tick in the bluish darkness of the mouldering mood in the kitchen.

Cahill stood up. "Come with me."

She turned and walked out. He hesitated, then bent and picked up the plastic handle of her case.

When they were gone, Njanja came to life enough to move to her chair and sit down in it. Her hard-working swollen hands lay on her white apron like red buff-leather gloves in snow. "Fifty pound zr week," she muttered and got up again. Out of the Staffordshire Toby jug on the shelf she took a little vinegar bottle. Pulling out the pale narrow cork, she took a medicinal tot from the small supply she kept for emergency moments. The vodka shot through her old body like a blaze. The Brodskys could not afford a private nurse, not at that salary.

Someone knocked at the tradesman's entrance. She pushed the cork into the neck of the bottle and hid it in the jug again. Slowly she walked to the door.

A tall young man at the threshold in jeans and studded leather jacket said, "Pegasus Saddlers. Better late than never." He held a fawn saddle draped over his arm. At his feet was a large box. "In that are the hand-stitched harnesses, the hunting coat and boots, which the countess ordered." He put the saddle down and pulled a folded piece of paper from his breast pocket. "Four hundred and fifty quid, cash on delivery, plus a fiver for the trip all the way out here."

Njanja stared at him with her china-blue eyes, and her jaded senses were quickened by the vodka churning still. "Moment," she uttered, turned and left him standing there.

In the kitchen she stood stockstill with closed eyes. *Miss Valentina, the child in the starched petticoats pointing to what she wanted; the three-year-old girl who flirted with the soldiers on the Red Cross train out of Russia.* Durov opened her eyes and breathed deeply. *Miss Valentina could not point at what she wanted any more, not now, not with a nurse as well.*

"*Nikogda* – no way!" she exclaimed, returning to the tradesman's door, and shook her hands in front of her. "*Nikogda!*" She made movements to brush the young giant away from the house.

"What's going on?"

"Zr viscount is ill. Fifty-pound-nurse ill. She not want zr riding things now."

He stared at her with hard eyes, shaking his head slowly. "You ought to be in a dolls museum."

"Go, please go."

"Some people really fuck you up," he complained, but bent down and slid his arm under the saddle to pick it up. He carried it to his chocolate-coloured van *Pegasus Saddlers*. He came back and lifted the box too. Under his boots the gravel crunched. He threw the box into the open back of the van and slammed the panels shut. Revving the motor, he drove out of the park.

In the kitchen Njanja wrung her hands.

Cahill came back. "That's a brazen hussy. Do you know that she…?"

Njanja knelt before the open larder door.

"What happened to you?"

Durov kept crossing herself, while her eyes were on the picture of the saint pinned to the wood with drawing pins. "I have sinned. I sent away zr Valentina riding things she ordered. Four hundred fifty pounds!"

Slowly a grin spread on his face. "Well done, Njanja."

She twisted her head to throw him a look, and then crossed herself again and bent to touch the flagstone floor with her forehead.

"There is something burning in the oven."

"Oh, *bozhe moy*!" She grappled up and closed the larder.

When she slid out the baking tray, the kitchen filled with the smell of drowsy rich warm autumn. In the encrusted square nestled sizzling apples filled with ground almonds, cinnamon and demerara sugar, whose skins had shrunk in the baking and meat split. Njanja spooned the lemony juice over the burns and bruised bubbling lumps, coating their agitation into submission.

"Will there be cream?" Cahill asked, watching her.

"Get out of zr way." The big round lid came down on the apples on the hot-plate.

"There are only five apples," he said.

"We are five."

"How about the nurse?"

"Zr nurse!" she growled.

CHAPTER
TWENTY-ONE

On Governor's Island the early morning cannon boomed for the thirty-second motionless silence. Irina ignored the military salute and, at the door to her house, pawed Antonina in an attempt to keep her close. "We old Russians are dying out, and the stories of our stolen lives will be lost."

Antonina detached herself from the attempted embrace.

"It is not your fault, dearest, and my son understands that you want to go out there somewhere, but I must tell you that you are abandoning your family." Irina fingered the strand of pearls around her neck.

Antonina had to nerve herself to walk away. At the ferry pier a coast guard unit was boarding, and she pushed herself on, jostling the men.

In front of the Catholic Centre in Manhattan she alighted from her yellow taxi. She picked up her Vuitton suitcase, the sleeping bag she had found in Ricky's bedroom cupboard and the autoharp in its case, and went into the building which had a large stone cross over the entrance. Inside was Father Bernard, dressed in jeans and a T-shirt that took her by surprise.

"Hello there," he hollered. "Let me introduce you to Father Larry and the other travellers."

Father Larry was a worn seventy-year-old. He stood stooped and fiddled with a map of North America coming apart along several seams. He acknowledged her briefly through rimless spectacles which enlarged his eyes.

The four students participating in this cheap goodwill trip around America were introduced: two girls and a young man in their mid-twenties, and another man who was slightly older, probably mid-thirties. Once ready, Father Bernard got them to pick up their bags and follow him outside to an old white and lime-green Ford Country Sedan no-one had taken the trouble to clean.

The seating allocation was awkward; they had never met before. Inevitably they would sit compressed against each other in the confines of the vehicle for hours on end, and Antonina had only ever pressed against her identical twin. Perhaps physical intimacy came more easily to others, but she would have to give herself over to it if she insisted on undertaking this adventure.

In the car she ended up in the front near the door, next to Maria, a language student from Bologna who sat covering a triangular tear in the upholstery. At the wheel Father Larry in a mottled grey cassock searched with his key for the ignition. He smelled strongly of Brylcreem. On the back seat, in the middle was François from Paris and "studying women", with Manfred, a qualified architect, on one side, and Helen, a Swiss student of hotel management on the other. The luggage had been stuffed into the back of the station wagon by the priests. The Vuitton case, which did not fit in, was strapped onto the roof. *What if it rains*? worried Antonina but did not dare say anything.

"The priest," Maria whispered to Antonina, "washed his cassock with too much bleach."

"That's it then." Father Bernard's loud and cheerful "May the Lord be with you" sent them on their way.

Father Larry started the motor which rocked in neutral. His map slid off the dashboard. Antonina caught it. "Well done," he said. "You can be my navigator. First, tell me how to get to Washington."

"Hold your horses!" Father Bernard came running after them, brandishing before him the black case with the autoharp. It was pushed through an open back window. They took off.

Antonina studied the map. "I guess we have to get off Manhattan and head south. Do you really not know the way?"

"Boy oh boy," came from the back seat.

"The priest," Maria leaned towards Antonina again, "has really poor eyesight."

Antonina ground her teeth from stress, then called out, "There's a sign: the Lincoln Tunnel. And look! Washington. Yes, it says Washington!"

Antonina was shot forward in her seat as Larry yanked the sluggish car to the right for the entrance to the tunnel.

"Watch out!" shouted Helen. "That truck will hit us."

Maria crossed herself while the elderly priest's bloodless fingers gripped the wheel and his frantic myopic eyes searched for signposts.

"Shouldn't we be in the right-hand lane?"

"I know. I know."

It smelled of carbon monoxide in the tunnel.

"The window on my side won't close," complained Manfred.

The car swerved. St Christopher on the medallion hanging from the rearview mirror swayed drunkenly. Nobody said anything more. The girls in the front protected their chests with crossed arms, and their breathing was fast and shallow. Manfred had propped the autoharp case against the open window to shield himself from the draught.

They emerged onto National Highway 95 to Philadelphia and Washington. It was reassuring. Father Larry overtook a slow van, and the Ford Sedan groaned with the effort. They were now cruising along in the correct lane. Antonina had not noticed the blue Rambler follow them out of New York.

The stress eased as they drove southward. On the back seat a conversation started up from which Antonina learned that the three young people had each felt the need to go off on an adventure in order to escape from the limitations to which their lives were confining them – just like her. It sounded as if Helen might well have to overcome her Swiss idea of a tidy life being a good one. François clearly needed some rejections to mature him, and Manfred seemed to want to forget something which had gone wrong in his life. So what about her? What was she here to overcome or get away from? Her dependency on her family, certainly, in every way. But what about rupturing her consanguinity with Anna: could she break it? Should she?

Driving into the unknown with strangers was an opportunity to step back from herself, to discover a clearer view of things. The Brodskys in their *grandness* took it as given that unworthiness was innate in everyone else around them. Others did not have to earn this low esteem; their inferiority was an unjust absolute. Antonina knew that she should evaluate her fellow human beings on their merits, and be evaluated in her turn: a disquieting prospect.

Without warning, the car door next to Manfred swung open. He threw himself over François. Everyone shrieked and Father Larry skidded to an emergency stop on the hard shoulder.

The cop on his bike enlarging in the car's rearview mirror was awe-inspiring. With cunning eyes he assessed the case before him. He informed them civilly, but with a no-nonsense drawl, that the car's licence had expired a month ago, and that even with his naked eyes it was obvious that all four tyres were of a different size.

"Are you a Catholic?" Father Larry asked tentatively, after which he was ordered to step out of the automobile.

The cop contemplated the cassock. "Aren't you a bit old to go with hippies?"

Father grabbed the cross on his chest and yanked it on its chain. "I'm a priest at Saint Catherine's."

"And them in the car are your angels?"

The cop let them drive on with a warning and a threat. They had to stop at the next service station and get the door fixed and the tyres replaced.

With a trouser belt holding the car door in place, they carried on. In East Brunswick *Saint* Larry, as he was now called, pulled into a gas station.

While the sedan was hoisted up, they stretched their spines and loosened their muscles. Helen paced around voicing her complaints about the inadequacies of the preparations for the trip. François, robbed of attention, reverted to childish behaviour, and Maria fussed around the priest, hoping for his approval.

How was it that Antonina had never analysed people's ways so clearly before? Next she would have to find a way to relate to them. When Manfred asked what was in the flat black case, a first means presented itself in a simple form. She took out the autoharp, sat on the ground and strummed *Green Grow the Lilacs.*

They crowded around. "Where did you get that?"

"It was a gift from a young Russian – people I stayed with in New York."

"Don't say the word *Russia* around here; Americans freak out."

"Why?"

"Where do you think the Vietnamese get the weapons to kill American soldiers with? You're not Russian, are you?"

Antonina scraped across the wires roughly. "No, I am English," she said. "Just plain English."

They sang more folksongs from the music book and the mechanic, tightening the bolts on the hubcaps, whistled along. Antonina was not aware of the blue Rambler at the petrol pumps in the same service station, nor of the man holding the nozzle and continually glancing in her direction.

★

In Washington Saint Larry got them lost. Twice they circled the Lincoln Memorial as the light drained from a red-stained sky. Fatigue turned them cranky. The Gallic word for excrement was used often in the back seat. Finally they drove up to the steps of the National Gallery of Art, and Sister Theresa was sitting there, plucking a guitar, unaware of the time of day.

The night was spent in the sanctuary of a care home for the elderly. After more singing and strumming, amplified and eerie in the mock Gothic chapel, Antonina's head sank on a prayer cushion, her eyes fixed on the red eternal light in its suspended oil burner. It gave a glow to the stained-glass window on which were two elongated female saints, each with a hand placed on the hilt of a planted sword, two visible red hearts beating in their open chests.

★

The State of Virginia was announced by a road sign: *Help keep Virginia green*. Beyond Barboursville stood the Blue Ridge Mountains, and in the late afternoon the sedan cruised along the Skyline Drive on the crest of the ridge. Beneath them stretched the vast and luminously green expanse of the Shenandoah Valley.

"Virginia has changed little since the times of the Puritan settlers," read Helen from her guidebook.

"Puritans – we'll cure that," grumbled François. Manfred had caught a cold from the draught of the missing car window, and Maria attempted to mother him, but Antonina saw his chilly smile warning her off. Antonina expected Saint Larry to announce their visit to the Orthodox church centre but he didn't. Either Irina had not written to them or Father Bernard had forgotten about it.

Instead, the group spent two nights in a camping site, eating burgers and toasting marshmallows on the fire around which they sat on long benches, meeting young American people, chatting, drinking root beer and singing together. Saint Larry did not participate. He had complained of a stiff back and was said to have crashed out in some leader's camper van.

Antonina was getting more self-confident on her harp, and Maria and François had good voices. It emerged that François had been a choirboy in Lille, which had little to do with a daring Paris life and sex with hot girls.

She felt relieved about the Frenchman's *all show and no substance*. Now she was out of the family cocoon, her exposure to sex, her intentions about sex, would matter. So far in her existence, the subject had remained preciously concealed despite Valentina's regular crude allusions. The twins had protected themselves by being secretive about anything to do with sex. Now this reticence could prove to be an embarrassment in terms of knowing what was what. Blessedly, Antonina had been deflowered, by finger that is: a medical student at university. That awkward messy petting incident would have to serve for now.

That night the group slept under the stars, galaxies of them in that immense other world above. Pinheads of light were shooting and falling in the cobalt blue. "Good night *the other one*," Antonina slurred, needing sleep.

In Knoxville they were separated into families to learn more about the American way of living. Then they drove up the Great Smoky Mountains and, pushed along by wet and gusting winds, they reached Memphis. They had been on the road more than a week, time enough to shed part of their former selves. Antonina had even shed her Vuitton suitcase as it had come off the roof on the highway and tumbled under a juggernaut. A woven strawbag had taken its place. Memphis was all about Elvis and the sound of soul.

If you can't beat them, join them was Helen's opinion, so the group settled down behind the handpainted sign Antonina had made, saying *United Musical Nations*. They threw themselves into an impromptu busking session and, to their astonishment, they had collected thirty dollars by the time Sister Ursula identified them. "Heavens above," she exclaimed cheerfully. "I thought you needed to be shown our country."

The decision was made to spend the money in a music shop of which there were many. They purchased a secondhand guitar for Maria and enough was left over for a bongo drum for Manfred. The shopkeeper threw in a pair of finger cymbals. After that, the sister invited them to a soda fountain offering a choice of twenty-two flavours of ice cream; perhaps it was an attempt to sweeten the news that Father Larry could not go on and that the trip had to be abandoned. "The priest is seventy-two years old." Sister Ursula's tone was accusatorily concerned.

"And that's our fault?" coming from François started a rather unpleasant conversation involving *irresponsibility, danger, clapped-out Ford Sedan*. Sister Ursula, not being a practical person, only understood part of this. What she failed to grasp entirely was that they were without a driver, had paid for transport, not much admittedly, and would now have to buy plane tickets back to New York. Just because the good Lord had apparently always protected her, she assumed with sweet smiling confidence that He would do the same for them.

That night the group lodged in a summer camp for underprivileged children. The mood was sombre despite the excited kids all around them.

Only Antonina and Manfred had driving licences, and neither of them was insured for driving in America. They could in theory steal the sedan and go anywhere they wanted. They were free, even free of religion. Helen objected that if they planned to steal a car, they ought to consider a better quality one. Clearly none of them was ready to be defeated and fly back to New York.

"Give up? Now that we can do what we want…" Antonina untied the handkerchief from her ponytail and shook loose her long chestnut hair. She climbed over the wooden bench fixed to the table on which was their hamburger supper with coleslaw, and ran around wildly, shouting "Free, free", arms eagle-spread, hankie waving.

The kids left the tables and ran after her, around her, most of them black children, imitating birds flying, while the camp-leader watched, his fat pumpkin face glowing in the light of the kerosene lantern.

After pudding of candied apple, they decided that the following morning before sun-up they would drive off by themselves towards Fort Worth near Dallas. Helen put herself in charge of organising the trip from now on. They would pool their money. Maria started to panic from guilt but was jollied along.

Realising they had neglected their companions, the five travellers turned their attentions back to the children. Helen gave a yodelling performance to great applause. Maria with her Elvis guitar, Antonina on her harp, the drum, and the singing in canon, left the kids' mouths agape.

"Wow, guys; they do that just for you."

The next day one early bird chirped in the crude morning chill. They stood around the car, their limbs pitted with goose pimples.

"Okay then. Let's go," said Manfred naturally taking the lead because he was the eldest. "It's not stealing; we paid for it."

Antonina drove the first leg and found that, on those wide roads with little traffic and with the need for only one foot on the pedals, it was more like relaxing in a worn sofa. Olga of course would disapprove deeply. Valentina might not seem to care, but Anna would point out the need to worry about Father Larry. Well she, Antonina, spat her chewing gum out of the window and decided that she could not wait to find out what would happen next.

Next was Fort Worth, an uninspiring town which they enlightened with their street performance, *Yellow Rose of Texas*. No kidding, they were starting to shape up as a band. In America everything seemed possible in an easy kind of way.

Two men stepped from a green Chrysler parked close by, and one took photographs of the group. He was neither old nor young; he was wearing a canvas sports jacket. The other stood behind him watching the picture-taking. Noticing that Antonina was aware of them, the photographer dropped the camera to dangle around his neck and smiled at her in a tense way. She could not be sure whether or not she had seen them before.

Manfred paid for two rooms in a small hotel that night: girls and boys. The meal was paid for by their performance. They drank Californian wine and toasted to America. In the middle of the night Antonina woke and watched Maria and Helen breathe in deep sleep. These women had grown so close to her.

They had been en route for nearly two weeks and were only halfway to San Francisco – a long way from Podzhin Hall.

CHAPTER
TWENTY-TWO

Sasha awoke from a doze. The daydream had left his body cold and clammy. He lifted his heavy eyelids and saw the festoon curtains lowered at his bedroom window. He did not know what time of day it was. It felt like the bland in-between hours of late afternoon which offered no sudden change to snap him out of his floating solitude.

He had dreamed that he was in uniform, his head held high in the embroidered collar, marching up steps to a podium. The stiff metal of his scabbard pressed against his thigh. Awaiting him at the top was the general holding out a medal to him. It was like a rosette one pins to a winning horse's bridle. A long red ribbon adorned the stiff cardboard rose. Somehow the general and he were the only ones present. The decoration was affixed to his chest. Sasha looked down at it. The red ribbon wriggled, and the rose had turned into a rat pinned to his heart. Terror melted into consciousness; Sasha had woken up at that moment.

He reached for his bedside table lamp but his heavy hand knocked against a china cup of tea which toppled and fell. He heard the liquid trickle to the floor. Sasha closed his eyes and put his hand on his heart. Laboriously that damaged life-pump worked inside him. Faster and faster it seemed to strain, and then jerked. Panic seized him, and panic was bad and could be fatal. The heart missed a beat, plunged then surged, and a burning heat rushed through his veins. *I must not get excited*, he thought, and tears started to flow freely from his eyes. He was so weak, so lonely, and time slackened deliberately to punish him.

Perhaps it would be best if he jumped out of bed and leaped around the room. It would be his end, the cessation of dull suffering and memories of the past.

"Sasha. Sasha."

Yes, he was Sasha, the son of a duke, trained in the Corps of Pages, the Czar's most exclusive military school.

"How do you feel?"

He turned his head and saw Olga, a caricature of the young and beautiful Olga. Only the shape and strength of her eyes, enfolding him now with concern, had remained the same in age. He offered her his hand and she, sitting on the chair close to his bed, took it.

"I knocked the tea over. I am sorry."

"The nurse will deal with it; don't fret yourself."

"I am so clumsy, so useless. Olga, what has happened to me?"

"What has happened to us?"

Sasha had known Olga from childhood for their parents had been close friends. To his chagrin she had married his brother and not him. Often he wondered whether she had done this deliberately so that she would not lose either man.

"What time is it?"

"Never mind."

"For a fool like me the time of day is immaterial."

"That's not what I meant."

"Olga, do you remember the day of the coach accident?"

He willed her to say *yes*. They had been teenagers. He knew that, once she had married Ivan and became a mature woman, she had submerged all memory of his efforts to woo her with innocent clumsiness. But for him his youthful romantic infatuation had meant so much more. Thinking about it now, he recognised that he had never experienced such devotion to any other woman, not even his wife.

"Olga, do you remember when we drove back in the coach from the reception at the Vorontsov Palace?"

"You tire yourself, Sasha, and it was at Countess Brassova's."

She remembered; he knew and tried to squeeze her hand as an ally. It seemed important for him now that he eradicate all jealousy of her love for his brother and of her coquetry with other men. He needed her to acknowledge her part in that event with him. For if she denied it, would he not have to admit that he had duped himself most of his life?

"The coachman drove the horses too fast for he wanted to be home. Do you recall how we enjoyed the excitement of being jolted through the star-filled glass-clear night? Even the snowflakes hung frozen, immobile in the air."

"It was the first time my father allowed you to take me out."

"The horses' hooves struck sparks from the ice. I slipped my hand into your ermine muff. We kissed," he whispered, and tears filled his eyes.

"Yes, we sort of did," she admitted.

"I remember feeling your warmth right through your furs. You were like one of those coal stoves the peasants erect in their farmyards."

"A brazier."

"Yes, you were a brazier, with eyes glowing like smouldering coals."

"You wore your cadet uniform, and the cap was too big. It bent your ears and made you look silly."

"I was silly, Olga, and for the first time yearning for the heat of a woman's body." Sasha tried to move into an upright position on his pillows but Olga did not let go of his hand. "Suddenly the seat underneath us flew sideways as the coach toppled; one horse had fallen and broken a leg."

"My father dismissed the coachman the same night."

"They had to shoot the horse. You can't possibly know how dear I hold the way you lay in the snow. I turned your face, and your cheek was toasted with glittering crystals. I thought you were dead."

"I was hurt."

"You opened your eyes, and I could have shouted out with joy."

"My enraged father was sitting on his ottoman in a cloud of cigar smoke by the time we finally got home."

"You were pampered to bed, and the doctor summoned."

"I was bruised all along my leg for days."

"I had to sneak into your room to find out how you were."

"Did you really?" Olga asked, turning her eyes away.

"You waited for me?"

"I can't remember."

"Oh, but it happened, and it is still with me." Sasha let himself glide into the scene:

On her satin bed, the sixteen-year-old Olga whimpers theatrically, her tousled hair entangled with the dolls she has outgrown. They are without a chaperone, and there is an aura of magic and danger.

"Kiss it better," she orders, giving him an impish look while pulling up her nightshirt higher than is needed for him to put his lips on her firm warm flesh. Her little shriek shocks him and he sees her teeth have left indentations on her moist bottom lip.

He is shaking from desire and for the first time in the presence of a woman his male member rises to its full size. She does not seem to be put off, nor gives the impression that he should be ashamed. The blaze in her green eyes contains the knowledge of his early morning shameful practices. He is not yet eighteen years old and cannot stand the pain of pleasure any longer. As his body releases him from torture, he stares into the glass eyes of her dolls.

"Olga!"

"You're making up stories in your head. It's time for your medicine."

Sasha focused. It was the nurse who stood at his bedside. Olga had left and he lay on his sick bed alone and on his back.

Sasha thought that it was indeed a bitter medicine. Why was the brain not programmed to release a hormone that made one enjoy being old, revel in the fact that the

221

body withered? Why did one still wish so urgently to be capable and loved?

"You have got too worked up and talked too much." A strong hand was put on his forehead. Gratefully he felt Trish's youth flow through him.

"Let's see how naughty you have been." She shook a thermometer. He watched the strong flesh of her arm emerging from the short-sleeved uniform. The arm was pale and creamy. He did not like the fashion of tanning skin.

"I knocked over the tea," he guiltily confessed.

She pushed the thermometer under his tongue. It felt cold. Silenced, he gazed at her.

"Naughty boy."

He smiled weakly.

She walked around the bed. Her bosom was trapped in the strong cloth of the uniform. He imagined creamy breasts, cool to the eyes yet warm to the touch.

The nurse picked up the cup. Njanja would do the mopping up. She pulled the thermometer from his mouth and inspected it, rolling it in her fingers. Her face was unlined, her temples wide and smooth before ceding to dyed blond hair. She was not pretty, her features coarse, but she dispensed energy and hope. He thought he could smell her like lemon balm. She grabbed his wrist. A moment ago the ageing hand of Olga had held him. Or was it much longer ago and he had fallen asleep in between? Trish's touch carried vibrancy, reality.

"Naughty man."

He smiled meekly. *She had called him a man.*

"I will have to give you two milligrams of Mogadon."

She dropped his hand and he was sorry. He reached out to touch her forearm. Her arm lingered. She looked at him, her eyes mocking gently. "What next? Am I going to find a surprise under the cover when I give you the bottle?"

His spirits sank. *Oh no!* "I want to go to the lavatory by myself."

His hand was slapped. "You do as Trish says."

He smiled bravely. Tears formed. He was jolted between pleasure and degradation. She saw the tears and bent over him. The uniform crinkled. "You'll pop up again. Soon you'll be your naughty old self. I'll wheel you around your nice park."

He felt like crying more. She straightened up and brushed his tears from his cheek.

"We'll elope into the woods." She suddenly bent and kissed his cheek. The firmly pressed lips stiffened his own face muscles. His tears stopped. Her strength ran into him.

"You would be behind me pushing, and I couldn't see you."

"We'll stop and I shall be at your feet. Okay?"

"There is nothing to kneel to."

She laughed. "You wanna bet, you old lecher!" She grabbed the goose-necked bottle from the bedside table and held it up. "Water games?"

He nodded. She gripped the covers to pull them off him. He clung to them, the diamond signet ring sparkling.

"That's what I thought: a naughty man underneath there."

They fought over the blanket. His heart beat fast but happily, regularly. *Perhaps his heart wasn't sick. Perhaps it was his troubled mind letting his body down. Trish could make him better, younger again.* "I'll let go if you promise not to peek."

"I want to peek." Her eyes widened.

He imagined her stroking his withered sex. She had won; he let go.

"Not bad, not bad at all," she said. "Could be a lot better still when you're off the dope." The glass jar chilled him. He tried to release himself. The sensation for a moment was like before ejaculation. The dreaded exercise turned into something nice. Trish held the bottle, and her eyes challenged his cheekily. A door was slammed somewhere in the house.

"We'll be caught," he whispered. She removed the bottle. He did not look at it, but checked whether she did. Then she pulled his nightshirt down and flattened it, brushing lightly over his genitals.

He loved her.

She made ready to go.

"Stay a little longer," he pleaded.

"I'll bring your medicine and supper." She bent and suddenly kissed him on his mouth. His erupting sob was stifled. She was at the door.

"I'm an old disgusting man to you. You must kiss so many young and healthy suitors."

"Suitors died out a century ago, and young men are boring. They've got no manners or class. You're a real elegant gent, you are. I like that."

"Trish." She turned at the door. "Do you mean that?"

"I'll show you when you're well again." The door shut behind her.

On the landing, she bumped into Valentina who appeared to be idling as if she was in search of something. She straightened up and grabbed Trish's arm. "I am watching you, Nurse Trish."

With a snort Trish walked to the top of the stairs, Valentina's disapproval like needle pricks in her back. Jaws clenched, Trish thundered down the stairs making the wood creak and the chandelier dingle.

In his bedroom Sasha lay happily on the pillows and felt inconsequentially light. Trish had not shrunk at the sight of his sex and it had been wonderful, so wonderful, and nobody knew about their secret.

Nights, and now days, were nothing more than an assailment of memories but now with Trish's soothing… When the nurse had started work, he thought he would die of shame because she was the same age as Antonina and Anna, upsettingly young. But she was fascinated by his Russian stories. The twins never listened; they were always in a hurry to leave and when he gave them important advice, their eyes glazed over and he saw himself as an unfit old uncle. There was no place for him amongst the young and their ideas, their noises and thoughts. There was only Olga's love but she could not help or explain because she too was old.

Depression returned, like the pain when the analgesics wear off. With a sigh he let the thought in – *Fydo*.

His son was the greatest disappointment of his life. Fyodor Alexandreich, after a childhood of unfounded tantrums later diagnosed as epileptic fits, had turned out spineless. The fits had ceased, but so had any ambition in him. Fydo was his only heir, the sole surviving male carrying the name Brodsky and the title given to them by the Prince of Varsovie. Despite all caning Fydo had refused a military career. He had studied philosophy. Sasha would have accepted that if he had then written a novel, become a famous Russian writer, but no – Fydo dallied through life aimlessly. Was it because his mother had died before he had reached one year – because the strain of giving him life had cost hers?

Tatyana! The clamp on Sasha's head squeezed a little tighter.

After Tatyana's death he had wanted to see nobody, not even the infant son. Apparently according to child psychology nonsense the twins talked about, this had damaged Fyodor's future. Back in Russia a wet-nurse was hired until a child was acceptable to its parents. Obviously those were the olden ways.

Fydo's moping around and solitary walks could only be blamed on a lack of discipline and authority. That was it. Fydo needed someone to tell him what to do. For a start he would have to be betrothed to a suitable wife.

That's what Tatyana had been to him: suitable, from the moment he had first laid eyes on her. In full regalia he had waited for a servant to call him downstairs to be introduced to his bride-to-be. Sasha's moustache then was only a fledgling, slightly curled up over the corners of his lips. Tatyana had sat on the sofa, small and dainty, and her thin ivory arms had emerged from the loose lace of her frock, her hands joined in the vast material of her skirt.

Throughout the introduction she had not dared to lift her eyes once to him. All he had looked at fondly were chestnut curls either side of the crown of her head and a small pointed nose. He had thought her endearing.

His father had chosen well because he had cared for him. Now it was up to Sasha to do the same for his own son. It was high time: the boy was mature now, very mature. Trish had made it clear that young men were without interest to her. So all was well.

The only drawback was that Trish had no money, a fact she had repeatedly alluded to. Her parents owned land, were therefore landowners, gentleman farmers, solid stock. What Trish needed were nice clothes, a few baubles to appeal to Fydo, especially since Sasha had always insisted that a wife ought to have money of her own. Well, he had to think about that. Not now. He was too plagued by returning pain. Where was his medicine? He would think about it another time. Perhaps he would ask for the family lawyer to come and see him, and discuss a regular income for Trish, secretly. Yes, yes.

The door finally opened. Trish put the tray down. She smiled at him and, oh God, touched him. He adored her. He picked the painkillers out of her hand. He would do anything for Trish, give her anything in gratitude for her mere existence.

CHAPTER
TWENTY-THREE

The family lawyer sat at the Regency table in Sasha's bedroom and contemplated the annuity covenant in front of him. "With all due respect, Viscount, but given the family's present financial situation, I advise against it. Bankruptcy could be less than a year away."

In the bed Sasha tested the elasticity of his moustache. "My dear man, the Brodskys' finances are on the point of returning to spit and polish."

"This is not the impression I received from the countess."

"First of all, there is the sum from the Ikon about to be realised, surely. Secondly, we have asked for compensation for our losses. A piffling monthly appreciation to a loyal girl would be hardly noticed."

The lawyer pushed his glasses higher on his nose. "I have prepared a covenant in perpetuity and standing instructions for your bank, but have not filled in the figures. How much did you have in mind?"

Sasha sat propped up by several pillows and seemed better than he had for days. "Two hundred pounds a month."

"Two hundred pounds!"

"That's what I said. With this she can get a good seamstress, travel to London for tea, and the sort of things a lady requires."

"That is two thousand and four hundred a year."

"I wish I could increase the sum but I have responsibilities towards Podzhin Hall."

The lawyer turned. For a moment the light from the window caught in his crystalline lenses and made him eyeless, blind. "Two thousand four hundred pounds is a large sum. There are already threats of legal action on outstanding bills for the property in the region of twice this… this… hem… annuity."

"Come over here." Sasha beckoned the solicitor to his bedside. "This is top secret," whispered Sasha up to the bent head of the lawyer. "But my son is to marry Trish Worship."

The lawyer nodded, straightened up and with a perplexed shaking of the head walked back to the table and sat down. "So…" he said and stopped. "So…" the lawyer hesitated again, "the money would stay in the family, as it were."

"Precisely."

"In which case, I will fill in the sum." He picked up the fountain pen from the bronze writing set and wrote down the figure. Then he fanned the paper in order to dry the ink. "Still, I would like you to take some time to think about it before you sign. I will wait for your phone call to return for my countersignature."

"Don't you dare do that to me! I can't wait one minute longer. Give it to me."

229

Hesitantly, the lawyer obliged.

"Beautiful, beautiful." Sasha wriggled in his bed, reading the text. "Hand me the pen please." Holding the paper under the light of his bedside lamp, he put a jittery signature on the document. "Now you countersign it."

Unwillingly the lawyer signed the paper at the table, filled in the banker's order and signed that too. Finally he lifted his leather briefcase from the carpet. "It would have been wiser to sleep over such signatures. I refuse to post these forms for forty-eight hours, and even then will only do so with your personal confirmation that you wish to go ahead with it."

"All right. Leave the contract with me, and come and pick it up tomorrow, if you like. It will allow me to show it to someone." Sasha ignored the lawyer's civilised parting wishes as he was engrossed in re-reading the document.

★

"Is the coast clear?"

"Come here."

Trish approached the bed.

"If you kiss me properly, I'll show you."

She clambered onto the bed and pressed her upper body over Sasha's maimed heart. Their lips met. She tasted of apples stored on straw; her hair smelled like newly cut grass.

"Get off me, and I'll read it to you."

Trish let go of him. He grabbed the paper from the bedside table. "… and theretofore, I do herewith order the payment monthly and in perpetuity, so long as she shall live, of two hundred pounds sterling to my devoted nurse Miss Trish Worship, of Brampton, Oxon."

The nurse sat on the bed, clipping dead skin from around her index nail with her front teeth.

"This will give you possibilities for nice gowns, some trinkets, hair-dos: things to charm my son. You do like my son, don't you?"

"The old guru?"

"The future Viscount Fyodor Alexandreich Brodsky, the one to carry our title forward."

"Now, now, don't cry. I promise I'll be nice to your son."

"Do you think it is enough?"

"Oh, Sasha! You shouldn't have."

"Trish, you give me more joy than I can spell out on any document. Stop biting your nails." He took her hand in his and playfully nibbled at the wet finger. "It's a bad habit. Don't take anything off you."

"Not even dead skin?"

"Not even dead skin."

Saying silly basic things thrilled him with joy. He felt elated at having done something to secure the continuation of the pleasure she generated in him and would give to his son later. After all, it was only a contract, and what was a piece of paper when it could be traded for such happiness? He had plenty of worthless documents downstairs in the study, none of which had given him any pleasure in return. He let go of the hand. "I need you, you know."

"It's getting worse, is it?"

"Definitely."

"Can you do it, or is it the old prostate?"

"I diagnose prostate, nurse."

Trish didn't take out the bottle. She pulled back the sheets. "In order for you to piss, Viscount Brodsky, you need warming up."

"Without any doubt." He lay back on the pillow and spread his legs. Her firm hand stroked down his stomach and over the pelvic region, sending waves of sensual warmth through him. His moan transformed into a spreading rubbery smile. "It's bad today. Very bad."

Expertly she touched his shrivelled masculine limb – the royal treatment making him feel so good that he wished he could give Trish everything he owned. His thrilled heart jolted around yet he knew that it was bad for him. "Very bad," he muttered again, enfolded in thousands of embraces, hundreds of imagined women's passions and indefinable physical comforts. She stroked gently while the sick heart in his chest beat as if to burst out.

There was a knock on the door. Trish jerked up and yanked the covers back over him. He closed his legs.

"In the side-table," he hissed just audibly. She grabbed the covenant and shoved it into the top drawer. The door opened. Trish had moved to the window and was shaking the festoon curtains straight. Sasha's heart thumped like a piston in a diesel engine.

Valentina wore a turban; blade-shaped earrings dangled from the emerging lobes. A kaftan made her look like a fortune-teller. Sasha noticed his niece's sharp eyes on Trish. A deep frown was chiselled into the hard-set face.

"Leave us," Valentina barked at the nurse.

"Very well." Trish let go of the curtains and flounced out, pulling out her tongue at Valentina's back before slamming the door. Sasha chuckled.

"What's funny?"

"Oh nothing, my dear."

"Those drugs affect your brain."

Sasha still felt Trish's warm hand on his private parts.

"I came to tell you that the Russian Embassy may be going to support our claim for compensation. Mr Vasily Voronov is coming to pay us a visit later today."

Sasha edged himself higher and more comfortably in his bed. With a shock, he noticed that the corner of the covenant was protruding from the bedside drawer. Tilting his body, he reached out with his left hand but could not stifle a little groan of pain, as he managed to push the paper in and re-shut the drawer properly. "The lawyer will be pleased about the compensation," he grumbled, feigning calmness. The contortion had given him a cramp in the left arm. He needed a massage. *Trish!* He would increase the sum of the annuity to three hundred pounds a month, he decided and felt curiously elevated as if he was drifting like a dab of foam on the Neva in summer, only to be punished by the sharp stabbing of yet another angina pectoris attack. "Trish," he croaked. "Medicine, my dearest Trish."

"Your dearest Trish!" Valentina clawed the turban from her head and threw it on the foot of the bed where it lay like an unoccupied nest. In times of stress she needed her hair free. She dashed to the bedside table, pulled open the drawer and took out the covenant. Her eyes flew over the text. Her hand went to her mouth. Viciously she tore the contract in half, then each half into halves again. "Cheap bitch," she hissed.

Trish had come back in response to Sasha's call and was guardedly closing the door. Her youthful bosom pulsated under the uniform. "If you think you can get away with this…"

"Slut!" Valentina grabbed her headgear and tossed the shreds of paper into it.

Trish's arms hung at her side but her hands were balled tight. "Thief," she panted. "That was for me. I've earned it with the trouble I take over him. I'll get you for stealing it. I'll make you suffer for the rest of your life." Trish's shaking voice had turned deep and was laced with the menace of curses.

Without a further glance at her groaning uncle, Valentina swept out of the room.

Trish bent over her patient. With her voice unnaturally strained, she proposed something which cannot have been recommended in her training. "I will take you for a walk in the park," she suggested, wanting to escape the suffocation of the airless room but unable to leave the sick old man. "And afterwards, we'll call the lawyer again."

★

In the park, by the family graves Fydo chewed on a grass stalk, unaware of Valentina dispensing paper fragments from her turban into Cahill's bonfire of raked leaves. The stone slabs at his feet lay tilted and earth clawed at their drowning edges. The chiselled name *Mikhail Alexandreich Brodsky* had lost definition. A woodlouse scuttled from the date 1849 to 1918. Fydo tickled the insect with the tip of the grass. The louse was instantly transformed into a pellet, making an embossed full stop after the year of his grandfather's death. Next to Mikhail lay buried Ivan Brodsky, his uncle and Olga's husband. The date of death showed 1954.

Fydo shambled on and bent to touch the cold tablet of his mother Tatyana's grave. He could not remember touching her when she was alive; she had died before his first birthday. *Requiescat in pace*. The distress that this heavy stone crushed his mother's delicate body still lingered in him, as it had as a child. He had seen only one photograph of his mother, taken on her wedding day: staring self-conscious and slightly frightened into the camera lens, her narrow shoulders decked in ruffles of lace and her waist breakably thin. She looked like a child-bride next to Sasha in the Imperial uniform, strong eyes expressing male dominion over the butterfly creature joined to him in arranged matrimony.

The oldest grave bore the remaining readable letters *nasta* and the date 1884. That grave belonged to those who had owned Podzhin Hall before the Brodskys.

Fydo discarded the split grass and strolled barefoot into the woodland area. The soothing of cool air relaxed his face, slackened his firmly clenched jaw. Amongst the family, even the dead ones, he could not but tauten his features, contrary to the inner peace and serenity that he preached; but alone in the woods and their obscure mingled shadows, he softened. He glanced up yearningly at the autumnal foliage above him: November would impair this vitality, as illness had damaged his father.

"And summer's lease hath all too short a date," he murmured and knew that his father would not live to next spring. Fydo sat down on an old log, his favourite place. Around his feet the ground was alive with purposes pursued on a small scale. An ant climbed onto his foot. It hesitated, faced by the tuft of hair growing on his big toe.

"The bitch!"

His meditative calm was cruelly ruptured and replaced by the dread of facing Valentina. His cousin approached him eagerly, her face flushed. She dropped onto a tree-trunk. "The trollop extorted two thousand pounds a year from Sasha. Do you hear me? Per year! Annuity, my foot!"

Oh, how I hate people, thought Fydo, gently brushing the ant from his foot.

"Snap out of your lethargy and have her arrested."

The colours of Valentina's kaftan clashed with the tints of the wood. "Lucky I didn't go riding this morning," she puffed.

"Horses should gallop free, roll in mud and…"

"Oh, shut up!" Valentina ground the heel of her shoe into the soft soil, and Fydo winced. "Why do you sit around like that, not understanding a bloody thing anyone says to you? You should be married, have a family and work – be normal for God's sake!"

Fydo watched a chaffinch expel a dropping before flying from a branch. "Is it normal to walk through life, sexual pride in one pocket, the key to the Jaguar in the other? Normal to whang my sex three times a week into my prostrated legal woman, who suffers it for the sake of the children and her pride in the bargain?"

Irritated, Valentina checked his face partly hidden in shadow.

"I would soon dream of driving a better model of Jaguar down success lane, where women, younger than my wife, stand by the roadside, nubile and available. My wife would walk from one specialist in Harley Street to the next, enjoying the spatula in her vagina, bargain alley to pearls, fur coats, and crocodile leather shoes."

"Now you sound like a homosexual."

"Oh horror! The shameful word in the mouth of an unkissed woman."

"Talking about kissing, the nurse is sexually abusing your father in order to extort money from him. What do you say to that?"

"I will have to leave," he declared with conviction.

"Leave? Where to?"

"Where there are no fateful sacrifices expected."

"There is no such place."

"In Thailand, they have temples and Buddhist monks."

"Oh no."

"Oh yes. Meditation removes the soul from the body. After years of practice, you can see your soul detached, outside yourself."

"What good does that do?"

"Then I would be able to ask my soul to free me."

"Fydo, it sounds stupid. It comes from all that sitting around doing nothing all day."

"There will be years of sitting around, learning to do nothing."

"You're already quite good at it."

"At times, the gong is beaten by brothers, and we assemble in the temple for collective meditation. Prayer coils burn slowly, and their smoke corkscrews to heaven."

"There won't be any wine, or other luxuries you're rather used to."

"We'd beg for food in the villages, and during droughts we'll eat frogs and cicadas."

"Don't count on the family to send you food."

"I will not be a Brodsky. I'll be shaven and wear a saffron robe. My name will start with Phra for brother."

"Like Phra Batinabelfry. You know what this is all about, don't you? You're afraid of taking on responsibility. Maybe it's just as well you will never have children."

"I would despair, watching my children sentenced to the pain of childhood, while I could offer only plasters of deception for their gaping emotional wounds."

There was nothing wholesome left in the woods for Fydo. He walked back to the house with her. On the way they passed the nurse, advancing slowly, pushing a crumpled Sasha in his wheelchair.

"Bitch," Valentina spat sideways.

It was clear that, apart from Anna and Sasha, no-one in the family had taken to Trish; they accepted though that her presence was a necessity. Olga had insisted the nurse ate in the kitchen. Anna had waffled on about social equality and exploitation. Olga would not discuss the matter further.

Now Valentina and Fydo entered through the French windows of the music room. They found Olga sitting at Sasha's roll-top desk, writing.

"I am glad you're back." The pen poised. "You do remember that this Soviet diplomat is due any minute."

Fydo said nothing for he had forgotten.

"Vasily is rather sexy, I seem to remember," said Valentina.

Olga put the pen down and closed the desk. "We want no more of that flirting."

Valentina, rebuffed, consulted her wristwatch. "He's five minutes late."

"It is polite to be five minutes late," retorted Olga, putting both hands against the samovar, checking its warmth.

"Ten minutes is extending politeness, and a quarter of an hour is rude. Half an hour means he got lost. One hour means he's not coming," recited Valentina.

Olga paid no attention for she was rehearsing in her head what she would say when he arrived. Suddenly she noticed Fydo's feet. "You, go and put on shoes at once," she ordered.

Slowly Fydo padded out of the room.

"And hurry. I want us all to be here to receive him."

Olga at the French windows rubbed her questing fingers along the cushioned seam of the drapes but no-one drove up to the Hall.

"This commie is playing us up." Valentina shook the tambourine.

★

Vasily Voronov had laid out his map on the passenger seat. Once in the centre of Hatley, he stopped and studied it. A tiny dot had been made where Podzhin Hall was situated. He drove off down the street going west. As he emerged onto the road to Drayton, he knew that he was on the right road and the Hall close by. Suddenly two imposing stone pillars appeared, supporting ornate metal gates. Hastily he drove by and stopped the Vauxhall a little further on. He was late and could not explain to himself why he had not driven in, except that the opulence of the stately entrance had put him off. *What effect might the house have on him?* He made a three-point turn. Hesitantly, foot gingerly on the accelerator, he drove up the curved drive and faced the worst of his expectations: an oval fountain tinkled in front of the portico of a splendid old house, haughty and cold-shouldered. Vasily parked and walked to the door. There was no bell, but a brass knocker. It resounded in the interior. He heard equally hollow steps approaching, and wished he could run away and hide. The woman opening the door he recognised at once as an old *babushka* and he relaxed somewhat.

"Mr Voronov," he announced himself.

"You are expected," she said in Russian and let him in. As he followed her across the vestibule to a door on the right, he gazed up at a chandelier which appeared to be made of a monsoon of frozen raindrops. She knocked and he braced himself.

The *babushka* opened the door for him and pulled away. Vasily stepped into the music room.

"Mr Voronov, what a pleasure." Valentina reacted first.

He remembered his character description of her – *a man-eater* – but took a step forward. "How do you do?" He did not smile nor did he touch her hand.

"Away from your embassy, you're a bit of a fish out of water." Valentina challenged him shamelessly.

"So good of you to come," said Olga civilly. "Please have a seat."

He obliged but the shock of Valentina's frontal attack caused him to forget the opening words he had prepared for these degenerate creatures. The only noise in the room was the gurgling of the silver samovar. Annoyed by the cushion pushing into his lower back, he extracted it and placed it into the armchair next to him.

Valentina picked up the cushion and tossed it into a corner before installing herself. Olga remained in the wooden swivel chair, twisted away from the bureau.

"We were so much looking forward to your visit," Valentina said, and her cherry-coloured enamelled fingernails crawled onto his upholstered armrest.

The quiet man in the corner of the room was introduced by Olga as Fyodor Alexandreich Brodsky, son of the viscount. This balding middle-aged aristocrat in a sackcloth shirt and canvas trousers wove his hands into each other and appeared to be living in a world of his own. That was perhaps a ploy and he would have to be watched. Vasily also needed to keep brash Valentina at bay, while misleading the pompous old woman into believing that Mother Russia would consider giving them money. The physical challenges of his youth had been easier to handle. Oppressed by the stuffiness of the panelled room, he nevertheless had to perform his job with dispassionate rigour.

"What a mild autumn day," he heard himself say, pleased there was no stutter for he had concentrated on the practised inflection.

"Indeed." Olga reached up to her forehead to heft her fringe.

The day before, Vasily had been briefed by Turchin. The overall message from Georgi Miliukov in Moscow was, *Establish yourself with the Brodskys.*

He peered around the room. In the bookshelves were no tennis trophies. Painted porcelain plates leaned on wooden stands and there were books bound in pigskin. He twisted his head to read the spines of the books. *Oh no!* Chekhov, Tolstoy, Princess Dashkov Romanovna, and Boris Pasternak: shelves weighed down by the lies of despicable traitors.

"*Dorogoy moy* – my dear chap – why do you look so serious?" Valentina was on him again.

"I am admiring this room," he said, using *small talk* speech. To prove his point, he indicated the mantelpiece where hung a modern painting, a piece of degenerate art characteristic of the particularly undiscriminating muddle in which these Brodskys lived. In the whirl of abstract shapes the only recognisable thing the artist had painted with application was a coat-of-arms in minute detail. "An interesting choice of painting. I would have expected something more traditional."

He sensed Valentina rearing up next to him. Opposite, the theatrical old lady eyed him calculatingly. He had touched a sore point: the Ikon. His ultimate objective was to get the Ikon back for the Soviet Union.

"The painting you see over the mantelpiece is a work done by Paul Malloy, a gifted artist," Valentina said in the uninvolved voice of a museum guide. "The Tate Gallery have offered Paul a price for one of his works." She stood before the swirly mess in glossy oil. "I seem to be the only one who understands the message of this art but then I, the artist's muse, was there when he created it." She pointed to the detailed inset. "It is the emblem of the Prince of Pozharsky, one of the greatest noblemen in Imperial Russia."

Almost choking on hearing *imperial* in the same breath as *Russia*, he nevertheless managed in a detached manner to offer, "Bold brushstrokes. This artist is obviously talented. The new Russian art is also based on generous brushstrokes, perhaps a little more confined in structure."

"Mr Voronov," started Olga, "to take your mind away from art, what would you say to a cup of…"

A window-pane shattered as a projectile flew into the room. Valentina cried out and clasped her shoulder.

"*Bozhe moy!*" Olga threw her spread hand against her chest.

"I've been shot!"

Fydo woke to his surroundings and picked up the projectile from the carpet. It was a stone, as big as a child's fist. He showed the stone around.

"Are you all right, dear?" Olga asked her daughter, who was still rubbing her shoulder.

Vasily was on high alert. Turchin had not thought it necessary to send a bodyguard along with him. *Was he safe in this house?*

"This time, Sasha has gone too far!" Olga stated, as if relieved that it had not been anything more serious.

"What is happening here?" Vasily had not yet untensed.

"Please excuse us, Mr Voronov, and don't be alarmed. It's only my brother-in-law." Her arm with a glittering bracelet mopped threat from the air. "He is a little old now, and he hates that painting. He often threatens to destroy it if it is not taken down. It injures his aesthetic sensibility. I saw the nurse wheel him into the park earlier on. Would you like a sherry, rather than tea?"

Valentina still massaged her shoulder, her dark eyes frothing.

Vasily dared to analyse her as she was preoccupied with herself: *fifty-three years old, divorced, tough, drinks, crude female, catches men for sex, ostentatious dress.*

Yet there was something touching about her posture of self-concern, the outline of her chignon from which some dark strands had come loose. Perhaps it was merely the sweep of her white blouse from the belt of her ample skirt to the gathered oval neckline. Strangely, it brought back visual memories of the girls of his youth in the Ukraine.

Slowly she turned her dangerous attention back to him. He could not help an involuntary nervous grin. His nostrils flared wide. He tried to master his face, to keep his lips closed without trembling.

"Perhaps we ought to go to the park and introduce you to the viscount, Mr Voronov," suggested Olga and saved him from further exposure.

Vasily had by no means come to terms with the incident of aggression, but was now civilly invited to meet the aggressor. The only desirable thing about this was that it would get him out of the suffocating space.

As they stepped into the vestibule following Olga, Valentina made sure she brushed past his body.

"*Shabarsha*," he thought he heard her whisper conspiratorially. Shabarsha was a game of tag based on an old fairytale, now banned. Why did he know it? And why was the Party punishing him with this atrocious assignment?

★

Sasha felt the wheels of the chair run smoothly across the lawn. For some reason the colours had left the park and the shapes were gone. It was all lidded with a cataract skin. *I am dying*, he thought. *Is death shapeless and without tint? Will the last memory of life be no more than diffuse pain and fear? Surely one was not slipped whimpering into the slot of* death *without some glorious moment of recognition, edged in gold.*

He suffered but he had to prepare for pain, so that once he got there, he would be strong. Some old military discipline had to serve here. Terror had to be controlled. That was the first rule for a soldier and the last.

The chair rattled over stones again and approached the house. Before him was a crowded scene of people in some sort of painted cave. Above them hung a crystal moon, frozen. His father, Mikhail Alexandreich, came down the steps first in fragile light; he grew larger and approached smiling. And there were others coming down the stairs, pouring out of rooms, the backquarters, all the others, the old others. They bowed before him, and he pressed their hands in friendship, as he sighed and the water from his eyes dropped off his chin.

★

As Trish rolled Sasha back to the house, and Cahill helped lift the wheelchair into the vestibule, they were met by the party setting out from the music room in search of them.

"Here you are!" exclaimed Olga. "My dear Sasha, may I introduce the envoy from the Russian Embassy, Mr Voronov, and please be civil and leave that painting alone. You hit Valentina with your stone."

The trembling spotted hands holding the silk border of the rug kept contracting as if gripped by the handshakes of friends. At last they relaxed gently.

Sasha emitted a profound moan that echoed around the vestibule. The crystal drops on the chandelier clinked although there was no draught in the house. Olga touched his forehead. A sensation of dry ice, burning hot and cold, seized her. She saw the still lips, the fallen-in old body. And there was a gloss on the eyes which seemed pleased. Hundreds of pieces of cutglass played in them.

"The Viscount Brodsky is dead," Olga declared with dignity. Then she turned away to stifle her sob.

With stiff anger Fydo turned to the nurse. "You took my father outside when he is so poorly? Didn't you notice?"

"He was no worse today than yesterday."

Vasily had no idea how to handle this new situation. He was standing in a pompous corridor facing a dead man in a chair, while Valentina prowled around the nurse. Countess Olga had disappeared into the backquarters. Vasily decided to leave and nobody took any notice of his departure.

★

"Durov." Olga, blinking her tears away, tried to say more but could not.

The old nanny instinctively knew, perhaps had seen or perhaps not. "Countess Brassova's party," she said. "You danced, zr viscount and yourself, zr Herzegovina Waltz, so young, so happy."

Numbed still, Olga stood in the dark magic kitchen. "He is dead."

"He could dance like a prince, I remember."

Olga bent her head.

"Is zr goodbye for little while only."

Olga gently stroked the face of her servant and friend; Njanja's cheeks were wet.

"Do our lives go on? Without Sasha, Podzhin Hall will not be the same again, Durov – never, ever again."

Njanja held her hand over the one against her face. "You zr countess. Podzhin Hall will be zr same."

"Thank you, Durov."

CHAPTER
TWENTY-FOUR

Antonina and her travelling companions had left Texas hundreds of miles back and were making way in New Mexico, where early October temperatures were still around thirty degrees Celsius. The first stop of a new day was a late breakfast in a diner in Albuquerque. From rubber bottles they drizzled maple syrup onto pancakes, drawing lazy loop patterns. Weak coffee was poured from a perspex glass jar.

"It is a sweet sort of plastic experience," Maria rated their meal.

The lavatories were round the back of the diner. Antonina was given a key from which dangled a large lump of wood. On the way she encountered a black man, skulking around. His face was thin, a little wolfish, and the cheeks sunken but the eyes had a bright blue-grey glint.

"Ma'am." His clawlike pink-black hand reached out of a dirty sleeve towards her. "I need a dollar."

She quickly unlocked the door to the toilet. He was not the first homeless beggar she had noticed since arriving in this town. When she had to emerge, he was still there, his anguished feverish eyes on her, still begging for a dollar. It was one thing to travel through America as a lighthearted tourist but a wholly other thing to get involved with the dark side of the country.

When she returned unharmed to the others, after giving the beggar two dollars, Manfred made things worse by telling them that under the desert were stored masses of indestructible radioactive waste.

It was possible to take a funicular railway up to the ridge, but they did not care enough for that, and lingered for a moment undecided and silent in the rising heat of the day to come.

Eventually François said, "Let's go to the Grand Canyon. It's almost next door, isn't it? Maybe one day, we'll come back here."

"Next door?" Helen consulted the map. "Same as across France."

Manfred drove the next lap. The group had started to nestle into the cocoon of the car with their intimacies shared. Each accepted the other as a familiar feature and, with the miles driven, the acceptance was turning into affection. Antonina had come a long way, a long way inside herself as well. The scar inflicted by her separation from her twin was healing. A tender sense of responsibility for Anna remained but the itching of the scar tissue brought the sober recognition that what there had been between them could never be again. And today was their birthday: twenty-four times two.

★

It was Antonina who drove up to the Grand Canyon visitors' area. Exuberantly she wrenched at the wheel and, as the sedan swerved into a parking space, the back wing knocked over a wooden pole on which was carved *Kodak point* with a gopher with a camera to its face.

"I haven't gone crazy. Lots of life-changing thoughts have just caught up with me."

"Life-lust, ja?" Manfred replanted the signpost into the ground.

They stood at the rim of the Grand Canyon and the breathtaking red-earthed valley lay in awesome stillness at their feet. Here and there, glimpses of the Colorado River showed like a thin silver snake.

"Just like the mountains in *Alpenglüh*, but in reverse," observed Helen.

Antonina, sobered by the magnificence of the natural phenomenon, quietly admitted that today was her birthday.

"Why didn't you say?"

"Maybe because I am not alone in this," she said. Then she picked up a round white pebble close to her feet. *Happy birthday, Anna*, she mouthed and tossed the pebble into the canyon.

"Are you mad? It took the river two billion years of erosion to get to this point, and you start filling it up again?"

"You," she snarled and, as Manfred ran away, she chased him. They returned to the others, his arm around her shoulder.

The twenty-fourth birthday party that evening took place in a Mexican taquería.

Las Vegas was a *Fata Morgana* town of cheap glitz amid the desolate landscape. In mid-afternoon rows of hard-bitten women in evening wear pulled at *the slots*, grim determination on their faces. From buckets of coins they fed the dream-making machines.

On his knee in front of the Sweetheart Chapel, Manfred proposed to Antonina and she said "Yes". Tapping at the brass plate of a lawyer's practice next door, she said, "No".

One more day's drive west and they would be in the Sierra Nevada. California was just beyond that bump. However, there was Death Valley to cross first.

They cruised in heavy silence. The wide-spreading desert throbbed under a fireball sun in a cinereal sky. The metal of the car crackled as if it were breaking up to melt. The temperature gauge was rising. Dazed and threatened, they peered around: no other cars were on the road. A sign read: *Furnace Creek is closed during the hot season*.

Fifty miles later Antonina took over the driving. The gauge had risen to red. Eyes pinched together, she concentrated on the shimmering road. Steam was starting to escape from the bonnet, wrapping them into white fog. She was forced to stop. Although she had turned off the ignition, the engine ticked like a time-bomb. Nobody dared lift the bonnet.

Walking a safe distance away, they sat down by the side of the road and passed a hot bottle of Coke; each was allowed two sips. They protected their heads with their T-shirts.

In the first twenty minutes, two cars passed. The boys jumped up, waving their shirts, but the drivers sped on to get the desert behind them.

Gradually a heat lull came over Antonina, dulling her senses. She slipped into a kind of trance, and a feeling of doom grew as familiar noises filled her brain: the rattle of mail dropping into the letter-basket in Podzhin Hall; the murmurs and creaking of the ageing house's secret wounds. She heard the padding of her feet on the carpet in the music room, and the crunching of the brass latch closing the French windows. It smelled dusty and dry, like the landscape of this deadly place where they were now slowly expiring.

Vaguely, through tremoring haze, a black car materialised, slowed down and pulled up.

Two men emerged and came over to ask whether they could help. Antonina realised that she was laughing hysterically and could not understand why.

The man wearing reflective sunglasses and a canvas hat pulled low over his face, went back to fetch a jerry-can. He opened the bonnet of the Ford Sedan and filled the cooling tank with water before offering the can to them.

Had it been neat gin, the effect on Antonina could not have been stronger. Scare had nearly wiped them out; salvation caused hilarity. "Polly Wolly Doodle," Antonina intoned, and they all sang out, loud and coarsely.

The men who had saved them remained sober and serious. Instead of joining in, they asked questions about where they had been, who they were, where they were heading to. Since the group had played truant to the

Catholic cause, all Antonina answered was, "Polly wolly doodle, and thank you ever so much."

Despite the brush-off the black car followed them all the way through Death Valley and kept behind them stubbornly, probably to make sure they were all right.

Two days later Antonina drove the hiccupping Ford down to join Highway 101. Abundant flowers bloomed in the central reservation, mingling their scent with the salty sea breeze. The turquoise Pacific appeared and reappeared with the bends of the road along a coastline bright and hard-edged under the perfect blue sky. Antonina drove slowly, taking it all in. She felt reborn.

As she passed a lay-by, she saw an old couple wrapped in coats against the breeze, standing, facing seawards. He gazed through binoculars. She was at his side as if holding him up, her coat in gauzy material tearing in the wind like museum silk. His sparse white hair lifted to flutter. He had a white handlebar moustache. *Sasha and Olga!* The vision shocked Antonina into guilty longing, that composition of love and resentment which is a most painful sensation. She drove on, rejecting the picture. *Not now, not when I am just about to start my own life.*

★

In the second week of October they drove into San Francisco, leaving the coast range and Sao Alto behind them. Here, three thousand miles further away from the Brodskys, in the city of flower power, she could indulge in new sensations, untainted, and she could at the same time experience what life was like for a girl without an aristocratic background. She was ready to take the rough with the smooth because she would stay here for as long as it took. The temperature was still balmy and whitewashed houses looked friendly, as if they had been expecting her.

"You are so gutsy to get off the trip here," admired Helen. "We have to drive all the way back, and this time, let's guess: with another Catholic father."

"Teach him to yodel."

Less than fifty metres from the Priory of St Sophronia the sedan buckled, choked and rocked on its suspension. No coaxing or kicking would bring it back to life. Resigned, they pushed the jalopy along the road. Luckily they were not on a hill.

The reception they received at the priory showed a controlled chill. Father Bernard had been frantic in telegrams and calls from New York. Father Larry was back in New York and indisposed. A mature priest of St Sophronia would drive the group back. When he saw the Ford, he crossed himself.

"The wretch is dead," explained Antonina. "But with the help of good-humoured angels, we made it here, and not thanks to the quality of Father Bernard's motor vehicle."

"Dear, oh dear," he kept repeating.

"Manfred and I deliver the group and I, personally, hand in my resignation."

After a lunch at the priory where Antonina tasted Californian abalone, she said goodbye to the young people she had grown fond of. "I'll have to be a one-woman band now."

"Use St Sophronia's as a port of call in whatever you

do," Antonina was offered. "In fact, I ask you to check in once a week, promise? You seem to be a special protégée of Father Bernard."

Antonina thanked everyone and, armed with an airline ticket back to New York, twenty-five dollars in her pocket, her harp and a rucksack with a buffalo head on it, plus the long-handled wicker basket over her shoulder, she left the group. Around the corner she stopped and took several deep breaths to absorb the shock she had just inflicted on herself. She was going to stay in San Francisco without knowing anyone. There was a grim simplicity about her right now. Whatever move she made next would decide a direction, entail an involvement, pain perhaps, physical suffering. To avoid the last, her first step had to be to find shelter for the night; this was basic. She was who she was, without frills, and was ready to discover what she was worth as herself. Surprisingly, from this new down-to-earth awareness came a sensation of exhilaration. Antonina could not wait to experience precarious survival.

In Grant Avenue an illuminated box advertised Hotel Angel. The night cost eighteen dollars, too close to all she owned. She continued up the hill to California Street. Cable trolleys passed her, *ding-a-ling*. She eyed them with envy.

In China Town she found a hostel which was not clean and smelled sickly sweet but where the night cost only five dollars. The room had no window but the manager pointed out that she had her own sink. It was triangular, in one corner and with a dripping cold water tap.

"Perfect," exclaimed Antonina and slid her buffalo bag into the dust under the iron bedstead.

CHAPTER
TWENTY-FIVE

In the three months Vasily had been attached to the London embassy, he had learned the vital secrets of its operation.

The Referentura was the nucleus of the embassy with its own security measures. In there, each senior diplomat had a locked filing cabinet for papers on which he worked. At a desk at the entrance sat the Resident of the Referentura like a sentinel to the fort. If Vasily needed to work on the Brodsky file, he reported to the Resident, opened his cabinet and took the file to a writing cubicle. Reports were written in manuscript and had to be signed by the Resident before the file could be put back into the safe. If Vasily wanted to send a telegram to Moscow, he drafted it in one of the cubicles and brought it to the Resident to check and sign. Then it was passed into the telex room where the cypher clerk fed it through the coding machine and sent it by teleprinter to Moscow. When a telegram came in from Moscow, again it was fed through the decoding machine. The cypher clerk never left the compound of the embassy during his posting.

Some of Vasily's time was spent attending leadership meetings where important matters and messages from Moscow were discussed. Usually these were confined to generalities. Then there were the operational staff meetings and information lectures on the country in which the embassy was stationed. Vasily, like anyone else posted abroad, had to produce reports on observations made of all aspects of the host country.

Now he was heading to the safe speech room of the Referentura for debriefing on his first visit to the Brodsky family. He punched in the combination at the door and made sure the Resident saw him. Vasily stepped up into the wood-clad room resembling a Finnish sauna. There were no windows but the susurrus of an air-conditioner. Counsellor Turchin joined him. Neither had paper or pen.

During Vasily's oral report, Turchin interrupted him several times. "Have you assessed the situation correctly? Have you interpreted what she said carefully enough? Do you think the stone could have been aimed at you?"

"I have not seen or traced the Ikon so far but then I have not had the opportunity to inspect many rooms. I have drawn up a plan of Podzhin Hall as precisely as possible without a more detailed study."

Turchin had many questions to ask.

Finally Vasily explained, "When the family grasped that the viscount was dead, I thought it right to depart. Also, frankly, I couldn't take much more of them."

The counsellor scratched behind his ear. "According to my instructions from Miliukov, your first visit was only for reconnoitring and warming up contact."

Vasily left the room feeling that he had been disappointing. Outside, he was able to breathe normal air again and he concluded that patience and adaptability were needed in order to reach his objectives.

He returned to his own office where a new analysis of the British middle class was brought to him. He found this work mechanical and boring. The reports stuck closely to the official line. Vasily modified a fact repeated twice and found no contradicting observations. His work in Moscow had been more important, and he let his mind wander back to yesterday's visit to Podzhin Hall and to what had shaken him most amongst the unnerving events. In no other reports shown to him had he ever found similarly observed behaviour. A dead man pushed in a wheelchair? A stone hurled at a painting?

The painting! Vasily should have found the Ikon hanging in its place. Instead, it was something incomprehensible and modern.

Last night on his return from Oxfordshire, he had sat on his bed unable to banish the discomfort of what he had seen. He had been warned about exposure to bourgeois decadence, the necessity to walk upon shifting sands. But it was just a picture on a wall, one with swirls of wildly applied colour as if the painter had suffered a seizure. Or that is all it would have been were it not for the part in the painting representing with careful exactitude and tiny details an old chivalric insignia. And Vasily had seen this crest before.

He extracted the handkerchief from his coat pocket, flattened it out and with a pencil started to reproduce what he remembered: the bearded head with a conical hat trimmed with fur, the shield with the red and blue lozenge design.

The light was switched out on him; electricity was controlled in the building. Vasily had no choice but to undress and go to bed. Sleep did not come. He tossed and turned, trying to think where he could have come across the insignia. He had shown visitors around the Kremlin Museum. And there, yes, he had seen regal shields in that style.

He pressed his eyelids closed and told himself to go to sleep.

Assailed sneakily by a dream however, he struggled to cross a churning and foaming torrent. On the other shore was his father watching him, with another man by his side. Neither showed willing to save him. He was being swept away and the strength withdrawn from him. He moaned and cursed aloud which woke him up.

His father! His father had kept uncomfortable things in a box in the roof-space of their cottage in the Ukraine. Those articles were obviously dangerous for the box was at all times hidden under a sack and a pile of straw. Shortly before Vasily had become a pioneer, his father had taken him up and shown him some newspaper cuttings from the box. There had been a picture similar to what was on the painting in Podzhin Hall. There had also been a gold pen, solid to the touch. His father had acted strangely, his voice husky with earnestness as he asked Vasily to hold the pen, just rolling it on his palm, while tears had risen in his father's eyes. Dislike of this secretive behaviour for which his father had offered no explanation or interpretation had obviously left a mark in Vasily's subconscious as it just now had risen in a dream.

Giving in to dreams was aligned with letting oneself go. *Stamp it out in you*, he had been taught. *When you wake, replace it at once with what matters.*

Vasily left his bed. At the kitchenette sink he pushed the handkerchief under the sink tap and rubbed his drawing out. His desk was periodically checked and so were his pockets.

At work he appeared, using his nonchalant walking technique. His father's treasure box had been and possibly still was a dangerous secret. Secrets withheld from a superior were bad, very bad. They brought one into trouble sooner or later. He decided to mention the insignia on the painting at the next debriefing but omit the source of the recollection. After all, truthfully he had only an unconfirmed sensation of *déjà vu*.

He felt a little better. He drank many glasses of water and used the facilities three times, each time flushing down strips of his handkerchief. At closing time he checked his watch, pushed the disturbing Pandora's Box of his father out of his mind and flushed the last bit of handkerchief down the toilet before the search on leaving the building.

CHAPTER
TWENTY-SIX

Olga wrote with her fluent generous calligraphy on the embossed death announcement cards. Outside the French windows gusts of wind caused the old trees of the park to grumble and growl.

A car drove up to the house. The door in the vestibule banged shut. Olga was taken aback; the whole house seemed to have quivered.

It didn't sound like the Rolls Royce nor did it sound like Lady Mortimer's car. Frowning, Olga put the fountain pen down, and the nib bled a black tear on a new card. Irritated, she walked to the door and pulled it open.

In the vestibule stood Anna in a long charcoal cardigan, her short hair askew from the wind. "Hello, Grandmother," the girl said, surprised at the vehemence with which Olga had torn open the door of the music room. "Sorry, I did not have anything black. A friend…"

"Who brought you here?"

"Mummy saw me at the bus-stop in front of Christchurch and gave me a lift."

Olga said nothing. She crossed the vestibule and opened the oak door. In front of the pond stood a gleaming eggshell-coloured Jaguar with silver hubcaps. Valentina was studying the papers on a clipboard held out to her by a young man in a grey suit with lapels flapping in the breeze.

Olga stepped outside and walked towards them. Anna held the door open a crack to watch.

"How do you do?" said the man politely when he saw the old lady. "This beautiful baby is just the thing for this imposing property."

"Are you referring to my daughter or the car?"

"May I introduce Mr Last from Jaguar, Oxfordshire?" said Valentina. "Countess Brodsky."

"Oh, pleased to meet you," he smiled lopsidedly and a little nervously. Olga's face was not inviting. "This exquisitely styled car is for all generations, but only for sophisticated society. It rides quietly; handling and performance are…"

"Don't slobber that sales nonsense over me. Tell me, has my daughter signed any papers?"

"She drove herself here as a test drive, so that we could sit down and discuss the payment arrangements."

"That should take no time at all. Mr Last, take your *baby*, and get out of here and never ever contact my daughter again."

He hesitated, looked at Valentina, then unclipped a brochure from his board and held it out to her but she did not take it. He shrugged his shoulders, threw his clipboard onto the leather passenger seat, got in and closed the door with a soft noise. The purring of the engine as it drove out of the park was subdued, elegant, and Valentina twisted on the gravel. "I hate you, Mother!"

"We will talk inside, and remember this house is in mourning."

★

Anna quickly pulled the door open wide. Crackly dry leaves were blown into the vestibule. Neither Grandmother nor Mother gave Anna any attention as they sailed by, and the girl had sacrificed a morning of two special lectures on Trotsky to come home and comfort Olga in her loss.

Olga and Valentina disappeared into the music room. Anna took off her cardigan which was heavy and smelled unwashed. She laid it on the first step of the staircase and sat down on it.

"What do you think you are doing?" Olga shouted behind the closed door.

Anna held her head between her spread fingers.

"Anyone can see that we need a new car. Smelly Ben is a disgrace. We rattle through the village, and they laugh behind our backs."

Anna could have gone upstairs to her room but something kept her within hearing distance. She had missed enough lately. Perhaps today Olga would tell Mother about the broken Ikon.

"Any minute now it'll give up the ghost, but you can't see that. Because it's old and dear, it has to do."

"Valentina!" It sounded like a dry shot. "We cannot afford a new Jaguar." There was the sound of a flat hand smacking a hard surface.

"Where's the damn money from the Ikon?"

Anna lowered her head and stared before her at the *nervure* pattern in the marble tile. It resembled a road through mountains. *Antonina*, she thought, *where are you?* Her twin would miss Sasha's funeral; she probably didn't even know he was dead.

"There is one chance for us to keep Podzhin Hall and one only, and that is to convince Voronov that we deserve to be recompensed. But no, you are blinded in your egotism. You casually, just for fun, flirt with a Soviet envoy on whose benevolence we depend. I tell you something, Valentina: you're going to buckle under this time, or I'll have you disinherited."

Anna took her head out of her hands. She had never heard Grandmother talk with such anger.

Anna knew that the diplomat had visited Podzhin Hall. She would have loved to have been there. A communist grown and trained in the new Russia was a rarity to meet and talk to. At first she had been disturbed by the news that someone would be sent to examine the possibility of compensation. *Why would the USSR even consider such a move? Had the Brodskys not truly terrorised the lower classes and denied them their rights back in Russia when they and other aristocrats had ruled?*

In the music room the argument went on. "Voronov was shocked at your behaviour. He is not used to flirting; one can see that."

"I can't help it if I am the way I am. And I am attracted to him."

This is just Mother's tactic to annoy Grandmother, thought Anna with despair.

"Until we are compensated, you keep your hands off Voronov and stay with your painter fiancé."

"He bores me to tears."

Anna thought about Ned. *Where did she stand with him?* The last time she had seen him in the village shop he had ignored her. When she had loaded her shopping into the bicycle basket, the front wheel ran away under the weight and a bread loaf had fallen out. Ned had stood there watching, his hands in his pockets.

"We must see each other sometime soon and talk," she had urged, reloading and twisting the bicycle away from the trunk of the chestnut tree.

"Why?" he had asked. In his grimace she had seen for the first time that he was ugly.

With Trish at Podzhin Hall, Anna had hoped the relationship would deepen but in fact Ned seemed even more defensive. *Well*, Anna thought, *she had done her best for Trish*.

The door to the music room opened and Mother came out, brushing herself down as if the angry words adhered to her clothes. She noticed Anna.

"Why are you sitting here snooping? I fancy Vasily Voronov because he is a dashing Russian, and I can do what I like with my life."

Olga appeared at the door and Anna saw that she was flushed. "We save Podzhin Hall first, and then you can do what you like." The door was closed with a bang.

"Mother?" asked Anna tentatively.

"Stupid old goat. What?"

"Mother, I don't have anything black to wear."

"Why black?"

"The funeral."

"Ah. Come to my room."

Valentina's room shared the top floor with Fydo's and three unoccupied visitors' rooms. It was furnished as a mixture between a nomad tent and a classical French boudoir with rosewood furniture. The bed was a tangle of colourful rugs and cushions, and from a hoop fixed to the ceiling fell richly gilded, tasselled curtains which could be pulled to give the sleeper privacy but not much air. When Valentina had ordered the firm to install it, the twins had been children and enjoyed playing in the exotic bed.

Valentina rifled through her clothes in the armoire. She pulled out a black dress with volants and velveteen top.

"No!" exclaimed Anna. "That's a cocktail dress."

"How about this?"

"No, Mother, really."

"Why didn't you buy something in Oxford?"

Anna said nothing.

"In Cherwells. You could have charged it to Olga's account."

"I heard you in the music room," said Anna. "We must all try to save Podzhin Hall."

"Don't you start as well."

"Mother, I know it is none of my business, but please don't flirt with this Soviet man. We need the money."

"Oh, I've got my own ways with Voronov, you'll see. God, even you don't trust me."

"Yes I do, of course, but he's a communist."

"Fiddlesticks. Vasily is a true Russian, tall and attractive. It is not my fault if he has been warped by a criminal government."

Anna sighed. "One of those who can grab a woman with poetry?" She forked short hair strands behind her ear. "I'd better go and ask Njanja for something black."

"You do that, Anna, and don't meddle with things that aren't for you. Do you understand?"

Anna left her mother's bedroom. "A real red Russian," she mumbled to herself.

CHAPTER
TWENTY-SEVEN

Antonina sat on her mattress in the hostel in San Francisco and dangled her feet in moccasins that had come unstitched. From somewhere she could hear plaintive yells. It was best not to imagine what the other residents were like.

The next hurdle was to find a source of income. She set off with hopeful energy and applied in a Chinese grocery store which had a notice in the window. She was not taken seriously. She tried a Ladybird Kindergarten and was told she needed qualifications. At a job centre she was reminded that she had only a student visa. Antonina filled in an application form but the female interviewer slipped it under her coffee cup to protect the desk before Antonina had even left her office.

Outside she boarded a street trolley because she simply had to try it out. The driver manipulated the long iron-bar brake by applying his weight against it to force teeth into the gearing of the rack-railway. Antonina peered down the steep hill and fought the panic of vertigo as they seemed to be hurtling out of control. The brake smoked and smelled of burning. On the sidewalk she noticed that hippies, female and male, were mostly barefoot. At a random stop she jumped off and someone handed her the harp case she had taken along to qualify as a *hippie*.

In a nearby drugstore Antonina ordered a jam doughnut and a strawberry milkshake from a young man in a white paper side cap.

"You're not from here." A customer sitting at the bar on a plastic stool turned to her. "England, am I right? I knew, the nifty way you asked for a doughnut." He was a middle-aged man with robust features and weak watery eyes.

"Would you, by any chance, know of a job for me?"

He thought about it, sipping his glass of milk. Antonina would have expected him to sit behind a pint of beer.

"Your accent is just so cute," he went on, and she knew he had thought of something. "My sister is an invalid, and I guess she could do with someone doing her shopping. How about that? My name's Pace, by the way."

She finished the doughnut and licked her fingers fastidiously. "I would appreciate that very much."

"It's the way you say *appreciate*."

Antonina smiled despite herself. He was a total stranger and yet she trusted him and agreed to go with him in his car to meet the invalid sister right away. Californians seemed to give and take with ease. Life was lived almost casually and its more serious aspects touched upon lightly and woven into everything else in this young country. *What a change from Podzhin Hall's eternal burden of the past, filling every room like the heavy dark furniture, the grey park rendered sinister by its rotting graves!* Without a thought, uncaring she had left her twin behind in that old world from where Anna now seemed to point accusingly at her many thousands of miles away.

"What do you do for a living?" Antonina started a conversation with Pace.

"I'm an undertaker."

"No job there for me?"

"We could do with help. All those nuts jumping off the bridge, but that's not something for a pretty young lady."

"Do they really jump off Golden Gate Bridge?"

"Some folks have loads of problems. It solves them I guess."

The invalid sibling lived in an Edwardian-style house with a wrought iron porch and well-trimmed wisteria: all very neat. She introduced herself as Cynthia and explained that, wheelchair-bound, she spent her time writing novels. A maid did the cleaning and cooking. Brother and sister talked and it ended with the novelist agreeing to Antonina helping in the mornings with shopping errands and trips to the post office. The job could start the next day.

Magic! – although it was her elocution, the result of her stifled upbringing, that had procured her the job and not her daring independence. Whatever, now she would have *bread* and could survive. That evening the Italian woman in a shop in Little Italy let her buy a bottle of Chianti on credit. Antonina celebrated in her windowless cubicle. She started to write a letter to Anna but the words did not come; letter-writing home would have to wait. By the time she had drunk the bottle, she could swear the room had large windows. "There are more miracles in a bottle of Chianti than in a church full of saints," she muttered and fell onto the thin mattress.

The next morning Antonina was given a shopping list and a purse with money by Cynthia who did not seem to mind the dusty bare feet. Antonina set out following a drawn map. In the supermarket, however, when she compared the words on her shopping list with what she saw on the shelves, she was at a loss. *Two packets of Spic'n'Span.* Antonina had no idea what this could be. She asked a store assistant who checked her up and down unpleasantly. They were in an affluent area and shoeless customers were scorned. In the end Antonina left with a packet of spices and two cans of spam. In the carpark a man civilly asked whether he could help her carrying. She declined and hoiked up the brown paper bags, one in each arm. He disappeared rather too quickly and she was glad that she had not trusted him.

Back at the house the author was sitting at her specially raised desk, engrossed in typing. She waved away any interruptions; inspiration had clearly struck from the way Cynthia pounded the typewriter. Quietly Antonina stored away the shopping, put the change on the kitchen table. She also washed up the dishes in the kitchen. The writer was still preoccupied when Antonina let herself out of the house.

The same man who had offered to carry her groceries was standing over the road, smoking a cigarette and pulling ivy strands from the hedge. *He lives there and saw me go shopping*, she thought, feeling foolish for having been scared. Acknowledging him with a smile, she sauntered down the hill.

★

"You brought me some strange things." Cynthia rolled her chair into the hall when Antonina arrived for her second day's work. "And you forgot some."

"I am sorry. Could you please pay me daily?" It was difficult to ask.

Cynthia noted Antonina's loose-sleeved cotton minidress, the plastic pink sunglasses stuck in her hair, and her dark toes, and shook her head. "Impetuous youth," she said and rolled herself to a Chinese ginger jar on the hall table, from which she removed a five-dollar bill. Gratefully Antonina took it from her.

"Today, I want you to go to the post office and dispatch this manuscript. Remember, by air, registered and first class, and for the love of God, don't lose it."

Antonina promised to treat the parcel with royal care. Another five-dollar note was handed to her and a brown packet addressed to a publishing company in New York.

"Please buy some Spic'n'Span today."

"Will do," said Antonina leaving the house. The neighbour was still poking around in his hedge. *I feel nearly at home here already*, she thought.

The woman Antonina accosted to ask what Spic'n'Span was shrugged her off. Antonina encountered the same unwillingness in the next woman and decided to go back to St Sophronia's and ask there.

To her delight the student group had not yet left. They were readying themselves for the long journey back. Father Anselm who would drive them was ineffectively bustling around in his starched black cassock. The sedan had gone through a garage's intensive care unit but was still unwashed, with the back window missing and the door loose.

"Some things never change," mused Manfred, and Antonina helped fix the door handle with a rope. Father Anselm insisted on a small prayer session before departure, and François rolled his eyes. After that the young travellers, resigned to another adventure across this vast country, waved from the car as it drove out of the compound.

Antonina turned to a nun. "Sister, do you know what Spic'n'Span is?"

"It's a cleaning powder for bathrooms, my dear."

"Oh. That makes sense. Thank you, Sister."

At that moment Antonina realised that the manuscript parcel was not with her any longer. She forced herself to calm the onrush of wild blood. When she was able to think straight, she recalled how she had put the parcel on the back seat of the car to be able to help fix the rope to the doorhandle. Cynthia's manuscript was still there, being driven to New York. The only consolation was that Antonina had dispatched it to its intended destination.

Back at the supermarket she bought two packs of Spic'n'Span and returned to the author's house. She put the cleaning powder on the kitchen table, the change and receipt, then left the house noiselessly never to return.

Passing a church on her way to the hostel, she went

in and with all her might implored the Holy Spirit or any affiliated powers to deliver the manuscript safely to its rightful addressee.

When she came out feeling a little less guilty, she was out of a job again.

CHAPTER
TWENTY-EIGHT

Six hired pall-bearers carried the coffin across the lawn. Blustery winds persisted in shaking trees which had already shed their testimonies to summer. Olga's black cloak ballooned, and the ribbons on the wreaths ruffled: *Dear Uncle – Father – Sasha*. A rose-bud cushion had been sent through Interflora by Anna in the name of Antonina from whom they had not heard for weeks. Artemis watched them pass with stone-cast eyes, her bow poised, an arrow inserted. Valentina wore a black deux-pièces, copied from Jackie Kennedy's mourning outfit, with a pillbox hat enshrouded in a veil. Rasputin whinnied and rain was predicted.

The procession reached the grave Cahill had dug. The cluster of family gathered at its side, shaken by wind and pain. The village vicar stood at the narrow end of the trench, his thin hair toying in the gusts. He held down the page of the prayer-book with applied thumbs. "We are gathered here…"

Olga's sobs and the noise of the trees drowned the vicar's words.

Anna sneezed for a second time. After a sharp glance Valentina took out a handkerchief and smuggled it into her daughter's hand. Fydo gazed into fast sailing clouds as if he envied the wheeling birds. Vasily, who had sent a formal letter of condolence, had been invited and stood a little apart.

Anna dared to shoot glances at him. It was disconcerting: how could he possibly be a communist whom she imagined in rough shirts, baggy trousers, and a scarf at best for special occasions? Through tear-filled eyelashes she observed him during a prayer when other heads were bent. The *comrade* was tall, and stylish in a charcoal suit and a grey felt hat, his coat loosely over his arm. The dark hair curled up around the rim of his hat, and in his evenly tanned face there was a slight drooping of the brow over one eye giving it a fortyish runkle, and Anna understood completely why Mother was taken by him.

Anna's nose tickled, and she knew that she would sneeze again and draw attention to herself.

Slowly the flower-laden coffin was let down on two thick ropes. With taut grief Anna watched the remains of her great-uncle sink under the surface of the earth. The vicar spoke his words of final goodbye, almost torn from his mouth. Anna checked the Soviet diplomat once more and found his head turned. Their eyes met. She felt giddy, and a gust blew a brittle curled leaf to rest at her feet, then picked it up again to tumble it through the air as if it were alive, had sudden feelings and possibilities. When it came down again, it had settled close to Voronov's polished black shoes.

Valentina from under her black tulle watched every move of Voronov. Today he looked just like any boring Englishman in mourning clothes. She imagined that the next squall took off his hat. Then she thought of unbuttoning his outmoded dark suit jacket, of ripping away his shirt, to find a dark-haired, bronzed chest. Yes, well, the shoes too were awful. They would have to come off even before the shirt.

The vicar finally wound up in a wind-shredded voice. In Valentina's imagination Vasily wore only trousers now, and his hair was long and tumbling like a gypsy's. He hightailed it over the lawn, escaping her, laughing, teasing, playing *Shabarsha*. At her touch, he would be the tig and she would run from him.

Through her indulgent fantasy, Valentina caught sight of Trish, half-concealed behind the plinth of Artemis – Trish in a red jacket, a grimace on her face. Valentina drew a deep breath to contain her outrage, and closed her eyes to dispel the derisive vision. As she gasped loudly, the coffin reached the bed of the grave with an inelegant hollow boom; one of the pallbearers had lost his grip on the rope. The vicar said "Amen", and Olga bent down to pick up a handful of loose earth.

When Valentina checked over her shoulder again, Trish had vanished.

Anna made to help Olga back to the Hall. Olga, instead of brushing the support of her granddaughter away, clung tightly onto her with a liver-spotted hand because she was busy weeping inside herself.

The mourners hastened into the shelter of the portico out of the elements now spotted with rain. Apart from the lawyer, Baroness Aksakova and the vicar, Vasily was the only outsider. In fact Olga had suggested he stay for the weekend. After discussing it with Turchin, Vasily had been persuaded reluctantly to accept the invitation. "An excellent opportunity to penetrate deeper," Turchin had called the occasion. "Grief brings out the real stuff they're made of."

In the vestibule Cahill relieved Vasily of his coat and, tense and irresolute, he joined the conversing mourners in the drawing room where the *babushka* offered around small pieces of food from a silver tray. This was his second visit to Podzhin Hall and he felt extreme disquiet at the thought of spending two days. In London he had been startled at the confidence the embassy put in him. Now he was stuck with it.

The *babushka* in a white apron passed with her tray. He read her expression: *This isn't your business, is it? You aren't welcome.*

The canapé he picked from the tray was of salmon. Cahill, from another tray, offered him a glass of white wine. Everyone else seemed to be conversing animatedly but in lowered voices as if this were a conspiracy. Vasily averted his eyes from shelves with more books of vile content and studied the artefacts in a lacquered display cabinet. A diamond-garnished pendulette was clearly Russian, as were the various decorated eggs. He bent to a minutely executed female reclining on a pouffe, adjusting her garter. Under lace-thin porcelain petticoats she displayed her underwear.

"We call that one the strumpet," explained Valentina, sidling up close to him. "Meissen."

Vasily lowered his eyes as he wished the vulgar figurine would lower her skirt. He did not know the meaning of *Meissen,* and he felt the stale taste of defeat. One of the first words said to him and he was at a loss. He excused himself and was directed to the cloakroom across the vestibule. Sitting on the toilet seat, he fingered the crocheted mushroom concealing the extra toilet roll. The Brodskys' tastes were appalling, yet it was his duty to display polite curiosity, amiability even.

Inevitably Valentina was at his side the minute he returned to the drawing room. He forced himself to empty his eyes of prejudice. She seemed to have the power to re-fill them instantly with anxiety, vulnerability, and he comprehended how strong she was.

"Come, Mr Voronov. I'll introduce you to the vicar." Her eyes danced mischievously.

The vicar stood by himself, sipping wine and still wearing his black canonicals. Vasily imagined him in ordinary clothes to make him seem more approachable.

"Death is a wonderful event. It defies political adherence and declares the reign of God," said the vicar after being introduced to the Soviet diplomat.

Vasily nodded and decided to leave the vicar clad in black. He moved away and accepted another salmon canapé held out by Njanja who regarded him with open antagonism. Despite his discomfort the food tasted delicious and was quite a change to the open-faced ham sandwiches served at the embassy. Vasily felt Valentina's calculating glance on him and he had to admit to himself that, unless he stepped over his dread, he would fail in his assignment. Whether he appeared clumsy or not, no matter what embarrassment he might be caused, he had to set out in search of the Ikon. Half a canapé in hand, he left the room. Crossing the torrent in the gorge in the Ukraine with a rope on his back had been child's play compared to this.

★

"Oh sorry, I didn't know." Vasily half-hid in awkward hesitation at the door to Sasha's bedroom. The lawyer sat at the Regency table with a pocket knife in his raised hand.

Vasily dared and stepped into the room. "Sad for the family," he ventured.

"Indeed." The lawyer clapped the knife shut and put it into his jacket pocket.

The roof had not caved in on Vasily, who crossed to the window dotted with raindrops. Down in the park near the woodland area, two men were shovelling earth into the grave – the end of a despicable aristocrat.

The lawyer had left his position at the desk and was now on all fours, searching under Sasha's bed.

"The legal system in England is of interest to me." Vasily let the festoon curtains drop back into place.

"Yes?" The lawyer straightened up and, still on his knees, opened the bedside table drawer. Vasily saw the viscount's pearl-handled revolver and his pills, nothing else. The lawyer pushed the drawer back.

"Did the late viscount in fact own Podzhin Hall?" Vasily was pleased with his *in fact*. It was one of those to pronounce with a honey-coated voice, like *incidentally* and *by the way*.

The lawyer had opened the lower door to the

bedside table and was inspecting its contents which were nothing more than a pair of velvet slippers and a male urine bottle. "As a matter of fact, with his death the estate belongs to his niece alone."

"Valentina Brodsky?"

"Yes."

"Isn't this unusual?"

"Oh, you see the property was bequeathed to Valentina when she was a child; it was held in trust during the viscount's lifetime." The lawyer lifted the bedcover and his hand explored under the pillows.

Strange, thought Vasily, *that the house did not belong to Olga.* "Surely, the viscount left some valuable antiques," he prompted, riding on the lawyer's candidness produced by his strange preoccupation.

"Yes, he did."

"Are you searching for something?"

"Me? Not particularly." The lawyer got up. He appeared flushed.

"In England, I understand that family lawyers, like yourself, are entrusted with the safe-keeping of papers and valuable objects. Am I right?"

"All the papers are in my safe, yes, or should be."

Without any warning the door was kicked open; the two men stiffened. Trish eyed one and then the other, and a tear rolled very slowly over the curve of her cheek. "Don't bother to search for the covenant. It's gone." She turned and collided with Olga. "Damn!"

"What are you still doing in my house?" Olga cupped her jolted curl. "Pack, girl, pack. Your service is not needed any longer."

"That's not fair. Mister Fyodor Brodsky gave me a three months contract."

"My brother-in-law can hardly be blamed for suddenly…" Olga sniffed delicately.

"I'm staying right here until the end of my contract." Trish squared her legs.

"No you are not, insolent *muzhik*."

"I've still got things to do here."

"Then put your uniform back on and start by helping in the kitchen."

Trish left, trudging down the stairs and emitting isolated objections.

"My father used to whip the servants." Olga smiled at Vasily grandly, then her face sombered. "What is the meaning of your presence in Sasha's room?"

"Homage, Countess, homage to the departed."

Olga hesitated for a second as if calculating her next move. "How charming, how elegant. Good manners will make our business dealings so much more agreeable." She gave him a winning smile back over her left shoulder.

From below came a shout from Valentina. "Mother, could you come down please? The vicar is leaving."

Olga encompassed Vasily almost possessively and then propped out her elbow. He hesitated. His mind flicked through the pages of the etiquette book. He guessed that she wanted him to take her arm and guide her – the pathetic pretence that she was unable to move around with self-sufficiency. Vasily lurched forward with a gauche movement and slid his arm under the countess's, to escort her back downstairs. On his forehead was cold sweat.

In a corner of the drawing room Valentina was assailing Fydo. "You're now the head of the family. I ask you for God's sake to fire that nurse."

"But I gave her a contract."

"Then buy her out."

"Couldn't she be helpful in some way?"

"Get rid of her."

"She was good to my father."

"Too good, as far as I am concerned, and don't be such a coward." Valentina high-heeled away in a huff.

★

Anna escaped into the music room. The samovar was bubbling in a cosy way. Tea would be served later. She plunged with grateful relaxation into the armchair.

It had been shocking the way in which Sasha's coffin had reached its final resting place. The boom of doom had echoed all over the park. Only six months ago Sasha had popped champagne corks for Olga's birthday and marched about, regaling them with his lost glory stories of the Czar. Anna realised that, although during his life she had never been close to him, now gone she would miss him sadly.

Had Sasha used the time to review his life during his long hours in bed? Had he perhaps even understood that his military glory was founded on lives and freedom taken from others? She doubted it. Her family was not generally known for truth-seeking metaphysical analysis.

Now that the money for the Ikon was lost to them, it was imperative that this Soviet envoy be coaxed into being sympathetic towards the Brodsky dilemma – and Mother was flirting with him. Anna had seen her do it in the drawing room, showing him the porcelain collection. She had also seen Grandmother becoming frosty and dignified, on the verge of losing her temper as she watched Valentina nuzzling her shoulder close against the Soviet's.

She, Anna, was responsible for everything that was happening, because she had broken the Ikon, but talking to Mother would encourage her wilfulness, and nothing more. It was a miracle that the Brodskys were being given any consideration by the USSR at all. Vasily had to be protected from Valentina, and Grandmother had to be supported. After all she, Anna, was the only one in the family who knew about socialism. Somehow she had to demonstrate that her studies were not wasted, get the communist to trust the Brodskys and thus save Podzhin Hall. To achieve this, Anna would have to find opportunities to talk to Comrade Voronov alone.

If Antonina were here, would Anna confide her true feelings about this? Probably she would conceal them from her sister. Well, what could Antonina expect? Was it not she who had left? Anna's resentment at Antonina's desertion quickly melted into guilt for doubting her.

With a prolonged sigh the silver samovar announced that it was ready to be drawn from.

Anna took a sheet of writing paper and an envelope from the roll-top desk and left the room through the French windows, protecting the stationery from the rain by holding it under her black cardigan while she ran around the house to the back door. In the boiler room she paddled her hand through her hair and pulled a stool out to sit at the narrow table to write.

The bulb hanging from the ceiling flickered and she hoped it would not give out, used up as it probably was.

My dearest OTHER,

It is hard to bear that you are not here, especially today at Sasha's funeral. I feel cut off from you and have to make decisions for myself without you. I hope this is OK. In your name, I contributed a pink rose cushion which looked dear on the mahogany coffin Grandmother had chosen. Everyone is taking it bravely, and we are now all gathered in the drawing room for refreshments – except for you of course, and me. I sneaked into the boiler room to write to you right now, because I want you to have the feeling that you are part of us and share this sad and important day. Fydo is now the viscount, and perhaps we should call him Fyodor, but I fear…

Anna jumped from her seat in surprise. Vasily Voronov had opened the door. She stared at him as if caught in a trap, and then felt ablaze in the heat of her blushing. Nobody ever came in here; it was a safe hideout. "Can I get you something?"

"No. I opened this door by mistake. You are, er… We have not properly met."

"Anna Brodsky." She edged herself along the table, her hands behind her back testing along the table rim. Imagining being alone with this Soviet communist was a brave dream; being closed into the boiler room with him, crude reality. She thought of how Fydo had muttered, "He is a snake in the grass, a cunning, well-trained communist" – as if Fydo were the realist in the family.

The communist and Anna measured each other.

"You are hiding here to write a secret letter."

"No, nothing like that. It's to my twin sister, who has gone to America and must be now in San Francisco, but we don't have an address for her yet, and it's a terrible shame that she is not here today…"

Anna was aware that she was waffling. She was alone in this tiny utility room with an attractive man dressed in charcoal, from a country they should have in common. It was unnerving.

"Do you cherish Russian art, Miss Brodsky?"

She cleared her throat. "Call me Anna." She could not decently say that she did, since she had broken the most precious object of that art. "Yes, I love art."

He leaned against the table. The fact that they were both touching it bore an intimacy in itself. Anna kept tucking her short hair behind her ear.

"I thought I heard Fyodor Brodsky say that you were in charge of a family ikon."

"Oh, that ikon," said Anna vaguely, as if some other ikon had been in question. Valentina had told them about the Ikon in the embassy. Anna knew that their interest in it had to be thwarted.

"Isn't it important to you?"

"Well, you know."

"Em. Tell me about it."

"There is really nothing to say." She had to bring him onto another track. "However, there is the problem of some women in our society who can't quell the need to flirt. It does not mean anything; it's just a game. You must know that."

He looked at her baffled.

Surely he knew what she meant. Anna suffered because she had to tell him this and because his eyes on her face were so brown and troublingly familiar, as if she knew them, their colour, their shape.

"And you are a woman who does not flirt?"

At least the Ikon subject was gone, replaced by the delicate subject of her mother endangering everything.

"Life is too serious to play with emotions," she said. "Maybe all women in the West flirt; it's a fault in the society," she bumbled on. "I am probably doing it right now too, but am not aware of it."

With a brusque about-turn, he walked back to the door. Perhaps she was upsetting him. "Sorry, I won't talk about it anymore."

Lifting up his arm, he checked his watch.

"Do you need to leave?"

She saw him frown; saw sweat pearls on his forehead as he turned into the light. He was caged too, it occurred to her, and she felt elated as she had when she first saw him at the graveside. How could Fydo think Vasily was a cold and cunning communist, when she reacted so positively towards him?

She pulled the other wooden stool from under the table. "Please sit down. I assure you, I understand you and your people in the Soviet Union," she said quickly and with animosity.

"Really?"

Anna blushed furiously again because he was mocking her. But to her surprise he smiled. The fold over his eye tilted. With slow movements they both sat down on the stools. Only Antonina had ever sat like this with her. The room, everything around them, started to have its secret and abstract meaning, as did the alertness of his face, the quizzical mouth, his unblinking eyes. There would be a secret between them; she could predict it. He was a mystery: hers. She loved it, she liked him. Oh yes, she had fallen for him the second she had seen him.

He was not only a *well-built mature Russian, who could marry passion to poetry*, but he was a Soviet Russian of no doubt peasant background – someone who had moved up into an important position but who had done so for the good of the peasants, the workers, for Russia's underprivileged Neds. Ned – compared to Vasily Voronov's aura, Ned Worship suddenly appeared glum and grubby to her. In Russia Ned would bloom. Russia was the answer somehow to everything. "Sorry, what did you say?"

"We would mutually benefit if we learned more about each other, Anna."

Anna. She focused on the *boiler beast* to hide her emotions from him. When she faced him, her cheeks had calmed down to their normal temperature. "You must feel ill at ease in Podzhin Hall, bumping everywhere into telltales of a past that must be offensive to you."

She read the surprise in his eyes. He uncrossed his legs and seemed to relax a little.

"Do you often go to St Petersburg – I mean Leningrad?"

Vasily did not reply but he made no move to leave. At least he trusted her company that far.

"Have you ever been in Leningrad?" she tried again, more confidently.

"The first time I saw the city was in 1930, when I was five," he said and smiled at her.

"The Brodskys lived on Bolshoy Prospekt with the famous tall elms, on Vasilyevsky Island."

"The elms are gone. I was shown mostly the Leningrad side, but I remember gold-winged gryphons staring down at me and the wriggly iron railings of Leytenanta Shmidta Bridge."

"It used to be called Nicholas Bridge."

"I believe so."

"Have you been back since you were five?"

"Later, when I thought the Neva had shrunk, or perhaps I had grown, but the railings on Nicholas Bridge had not changed."

Anna was touched by his delicacy at using the Imperial name for the bridge.

"A lovely city," he said softly.

"The revolution changed a lot of things. It felled the elms." She started with something tentative.

"The revolution felled old elms amongst many other things, but planted new ones all over the country for everyone to enjoy. The planting is not finished; the Soviet Union will be a lush park one day. You too have elms in your park."

"It is a good thing to give the workers and peasants more rights. Unfortunately, the Brodskys are not peasants, and we are therefore somewhat helpless. Can you make it possible for us to be paid back some of what we lost? It's not for me I am asking. I'd rather not have it. I'd prefer to go to your country instead, to see it as it is now."

"We welcome foreigners."

"Somehow I don't feel like a foreigner. Perhaps I am a *Leytenanta Shmidta* Russian. I don't know yet for sure."

He examined her face.

"Will I like what I would see?" she asked, hoping he would protect her with his answer, value her courageous forthrightness, and even judge her pretty in some way.

"Being you, intelligent and aware, you will probably love it."

"Oh, Mr Voronov." She jumped up and spontaneously clapped her hands.

"Call me Vasily."

"Vasily." Anna walked over to him and impulsively grabbed the fine-boned hand protruding from an impeccable cufflinked sleeve. "Thank you. I want to love it, and I want you to show me today's motherland."

For an instant she remembered the feel of Ned's coarse green sweater. Was she unfaithful? Was she confused? She certainly was forward.

Vasily pulled his hand away. "Perhaps, one day."

"You hope?"

From the passage outside came the voice of Fydo, shouting, "Is the nurse down here?"

Vasily and Anna leaped in surprise and guilt.

"Valentina has fainted," Fydo declared as they emerged from the boiler room. All Anna could think about was the intimate time she had shared with Vasily.

★

In the drawing room Anna and Vasily found the family crowded around the velour chaise-longue on which they had installed Valentina, who was being vigorously fanned by Aksakova. Valentina lay, her eyes closed in apparent slumber, her face creamy pale.

"Poor child, poor child. It is all too much for us," the baroness sympathised. "I remember when the baron died, my daughter…"

"Cannot find zr nurse, but here is zr salt." Njanja handed Olga the bottle of smelling salts.

Valentina opened heavy-lidded eyes and groaned. "I am so tired. I need to sleep," she mumbled and fell back.

"Cahill and Fydo will carry you to your room, my dear," said Olga.

"As I said, when the baron died, my daughter felt the need to lose her grief in an excess of alcohol too. She…"

Anna closed the door on the scene. Her mother had behaved outrageously yet again, she thought grimly.

★

Vasily debated with himself on how to end the evening with the Brodskys and get himself to bed under their roof. A casual goodnight? A drawn-out parting? Some words added to conclude the sad day?

291

In the end he said nothing and went up to the room Njanja had allocated to him, the *babushka* with the hate-filled eyes, the one whom he would have expected to be the easiest to handle.

It was getting late. Coming out of the bathroom, with the guest towel over his arm and his sponge bag, he crept along the landing to the furthest room facing west. In a recess was a door revealing a narrow wooden staircase leading up to the next floor, clearly for servants. He made a note to go up there and nose around. Gradually, the house quietened down. Vasily took off his clothes and folded them neatly. He would have to wear them again tomorrow. He climbed into the bed which belonged to Antonina. It creaked under his weight.

On shelves and the polished surfaces of furniture were displayed the belongings of the spoilt capitalistic young woman who was in America. He stood up again, despite his fatigue, to turn a framed photograph of President Kennedy to face the wall. Then he climbed back into bed.

He had been able to check a good part of this vast house but had not found the Ikon. He had seen many unpleasant objects but gained little understanding for their owners except for Anna. Her approach was unexpected but he classified it as intelligent. He didn't doubt her good intentions, and he realised that she had succeeded in breaking through his passive-aggressive reserve for which Turchin had criticised him. However, the poor girl seemed quite muddled emotionally. It crossed his mind that competing with the other strong women in the family made matters difficult for her.

Anna was definitely the door for him to use. Each time he sought her out, she became flustered, the opposite of his experience with the rest of the family. Turchin would approve of the way he had played her along. He had to find more time to talk with her alone. She could help him with the mannerisms, words, expected of him in this foreign assignment. She could guide him through all those hateful ugly treasures stolen from the workers, sitting in this bombastic house so confidently, so pleased with themselves.

The Virgin of Kazan. What a fuss over some wood, stone and paint! He hated artefacts, especially Czarist stuff. At first he had not understood his government's wish to re-appropriate these old treasures but now, moving around in the obscene wealth of the émigrés, he saw that some had to be taken away from them, perhaps just to put one's foot down.

With the help of Anna he could do this job well, find the Ikon and live up to Georgi Miliukov's expectations. *Anna. The way she had blushed!* He grinned as he fell asleep.

CHAPTER
TWENTY-NINE

"Imagine! Someone slipped a Mickey Finn into my tea yesterday!"

"You were overwrought, that's all." Olga stood pensively at the mound of earth on which last night's rain had tattered the flowers. It was hard to accept that Sasha was no more. Now though, he was at peace with those who had preceded them while she felt cold and abandoned.

"Mother, you think that I was just drunk, don't you?"

Several suspicions had crept through Olga's mind concerning her daughter's collapse, the obvious being that Valentina had found it necessary to draw attention to herself.

"You've recovered, and it shall not be mentioned again."

"Is that all you care?"

"Remember, we have an important guest staying with us."

"Well, *à propos* guest, have you noticed that Anna has taken a shine to Voronov?"

Ah, perhaps that's what it was – Valentina's jealousy. "He is in his best years; nobody could deny that."

"Mother, given Anna's warped opinions, she could seriously hamper our dealings with Vasily."

"Don't you think you're in a bad position to judge? Or is your concern based on pure jealousy?"

"Certainly not! I was thinking of the money, that's all."

"I believe Voronov is able to make his own judgements." Olga returned her eyes to the last vestige of her brother-in-law's existence. If she was indeed destined to remain behind, she was determined to fight all the harder to preserve in the present all she could of the past.

"You give me no credit, because you think that I am drunk and disorderly. Behind my back you turn away things I desperately need."

Almost reluctantly Olga contemplated her daughter. "I do not know what you are talking about."

"The hunt! You made Njanja send back the few things I had ordered, and then the saddlers flooded me with abuse. Without the right coat, I couldn't go. You won. Bravo!" Valentina clapped her hands.

"Keep your voice down." Olga pulled a handkerchief from her sleeve and dabbed her temples. Her daughter's angry passion was that of someone else who was dead too; the blooms on his grave had wilted long ago, despite the tears shed.

"In the summer we rode in shirt-sleeves through the Crimea," Olga said in reverie, as if her indignant daughter was not next to her. "The immense wild plains and the clear still water, so different from here. I wonder who is living in our summerhouse now."

"You never listen. You ignore my problems. The next time, I'll have the saddler send things to Lady Mortimer and pick them up from there."

"I hope Lady Mortimer will consider paying for them too."

"That's typical of you: insensitive and cruel. That's how it's always been." Valentina reared up her head and sniffed the air. Abruptly she turned to Olga. "There were daffodils in the garden of that summerhouse. Carpets of them," she said and walked away.

As the countess crossed the lawn to the Hall, she noticed the moving figure of Vasily further along. He was walking briskly in physical exercise. *Had he overheard the argument between mother and daughter?*

On a collision course, Vasily slowed his steps and waited for Olga to catch up with him. He bent slightly as if performing an official bow. It was becoming, and she felt irritated. Clearly the elegant gesture befitted his stature. He would have the physical build for a Czarist uniform: high collars, gloves and stylish poses.

"A new crystal day and a beautiful park." He voiced his compliment.

"It's a clear day, and we are sorry that you are inconvenienced by our mourning and my daughter's malady. It will take us time to accept the loss of the viscount." Olga smiled benevolently.

"Perhaps it would be better if I went back to London, under the circumstances."

He had heard their arguing, decided Olga. "Not at all, not at all. We much appreciate your company."

Trish snickered defiantly. "I know exactly who asked you to talk to me."

Caught in the kitchen, his back against the sink, Fydo mulled painfully upon the task ahead. "Miss Worship," he started, breathing deeply, "my father is dead and buried, and surely you want to attend to other patients, as you did so admirably to my father."

"*Admirable*, is that it? I have a contract signed by you."

He found her slightly sluttish appearance, her self-assured ignorance, tough to deal with and wished Valentina had agreed to fire her. "Surely, your dignity will not allow me to order you to leave?"

"Dignity! Look who's talking. You're all a load of crap."

Fydo winced. He turned and tightened the dripping tap behind him, for it ground on his nerves. "I shall pay you the full amount until the end of the contract."

"I couldn't care less about that pathetic salary."

"There is no need to be shy." Immediately he recognised that *shy* was the wrong word.

"You're in on this with her. Shut the nurse up, smooth things over and the posh Brodskys rule!"

To his relief Njanja appeared. Seeing Fydo near the sink, she said, "Is zr tap. It is no good. It goes bing, bing, bing."

"Well yes, it needs someone to do something about it," said Fydo.

Njanja left through the back door, banging it as she went.

"All it needs is a new washer," commented Trish.

Fydo looked from the tap to Trish. *Why were things so clear to others and always so obscure to him? If the tap simply needed a washer, then why should his handling the nurse be so complex?* "Look here, Miss Worship," he said, "I don't know what you want from us, nor what your insinuations mean. We wish you to go. I shall leave a reference letter and your money near the telephone in the hall in one hour's time."

"It'll be filched and torn up, I bet."

"Who would want to do that?"

"Madame Valentina."

"Valentina?" He stared at her, uncomprehending and uneasy. He had not been aware that some feud had matured between the women during his father's illness.

"Or that snooping Russian spy," Trish shouted after him as Fydo escaped from the kitchen. *Women,* he thought. *Women were the most depressing creatures ever begotten.*

★

"I understand you wish to see me." Vasily was at Olga's bedroom door.

"Come in and divert me. I cannot find any comfort, knowing that there is so much discord in our family."

From her beguiling smile, he deduced that the day after the funeral of her brother-in-law she was not beyond bidding for admiration.

The countess sat draped on the stool to her vanity table, the folds of her long black skirt layered. The visible tip of a suede shoe tapped idly on the carpet. Heavy fragrance must have been sprayed around, to compete with the sickly scent of lilies. On a tripod table stood a large palm in a Chinese pot. The misgivings the Brodsky assignment caused him were intensified in this room. He took in the solid four-poster bed, the tapestry bergère, the voluminous wardrobe. This was the perfect example of what he, his family, his country, despised most. He smiled.

"Come, let us have a cosy chat." Olga pointed to the tapestry-upholstered short-legged chair.

"A pleasure, Countess." He hitched up his trousers, folded his knees and sat down.

"Shall I ring for tea?"

He tried to find an acceptable position for his long legs.

"Perhaps tea is not the right thing after my daughter's recent ailment." A theatrical flick of the head showed him her profile. From the lower cavity of the vanity table she produced a crystal decanter and two glasses. "Cream sherry," she pronounced as if she was tempting him to adultery.

"Let me." He worked himself out of his seat and poured them both a glass.

"It is incomprehensible to me that you or anyone else would wish to belong to modern Russia."

"The Soviet Union is not a difficult land to explain."

"Economic plans devised by an impenetrable régime of Party members and other nameless doughheads?"

"Today's Soviets are not more humourless or puritan than in the past."

"The past. Ah, the rebellion." Olga rolled the knobbed stem of her sherry glass between her fingertips. "Such an expensive, ridiculous means of taking revenge for a fate decided by birth."

He clenched his glass. "Soviet society interprets Western terrorism as revenge."

"Is there such a thing as Soviet society?"

"Had you remained in the motherland, you would probably be part of it."

"Denouncing my closest friends?"

"A less vain, perhaps more honest society."

"Vain pleasures are healthy and necessary. Organised societies turn irksome and dour."

Vasily's voice was even. "The pleasures were for few only."

"The high-born, the elegant, the witty." Olga's skirt rustled as she bent towards him. "Do you not think so?"

"The perceptions of a misguided class."

"You, my dear Vasily, have some ornateness and acumen." Her eyes challenged him.

The sip of sherry tasted like the medicine administered by his mother when he had a cough.

"Nobility equals culture, never forget that. We knew many cultivated people in St Petersburg. The Brodskys were close to the great Kavinsky family."

Vasily frowned. *Kavinsky*. That was a name he had heard before.

"The first baron was the generation of my father. Dimitri, his son, lived on the Nevsky Prospekt. You should have seen the receptions they gave. You and your *comrades* believe that with your Five Year Plans you have

300

started a new history. Can't you see that you are starting it from the end in order to reach the beginning? I am over eighty years old and know both ends of the history book. Russia is a country mired in its own history. The Russian soul cannot change; it is made of patriotism, eccentricity and vanity." She finished her speech with a devastatingly antique smile and added, "Foolish sentimentality on my part, no doubt."

Vasily faced her glinting malachite eyes. One thing was certain: the expensively clothed, perfumed, self-possessed countess sitting opposite him was neither sentimental nor foolish.

"There is so little left to remind me of precious memories. All yours now, young man." A controlled sob escaped from her chest.

"I will do my best to persuade my government to offer you some compensation for what you had to leave behind."

"You cannot give me back the Kavinskys' friendship, nor the Neva or the life we led."

Vasily twisted himself about on the bergère. "Anna mentioned that you take great comfort from the elms in the park, as they are the same as those in Leningrad, and there is of course your Ikon mentioned at the embassy lunch. According to your charming granddaughter, it is of great sentimental value to you."

"My grandchild Anna lives in the *Novyi Mir*, a new world which confuses vital values."

"But they do represent the Russian heritage. We still value them, for history has led today's Soviet Union to where it is."

"I wonder why I have the impression that ikons are more than that to you?" she said slowly and appeared to him like an old experienced bear ready to go for his jugular.

"Who would be gross enough to deny the value of antiques?"

"The new motherland would."

"Madam, we encourage Soviet artists more now than the old régime ever did."

"I have seen reproductions of garish oversized propaganda paintings."

"Art styles change; they move with time away from religious concepts. You have one such example hanging in your music room."

"That isn't art. That's a result of my daughter Valentina's insatiable sexual hunger."

Forcing down the knot in his throat, Vasily bravely persisted with this difficult interview. "Yet in its centre it depicts an old Russian insignia, I believe."

"Does it?" He knew that she was going to change the subject and she did. "In a complex way, my daughter has suffered most from the loss of Russia." She switched to a doe-eyed vulnerability.

Damn it. He had lost his opportunity. He decided on a desperate stab at it. "Countess, would you allow me the pleasure of seeing your Ikon of the Virgin of Kazan?"

"I believe you are requested downstairs."

Valentina was standing at the door.

★

"Olga gave you a hard time; I can tell from the way you smoulder." Valentina escorted Vasily down the stairs.

In the vestibule she unhooked a short coat from a stand. It was made of Siberian squirrel. She pulled it over one shoulder and then expected him to help her into the other sleeve. "It's simple really. We accept your ideas as little as you accept us. I bet you're yearning to get back to your embassy and vile KGB work."

He helped her into the squirrel skin. "Staying with your family is a valuable experience for me," he said dryly.

"Valuable experience, general principles, restrictionist policies – what hogwash! Come and walk in the park with me. I feel threatened in this house. You do know the stone was not aimed at the painting, but at me."

He was exhausted from the countess, and Valentina was even more challenging, but he could not think of an excuse to avoid having to walk in that park again.

"And that my tea yesterday was poisoned?"

"I do hope not."

"If I'm dead, you can cross one more aristocrat traitor off your black list."

This was obviously a rare moment when an émigré saw the truth quite clearly.

They marched rather than strolled in silence across the lawn. She kept her head turned towards him and her eyes scanned his face, not letting go. They were so probing as if they could penetrate all his secrets. He had to report all of this to Turchin. She walked briskly by his side, so close that her wide yellow dress, swelling out under the coat, brushed against his trousers with

303

each step. She was the only one who had changed out of black.

"If I seduced you, you couldn't do your spying stuff any longer, could you? They'd send you to Siberia."

Seduce (transitive verb): to draw aside from Party, belief, allegiance, duty. "I am sorry, but I do not understand what you're saying." He had stopped in his track.

She stopped and slipped her thumbs under the lapels of his jacket, sliding them up and down. "You're my kind exactly, despite your heathen upbringing." She let go of his jacket.

He checked whether she had fixed her verbal declaration somehow onto his lapels. But she had not. "I rather doubt that we have a lot in common."

"My gut reactions are never wrong. You'll see. Now let's get further away. I'll show you my favourite place in the wood."

He dug his hands into his pockets, straightened up and reluctantly walked on.

"Sorry for being so beastly to you. I'm always like that when I am interested in a man."

Alarmed, he shot a sharp glance at her. If he suggested turning back now, she would make beetroot pulp of him.

"Have you ever felt you've known someone for a long time without having met them before?" she continued.

The paling sun, filtering through the naked tangled arms of trees, polished her long black lashes to a silky gleam, her hair to the black of elderberries. She was ten years older than he was but her skull formation had kept the face deceptively youthful. Her passionate eyes were the same dark brown as his unpassionate ones. This was not a welcome discovery.

"Vasily, I cannot tell you the hell I am in."

He waited for this to expand into a rant, probably nauseously sexual. His aversion had to be kept in check. It was an assignment from hell, and the day not over yet.

"Alone here." Valentina blew the words into his ear. "Let's relax." She spread her arms wide. The coat was pulled apart to reveal that the yellow dress had a crocheted bodice. "You don't like my dress?"

"Yellow."

"Yellow is the colour of bile and jealousy." A dangerous boldness glinted in her eyes. "You think that I am dangerous and frightening, but hopefully interesting."

"Hardly." *She can see through me.*

"Don't look so wide-eyed. It's just that something about you gets to me. It's all to do with my past somehow."

"Mrs Brodsky, don't get us into a stupid conversation."

"I suppose you wouldn't cheat on your wife."

"What wife?"

She grinned broadly, showing her cared-for teeth. "Is it realistic to hope to get some of our lost money back?"

"Soviet policy is to be co-operative."

"I'll lose Podzhin Hall if it isn't possible."

"How come Podzhin Hall belongs to you? Didn't your mother inherit from her father, or Sasha?"

"You know a lot about us. Of course, the communists always know everything."

"Why you? You see I don't know."

305

"Not been attentive at your brainwashing sessions?"

He shrugged his shoulders as if he did not care.

"Olga never told me why. Podzhin Hall was some kind of an endowment trust from someone important. It's all vague, and linked to some old family secret: *un vice caché.*"

"A hidden flaw."

"You also speak French. You are obviously chosen to do important things for your country." She moved closer. "Do you like gypsy music?"

"I grew up in the Ukraine, the land of gypsy songs."

"Never been there, yet I feel myself when I hear it."

"You dress like a gypsy."

"Vasily." She held onto both his forearms. "Someone is trying to frighten me."

"Who?" He peeled her hands off his arms.

"Why don't you pity me? I told you that my life is hell."

The tension which had been building up between them was almost tangible. With a shock he realised how much, even in the last ten minutes, the prospect of closeness, the mere thought of intimacy, had gained ground. She stood before him and they were the same height.

Valentina pulled a hairclip out of her chignon. Long strands of hair fell and untangled in the shaking of her head, bent backwards. Without warning she locked her arms around his neck and kissed him on his mouth. He nearly lost his balance. "The first time I saw you, I knew I was going to do that."

"Because you want to humiliate me?" he pressed out, noticing that she smelled as he had expected her to smell: healthily sensual despite an expensive perfume.

"No, because you are you." She moved to kiss him again.

"Please," he remonstrated, pulling away from her embrace.

"I could pretend to be afraid of you. In 1917, your people were my enemy, executioners. I was only three years old. You stand for what we lost and yet – and yet you are a Russian." She took his hands and bent over them; there were a few silver strands buried in the dark mass of her hair.

"I can't give in to sentimental games." He was cross with himself for having dropped his guard. He yearned for the safety of the embassy, where he could get all this off his chest.

He retrieved his hands to put them non-committally on her shoulders.

When Vasily drove out of Podzhin Hall in the embassy car later that afternoon, he pulled the tie from his neck and groaned. Would he disclose his feelings for Valentina? He blanked out that question. Nothing had happened to compromise him. He drove on towards London and his debriefing.

★

Anna, still in Njanja's black skirt and blouse, stood under an umbrella in front of the Hall, gazing down into the ornamental pond, in the middle of which the thin waterspout's water cascaded over moss-covered stones. With the light fading, rain had returned. She recoiled in surprise on seeing several toads squatting on the stone rim, slithery in the damp gloom.

"Oh, not again!" Valentina, returning from the stables with the hood of her macintosh over her head, stopped in her tracks. "Those disgusting toads are crawling out to hibernate."

Anna gazed in fascination at the amphibians. The first pustule-covered pouch flexed its cushiony hind legs and, in an elongated stretch, jumped off the rim onto the gravel. Anna stood back. "They will hop to some muddy ditch and bury themselves in for the winter. I'm sure there is poison in those sacs."

"Anna, you say that every year."

"Antonina does not believe me either, but I am convinced they are a bad omen."

"Stop being so sinister. I'll ask Cahill to clear them away."

"More will crawl out. There is nothing we can do. Nothing at all. And we don't even know where Antonina is. Perhaps she had an accident and is in a hospital, thousands of miles away."

"No news is good news, remember."

"I need Antonina to come back. I can't do it without her."

"Do what?"

"Live. Just live."

Valentina turned and sprinted towards the porch. Anna remained. The rain tapped on the taut rayon over her head. A dark glistening hump surfaced at the waterline. She shuddered.

CHAPTER THIRTY

"I need a job to survive in California," said Antonina to the girl at Manpower.

"All I can offer you is a one-off secretarial job in a bank this evening. None of my *white glove* regulars is available."

"I'll take it." Antonina nodded eagerly. She had six dollars left.

That evening the night-watchman let her into the impressive CA Trust Bank building. Her second-hand shoes clicked on the inlaid floor. She had taken her autoharp along for moral support. It was a quarter to eight.

The door on the tenth floor was opened by Mr Adams himself, deputy director of the bank. All the staff had gone home. He led Antonina to his secretary's desk.

"I'm catching the nine-fifty flight tonight to New York for the annual general meeting tomorrow morning. I want you to type the title and contents pages of this report. You'll find everything in the drawers." He gave her his hand-written draft. "The title in large capitals."

"Yes," said Antonina and put the harp down.

He left the room. Squat on the desk before her was an electric IBM typewriter. She had never sat before such a machine before and could not type. *Only six dollars left,* she thought. The white gloves given to her as the badge of good temporary service lay on the desk. She tried to pull a sheet under the roll. It would not move. With a pair of tweezers from the top drawer she managed to squeeze it under at the expense of one corner of the page. She pressed a switch and the paper rolled nearly out. The machine hummed. Her fingers touched the keys. *ZXCV* was printed in a flash at the bottom of the page. She managed to thread in the next sheet only because her elbow brushed the right key. Typing tentatively produced *TGE* in italics on the left hand side of the page. She tried on a new sheet. *THE ANNNNNNNU.* She crumpled up the paper, threaded in a new one. The door opened.

"Finished?"

"Er."

"I leave in an hour and I need you to bind the report as well." The door closed.

Antonina made many interesting samples. Once she managed to type *The Annual Financial* before it went wrong. It was twenty past eight on the clock.

The door opened. "Ready?"

She put her head on the infernal machine. Mr Adams came in and picked up her latest trial. She met his eyes.

"You can't type."

"I am nervous," she whispered.

He collected some pages and un-crumpled them; then he sighed and looked at his watch. "Go and make us some coffee."

She switched on the kettle with shaking fingers and poured Nescafé, sugar and milk into mugs. The knob popped; the kettle hissed. She opened the lid. She had forgotten to fill it with water and it was burnt out. She filled the mugs with hot tap water.

In the office Mr Adams sat behind the IBM. He had typed *Annuelllll*. Antonina gave him the coffee. He took a sip and spat it back into the mug. "You can't make coffee either."

She shook her head.

"What *can* you do?"

She was very close to tears, and it was nearly nine o'clock.

"I can't believe this is happening to me." He lifted the phone to change his flight to half-past eleven, the last shuttle to New York.

"Young lady, this is the Charles Adams Trust Bank. My father is the founder and chairman, and you are going to make me a title page to this report. Now!"

Antonina flinched and sat down behind the machine again. "Do you think this is the right sort of bubble?"

"They are called golf balls, and at this stage I don't care as long as it says the right thing."

Resigned, Antonina threaded a new sheet into the IBM. With twitching fingers she typed *THE*. The print had moved far too much to the right and would never fit. His eyes fixed on her were dangerously dark.

"I'll try." He sat down. His *T* was even further to the right. "Christ!" he exploded. "Do you know what you're doing to me?"

"Sorry."

"Sorry? I should think you're bloody sorry. Where am I going to get someone who can type at this hour of the night?"

"I don't know."

"I believe you."

"You see, from my twenty dollars I've only got six left, and tomorrow I will have only one left and that's without eating."

"So, you told them you were a typist."

She nodded and started to cry.

"Jesus," he said. "I can't believe this."

"Mr Adams, I could draw the pages for you."

"Great."

"Please. I did art for my O Levels."

"Draw some flowers in the corners; the board will love it. My father will think I have turned into my head-in-the-clouds brother."

Antonina pushed the IBM away and took a new sheet. Carefully with a ruler and a sharp pencil she started to work on the heading while Mr Adams paced up and down behind her.

"If you weren't so pretty, I'd hit you," he declared.

She drew a beautiful *T* in pencil and filled it in with ink. When the title was finished she handed her work to him.

"Can you do the contents in the same way?"

She had already started.

Mr Adams called the night watchman and ordered a Chinese take-away to be brought up.

By the time the cardboard boxes were delivered, Antonina had finished. She had drawn three nice squiggles under the table of contents. There was more than an hour left.

Together they perforated the pages of the report and threaded them into a spring fastener. Then they sat down and ate the meal. Mr Adams kept glancing at the drawn pages.

Antonina had slipped off her high-platform sandals. "I got them from a yard sale. They're killing my feet."

"You're one of those hippies, make-love-not-war people, in Haight-Ashbury, and all that. I sincerely hope you are not into LSD." He scooped noodles into his mouth, and she saw him splatter his tie and tie-pin.

"What's wrong with your brother?" She changed the subject, and he stared at her uncomprehending. "The dreamer?"

"Yeah, dreams up new designs for faster automobiles, together with a buddy."

"What is wrong with that?"

"He hasn't got a job; drives around in sports cars."

"What's his name?"

"Lucius."

"If you admitted it, you actually love your brother."

"Yeah, I guess I do, nosy Miss Flower Power." He rose, and she started to stack the cartons.

"Will you still be in San Francisco when I get back in three days' time?"

"It depends on how many typing jobs I am offered."

"Well, let's hope they appreciate art." His mocking was kind, and he reached into his breast pocket to take out a wad of notes. They were twenty-dollar bills. "For the artwork," he said. "Invaluable."

She did not take the money from him.

"How about the one dollar left for tomorrow?"

"Then that'll show my commercial worth."

"Surely you have a family somewhere."

"I have to find out how to make it on my own merits."

"Gee, what's your name?"

"Antonina."

"Antonina, I've never met anyone like you." His eyes scanned the desk, the bookshelf. Finally he picked up a geode rock paperweight and handed it to her. The cavity inside was lined with amethyst crystal spikes. "That's the best I can do. After all, you offered me a few unforgettable hours."

The watchman rang; the banker was ready to leave.

She held the crystal stone. "Thank you, Mr Adams."

"I guess you can always sell it. By the by, where can I find you if I need more typing done?"

"The Priory of St Sophronia."

A last smile warmed his handsome face. The door closed behind him.

Antonina left the bank with her harp and the amethyst crystal in her white-gloved hands. In the flashing lights of the advertisements, it sparkled like a miniature Manhattan at dawn. She did not feel tired; she felt uplifted. Her performance had of course been a disaster but she had got away with it. That in itself surely counted as a success. In fact the important, no doubt rich, no-nonsense Mr Adams had been thrown off track by her. He was right now in an aeroplane to New York with a dirty tie and childish drawings on the annual report, wondering whether he really liked his brother, Lucius.

The few people she passed on the pavement were grubby.

"Taking the governor's pet rock for a night out on the town?" The tramp had a wisp of white beard and seemed installed for the night in Union Square.

"Afraid not. It's sleeping like a rock," said Antonina.

He chuckled.

In a 24 hour café Antonina ordered a bagel and hot chocolate. More jokes about the crystal came her way. Now, apart from her night's lodgings, she had exactly one dime left. How could she survive? She put half the bagel into her pocket.

"You wanna rocky bag?"

She walked about town for hours. By 5am a queue of people had formed in front of the staff entrance to the *Emporium* store on Market Street. One of them told her that sales jobs could be had. She joined the queue. At seven, the door opened. They were let in and had to box-tick an intelligence questionnaire.

Later, after some waiting and fretting, a few of the applicants were called into an office. She was one of them, probably on the merit of her university education. She was given a dark blue overall and a sales job in the stationery department starting right away.

She had never stood on the other side of a counter before. During the first hours, she dreaded anyone heading towards her.

"Say, I'm lookin' for a present." The Texan lay his stetson on the counter.

"We have assorted monogrammed papeterie, or perhaps a fountain pen or writing accessories?" suggested Antonina.

"Whaddya say?"

"It's for a gift, isn't it?"

The floor manageress's sharp eyes had caught them. "Is there a problem here?"

"This young lady here talks some kinda kangaroo."

The manageress called the other girl on the floor. "Sharon, please help this customer."

"Mighty pretty girl, mighty bad English."

Antonina was taken aside by the manageress. "This is the second complaint we've had, and you haven't been here a full day yet."

Antonina knew she would not last two days and was proved right when at closing time she was ordered upstairs. She returned the blue overall with the embroidered *E* and received a thin envelope. No regrets nor thanks were uttered. In front of the *Emporium* there was still a small queue of hopeful job-hunters when Antonina stepped into the street.

Now she had eleven dollars and twenty cents and half a bagel, a pair of white gloves, a crystal stone, and *bloody* painful shoes.

Further up Market Street a colourful brass band was playing. Businessmen in suits surrounded an official with a red sash who lifted a shovel and hacked it symbolically into the asphalt. "I hereby start the construction of the San Francisco subway."

The considerable crowd cheered. *Tea for two*, played the band.

My gosh, to think they'll dig right under the Bay to Oakland, thought Antonina.

Tired, she dragged herself up the steep road to the hostel.

As soon as she opened the door of her room she knew someone had ransacked her belongings. Her rucksack was open on the floor, clothes pulled from it, music sheets discarded. She threw herself onto the bed and whimpered from exhaustion. It was not as easy to be poor as she had imagined.

The next day she stood in queues and filled in questionnaires but could not get work.

The day after that was worse. She now owed the hostel ten dollars and still did not have a job. The manager gave no credit and insisted that bills were settled daily. Antonina dressed in all the clothes she possessed, one over the other, packed the harp into its case, and her passport and airline ticket into a beaded stash pouch. Picking up her buffalo rucksack stuffed with the bed pillow, she went down into the grubby lobby.

"You owe me ten dollars," shouted the unpleasant woman at the reception desk.

"I'm going to the bank now. Look after my things."

"Yeah, yeah. That's an old one."

"Of course, you'll have to put this in the safe." She placed the crystal on the desk. "It's amethyst. Worth a fortune."

The woman poked her fat finger into the cavity.

"Back in a jiffy." Antonina left the rucksack and walked out of reception.

Easy come, easy go, she thought on her way to St Sophronia's.

317

At the priory a nun with a dimple in her chin pulled two Western Union telegrams from the pigeonhole. "It's my chin, isn't it?" she said. "That's why I am Sister Dot." The nun put her finger to the dimple.

"Pleased to meet you, Sister Dot with a dimple."

"I hope your telegrams bring you joy. Sometimes they can be distressing."

"Sister Dot!" came a stern voice from the office.

"I'm babbling too much," the sister whispered, and Antonina opened the first telegram. *Today is Snoopy's birthday stop Love stop Ricky.*

Antonina burst out laughing and handed the piece of paper to the nun.

"Oh my, and I haven't bought him a present."

"Dot, come in here right now!"

The other telegram was from Anna. Uncle Sasha had died. The old world seemed to fold itself up around her like some trick of stagecraft. She had not been with them for this sad occasion. Anna was imploring her to return home. All that in twelve words. Antonina knew that she was not ready to go home yet. She left the priory and headed towards Haight-Ashbury. She had not eaten since yesterday lunchtime and felt restricted in the layers of clothes she was wearing. Kicking off her platform shoes, she climbed onto a garbage can pushed against a wall and started to strum her harp.

"Here I sit on Buttermilk Hill
Who could blame me? Cry my fill,
Shul shul shula roo."

A few hippies stopped and listened to her. One with

318

bells on elastic bands around his ankles climbed onto another garbage can close to her.

Antonina kept singing and playing. After a while she ran out of songs.

Summoning all her courage she faced the blond young man. "If you give me fifty cents, I'll give you my shoes – for a girlfriend perhaps?"

"Who needs shoes?"

"Please."

"You hungry?"

"Yes."

"You got somewhere to live?"

"Nope."

"I'm Elf. Let's go to the psychedelic heaven."

Antonina wondered what he meant but climbed down from her undignified seat and threw her shoes into it. "Okay."

If he hadn't been called Elf, had his eyes not been so blue nor shone so cleanly, she would not have agreed to something so uncertain.

Without speaking they padded along to Haight-Ashbury. Up four flights of a fire escape ladder, they climbed through a window into a large room not unlike a market of Turkish carpets; they covered the floor and were hung on walls. Young and old hippies sprawled on large cushions and rug-covered mattresses. There were pieces of cloth strung across the windows and the light was dim.

"Who's this?" A balding bespectacled hippie pointed at Antonina. "You wanna toke? You wanna freak out?"

Elf introduced her while Antonina was lost in the stifling herbal aroma.

"Nina, Nina, ride a cock horse like a concertina,

A fine lady upon a coarse horse called Hyena,

With rings on her finger and bells on her toes to make me keener," the hippie sing-songed.

"Just tune out. That's Gerry, a badass," explained Elf.

Thin hand-rolled cigarettes were passed from dry lips to dry lips. There were drawn-out moans as of expiring humans and whispering like rustles, but no music.

"Hi guys! Antonina sings and sells her shoes."

A lean girl unrolled from an all-fours position and threw her long hair back to free her face. Taking Antonina by the hand, she led her into a shockingly dirty kitchen.

She assembled a glass of milk, stale crackers and hard cheese, plus an orange. Never had sour milk tasted better; every gulp was a treat. Antonina stuffed crackers and cheese into her mouth with both hands.

"I'm Roxanne. You're real pretty." Antonina chewed. "Why are you wearing so many clothes?"

"Lost my suitcase."

"For you." They were two ribbons on which were sewn metal jingle-bells. "I make those, garlands and cotton flowers," Roxanne said proudly.

"Do you live here?"

"Down the block with Elf."

"What's his real name?"

"Randolph Fletch."

"Like the drugstores?"

"Yes, but never mention it. He's family. You can stay the night here. Everyone who sells their shoes does. To be groovy, you need a braid in your hair." She started to wind one into Antonina's hair while Antonina peeled the orange.

"Tonight, we're planning a demo. In a couple of days, we'll be out in force to bring the governor a coffin."

"Cool," said Antonina and ate the orange.

CHAPTER
THIRTY-ONE

Georgi Miliukov's official Volga swept him through the traffic to Kursk Station to catch a west-bound train to his father's dacha. He was oblivious to the vastness of the grey and ochre buildings, the commuter crowds, and later in the train he counted the halts by habit. His mind ran over the wording of the message received from the embassy in London.

"Oh, that's a new look," Georgi said in mock-surprise, as he entered the verandah.

"I had someone in to style my hair and massage my scalp."

"You smell like a brothel madame."

"Eau de Cologne from France."

"Did a sexy widow move in next door?"

The carer came into the verandah, three young cats playing about her feet. Mouth corners in a droop, she asked whether the men wanted tea.

"The bottle, and a plate of cold smoked sausage. And then go to the village and find yourself a husband."

"I'm not to be ordered around. In fact, I complain about bath time. Your father forces me to give him a rub down with almond oil. I'm only required to assist with bathing – Caring Level 2."

She turned and walked away leaving the door ajar long enough for the cats to go back with her.

"How can you force her to pummel your old flesh?"

"Ah, it's all about negotiation. If she refuses, I give her a cat as a present to take home."

"I knew you would go senile on me."

"I'm just positive." Pavel rubbed his dry old hands against each other. "Things must have gone wrong for Voronov. He had to spend a whole weekend with the Brodskys. Give me every detail."

"Vasily at target B2's funeral…"

"No, no, give them their names. I can imagine them better."

Georgi hung his jacket on the back of the chair, sat down and then walked the chair closer to his father to tell him about the report.

Pavel caressed the scar on his chin and concluded, "So Vasily's antagonism with Valentina has intensified, Olga is unmanageable, Fyodor only semi-normal, and the servant hostile, right?"

"At the moment, the only approach for him is through Anna."

"Maybe he should be instructed to woo her."

"Anna? No, that would blow the girl's usefulness, and cause complications."

"In Voronov, there is one Soviet cadre who will not defect for the love of any of the Brodsky women, trust me." Pavel cackled.

323

"Oh incidentally," started Georgi, "Turchin is in Moscow for the fiftieth anniversary of the October revolution."

"They flew him from London to Moscow just to see a parade! Too much money is spent in the wrong places," grumbled Pavel. "Or do you think there is another reason for it?"

"There is also Antonina Brodsky I haven't told you about. By lucky coincidence, Snell's report landed on my desk this morning as well. According to Snell, Olga made a call to Irina Potresov in New York."

Instantly Pavel started to show off. "Profile – Irina Potresov: played a minor role in Leningrad. Baronetess, probably a bought title. Husband a gambler, dandy, wore a gold monocle. The couple were at the Winter Palace ball when we stormed it. They fled to New York. Husband died ten years ago. Potresov is of no interest to us."

"That's where you're wrong. Antonina stayed with her on Governor's Island, I'll show you on a map, but has left to drive through America heading west."

"How come I don't know this?"

"I told you, but you forgot. No doubt that scented hair oil makes you dizzy."

"You're implying that the old women are close friends, and Potresov is in on this Ikon plot?"

Georgi unbuttoned his shirt down to the height of his nipples and reached into his vest to pull out an envelope.

"Taking chances," said the old man.

"Pleasing you, more like."

Pavel concentrated through his spectacles. "All I can

make out are boulders on a shore and the silhouette of a person."

"The picture was taken from a rocking boat."

A new photograph was offered to Pavel.

"Is that Antonina with her mouth open at a gasoline station?"

"She is singing."

"Who are the others?"

"Her travelling companions. And before you say anything, those people are irrelevant, checked and double-checked."

"All right, what are they doing on the next picture, sitting in sand on a road with their clothes on their heads?"

"The car she was driving overheated in Death Valley, and Snell offered them water. Notice the black case filling the window of the car. She goes nowhere without it, and it is about the size of the Ikon."

"Well, well, well."

"She has now arrived in San Francisco, left the group and booked herself into a dubious hostel in Chinatown, still with the black case."

"And…?"

"Snell's report ended there."

"I'll be damned if I understand what the stupid girl is doing in San Francisco with the Ikon."

"We'll soon learn more."

Pavel handed back the last picture showing an attractive young woman walking down a street in a mini skirt with the black case but without shoes.

Georgi got up and picked the jacket from the back of

the chair. "Shall I open the window a little? It is stifling in here."

"Open, close. Do what you like."

Georgi let the crisp air in to mingle with the stale. Then bent over his father's brow and kissed it. "Phew – that hair oil!"

"Off with you."

Inside the dacha Georgi poked his head into the kitchen. The carer sat at the kitchen table playing dominoes with herself, eating cakes she had obviously bought in the village.

"I opened the verandah window. Go and close it in half an hour."

"Interfering, interfering." Her fleshy hands scooped the black white-spotted bricks into a heap.

★

The following day Georgi's Controller was loitering in the North American Section, chatting with the Section Chief about the October parade that afternoon. As the Controller had anticipated, Georgi came in and requested the key to the safe-cabinet. He went to the adjoining restricted filing bay.

The Controller kept up his pretence of being on a social call until Georgi emerged and, without a sideways glance at him or a word of greeting, handed back the key and slipped out of the room.

Ending the conversation, the Controller asked for the key himself and went to check. He grimaced on discovering that the photographs of Antonina Brodsky were back in the file. "Gotcha." Now he had proof.

For four months he had been watching Georgi. Ever since Vasily Voronov had been chosen for the London embassy, he had smelled a rat. Georgi had obtained approval for Voronov's posting without the normal clearance process.

Each time a report came from London, Georgi went out to see Pavel. *Suspicious? Oh, yes.*

Irked, the Controller had started to dig around in Voronov's personal file and had found a letter to Pavel from a Komsomol leader who had trained Voronov as a child; the wording implied that the training had been at Pavel's special request. The following twenty years revealed similar examples of Pavel's involvement in Voronov's life. *Could Voronov have been specially groomed over decades for this job? And if so, why? Was it the Ikon that was important, or the Brodskys?*

The Controller leaned out of the window in his office. The whole of the city seemed clad in red flags as if the city bled. In the afternoon was to be the biggest parade ever but he would take this unique opportunity to convince his trusted friend in the Military Revolutionary Committee to give him access to the old archives. Minds would be on having the afternoon off, on the special ration of vodka and lastly on the military display.

With the findings he dared to expect, Voronov's posting would be the result of further manipulation by Pavel Miliukov. *What could he possibly be up to?* Turchin had come from London to Moscow. That was convenient.

The Controller lifted the receiver of his telephone. "Is Comrade Turchin in the building? Excellent! Make an appointment for him to see me tomorrow morning at ten o'clock sharp."

CHAPTER
THIRTY-TWO

The following afternoon Georgi was so angry that he wondered whether he would be forced to dash to the lavatory and vomit. He had received confirmation from a contact in the Politburo that the Controller had been sniffing around for months. And yesterday while all of Moscow was watching the parade, the Controller had gone through the archives until the early hours of the morning. He had arrived late at the office and immediately gone into a private meeting with Turchin. Georgi, tight with dread, did not dare to make rash movements; all he allowed himself was his clammy hand checking his burning forehead.

Despite all the care they had taken, the Controller had obviously set out to investigate the choice of Vasily for the Brodsky task. He must have pulled major strings to obtain access to archival files which were not even for his eyes. The little grey-eyed rat had spent much energy working against the cause instead of serving it.

How would Turchin have reacted to learning that Vasily Voronov had been posted to London with hidden motives?

"*Kak tak?* – How come?" he would have asked, bewildered because he was a man who trusted the system, but the Controller would certainly have suggested that Vasily might be a plant, an interloper.

Georgi lit a Western filter cigarette which he usually reserved for good moments. Perhaps he could come up with some legitimate explanation for Vasily's posting but the whole point had been to keep the trump card for the master-stroke on émigrés in his and his father's hands.

His father! Oh shit. He would have to tell Pavel that the truth was being undug.

His father would say, *We'll put it down to coincidence, malicious rumour. Turchin is a little man, weakened by his exposure to London, and can be persuaded. If he touches one hair on Voronov's head, we'll destroy his career.*

Georgi forked with his hand through his greasy hair. *Father*, he thought to tell him, *the garrotting and bayonet-stabbing revolutionary ways are in the past. You can no more just think what you think, let alone say it. For forty years you were lucky that everything went well, as you worked on your Vasily communist sculpture, ideally to bear your name on its plinth.*

The crime of withholding essential information had been committed. Just at the culmination of their labours, a bureaucrat risked spoiling everything.

Perhaps the Party or KGB might not take reprisals; they might understand the attraction of his father's arguments. Perhaps nothing drastic would happen, and Vasily be permitted to continue with the Brodsky operation. But this happy prospect could only be possible if Turchin were brought on board. *Perhaps* was not much on which to bet one's survival but it would have to do.

The expensive cigarette tasted stale in Georgi's mouth. He stubbed it out with a brutal jab.

That was it – the only way for Georgi to mitigate this disaster was to take the sting out of the scorpion in its infancy. He had to do it right away and there was no time to consult Pavel.

★

Comrade Turchin sat forward in the visitor's chair in Georgi's office. The car which was to bring him to the airport for London was already waiting.

Georgi shouted into the receiver of his phone, "I need a few minutes with him, that's all."

Turning to Turchin, he smiled with confidence. "The Voronov case should not have been messed with. It is a top secret mission, and Vasily's background has to be concealed, even from him, so that we can use him for an operation no ordinary Party member could do. You are intelligent enough to understand these subtleties."

"It's unheard of." Turchin was puzzled. "I confess that I fully understand the Controller's objections," he went on, "even though I don't approve of the way he came by the information."

"Pavel and I knew that it would be difficult to keep it secret. But it was the only way to make Vasily a great exemplary showpiece of Soviet achievements. Coinciding with our anniversary year, we are confident that it will be achieved."

"I did not expect another layer to our work procedures. You tell me that Voronov does not know who he really is? Do you intend to ever tell him?"

"Eventually, but first he has to succeed."

Turchin was visibly uncomfortable. "The Controller will not stop digging. You must know that. It will put your operation at risk. Voronov is bound to hear something. And then what?"

"If we, you and I, take measures to protect this operation…"

A woman appeared at the door. "Comrade Turchin will miss his Aeroflot."

"One more minute, damn it." Georgi flicked his hand at her. She pulled away.

Turchin's face was tense, his eyes clouded as he rocked in concentration. When he stood up, he had come to a decision and Georgi swallowed hard.

"If I'm to cooperate with you, we'll have to tell Voronov who he is. It is a big gamble, but the Party's triumph will be all the greater. That's the only way out of this."

"Excellent proposition, Comrade."

"You have given me no choice. I know you and your father. How Voronov will react, that is yet to be seen."

"Abroad with him, you can handle this the right way and make Vasily live up to our expectations."

"You ask a lot."

"It's what our glorious goal requires."

When Turchin had left, Georgi picked up the photograph on his desk: Pavel receiving the Star of Lenin. "I am sorry, Father, but this was the only way."

Georgi cleared his desk. It appeared that he had won over Turchin. There was no point sitting in his office feeling wretched. Before going home to his apartment on the elegant Kropotkinskaya and pretending to listen to his wife's dull complaints, he would have to walk the streets and think about how to neutralise the others to whom the Controller might talk.

CHAPTER
THIRTY-THREE

At the Manpower agency Antonina surrendered the white gloves onto the desk of a woman who read from a worksheet: "Antonina Brodsky, CA Trust Bank, typing job."

"I'm sorry," Antonina started. "You see, I…"

"Tell me what happened there. I must admit that I am baffled by the feedback from the deputy director personally."

"You see, I…"

"He telephoned to leave this message for you: *The board of directors was delighted with the presentation of the annual financial report.*"

"Strange man," said Antonina. "Confused."

"How about more temp jobs?"

"Never again. I already did the best I could."

*

The sun bathed the late October day, enhancing the blaze of the maples. Humming, Antonina in a sleeveless top and flowery bellbottom trousers strode down the street. Her chestnut hair was swiping across her back and Roxanne's hand-woven bracelet garnished her upper arm. She was heading for the hippie demonstration at the governor's residence.

A couple of blocks away a group of freedom riders and zonked-out youngsters exchanged disjointed conversations. Once the organisers judged there was enough support, they set off with a cardboard coffin in which bounced a grotesque papier-mâché corpse. They carried banners, paint on torn sheets; they shouted freedom. They yelled against the war in Vietnam, against the drafting of black people. Antonina, cushioned by those around her, just shouted utter nonsense because it felt good to do so in a loud voice in public. Elf had told her he could not make it; someone had to sort out money for the psychedelic heaven.

"Just like a bloody bank," she shouted.

"Bloody bank?" A girl with a knotted headscarf gave her a questioning glance. Antonina nodded. "Hey," shouted the girl, "we're doing banks now. Abolish banks. No more banks. Fuck the banks."

I believe that I have just outgrown demos, thought Antonina, her shoulders sagging. *How sad for me.*

The cortège moved on and slowly shed Antonina who edged herself away. Barefooted, she watched them pass. "Come with us," they called because she looked the part.

That afternoon at St Sophronia's, her poste restante, she found an envelope with a distinctive black rim around it. *My dear OTHER, (sorry about the smudge).*

How Anna-like this start was to a letter – Anna who was missing her, Anna who had contributed a flower cushion for the funeral in her name, Anna... *I want you to have the feeling that you are part of us in our grieving.*

The time it had taken for this loving message to travel from her sister's hand into hers, Uncle Sasha had already been in the earth for five days.

Antonina felt slightly guilty for having demonstrated with a coffin but realised that it had nothing to do with Sasha's death. She could not afford to call home, nor could she write because Podzhin Hall and their lives appeared as distant from her as if she saw them through binoculars held the wrong way round.

Just as she was leaving, Sister Dot came running. "This was brought for you at lunchtime."

Outside Antonina sat on a low garden wall and tore open the envelope from the CA Trust Bank. She hoped that Mr Adams had had a change of heart and sent her a wad of the twenty-dollar bills she had so grandly refused. However, it was just a note saying: *It is important that I tell you in person how the Board reacted to my flowery initiative. I will be back in S.F. Friday and invite you for dinner that evening. Please call Marion on 555-0846 for details, or to say you don't want to come. I would understand. Vance Adams.*

It would be pleasing to see Mr Adams again but the prospect of something good to eat made her call Marion straight away from a phone booth. She was told to be at the Sheraton Palace at seven o'clock the following evening.

As Antonina walked back to Haight-Ashbury, she noticed the days were getting shorter now and her feet were cold from the pavement. In front of the psychedelic heaven a crowd of people had gathered. Among them was Roxanne.

"Antonina, it's real bad."

"What happened?"

"You know Gerry, the bald hippie? He took an acid trip and tried to fly from the fire-escape ladder." Roxanne started to cry. An ambulance pulled away.

"Is he…?"

"Very dead. Now we've got to move camp."

"My harp!"

"I've got it. I've also got us each a bag of food. Goldie made dozens of jars with mash from stolen apples."

"Where can we all go?"

"Ocean Beach on South Bay."

"A beach?"

"We can set up near the cliff house."

The group processed along the road, carrying their possessions and chanting monotonously, "Turn on, tune in, drop out."

The sky had clouded over and the sand of the beach was dark when they got there. It suited their mood. Under a gallery of overhanging rocks they laid out their stuff.

Male hippies lit a fire with driftwood girls had joylessly collected. Someone opened a packet of chocolate-chip cookies and shared them out. Suddenly a girl ran into the sea. Her flowery dress floated around her. She stretched her arms up to the leaden sky. Another ran to join her, then another. It turned increasingly chill and their teeth clattered. It started to rain as evening rolled in on them. They huddled. A couple made love within reach of Antonina. The small dog someone had brought along vomited pieces of dead seagull. Raindrops drummed on the harp case. One girl hummed a lullaby, rocking herself, her arms around her chest.

"I have to give up," Antonina confided in Roxanne.

"You can't come unglued. Elf!" Roxanne shouted, "Antonina wants to leave. Come and give her some spunk."

"Can't. There's a storm coming."

A first roll thundered and the hippies scrambled tighter against the rocks, but Antonina moved away and climbed up the bank to the road with her few belongings.

Walking along the pavement in the direction of St Sophronia's, the rain prattled down on her. Jagged lightning shot down over the Presidio Golf Course. Thunder crackled and boomed. A passing car tossed a water plume over her as she slapped along barefoot.

In the priory the first person she encountered was the dimple-cheeked sister. "My child, you're soaked."

"Sorry about the puddle on the floor. I was wondering whether you could let me have a room for one night. But I have no money to pay for it."

"And what about tomorrow?"

"Tomorrow, I'm invited for dinner and then have to go back to New York. I do have a return ticket."

"We're not a charity. Our few rooms are for us and visiting clergy. Visitors can rent rooms in the next building. But…"

"It costs money. Sister, please. I give you – no, I dedicate this almost new autoharp to the priory. Surely

337

there is someone who can play it, someone who always wanted to learn?"

Sister Dot reached out and turned on the ceiling light. The downpour outside had intensified and a nun was laying newspaper under the door.

"I would have to ask Mother Superior."

"Please, don't do that. She'll say no on some principle."

The sister laughed. "Dead right you are."

"So what shall we do?"

"We?"

"Aren't you supposed to be doing good? I don't take drugs. I don't drink liquor. I'm not wanted by the police. And I am certainly not a hippie any more. It is time for me to get a job and to contribute in a constructive way. I'm now ready for it." Antonina sneezed twice.

"Gullible as I am, I believe you. Actually, I would love to learn how to play the harp, and we do have a vacant box room; we always do."

"And you can smuggle me in?"

"I will still have to confess to Mother Superior, afterwards."

"You're wonderful."

"I took a vow to obey."

*

The next morning Antonina woke to the sound of singing from the chapel across the inner court, assisted by the cheerful chirping of sparrows. The storm was forgotten. She lay, rested, relaxed and warm. The decision to return to New York to work spread in her a satisfying sensation of her altered self. It was invigorating and entirely new.

A rap on the door brought smiling Sister Dot, uplifted by morning Mass.

Antonina could stay in the room until later that day. With a shy movement, a buttered bagel on a napkin was put on the bedcover.

"Thank you, Sister. This gives me time to teach you the basics of the harp."

The nun showed quick learning and had long and thin fingers that helped depress several keys in fast succession. She was delighted by the sounds she produced. Harp and sister appeared to be made for each other.

Antonina explained that it was a director of a bank who had asked her for dinner at the Sheraton Palace.

"Will you go in what you're wearing? And how about shoes?"

"It's a problem. So big, that I have no option but to call and cancel. I don't really know Mr Adams."

"Nonsense. You must go. It'll be your last evening in San Francisco."

"Wearing what?"

"Perhaps I can help."

"Dress as a nun? Mr Adams is a perfect gentleman, I assure you. I don't need protection from him."

This made her laugh like an innocent child. "When we nuns take the vow, we leave our past lives behind and hand in our clothes. They are kept in storage just in case we lose our faith. You and I are about the same size."

"You don't have to do this painful thing for me. Really, I simply won't go."

The sister had already left the room. With pink flushed cheeks, she returned with clothes from the life she had left behind. Antonina got changed.

"We have no mirrors here." Dot pulled a soup spoon from her pocket. "This is our secret."

The oval reflection showed Antonina in a tulip-print dress with a cinched-in jacket from an earlier decade.

"Here are the shoes I wore with it." They were satin pumps, and they fitted. "You look just like me when I was about your age."

"I am glad I do. On my way to the airport, I'll bring them back to you, although I don't think you'll ever lose your faith."

In the bathroom, guessing the shape of her lips Antonina applied lipgloss, the only cosmetic she owned. Suddenly the bath plug chain caught her eye. *Should she?* Soaped and rubbed, the little round balls shone silver, and she wrapped them twice around her neck as a choker.

★

As she approached the Sheraton Palace, she saw in the lobby Vance Adams talking to another man who smoked. They watched her and must have thought: *Here comes Doris Day.*

Before she could greet them, she heard the younger man say, "Is that her?"

"I'm not sure," admitted Vance. "She seems completely different from the last time I saw her."

"Hello, Mr Adams," she asserted herself. "Good

evening." *Give me something large and expensive to eat right this minute, or I will scream*, seemed the wrong thing to say.

"May I introduce my brother? I was telling him about you, and he wanted to join us."

"Ah, the Lucius brother."

"Hey, you already know about me, and I haven't done anything yet!"

Lucius, considerably younger than his brother, stood with his feet apart in a linen suit which flattered him. It was easy to imagine him as a little boy. His ardent eyes scanned her with the puzzlement of a young savage. The siblings shared a rich mahogany hair colour, in Mr Adam's case cut recently short while Lucius's fringe played on his forehead foppishly.

Mr Adams asked, "Shall we?"

The men either side of her gallantly escorted her to the rotisserie room and their reserved table. Vance went to help Antonina from her jacket, holding the item for a moment with puzzlement before donating it to the seating hostess. Lucius ordered champagne.

"Groovy," said Antonina, and Lucius laughed out loud.

In a semi-formal toast after much throat-clearing, Vance explained that he had organised this supper to thank Antonina for her work for the bank.

"So, it wasn't planned as a date then," said Lucius, chuckling, and Vance stiffened in embarrassment.

The oysters, served on crushed ice, six lemony silky nothings sliding down the throat, made no impact on her undernourished condition. Vance's small-talk abilities were stunted. He felt safe talking about financial trends and figures, while Lucius with his chin in the heel of his hand gazed at Antonina with his pond-green eyes as if waiting for goodies to come from her. At that point her improvised chain-choker caught in the dress zipper. She excused herself. Both men rose and sank in their seats.

Vance turned to his brother with animation. "You're supposed to help me, help me make her out."

"You fell for her. You have to win your own battles."

"No, no, it's just she is so different from other women. Meeting her again tonight, I recognise that she and I would never work."

"Why not?"

"She is unbalanced."

"You haven't found out anything about her yet."

"I am not sure I want to any longer."

"Vance, you are thirty-six and run a bank, and I am twenty-nine, and you asked me here to fix your date. Don't be so scared of her."

Antonina returned to the table. "Just a spot of bother."

"Tell my brother where you're from, Antonina," encouraged Lucius.

"My home, Oxfordshire, England," she said and stopped talking, because she suddenly felt like a traitor to her family in mourning.

"I bet it is nice," helped Lucius. "Judging by your theatrical costume, your background must be significant in some way."

Antonina peeked at him from under her lashes. "I guess it is. We live in a Georgian mansion in a large park. There is a pond in the forecourt and a statue on the lawn. We also have a small wood." She drained her glass of white wine, and continued, "My mother has a stallion called Rasputin." Both men listened to her, Vance with a deep frown and Lucius with a mesmerised expression. Effusively she carried on. "We have a servant called Durov, who has been with us since she was seventeen and now she is about a hundred, and Uncle Sasha has just died and they buried him in his uniform in the park, and I was not able to be with them. The countess, my grandmother, is not happy that I came to America, and my twin sister is missing me."

"You have a lot of imagination," said Vance. This remark, Antonina knew, was an attempt to lessen his discomfort in her presence. She had not thought this dinner through, had only been aiming at free food. Now she felt vulnerably exposed and in a comical outfit. She excused herself again.

Lucius said to his brother, not without excitement in his voice, "She is a Russian aristocrat, White Russian. You do know that?"

"Rubbish. How could she be an aristocrat? Have you seen the necklet? Not exactly Cartier."

"I think it's a plug chain. Clever."

"Absurd."

"Vance, be honest; you are intrigued by her. If you weren't, we would not be here. Admit it. It's not to thank her for her work. And if you are not after her, hell, I sure am."

"Go ahead, my dear brother. She's all yours."

After ribeye steaks with garnish, the plates were taken away, and Lucius lifted his dessert fork and guided it along the damask table cloth. "Why do you think it is sliding so slowly?"

"Because you're pushing it slowly."

He took his bread knife and pushed it along swiftly. "Why is this knife so much faster with the same effort?"

"Enlighten me."

"Simple. The shape of a fork is unsuited to move ahead, aerodynamically. The knife owns no resistance curves, so it slices through. It's a question of resistance, volume, weight and speed."

"Should we ask the waiter perhaps for a snail clamp for your next demonstration?" asked Vance. "In case you can't guess, Antonina, Lucius is talking about sports car design."

"It is my ambition to see a fast trendy car driving in the road, one designed by me." Lucius snapped one of his braces with his thumb.

"Maybe she is not interested in cars."

"We have an old Bentley at home and its leather smells, has done from the start, and in your demonstration it would move as well as the cork coaster under that glass."

"The Bentley is a heavy car, but the British are able to build substantial cars adding a sports element to please."

"Here he goes!"

Antonina waved Vance's interruption away. "Aren't the Italians better at this with their Ferraris and Lamborghinis?"

"They are built to slice through, like the knife, but they're ostentatious with their noisy performance, and rather dangerous, actually."

"What's wrong with American cars? Let me guess," said Antonina. "They are large, to impress the eye."

"The customer gets a big metal box for his money. Sadly, he is satisfied with this. The British manufacturers try to give the customer a car to suit their personality, quite intimately with some models. In fact," and Lucius became agitated, "the factory producing some of the best sports cars in the world is the MG car company in Abingdon, which I believe is near Oxford."

"Abingdon is only twenty miles from our home!"

"Have you two finished with your cars?"

★

Back in the lobby, after the bombe Alaska Antonina had chosen for them, Vance offered to drive Antonina wherever she wished.

"I'm currently staying with the nuns in the priory," she said.

"Really?" mused Vance.

"I'll make sure she gets home," said Lucius quickly.

Vance, in a gesture borrowed from this situation rather than being a natural one of his own, threw up both arms. "I don't know what to make of anything anymore. Thank you both for coming. Do what you like."

Instead of taking a taxi Antonina and Lucius walked away from the Sheraton Palace, she linking her arm into his. The clear sky showed its stars brightly. She told him about Roxanne and the hippies, and her luck to have been taken under the wing of Elf alias Fletch. She told him about Dot, the dimpled nun.

Lucius stopped them abruptly, then pivoted her to

face him. "You think you were lucky to be picked up by the loaded Fletch, playing hippie? Your grandmother is a countess in a mansion, your home. Don't you think that's rather more lucky?"

"Living there, it does not feel like that. Anyway, we might not be able to afford it much longer."

He pulled her closer to him and circled her shoulder, shaking her amicably. "I don't want to pry or make you unhappy."

"Lucius, I was confused," she admitted. "The family has many financial problems, and I ran away to try and be a hippie, because I knew that I could not face it."

"It is important to be a hippie for a bit. In fact, it ought to be compulsory like military service or the Peace Corps."

She gave him a fond look he could not see in the dark. "I guess you too make sacrifices for the sake of your car ambitions."

"Oh sure, yeah. It's real tough having to share ownership of a whole bank with Dad and Vance."

"I see."

Moving his head forward, he pressed through his teeth. "Don't look to your left. There's a guy standing there reading the *San Francisco Oracle* which he cannot possibly see in the dark. He is checking us out."

She looked immediately and saw the man fold the newspaper and come towards them. The stranger had hooded eyes under heavy brows.

"Miss Brodsky?"

Antonina was startled. "How do you know my name?

A crease animated his face. Familiarly, he said, "I am

sorry about your great uncle. Your grandmother sends you her love."

"Who are you?" she demanded.

"A friend of the family."

"How could you have known that I am here now?" He shrugged, his chin close to one raised shoulder, which produced a triple chin. "I think you're making all this up. I don't remember you ever visiting Podzhin Hall. Few people do."

"You haven't been home for five months. They miss you. I expect I'll bump into you again. So long." He walked away.

"You are shaking," said Lucius.

"That was scary. I honestly have no idea who that is. Can we just forget about it?"

"Let me get us a cab. I'll show you the place in Golden Gate Park where the human *be-in* took place in January – over twenty thousand joined in."

They got out at the entrance to the Music Concourse. He draped his trenchcoat over her shoulders. At the rounded stone rim of the Rideout Fountain they sat down close to each other. Behind them a stone-cast sabre-toothed tiger fought with a snake.

"One day, these sit-ins will be written about in history books," he said. "Counterculture. Trying to reach higher consciousness with the aid of psychedelic drugs. The questioning of authority."

"Undermining banks," she contributed, as she had initiated that abolishment cry.

"Banks? No, never. Money was invented over beads and will never be questioned again."

"I love you." Her spontaneity surprised her. "You make things so clear to me, so obviously right. My family has always befuddled my thinking. Never a compromise; extremist, either black or white. It can drive you to frenzy or fatalism."

"You seem clear-headed, balanced and strong." He nodded his head. "And beautiful."

★

A taxi brought them back to the Sheraton Palace which they had left only a few hours before. The clerk at reception handed Lucius the key to a de-luxe room on the simple guarantee of his signature. It was close to midnight.

As an afterthought, he ordered a pot of Earl Grey.

By the time the trolley was rolled into the room Antonina was showered and in a hotel dressing gown.

"Luxury is heaven," she exclaimed, drying her hair in a downy towel. She pulled the belt on the dressing gown tight and sat down on the bed. "How is it possible to ride a horse in a suit of armour?" she asked, gazing at a reproduction of van Dyck's equestrian portrait of Charles I on the wall.

Lucius paced in front of her snapping his braces and did not let her distract attention from what was happening between them. "You must feel uncomfortable in this bedroom with a man who is a stranger to you. I hope you don't find me too fresh. I can do trustworthy and chivalrous, like that Charles guy on his horse."

She giggled girlishly.

"What am I to make of that?"

She laughed harder.

"From the moment you bowled up in that fifties costume, your chin theatrically pointed up, the bath-chain effort, I was smitten. You are gorgeous, Antonina: intelligent, fun and serious – all in one."

He came to sit on the soft bed and with care unwrapped the towel wound around her head. When the wet strands were free, he gently stroked them back over her head and slowly brought his face to hers, so tentatively she could have stopped it. She seemed poised as if unable to move and closed her eyes. He leaned in and kissed her on the tip of her nose. Her eyes opened, softened and smiled into his. She was ready.

Their lips met and instantly explored with passion what a man and a woman have for each other. Unleashing their mutual attraction, they almost fought to own one another, tumbling and rolling.

Afterwards, their bodies still heaving, their urges satisfied, she lay underneath him, and tears rolled out of the corner of her eyes.

"You are amazing," he said to her. "There is no need to cry."

★

In the morning Antonina awoke with a start, staring for a moment at the hotel décor, at the reproduction of Charles I on horseback, and then at the naked man next to her who feigned to still sleep but actually was alert to each of her movements. She plunged right back into the indulgence of his warm body in that luscious bed.

They ate breakfast sitting upright in the bed. She wiggled her ankles. He heaped strawberry jam onto his bagel. "I can't let you go to New York; I am far too comfortable with you."

"I have promised myself to find a job, one that matters to others and contributes to mankind somehow."

"That's hard for me to beat. All I can offer is you move in with me, but I share with a buddy, and it is a bachelor pad."

"I'll still be in the States. We might organise to meet somewhere again…" Her voice trailed off.

"Long-distance love affairs are pretty tough. They often fall apart despite best efforts."

"Sadly, probably so. But it is important that you know how I feel about you, despite my leaving. I love you, Lucius."

"Yes." He put half a bagel down onto the plate and pushed the tray from him. "And I hope you know how I feel about you, Antonina."

By the time they had to check out because it said so on a notice on the door, he had booked her a seat on Pan Am leaving later in the afternoon.

He grabbed his watch from the side table and concentrated, strapping it on his wrist. "You're still in your bathrobe."

"I need you to do me a favour and return the dress and shoes to Sister Dot at St Sophronia's."

"You serious?" He laughed shortly. "But you have nothing to wear. They won't let you on the plane."

"Yeah, this is my problem."

"You see that warrior Charles on his nag. He is rubbish. I shall be your knight in shining armour. Let's hit the boutiques in the lobby. Vance will get the bill. He won't even notice."

"Emergency shopping," explained Lucius to the surprised salesgirl in heavy make-up and high heels, who contemplated Antonina in her bathrobe.

"These glittery boutiques are too expensive for me," whispered Antonina.

"Never mind," he urged. "They are clothes and they cover you. No time to fuss either. I still want time to have a long lunch with you before the airport. Brassière, panties," he enumerated. She chose quickly.

"Stockings."

"No." She waved that away.

"Dress, or two bits?"

"Dress, easier," she said.

"Here's a cute one."

She picked up the price tag. "I can't."

"Yes, you can. Jacket over it? How about this one?"

"It does not go with…"

"Now it does. Handbag?"

"Handbag! The word sounds so funny."

"No, it doesn't. That one."

"It is a Hermès."

"So? Scarf?"

"This one has a beautiful design but is very expensive."

"Sold. That's the way men like to shop."

He did not interfere in her buying cosmetics. While she chose the essentials, he explained that nothing needed to be wrapped.

351

Antonina appeared out of a changing room, transformed. Lucius grinned happily. "You look like a million dollars, kid." She had no idea how much it had cost the CA Trust Bank.

They took a ferry across the Bay to Sausalito and she was glad for the scarf keeping the hair out of her face. The table in the waterfront restaurant overlooked fishing boats and all the paraphernalia that goes with catching sea creatures and bringing them ashore for men's consumption.

Antonina leant forward. "Lucius, this all went rather fast for me. Should we call our, er, love-making just a fling?"

He lowered the wine-list to see her face. "It's up to us, wouldn't you say? For my part, I don't feel as I normally do with a girl. Right now, I don't know what I feel, exactly. Do you think it could just have been a one-night stand?"

"No. I feel as if I have known you for ages, funny sort of cosy, a bit like wanting to snuggle up somewhere and close my eyes. You seem to be the one for whom I came to California. Sorry I make no sense."

"Let's order a bottle of Santa Clara County wine. Perhaps that will help us express ourselves more clearly."

"There is still the airport at five o clock."

"It's not three o'clock yet." Lucius ordered crab for both of them.

Fishermen lobbed around icechip-filled crates with twitching silver fish and crabs waving their legs in slow motion. It smelled strongly of sea.

"The poor things," she lamented as she saw the bluish crabs being tumbled from a tray into broiling bubbly water to die, scalded and turned red. "Please tell me that they are completely insensitive creatures."

He said nothing.

"You can't do that to me. Tell me they feel no pain."

"Let's put it this way," he said, "if I were one of those crabs, I would love to be sacrificed to be eaten by you."

"Stupid crabs, then. I feel better now."

She then told him that those last fifteen hours spent with him had been the loveliest in all her life. And he raised his glass to his brother, Vance, who had brought them together. She told him about her sensitive twin sister and things they had done together and how complex and guilt-riddled her tie was with Anna, while they both made a mess using crab-claw crackers.

The shadow behind the menu stand lengthened. Time could not be made to stop. They held hands over coffee, relishing their heartbeats passing from one to the other. Their eyes held fast, expressing so many things which there was no time to formulate. Their joined pulses told them how much they desired each other. They knew this moment would soon pass into memory. It hurt in advance.

★

"Goodbye," she said to him at the airport. "And thank you for everything." There were tears on her cheeks, tears running down her face. Her throat was tight and her heart thudded noisily under her ribs. They were past kissing. It would have been too painful knowing that it was their last time. The perfect had to be revered.

353

They had not exchanged addresses for further contact. Neither had a fixed abode right now. Lucius lived with a friend and she did not know when she would be back in England.

The flight was called again.

"For you. I got it while you were dressing in the shop." It was a small wrapped present. "I hope this will remind you of me. I love you," he added – and it was the first time he had said it – turned on his heels and started to walk away from her. The last she saw of him was his tweed jacket flapping as he walked briskly, his hair whipping, shining old copper in the airport neon.

"Lucius," she sobbed.

Once off the ground she clutched the courtesy rug closely around her. Down below was San Francisco and the autoharp she had had to give away. Down below was a man with whom she had spent few but magic hours, a man she would always love and never see again. Later, when the plane had taken on its constant purring noise and drinks were served, she tugged at the silk ribbon and the bow unwound. Unfolding the wrapping paper she revealed a small square black box. Slowly she opened it and her eyes grew wide. *Cartier* was embossed in silver in the lid. On a mound of velvet padding was pinned a jewelled flower, the leaves of mesh gold and the centre a cluster of cut diamonds. A tiny card was stuck behind it: *To flower power.*

"Classy," she said and pinned the brooch on her dress, closed her eyes and started dreaming of him with the luxury of seven undisturbed hours ahead.

CHAPTER
THIRTY-FOUR

Vasily sat in the canteen and poked at a potato with his fork. He checked his watch, then tilted back, rocking on the hind legs of his chair. "What time does the Moscow plane get in tonight?" he asked the cypher clerk, the only other man left in the canteen.

"An hour ago."

An hour ago Turchin had landed at Heathrow and Vasily had been waiting for three days to talk to him.

The receptionist downstairs confirmed that the counsellor was on his way to the embassy. On the half-landing, controlling the staircase, Vasily sat down on a cracked leather chair under Brezhnev's portrait.

The embassy was quiet; the security night-shift was in charge. Turchin would report in immediately on his return, as was the rule. Vasily checked his watch again; it seemed to have slowed down these last days while Turchin was enjoying the celebrations in Moscow. Like a spool of red yarn, the years ran back through the pattern of parades. Eyes closed, Vasily could see, feel, smell even the rejuvenating, reassuring occasions of mass displays. Columns of war machines advancing in rows of four drew impressive caterpillar and rubber patterns on the Red Square cobbles, and disciplined troops saluted, their heads locked to the rostrum from which motionless officials stared at the procession of power. Vasily remembered the peculiar hush over a red-flag-dressed Moscow, where the only noises were the growling engines kept in low gear and the rhythmical tramping of boots. What he had liked most were the women warriors dressed in severe uniforms, their hair twisted into tight buns.

Valentina had thrown her hairpins to the wind to let an avalanche of fragrant hair fall over his hands imprisoned in hers.

The telephone on the reception desk rang, a strident screeching bell. Through the staircase railings Vasily saw the receptionist reach out to answer. He spoke slowly, using trained English, then after listening for a while hung up. Vasily re-crossed his legs. He noticed two prints further along the wall. Standing up to investigate, he recognised them as wood-block prints of collective farm scenes.

He heard nothing but a faint scratching. He imagined the receptionist writing slowly and legibly the message the caller had left.

"… and the delay was minimal really." The door, opening brusquely into the lulled silence, brought Turchin's voice. A suitcase was carried in by the embassy driver.

Vasily stood up slowly and started to descend the stairs. "How was Moscow?"

Turchin put down his shoulder bag and took off his coat. "Tereshkova, the first woman to orbit the earth –

and forty-eight times! – marched before the triumphant Vostok 6 spaceship."

Vasily took the coat from the counsellor.

"Oh, and the Military Committee displayed the whole of the new fleet of anti-aircraft missiles: a twenty-minute parade, marvellous!"

"Will you need access to the Referentura tonight?" asked the receptionist, standing at his desk.

Turchin checked Vasily's face. "You stayed in to talk?"

Vasily nodded.

Turchin nodded.

The receptionist picked up the telephone to warn the security guard.

"So, Moscow looked good," said Vasily dreamily, walking up the stairs behind Turchin.

"At its best. A sunny autumn day."

The guard opened the Referentura for them. He checked the contents of Turchin's gift bag, then filled in the form: *Permit to enter Referentura after closing time. Reason for request: information from Moscow.*

The two men went into the safe speech room and switched on the neon tube.

"I've been waiting to talk to you about the Brodskys."

Turchin lifted an ornate gift box from his bag: *October Revolution 50 years.* "Special Party gift. I believe it is Tatar pepper vodka."

"I must tell you how excruciating it was." There was a desperate ring to Vasily's voice.

"What happened?"

Suddenly Vasily realised that his eagerness to confide in his counsellor came from guilt; he knew he could not tell Turchin about Valentina now. Had he lapsed, weakened by living in a degenerate society? He had to force himself back onto the old track. The smell of Moscow on Turchin helped.

"Damn them," he said involuntarily.

"Tell me."

Hesitant at first, Vasily told Turchin about the two days in Podzhin Hall, ending the debriefing almost with vehemence.

"Comrade Voronov, do not forget this is a Soviet routine you are well acquainted with. Moral evaluations will distort your analysis."

Vasily nodded.

"Exposed here in the West, our ideology appears to be misinterpreted. You are used to being part of a collective *we*, but here you are an unprotected *me*."

Vasily lowered his eyes.

"You would like to be sent back to Moscow?"

"Yes, I would."

Turchin smiled. "Georgi picked you personally. You are his golden boy. I did not know to what degree you were a special case."

Vasily frowned. "But I've only met him once."

"What I learned from the Controller and Georgi is extraordinary. You see, I was as impatient to talk to you as you were to me. Georgi has earmarked you for a great task. Of KGB agents amongst the Soviet emigration there are many. It is on descendants of the old Imperial families we now want to concentrate. Their superstition that Czarist Russia was something magical, destroyed by the Soviet, has to be eradicated. Only individual cultivation can achieve this. That involves stooping to their level, which you find so difficult."

"I see no effective way to approach them, let alone infiltrate their political thinking."

"The old lady had a point when she listed their characteristics as eccentricity, vanity and a kind of patriotism."

"They see a warped Soviet Union."

"Yes, but they keep thinking about it, about Russia. Plant the seeds in there."

"All I have come across is eccentricity and vanity."

"Comrade Voronov, try to forget that they are enemies when you deal with them."

Vasily shook his head wearily. "I have no idea where the Ikon could be."

"It might well be with Antonina in the United States. There is a possibility of her working for the Americans. We must gain influence over the family before it is too late. Antonina is a Brodsky before she is anything else."

All was quiet around them; even the telex noises had ceased, leaving only the noise of the air-conditioner. "I don't know whether I have the courage or the necessary preparation."

"You do. Those Brodsky attitudes and opinions are not immutable."

"I am afraid too much time in the decadent West has solidified them."

"Time for us is measured by progress. If ever time was well invested, it was in making you a Party member."

Vasily looked quizzically at Turchin.

"The Controller disclosed your past to me. I am authorised to tell you about it. Your father..." he paused, and Vasily, instantly alarmed, thought of Father's hidden box in the roof-space, "... your father was of aristocratic stock."

Vasily did not react.

"The man who fathered you forty years ago belonged to the Imperial family Romanov. His name was Kavinsky, a so-called baron."

Vasily repeated *Kavinsky* for the second time that week. Then he panicked. "My father is an old peasant in Obodovka. My mother was born there. How can there be any aristocratic connection? I want to be sent back to Moscow as soon as possible!"

"Not to panic, not to worry, Comrade – to consider and assimilate. You are living proof of what can be achieved with time. Now you can use this knowledge in your work against the Brodskys. A heavy burden has been laid on your shoulders: Moscow trusts you."

Vasily was too stunned to comprehend fully what the counsellor was saying. His father could not be an aristocrat; Moscow was wrong. Thinking back, there was no consolidated memory but fragments: Father's bouts of revolt against injustice, Mother's steaming cooking pots. Vasily grew up fearing his father's temper excesses and admiring his mother's devoted loyalty to a man she had picked out of the snow. She had always believed that Father would eventually open up and explain about himself. *Secrets*, yes, Vasily remembered the constant guarding of secrets, but an aristocrat – impossible!

Mother had died of pneumonia one winter without ever learning more. When the snow hardened on her grave-mound, the dog stood in the yard and yelped, muddle-headed and square-furry-pawed, as if he could call back the touch of her warm hand on his head. He couldn't. Father became even more hermetical and secretive. Vasily joined Komsomol in Moscow. The dog started to bite and was put down. Spring came. Yugina's grave was levelled into tender green.

Turchin opened the special vodka bottle, filled both glasses and started to talk.

★

In late 1917 the glittering aristocracy of St Petersburg met at a party given by the Princess Cherkanicha in the Winter Palace. The princess had chosen the Nicholas II room on the first floor for this event, because a large part of the palace housed the provisional Kerensky Government. Those who received the hand-delivered invitations had been chosen from the nobility, many of them *Knyaz*, princes of the illustrious lineage of the Romanovs. People only recently entitled by royal favour had not been included. The Czar and the Empress, exiled to Tsarskoye Selo, had declined with regrets.

It was a grey evening when the guests arrived by *droshky* at the main gate of the baroque palace near the Neva. For receptions the palace would usually have been all ablaze; now however light shone only from the first floor windows. Caped ladies were helped from their coaches by lackeys and hurried to the door.

Inside, the princess had spared no trouble. Along the staircases and at every door were posted troopers of the Cavalier Guards gleaming with silver and gold, and cossack Life Guards in red and blue uniforms. Palm trees and exotic Crimean plants sent from the greenhouses of Tsarskoye Selo belied the weather outside.

Olga was relieved of her cape and cupped her curl. Ivan took her arm. She shook out the folds of her hydrangea blue taffeta dress, gathered at the waist to build up to a balcony décolleté. Her husband wore his best dress-coat and white gaiters drawn deep over his lacquered shoes buttoned by mother-of-pearl drops. His moustache was waxed; his smile practised.

The hostess rustled forward in an ivory-coloured silk dress, the famous champagne diamond she had been given by Czarita Maria nestling in the little hollow of her cleavage. Ivan bent low over her hand.

"*Quelle magnifique occasion.*"

Olga and Ivan entered the vast reception room. It was in this room that Nicholas II, soon after his accession, had delivered an address rejecting the senselessness of those who wanted to limit the autocracy. Massive Corinthian columns ran along the inside walls and a row of chandeliers hung from the ceiling. The pearls gleamed creamy on the slender neck of Olga as she joined the guests. An atmosphere of feverish mania hovered, a desperate glittering attempt to deny the uncertainty lurking outside the palace in the grey of St Petersburg. Under the tapestry an orchestra played and candles toyed with the stucco reliefs on the ornate ceiling. Pale servants in white gloves stood in a row against the wall. Others served champagne in hand-blown flute glasses.

Politics were not mentioned, for if one of them had brought up the subject, the delicate structure of pretence could have turned to farce. On a gilded chair rested Gräfin von Holstein. She wore her three necklaces one over the other on powdered sagging skin, a desperate attempt to rally all there was left of the social life of Imperial and aristocratic Russia close to her bosom.

Baron Dimitri Kavinsky tall and poised walked in, his pumps clacking on the highly polished parquet. "You look mesmerising, my dear," he said to Olga and kissed her hand, glancing sideways at Ivan.

Then, fixing Olga with loving smouldering eyes, he led her to one of the bow-sashed central windows. Out there in the crystal cold night, the wide Neva seemed to have stopped flowing. Olga turned her back to it. "You must come and stay with us at Easter in the summer house. I can hardly wait for the trees to blossom," she said with frustrated passion.

"My dearest Olga, spring is far off, but of course it would be a great pleasure. How is your little daughter?"

Olga's malachite eyes fastened on his. "She is a pretty little baroness. Her eyes are turning more mysterious, and she has a temper."

"I want to buy her a Lipizzaner."

"She is only three."

"Well yes, perhaps next year."

"Perhaps next year." Her hand reached out to touch his wrist which she pressed hard.

"Help us all," muttered Olga, as she saw Irina Potresov heading straight towards them. "She is wearing white satin – and that hairdo: it is like a chicken fighting its way out of a pile of straw."

"Olga," Irina panted, tight in her corset, "everybody who is anybody is here. Oh!" With a shrill little shriek she twirled her hand in the air. "Good. My husband could make it. He is such a busy man."

Olga made meaningful eye contact with Dimitri Kavinsky.

Irina's husband, the gaunt lank dandy walking disdainfully towards them, lifted his gold monocle on a chain to his left eye to peer at Olga and Dimitri. No doubt that was how he inspected the horses on which he put his money and Irina's jewellery, for she wore glass copies.

Gräfin von Holstein using a walking stick slowly progressed towards them as well. "The last time we were all here was New Year's celebration. The guns booming in salute to 1917 from the Fortress of St Peter and Paul. I hope my bad chest will not prevent me from attending this year."

"You seem in excellent form," Dimitri complimented the ancient woman.

"At my age, winter becomes an enemy."

"Spring and flowers inevitably will come," said Olga with a ring of hardness. Her private time with Dimitri was over. It was a social occasion, and she had to conform.

The hostess passed them in a sweet powdery cloud of expensive perfume, the hem of her dress sweeping the carpet.

"The fashion is for evening dresses to stop at ankle height," Irina commented.

"Is that what your seamstress told you, when she was fixing the beige bow to your white dress?"

The hostess's progress was interrupted by Baroness Aksakova. "I hear that your beautiful Sophia will be introduced to the court next season."

"May that be so!"

Aksakova took on a significant air and continued in a lowered voice, her head forward and down, "Surely you must know that the Potresovs are taboo on the social list, and yet I find Irina here at your party."

"Excuse me," smiled the hostess sweetly. "Prince Zupov has just arrived."

"Prince Zupov!" Aksakova exclaimed in pleased surprise. Conversation stopped around them as a creaking wicker wheelchair was pushed into the room. The old prince sat slightly askew with a sable fur on his knees. One translucent hand lay on the fur; the other was raised in general greeting. A dry cough rocked his chest.

"Prince Zupov, *quelle belle surprise!*" Gräfin von Holstein bent and embraced him.

Dimitri commented, "He's been completely out of circulation for years."

Baroness Aksakova joined the group at the window, and Irina's husband let his monocle drop out of his eye socket and walked away leaving the three women with Dimitri.

"I remember he attended the famous Rimsky-Korsakov opera. We were in Riga at the time, unfortunately," said the baroness. "But of course we read all about it in the papers."

"Masini made history that night," commented Dimitri.

"Indeed," added Olga. "He got bored playing the dying tenor sprawled on the planks and walked off stage while the soprano was singing her lungs out. Eventually he returned and lay down in the same spot again, as if nothing had happened."

Irina laughed like a goat.

"He did have a twinkle in his eyes, you know – Masini." Olga glanced furtively at Dimitri.

The servants padding between them refilled their glasses.

"I wonder how she managed to organise it all."

"There is Sasha!" exclaimed Olga.

Sasha had come in through the gilded doors. He wore the bedizened uniform of the court, all epaulettes and braid. His legs were in stockings and his feet in pumps. His eyes took in the sparkling room and the guests. The sight seemed to wash through him and propel him in elegant steps towards his hostess.

"*Quel plaisir!* Just what we all needed." He walked over to the little group around his sister-in-law Olga and inclined towards Dimitri. "How is the poetry these days?"

Dimitri smiled enigmatically. "Some poets thrive only during times of turmoil."

"In which case, I hope your inspiration turns barren." Sasha exchanged his empty glass for a fresh one and raised it. "May this elixir quench our worries!"

"And may the only upsets be caused by bubbles of Moët et Chandon," added Olga.

"Bravo!" exclaimed the baroness.

Ivan came and drew Sasha away from the group,

leaving Olga with Dimitri, Aksakova and Irina. "I want you to greet old Prince Zupov. It might be the last time."

As the brothers crossed the room, a guest tugged Ivan's sleeve. "Tell us dear Vanya, is it true that there is a threat to the Imperial Bank?"

"Hush," said Ivan. "No talk of finance tonight." He raised his glass to his eyes to hide them.

The brothers moved to the old prince.

"My dear Duke," croaked the old man. Ivan was only a count, but his father was the ailing Duke Mikhail. "How is the Imperial Bank? I must come and see you there. We used to talk banking in the past so amiably."

"Sorry, Your Highness, you refer to my father."

"Oh yes, the passage of time confuses me."

"Ivan has been director of the Imperial Bank for nearly nine years," explained Sasha.

"Nine years, my dear, is nothing, a mere flicker."

Ivan offered the old prince a cigar from his silver case. Olga heard Sasha laugh.

The party was a success so far. Encouraged, the hostess pushed a lank girl ahead of her. "May I introduce my daughter?" Sophia blushed slightly under Dimitri's gaze.

"Soon it will be a hard choice between your beauty and your daughter's," he said. The girl blushed more.

"Charmingly put, dear Dimitri, but unnecessary flattery."

"It's never too late," said Gräfin von Holstein. "Did you hear that Countess Kubenskaya is wooed by Fokine, the dancing star of the Maryinsky Theatre?"

"Surely not! She's over forty."

"It is past forty that a woman truly blooms."

Olga smiled archly. "I did not know you liked autumn flowers."

The doors were slowly closed. "Everyone could come," whispered the hostess, "with one regrettable exception – Czar Nikolai and Alexandra Feodorovna." The musicians played a tune from Glinka's last opera. The window panes were steamed over, turning a blind eye to the events outside.

★

While Dimitri Kavinsky was at the Winter Palace, the doorbell rang at his fifth floor apartment on the Nevsky Prospekt. It was opened by Piotr, the baron's manservant. For a second the servant was suspicious, then he recognised the man wrapped in fur.

"Welcome to Petersburg." He opened the door wide to his master's longest and dearest poet friend, Yevgeni.

"O'er Russia a storm is prowling. Like a beast I hear it howling."

Piotr helped him unwrap.

"Tell me Piotr, where is Dimitri?"

"Sir, he expected you two days ago."

"The train from Moscow was delayed several times."

The servant showed Yevgeni into the salon. "The baron is at the Winter Palace but his brother, Stefan, has a cold and is just next door. Let me fetch him," he suggested.

"Do that, dear Piotr. I need company. All I've seen

for days are humans in barbaric uniforms, smelling like unwashed bears and talking nonsense." Yevgeni walked to a crystal decanter and poured himself a drink.

A few moments later Piotr returned with Stefan who hugged the visitor warmly, and they settled down.

"Since Dimitri does not consider my visit important enough to be at home, I shall show you what I have written this summer."

★

In the Nicholas II room, the hostess announced dinner. The double doors were opened. Each servant took charge of a lady and led her to her assigned chair, her husband to her left. Olga was seated diagonally opposite Dimitri. She smiled at him and he returned the smile. The taffeta of her dress played light and shade, her hair had a chestnut lustre and her remarkable eyes were wide, the pupils enlarged in the candlelight. The table between them was laden not so much with crockery and cutlery as with jewellery. The ornate gold candlesticks had belonged to Catherine the Great. The solid silver knives indented the lace tablecloth. Entwined violets lay, wound around Fabergé eggs and ornate animals of semi-precious stone.

"*Splendide, ma chère,*" Ivan complimented his hostess.

The music played softly as heavy tureens were carried in on upturned hands.

"To the Czar Nikolai!" exclaimed Sasha, half-rising and lifting his champagne flute, wishing it contained vodka to make him drunk faster.

"To our Czar and his family in Tsarskoye Selo!" Their glasses rose; their eyes glittered with tears.

"What a shame they could not be among us tonight. Other engagements, well…" The hostess's voice faltered. "May he and his wife and children be blessed."

The servants refilled the glasses. The yet-untouched soup steamed in Limoges bowls of delicate porcelain.

"Play a mazurka," instructed the hostess to the musicians who had followed them into the dining room. The music began, poignant and haunting to those at the table whose thoughts were with the Czar. The servants stood immobile against the walls, eyes bright with unshed tears.

★

Bearing terrible news, Piotr bluffed his way into the Winter Palace and ran up the Jordan Staircase to the carpeted corridor of the Neva Enfilade. After a whispered exchange with the cossack at the door, he pushed it open a crack and slipped inside.

The guests were on the main course of game delicacies which the hostess had miraculously obtained. Voices were raised and a hysterical gaiety lay over them.

"… and the cossack said, *not without my horse!*"

Laughter filled the table. Piotr worked his way along the chairbacks to his master, bent and whispered into Dimitri's ear. The baron paled.

He slowly rose, lifting his glass. The laughter still echoed from all sides. The noise dimmed and faces turned to Dimitri. In a choked voice he recited:

> *"And high above him, all undaunted*
> *By foaming stream and flooded shores,*
> *Deaf to the storm's rebellious roars,*
> *With hand outstretched*
> *The Idol mounted on steed of bronze*
> *Majestic soars."*

They all recognised the words of Pushkin.

"Long live the Czar! Long live the Empire!" Dimitri's voice was drowned in emotion. Olga sat in her chair as rigid as a portrait frozen for posterity. He gave her a long deep look conveying both love and despair, then he threw his glass against the columned wall behind him. The crystal crashed with the sound of a bell. Without a further glance he left the room, Piotr at his heel. As the door closed behind them, a tumult rose and many glasses followed Dimitri's to the wall.

★

Piotr led his master through the Rotunda, down the unlit corridor to the back stairs emerging on Palace Square. The muffled noise of gunfire came from all directions. Piotr draped his coat over Dimitri's shoulders, less to protect him from the cold than to conceal his finery. Raindrops with the falling night temperature had solidified into ice. The two men kept against the walls running along the barricaded Nevsky Prospekt. They crept up to the baron's apartment block. The cold blinded Dimitri's eyes; the champagne hummed in his head. The nearby streets were alive with hooves, clatter and uproar. Dimitri remembered the Bloody Sunday of 1905 of which the main battles had also taken place here – the year Grand-Duke Yerivanski had been executed.

Earlier all had seemed calm, but violent skirmishes could erupt at any time since the garrison had joined the insurgents. For two years the situation in Russia had steadily ripened and now began to ferment. Political winds fanned over the rotting ground, sweeping through the fences of the establishment, carrying the putrefaction with them. On the borders the army stood against the German enemy. Inside the country, discontent brewed. Fear and desperation clashed and merged in more violence, and it seemed a conflagration was imminent: a revolution that could not be quenched for it had gone too far and carried too many with it.

Dimitri understood the bourgeoisie had supported the Czar too blindly, too long. Hoarse invective came from many street corners. Jews were driven from their homes. Dispossessed and bewildered, they fled west and east from the chaos. Students joined the workers. All were brothers, comrades, but each distrusted the other. The police force drafted peasants from remote villages, struggling to regain some measure of order. The nobles were arrested, their silver and wealth distributed amongst the mob.

"Piotr, slow down. I can't run fast in these dress shoes. Tell me what has happened." Dimitri stopped.

"Armed men have broken into the apartment. Master Yevgeni is there."

"Yevgeni!"

"And I had fetched your brother, Stefan, to keep Mr Yevgeni company," added Piotr.

"My God. Are the thugs reds or whites, do you know?"

"I don't know, sir."

"Bolsheviks, most likely," whispered Dimitri in despair and took off his shoes, threw them from him and took up running fast again.

They turned into the courtyard. The silhouette of the watchman stood under the archway at the main entrance from the Prospekt on which the shadow of a demonstration could be seen in torchlight disorder. Banners fluttered like licking flames. Some demonstrators spilled towards the archway. The watchman spread his arms to defend the building. Shadows mingled into a confused, distorted pack. It fell apart. The watchman lay on the ground.

Dimitri followed Piotr through a door leading up the servants' stairs.

Is the flat already ransacked? wondered Dimitri. He was the treasurer of the Romanov jewellery. It would all be stolen from the banks, the palaces and apartments, tossed from hand to hand until it fell in the gutters with the blood of men.

In the safe in Dimitri's flat was the Ikon of the Virgin of Kazan, normally kept at St Petersburg's Kazan Cathedral. A ruby had been lost from the halo. In strictest confidence Dimitri had asked Fabergé to replace it. What if the intruders had got possession of it? And what had they done to his brother and friend?

In the fifteen years Dimitri had lived in this house, he had never used these stairs. On the fifth floor he felt completely lost. A narrow corridor ran along the inside of the building. Washing lines were strung.

Piotr opened a door. Dimitri found himself in a utility room. Stacked in the corner were the wooden crates from the move back from the summer house, their lids off and the crowbar lying on top. Now Dimitri stood helpless in part of his own apartment. Gently but firmly Piotr pushed him into a storage cupboard. "You stay safe, and I will go and find out."

★

"For the last time, Baron Dimitri Kavinsky, sign this statement confessing that you are an enemy of the people." The former soldier, in a torn uniform, reading from a list of names, pushed the form in front of Yevgeni.

The poet did not deny being Dimitri, nor did Stefan correct the mistaken identity. On the coffee table in front of them lay the manuscript of poems Yevgeni had been reading to Stefan not long before.

"Sign!"

Yevgeni's manuscript was pushed to the side. Slowly, the poet removed his famous gold pen from his jacket pocket and held it poised.

Stefan prayed that Piotr would not blunder in with Dimitri now. A window pane crashed in a nearby apartment. One of the revolutionaries stuffed a marron glacé into his mouth.

"Sign, both of you, or I shoot." A pistol pointed at them.

"Phew!" The man spat the chewed chestnut onto the carpet. The other cocked the pistol. From the Prospekt rose voices shouting the Lenin slogan: *Teper' ili*

Nikogda, Now or Never. It sounded like an approaching storm.

A thin young bolshevik thrust himself into the salon. A scar, the shape of a sickle, disfigured his chin.

"The pigs won't sign," complained the revolutionary holding the pistol.

"You are traitors to your country," said the scarred man sharply and distinctly.

Yevgeni looked up calmly into the ugly face of a man younger than he was. "I ask you to leave my property."

Fear grew behind Stefan's eyes as Yevgeni took the denunciation and tore it up. He dropped the shreds casually over the coffee table rim.

The armed man advanced one step closer. A scream was heard from the road. Another window shattered.

Piotr appeared at the door of the kitchen quarters.

"Please leave us alone; we have work to do." Yevgeni reached for his manuscript and started to read.

The scarred bolshevik turned to Piotr. "Are these your masters, Baron Dimitri Kavinsky, and his brother Baron Stefan Kavinsky?"

Piotr stood frozen. Yevgeni turned his eyes towards Piotr and smiled at him.

Piotr hesitated.

Yevgeni closed his eyelids once slowly.

"Yes," stammered Piotr.

"Shoot them!" shouted the bolshevik. Stefan jumped up, but Yevgeni restrained him.

"Shoot these pigs now!"

"Long live the Empire!" Yevgeni's voice was strong. Sparks leapt from the barrel. Yevgeni fell sideways and

Stefan caught him in his arms. A second shot exploded. Stefan's body jerked. A red stain grew on his white shirt.

★

From the cupboard in the utility room Dimitri heard the two shots. He could hardly breathe from dread. Trampling steps came up the servants' stairs. He heard the back door smash open. Through the keyhole he saw a policeman in the city uniform, a sabre at his flank. Loyalist or red, Dimitri could not take the chance. He sprang out, casting Piotr's coat over the man's head. In surprise the policeman struggled but Dimitri hit him with the crowbar. Dimitri's hands groped for the sabre. Pulling it from the scabbard, he raised it and jabbed it into the policeman's neck. Like a string doll the policeman tumbled and fell. He moved no more.

There was the rumble of more footsteps in the servants' staircase. Tearing at the corpse's arms, Dimitri pulled it into the cupboard and ran out again to fetch the fur toque with a ribboned badge. In the dark of the cupboard he undressed the warm body with difficulty, as the man was limp and heavy. When finally Dimitri had squeezed himself into the coarse uniform and the utility room was silent, he stepped over the body and emerged. With twitching fingers he put the cap on his head. Thus attired, he entered his own salon and his heart seemed to stop with shock.

The lifeless body of Yevgeni was being dragged by the feet through the room. Stefan had already been taken away; the smeared blood showed how. Piotr stood against the wall, his eyes bulging, the muzzle of a pistol under his nose. Yevgeni's corpse with inert arms was pulled along the Persian carpet, the gold pen clasped in his dead hand.

"Imperial swine," snorted the bolshevik with the scar. "We're going to feed them to the masses."

Dimitri managed to nod. One of the revolutionaries started to smash up furniture with the butt of his rifle. A framed photograph of Olga crashed to the floor. She smiled at Dimitri through crushed glass. Dimitri picked up Yevgeni's manuscript.

"Sentimental shit," said the bolshevik.

Dimitri threw it onto the carpet and trampled on it with his policeman's boots.

"Fancy rot," said another, kicking over a lamp. "Stolen, all stolen from the people."

With a swing of his elbow Dimitri knocked the fern plant from its stand.

"Let's go. The others will take care of that stuff."

Right in front of Dimitri was his desk. His own poems, letters and pressed flowers from Olga were at a finger's touch. He did not dare.

"What shall we do with this one?" asked the one guarding Piotr.

"Beat him up."

"With pleasure," said Dimitri, approaching the shaking Piotr. "I'll teach you to serve the imperialists." Dimitri closed his eyes and punched Piotr in the face with his fist. His servant fell to the ground, more from the shock than the impact.

The bolshevik watched with a smirk.

In Dimitri's fist had been the key to the safe. After the blow, he let it drop into Piotr's lap. Piotr's demented stare was on the baron, his master. Slowly, he reached to his lap and cupped the key.

"How many imperialists have you served, eh?" shouted Dimitri into Piotr's face. "Three, five, seven?" Dimitri willed Piotr to understand the combination number of the safe. The bolshevik turned to go, the noises from the Prospekt sounding much more enticing.

"For my love, all that is in there," Dimitri shouted in Piotr's direction from the door. "In a new clean Russia."

Piotr closed his eyes slowly once to acknowledge the message.

Dimitri left his apartment and followed the bolshevik.

A mob had gathered around the two dead bodies dragged from the house and thrown carelessly onto the wet road.

I must not weep; I must not weep, Dimitri kept saying to himself.

The Nevsky Prospekt was unrecognisable in the dancing torchlight. Armoured vehicles stood at its entrance, guns pointed downwards. Furniture was thrown from a window of the Stroganovs' mansion. Here and there bodies lay like dark Russian loaves.

Shouting "Now or never", the ringleaders dragged his brother and friend by their feet across the snow-toasted road to hang them over the railing of the bridge for all to see. The gold pen was jolted loose from Yevgeni's hand as it stiffened in death and quickly Dimitri bent to pick it up. In the chaos and dark tumult he stole away.

He emerged not far from the Winter Palace and pressed on along the Neva, past the bronze horseman. Gigantic sobs were wedged in his chest and Dimitri knew they would be frozen there forever.

CHAPTER
THIRTY-FIVE

"Dinner is on zr table!" called Njanja with less than the usual ceremony.

Valentina had dressed in a tailored shirt with a cherry cravat and loose flannel trousers gathered at the waist by a matching cherry belt. She looked sleek and took her place at the table with panache, tearing the napkin from its silver ring.

Njanja with her failing memory had laid the table for four as if Sasha were still alive. This *faux pas* did not brighten Olga's frame of mind and Fydo failed to appear, so the meal began in ominous silence between mother and daughter. The only contribution Olga made, between the French onion soup and the pork casserole, was, "Charming Voronov could prove a challenge, even for your talents." Thereafter Olga would not rise to any of Valentina's counter-sallies. By the end of the meal Valentina was bursting with contained aggression. She decided to seek out Fydo.

However, the minute she stepped into his bedroom, she knew that he would have little to offer as a disputant.

Cross-legged on the carpet, his concentration was on a poster: a young Buddha amidst flowering creepers above which it read *Know Thyself*.

Valentina circled her cousin twice hoping to arouse his irritation, but he just stared at the garish poster.

Fydo had changed. He was now a member of the Buddhist Society in Oxford and spent some nights with them. Each time he returned, he was more unsociable. He had turned vegetarian some time before, and the family accepted it. Now however he ordered Njanja to boil him gruel or brown rice, and he only ate once a day.

Over their family meals, Valentina teased him by holding succulent pieces of roast meat under his nose. At breakfast that morning Fydo had nearly given in when she wafted a freshly toasted, generously buttered crumpet in front of him. With an effort of self-flagellation and a sigh, Fydo had cited, "The student learns by daily increment. The way is gained by loss," and turned back to his brown rice.

Valentina wished he would say something similar so that she could argue with him, but he did not move. On her way out she slammed the door behind her. *He probably didn't even blink*, she thought, rushing downstairs, the hems of her soft trousers rippling around her shoes.

She swept into the music room to find it empty. A somnolent mood had installed itself there in the absence of humans. The neglected fire was merely glowing. She switched on the tasselled lamp and was aware that her intrusion into this drowsy room had an impact only on herself.

"Bloody boring." She contemplated the samovar

but would have to fetch water for that. Instead, she poured vodka into a small glass and lay down a new log. In the uncertain light Paul's painting appeared childish rather than a return to primal instincts. She dropped herself sideways into the armchair and lit a Sobranie. Why had she bothered to dress up for this wasted life? If only Vasily were here. His next visit was not for two days.

Perhaps Olga was right that Vasily would prove a hard case. In the wood he had let her hold him close, kiss him, but his heart and mind had not been engaged. Not even the grubby groom showed any interest in her since Olga's jack-in-the-box appearance.

"They're all useless to me," she told the room, but even as she said it she knew that Vasily was of paramount importance to her. He seemed to have put an end to her recurring nightmare, searching for nostalgic images and lapsed moments. "Vasily, damn you, Vasilyotchka; I need you."

She moved to the French windows giving to a lurid evening outside. He had pushed her away, but she would ignore that because she had felt a jolt of congruence with him – that and certainty; it seemed that she had understood so much at that moment. With perseverance she would eventually win control over him. It would be a hard struggle, mostly with herself because the minute she was faced with him, fierce aggression erupted somewhere in her.

A man's shape suddenly passing the window in the pewter-coloured park made her shiver. She strained her eyes and recognised Cahill, the gardener. There was definitely something creepy about a grave-digger slipping through mist ribbons on a November night.

Valentina picked up *The Daily Telegraph* to liven up the fire, but her eyes were caught by:

Drug Raid in Soho. Acting on a tip-off last night, the police raided three Soho flats and discovered undisclosed amounts of cannabis. Several people, including the artist Marcelle Silver, were taken into custody.

There was no mention of Paul but he could easily be one of those in trouble, as Marcelle was his next door neighbour.

Valentina decided to go to London and find out what had happened. Paul had almost slipped from her mind what with Sasha's death, the nurse and Vasily. Honestly she could not be expected to sit around here waiting for Vasily Voronov to condescend to pay a call. She crumpled up the pages and lobbed them into the fire. Excited flames licked up high. That was it; a re-animated affair with Paul could sharpen her talons for attracting Vasily.

*

The next day in Soho an icy wind blew litter along the pavement. Valentina was swept through, rather than entered, the small door in the house and nearly fell over a crate stored behind it.

"Paul?"

There was no answer. She climbed the rickety stairs.

"Paul?" The atelier was penumbral. She groped for

383

the light switch. Over the easel hung a laurel wreath with a black bow. There were other unfamiliar items: framed paintings she recognised as Marcelle's. These changes in the familiar place seemed to reproach her for not having come back. Now she had arrived unannounced, which felt like an illegal entry. Once this atelier had expected her at all times.

A rasping sound made her shrink back. With its repetition she recognised it as human groaning. Tentatively advancing, she found Paul on the floor behind the sofa bed, rolled into a blanket. The pupils of his glassy eyes were enlarged.

"I read in the papers," she said.

"Excellent! I thought I had run out of cheap thrills for you." She recognised that he was high on drugs. "Sorry, I'm not in jug. Didn't get a mention in the press. I can't even manage to get arrested." He unwrapped himself.

She calculated how to draw him back to her. "Arsehole." Her vulgarity often aroused him. He saw his role as bringing her down into his *real* rough world.

"Pretty close to the part of the anatomy you're most interested in."

"You're zonked out. I'm going." She turned and walked back to the stairs. Never had she seen his eyes so haunted, his body so neglected and his mind so desperate, as he glared after her.

He leapt at her, his surging hands grabbing her shoulders. They hurt through her coat.

"You came to gloat and judge. I'll show you what has happened to me."

"Don't!" she cried out, trying to twist away from his grip, and realised that Paul stank.

"It would be polite to take your coat off, Your Highness."

"Now that I've seen the state of you, I am in a hurry to leave. It's morbid around here with the wreath and all."

"When I arrived at the gate of your hall, all dressed up nicely with my wreath, that shit of a stable boy wouldn't let me in. He's probably having it off with you."

"You came to Podzhin Hall for the funeral?"

He let go of her and they faced each other.

"After all, I knew the viscount, didn't I?"

"How come?"

"We had a long chat when I brought the painting. Nice old blighter. At least he appreciated art."

"I see. You really did get to know Sasha Brodsky well." The sarcasm crackled in her voice.

"One of these days, I'll kill you, I swear," he threatened. "You've got no right to mock me."

"Paul, look…"

"I look, and I see a slut." He slapped her face.

The impact made Valentina recoil. "Shouldn't pot bring peace to the mind, or is that coke?" She cradled her smarting cheek.

"At first it does. It did. I saw you and me together, married. I saw us living in lovely Podzhin Hall." Paul's hand caressed the air with dramatic gentleness, the same hand which had hit her so brutally. "You waved to me from the garden while I painted the *Metamorphosis of Energy* in one of the hundreds of rooms you've got. You tossed me a dandelion through the open window, and I caught the gesture on the canvas."

"That's a lovely dream," she said soothingly and with caution.

"But it *was* a dream." He pushed her onto the bed and crawled after her. "Then came the ugly awakening. You pay for your dreams."

"If they find coke on you, you'll go to prison with Marcelle and all her lovely friends. That'll be the end of your dream."

"Who cares? What difference would it make?" he shouted.

"You know I care."

Paul exploded in hysterically shrill laughter. Valentina moved back on the sofa-bed against the wall and picked up a pillow to hold in front of her.

"Is there someone else now?"

"You're drugged, Paul; I worry."

"You were mine. You are mine, and you've got to marry me. Marry me!" His spittle sprayed her face. She did not dare to wipe it off.

"I will not," she said softly.

"We say *I won't* for we ain't got no posh private education and aren't born in palaces."

She tried to struggle up. "Stop. Please stop. You're not yourself."

"Baby, this is the first time I *am* myself." His face was a misshapen mask of flush and pallor above her, his red hair vehement. Then she saw that he was not erect and became seriously scared.

When he found out, he started to hit her.

Valentina screamed. He hit her with all his impetuous frustration and she shouted for help.

Light footsteps pattered up the hollow staircase.

"Help me," Valentina cried out once more.

An angular young girl in long white plastic boots stood on the landing, calmly watching the scene.

"I told you I'd punish her," Paul heaved.

"Is that her?"

Valentina rolled off the bedding and collected her coat and shoes.

"She doesn't look very upper-class to me," commented the girl.

"It doesn't show on her."

Valentina brushed past the girl, lifted her heavy hair and threw it back over her shoulder. "This was criminal assault. You'll be behind bars soon."

★

The first thing Valentina did back in Podzhin Hall was to unhook the painting from its nail. Despite her headache, her face hot and smarting, she managed to get it up to the loft.

"There you go, you bastard." She tossed the canvas behind a pile of odds and ends and dropped onto a dusty Louis Vuitton trunk. Touching her tender mouth, she felt her lower lip ballooning.

It seemed to require a breaking through, some violence, for her to establish contact with men – often her violence but sometimes theirs. *Gentleness is frightening*, she thought. She did not have the courage to be gentle for fear of receiving kind love back. She would be at a loss if that happened, and it would hurt.

Valentina noticed the damp-mottled sticker fixed to the trunk's flank: the red cross on faded white.

The train! This is the trunk which came with them from Russia.

She let herself slide to the dust-gritted wood planks. Kneeling, she started to drum her fist on the lid of the case. Furiously her hands hammered until they stung with pain. Fungal powdery spores rose up, coating the air with fumes like the breath of ghosts. She had never understood the source of her pain: something unknown but vital had been taken from her.

CHAPTER THIRTY-SIX

"Hard drugs, yes," Valentina said into the telephone receiver. "He lives at 42 Starkeley Street, in the attic studio."

Despite the sparse light in the vestibule, she was wearing sunglasses and a shade of blue shone through the heavily applied make-up on her cheek, and her lip was swollen.

A knock on the oak door reverberated around Podzhin Hall.

"Paul Malloy, a painter," Valentina spelled slowly into the receiver, undisturbed.

Njanja shuffled to the entrance door.

"My family knows him; we commissioned some work from him."

Njanja opened the door to reveal Vasily.

"We had our suspicions at once." Valentina turned to the wall.

"Ah, zr Voronov," Njanja greeted the visitor.

"Absolutely sure." Valentina hung up.

"Zr countess is expecting you in zr music room." Njanja led Vasily across the vestibule.

Apparently ignoring the visitor, Valentina ran up the stairs and out of sight. Vasily's puzzled look followed her. He had come fully geared once more to face the Brodskys. The disturbing revelation of his father's aristocracy would not sidetrack him. After all, his father was eighty years old, and his sordid origins played no role. Turchin had reassured Vasily that despite some concern back in Moscow over his selection for this assignment, Georgi had insisted Vasily stay in England. This was an act of trust, and it lay now in Vasily's honour not to let the Party down.

In the music room the modern painting no longer hung above the fireplace. Olga in a dove-grey dress, a sash draped around her waist, sat however as usual at her bureau covered in papers.

"Good morning. I hope you are well today," enquired Vasily civilly.

"I have made a complete list of all the shares and bonds we are owed. Unfortunately, some things have been destroyed in careless games." Olga faced Vasily abruptly. "I hope you bring us good news from the Kremlin."

"The signs are hopeful. If we could send your collated list, it would help."

"Would it? If you don't mind, I'll hold on to the originals for the moment."

"May I?" He picked up a bond. It was large; a blue decorative frame surrounded the conditions printed in Russian and French. A round watermark in the centre read *Imperial Russian Bank*. Two eagle wings crowned it. The bond was for one million roubles. There were piles of them lying on the desk. He appreciated how rich the Brodskys had been.

"If you don't mind giving me a little more time, I can finish drawing up the list of our properties. Feel free to go and speak to my daughter, or Anna who is here today."

"With pleasure." Vasily left Olga to her task. He mounted the stairs. On the second landing was a linen cupboard he had not checked out yet. From Valentina's bedroom came the distinct sound of weeping. The distress seemed to crescendo. He hesitated, then knocked on the door. It had no effect but increased weeping reached his ears. Eventually he turned the knob. In the richly furnished room, on a messy bed under an imitation Tartar nomad tent, was Valentina. Her face was puffed red and a dark patch, like a bruise, garnished her cheek.

"Vasily," she exclaimed when she saw him, and the wet red mouth opened while her arms were stretched towards him. "I am so unhappy."

He nodded only, still under the doorframe. She flung herself prone onto the colourful bed. "Don't leave."

The door opened a little wider. "Can I help?" he asked with stony determination to fulfil his duty, however difficult. Behind his mask he speculated about the nature of this strangely behaving creature before him.

"You could if you weren't a bloody communist," she sobbed.

He flushed, and his old desire to judge her flared up. He took a deep breath, then shook his head violently. "I'll go and find Anna."

"Don't you dare!" Valentina sprang up and came to pull him into the room by his sleeve. "Stay and talk to me."

He had glimpsed in her impulsive movement the top of her stocking and flesh of her thigh, before her skirt had fallen back into place.

"I am so unlucky with men. They are all so cruel and stupid."

"Surely not."

"Surely yes – but for you. Oh Vasily, help me sort myself out."

"I don't think I am the right person."

"You are. You seem to have cured my nightmares. It is because you are Russian and because we are one, you and I. I know it; I just know it."

"You only think so because you don't know me."

The white of her eyes was edged with red lines; her face seemed to have been brutalised but her expression was no less powerful as she begged him, "Please sit on this bed with me calmly for a while."

Her hand came searching for his. When he felt the warmth of her touch on his fingers, he lived up bravely to her brusque change of mood and sat on the edge of the bed, pretending to give in but remaining on high alert.

"Just hold my hand, and we'll sit here eyes closed."

He watched her eyelids which protected him from her intensity.

After a while she mumbled dreamily, "I can see a world where we don't have to fight. I see us walk in a wood, and it is not here. There are carpets of wild daffodils. A child rides on her father's shoulders. Blossoms fall in our path, and we just walk, hand in hand, with nothing to fight for, nothing to hide."

"Indeed."

"What sentimental rot!" She snatched her hand out of his.

He jumped up, fingers curled. He did not fear her physically. He would be able to snap her neck with one blow of his hand.

"It's dog eat dog, and fuck or be fucked. That no doubt applies to your life too. Isn't that so, Mr Voronov?"

"Stop playing games with me, using vulgar American words."

"You're just like all other men, but in red," she snorted and glared up at him from puffed eyes.

"I am like any other man, but I do not give way to egocentric hysteria, or bourgeois sentimental indulgence."

To his surprise, she asked seriously, "Would you like to?"

He held onto a thick tassel of the canopy and equally seriously thought about it, then said, "I see no merit in it. It can only be detrimental. My life is based on collaboration with the people and the authorities, contributing to the system in my small way." He gave the tassel an energetic clout.

"Rubbish. You are Vasily Voronov."

"And?" The tassel swung between them.

"And that's fantastic."

He shook his head. Time was his alleged friend; he would need a lot more of it to understand what she said or thought.

"Could you defect?"

"Pardon?"

"Lots of people defect, especially those who are let loose like you – unless of course you're only here to plant microphones in our rooms."

How did she dare? "Defectors are traitors," he retorted, shaken.

"Nice clothes, good food, freedom to be yourself, a house like this?" She reclined on her bent elbows on her cushion-strewn bed in a tempting pose.

He hated her for saying this; hated her for giving him so hard a task.

"If you pay us back, you will be admitting that it was worth something, something which communism destroyed, and not something we took from you."

"Aren't you arguing against your own interests now?" he asked dryly.

"There are choices in a free world. For you to survive, you have only the Party and its rules."

Despite his resolve, he could take no more. "I have to go downstairs and finish business with your mother."

★

"Just finished," said Olga. "I have generously left out details like coaches and our small servant's flat, confiscated by the state."

Vasily was still under the impact of Valentina. *Would you like the freedom to be yourself and to have choices? Why don't you defect? Many do.*

"Would you like some champagne?"

He looked blank, jolted from his thoughts.

"I think we deserve it." She rang the bell. "You see, we owned the whole mansion on Vasilyevsky Island, as well as the house next to it and a large summer house in the Crimea. We also owned a pied-à-terre on the Nevsky Prospekt for Ivan, so he would not have to cross the bridge on winter nights. Njanja, *shampanskoye*! Of course Podzhin Hall is not on the list. It was a present for the happiness I brought to someone." She cupped her curl. "An elegant gesture for my daughter Valentina, in fact."

"I see," said Vasily, understanding little of what she divulged. The champagne arrived. He took the bottle from Njanja whose set face did not return his false brightness. "Let me."

"Podzhin Hall, according to your Soviet law, still belongs to Baron Dimitri Kavinsky."

Vasily cut himself on the metal wire over the cork. *Kavinsky, Kavinsky...*

"You say that this house belongs to Baron Kavinsky?" asked Vasily, sucking his bleeding thumb.

"Such lavish gifts were offered by those who could afford them. What's the matter, young man? Can't you open the bottle?"

If Podzhin Hall belonged to the Kavinsky family, then the Hall belonged partly to him, it dawned on the stunned Vasily. The mushroom-cork popped out of the bottle. *Would you like a house like this? Would you like to defect? Moscow trusts you. We have elms in our park. Your Party work is to infiltrate émigrés. Miliukov stands behind you.*

"To our joint success," toasted Olga. "You are

very pale, Mr Voronov. Are you coming down with something?"

"I am dizzy," he admitted weakly.

"I shall ring for Epsom salts."

Sentimental indulgence. He was giving in to it. "Excuse me," he said and left the room rapidly to be confronted by the sumptuous vestibule. *Podzhin Hall belongs to the Kavinskys. My father was a Kavinsky. I am a Kavinsky.*

Vasily rushed to the boiler room for shelter.

★

Anna sat at the narrow table, turning the pages of a linen-bound library book. The new sweater she was wearing for the first time had a band of flowers around the neckline. A pinch of her hair was held together on the crown of her head by a horn clip, a first step towards coquettish femininity.

Through some pipes near the ceiling gurgled bath water: Fydo was cleansing his body again.

The door was torn open and Vasily burst into the room. She wiped her reading glasses off her nose.

"Oh," he exhaled.

"You sneaked away to come and talk to me," she said, as he stood panting, his back against the door, like a hunted animal who had found shelter. "Are you playing a game?"

He remained silent. *Oh dear, why could she never say the right thing, and why had she put this clip into her hair?*

He gulped and it occurred to her he might be sick – or, more likely, shocked.

Mother, thought Anna grimly. *Mother has done this to him.* She did not move from her chair; instead, in an attempt to help him she read from her book. "Listen to this profound social philosophy. *Every Leninist knows that individualisation in the personal sphere is reactionary – petit-bourgeois absurdity.* Correct, isn't it?"

"Yes, of course," he said non-committally and slowly came towards her. His eyes were stormy, and she nearly cried out because she felt his body so vibrant, so close, and her own so tingling in the desire to touch him. "Anna, will you help me?"

He put his strong dry hand over hers on the table. The last week's battle within herself, whether she was or was not infatuated with Vasily, resumed tempestuously. She put her other hand over his to keep him captured. These small movements bringing them into contact were at the moment all there was, but they were more intimate and meaningful than anything Anna had ever experienced with men.

Slowly he claimed his hand back.

To re-assert herself, she continued, "Lenin, Stalin were great men. They thought for the people. If only communism could successfully be applied for all. But then, not everyone sees…"

"Anna, I need a good friend, someone I can trust."

She dared to lean her head against him in the movement of a trusting child to an adult.

"I care for you as much as for socialism," she said. "You can trust me; in fact, I think I would do anything for you."

"Communism is not as idealistic as you understand

it from your books. It schools one for years to exercise total self-control and discipline."

"For the right cause, surely it should not feel like that."

"Some shocking things can happen in a life that threaten to pull the rug from under one and make one question oneself."

"You mean you? Something shocking has happened to you? Please tell me. I'll stand by you."

He attempted to stroke over her hair but the clip was in the way. She reached up and took it out but he had moved to the door.

"I'll tell you another time. First I need to do some more thinking."

"Of course Vasily, if that's what you want to do," she said sitting on her stool, the hair clip in her cupped hands like a trapped bird.

He left the boiler room.

★

In battle-ridden St Petersburg, Baron Dimitri Kavinsky headed along quiet side streets towards the Baltic train station. Under a gas-lamp he stopped and removed the papers from the breast pocket of the blood-stained policeman's jacket.

St Petersburg Police Identity Card. Voronov, Yuri. Born 3 February 1886, Korosten; farmer. Date of Issue: November 1916.

Slipped inside, the baron found a letter. It contained news about the harvest and a horse which had gone lame. Dimitri's eyes flew over the scrawled words. The last paragraph started, *Kuprik is growing up fast. He keeps asking when his Dada is coming home!* The letter ended, *With loving thoughts and prayers for your safety, your wife and son who miss you.*

Dimitri tore the letter up and threw the bits of paper into the gutter where the words drenched, darkened and finally were wiped out.

After the relatively quiet streets Baltic Station was as busy as the Petersburg summer fair. The crowd stretched from the platforms through the ticket hall onto the pavement and back into the street. Dimitri mingled with them. A station master in a red jacket, with the moustache of a sad walrus, kept throwing his hands into the air. "*Nye znayu!* I don't know!" Everyone pushed and shoved to get closer to the platform.

"No trains," said a woman with a basket, then saw Dimitri's uniform and turned her head away. Clambering over huddled figures on the ground, he managed to get into the ticket-hall. A group of policemen were smoking and talking. He took a deep breath; he wore their uniform. One policeman saw him and hailed. Dimitri stalked over sitting people and their luggage, and pushed himself through.

"Hello. Going to Novgorod?"

"Yes."

"We'll never make it. Trains still controlled by the labour army or bolsheviks, or neither."

"Chaos," admitted Dimitri.

"You can say that again. Got some vodka?"

Dimitri shook his head.

"That's our last." The short fat policeman slid a bottle out of his coat pocket. "Raided the swine, but this fancy stuff seems to evaporate. Have some." The bottle was handed to Dimitri. He took a tiny sip pretending it to be a gulp. The vodka burnt on his tongue where not long ago Moët et Chandon had lingered. He handed the bottle back.

"Did you hear? The bolshies shot the two Baron Kavinskys in one raid."

"I heard," said Dimitri.

"They've hung them on the bridge like herrings to dry. Great stuff, but I'm getting out of here, back to my farm."

Suddenly life came into the crowd surrounding them. Everyone scrambled up at once. "A train, a train!" They started to fight for space. The fat policeman lodged the bottle back in his pocket.

"Step back, step back," howled the loudspeaker. Dimitri pushed. A civilian spat on his coat.

The locomotive exhaled as if rendering its soul and came to a halt in the station. People ran for it. Only four coaches were attached and they were full to bursting. Faces peered from the windows. People were fleeing from Petersburg to their native villages. Dimitri did not understand how the train could already be full. Baltic Station was the end or the beginning of the line from Petersburg to Novgorod. In the shoving crowd he was separated from the other policemen.

His identity card said he was a farmer from Korosten,

which was hundreds of kilometres south in the Ukraine. Dimitri pushed amongst the compact body of people. The station master whistled; the pushing increased. Dimitri clawed his way through to the train.

"We're full, full," a voice shouted from a carriage window.

"Do you want to be thrown off?" The head disappeared.

Dimitri felt the step of the ladder under his foot. The whistle blew. He pushed in desperation. The woman in front of him carried a child. He pushed her aside. She screamed. His hand was on the handrail.

The locomotive hooted twice. People shouted in panic. Dimitri's other foot found the step. The train started to roll. The crowd swayed sideways. He held on with an iron grip. A man fell between his legs. Another let go. Dimitri joined both hands to the handrail. The train left the station. Like grapes, people hung from the coaches. Still some were pushed off, or fell. He hung on. The roof of the station gave way to a hard frosty night-sky. The overloaded train gathered speed as it left Petersburg and he was wrapped in coal smoke.

The train rattled across the flat marshes and rivers. Nine miles from Novgorod it slowed; the locomotive puffed out excess steam. They came to a halt. It was three in the morning. Huddled, frozen, the baron had ridden on the roof of the train with others who found no room inside.

Railway employees walked along the track with oil lamps. The passengers waited, crowded and silent. Some got off to stretch their limbs. Bolsheviks arrived waving rifles with bayonets. Dimitri lay flat on the soot-covered roof. They waited while the search for imperialists went on. Dimitri's hopes sank when he saw the stoker walk away from the locomotive. They waited. As time passed, more and more passengers alighted to stretch. The bolshevik guards searched the carriages. The hope for a continued journey faded.

A man in an astrakhan coat shuffled away from the train with a woman. "Halt!" A revolutionary pointed his rifle at them. The woman dropped her muff, screamed and ran. Two guards ran after her. The gentleman stood, a leather case in his hand, watching helplessly as they dragged back his wife. The couple were led away into the dark.

They waited.

"Train abandoned!" They all climbed off and started to disperse.

"How far from Novgorod are we?"

"Unbelievable!"

Passengers with luggage set off along the railway track towards the city of Novgorod.

Baron Dimitri walked at a right angle away from the train into bushes, his heart beating fast. He had to head south, as far away as possible from the turmoil in Petersburg and Moscow. It would be a ridiculous undertaking to attempt this on foot, in the vastness of the country; he needed to find the train line to the Black Sea. Stumbling through snow-toasted thickets in the pre-dawn dimness, he guessed where the sun would rise. The boots hurt his feet. He put a distance between himself and Lake Ilmen, on the south shore of which lay one of his summer-houses, his books, his poems. Dimitri put his hand over his eyes. The resultant darkness could not appease the horror pulsating in his brain. *I shall write it all again*, he thought.

As the day arrived, the baron reached a village. Farmers were letting their cattle out. He was hungry more than tired. A couple of hours' walk from where he stood was his summer-house with servants and a store full of food and wine. The same distance away in the other direction had to be Dno, a major train junction.

He asked a farmer the way, but he shook his head and scuttled back into his house.

In a shed Dimitri saw a white chicken egg shining on straw. He did not dare. He walked through the village in his uniform as faces in the windows watched him pass.

Approaching another village, he saw a flecked dog with a scrap of food in its muzzle, about to settle and eat. He threw a stone at the animal. The dog dropped the food and ran. Dimitri grabbed what had fallen from the canine's mouth. It was a dirt-encrusted piece of chicken. Slowly he ate it as he walked through the village. At the village well he drank. He knew midday had passed.

He skirted a small town and still had not seen any white cloud from a steam engine, nor the tell-tale of a straight telephone line. He walked on like a sleepwalker until he found a cattle shelter on a snowy field and curled up in it to fall into a comatose sleep.

When he awoke, before the birds sang, he set off. He needed to get onto a train to the Crimea. He thought of Anton Chekhov who had been exiled to the Crimea by his delicate health – Chekhov, whom he admired so much for his poetry.

At midday he saw the unmistakable straight incision in the fields. Shortly afterwards, his numb feet touched the iron tracks. He wept from relief. He walked along the rails. The shrill shriek of a hawk mocked him from a telephone pole. Dimitri's mind conjured up visions of food in rich sauces. *Raw hawk would do*, he thought, eyeing the bird of prey. His only weapon was Yevgeni's gold pen. How did Tolstoy's poem go?

"Haste to punish them,
Smite them from the sky,
Drive them far and wide,
Make their feathers fly!"

Dimitri recited, then wept, thought of food and put one foot in front of the other until the tower of the railway station was ahead of him.

Dno junction was a heavily guarded hubbub. There was no way to sneak in, so Dimitri had to brave it, straightening his uniform jacket and marching onto the platform, brushing aside a security agent. A fast green train from Moscow thundered through the station, steam pistons thumping.

"Get off me. I don't need a ticket. I am here to check trains."

He strode along the platform pretending to check the passengers tightly tucked into the carriages of a train waiting to depart for Moscow. Halfway down he ducked under a stone arch onto a side-line where freight wagons stood, and hopped into one at random. It was packed with jute bags of grain behind which he hid. All he could do was pray that the cereals were scheduled to leave soon.

They were. He was juggled about as the train was coupled up. They rattled south, while with stiff fingers he parted the spikelets of wheat heads, separating chaff from the grain to eat.

Through the night he sought warmth between two bales, but was plagued by thirst. His tongue swelled, and his mouth felt like raw wool. The longer he bore it, the further from danger he got.

When daylight came he banged the frozen window shutter aside and watched flat wintry countryside passing. The bell clanged at a level crossing and the name of a station flashed past: Korosten, the place the real Yuri Voronov was known. Dimitri pulled his head back and closed the shutter. Some state of sleep provided release from his thirst.

When he came to, the train had stopped. He jumped off and stole away from the station and its small town. He knew that he was in the Ukraine because of the style of the houses.

Across a field, he noticed the shivering of tall silver reeds: a river! He hobbled to it on frost-bitten feet, parted the rushes and crawled over mossy vegetation to be rewarded by the glint of ice on water. Moaning in frustration, with a stone he broke through the ice, and dipped his face into the river. He felt his head shrink. He had to detach his tongue from the roof of his mouth before he could gulp the river water, from time to time pulling icy weeds from his teeth.

Afterwards he lay on his back, rocking in shivers as the torment of hunger took over.

He followed the flow of the river, necessarily towards the sea. On the way, he stole a piece of buttered bread from boys, busy skipping stones across the ice.

Disappointingly the river bent away from his direct line south and the railway, which he hoped to use one more time to make absolutely sure he was far away from Petersburg and from who he had been.

The rising moon shone full, and by midnight Dimitri was back on the train track, glinting like two silver guidelines leading him to a station. It was unlocked and unoccupied and, in luxury, he slept on a bench out of the elements.

In the morning the station master arrived and appreciated Dimitri's police uniform, because he had two sons drafted into the police force in Moscow. He shared his porridge breakfast with Dimitri who invented details of police work in the city. The warm oats in his stomach nearly made him faint. A train to Odessa was due but delayed, and passengers were slowly accumulating. Delayed by thirteen hours a puffing engine finally materialised. Dimitri got on with the others. He avoided the ticket collector by constantly moving from one carriage to another with stops in the toilet – which had paper! Dimitri stole a wad and started to write as the scenery fled by.

Restless as the rain when twilight quivers,
Pressed on the earth I lie and shiver,
In dread of anguish and despair.

At the next station the ticket collector finally caught up with him and threw him off the train.

He realised that he was in the heart of the Ukraine and that behind the mountain range lay Moldavia, where his father had been governor in Kishinev. He also knew that he could not bear yet another hungry train ride.

He slept in a barn with a warm cow. The snow lay quite shallow; he had gone far enough south. He walked across a field towards a small village and behind him his boots left dark bean-shaped prints. He bent and scooped the snow until he reached the stiff earth beneath. The colour of the earth was black.

"I shall sow my tears in the furrows of this black soil," he wept.

Behind an orchard stood a neat white-walled cottage. The roof was thatched and the paintwork of the windows and the doorframe was blue. He crossed some planks over a frozen brook. The naked pear tree in the orchard stretched its branches into the white sky in yearning, like the dead fingers of Yevgeni after dropping the pen.

Baron Dimitri Kavinsky could go no further. Of all things he wept "Nikolai", the name of his doomed Czar.

CHAPTER
THIRTY-SEVEN

Njanja polished the brass stair-rods one by one. Scooping cream from a flat tin with a soft yellow cloth, she smeared it onto the metal. Slowly, hunched, she ascended, rubbing with care and leaving behind her a curved shiny brass ladder, as if she were earning her way up into heaven.

At the park's gate Cahill pulled up the drop-bolt from its cement hole and pushed the cast-iron gates aside. He grinned as he heard the creaking pedals, turning slowly, approaching on the other side of the wall. *Smack on!*

The young post-lad in shorts skidded as he swerved into the property. "Morning." With a muffled crackling of tyres on pebbles, he rode up the drive.

"See you." Cahill pulled the knitted cap straight on his gingery hair and picked up the handles of his wheelbarrow filled with mulch from the compost heap. He pushed the squeaking load over the tufty grass which still had the silvery shine of nightly frost.

By the rosebeds he stopped, set down the barrow and tilted it to unload the moist dark peat. He had to ready the beds for wintering. Hacking away, he hoed the mulch into the scummy hungry earth.

He looked up. Whistling, the postboy rode down the drive again, raising one hand. "Cheerio." Cahill reached out to hit a clod of earth with the back of his hoe.

★

Inside the hall Valentina checked her watch, then she rushed down the stairs, her hand raised from the railing for a few bars to pass Njanja before resuming its smooth slide. Njanja grumbled but Valentina was already rifling through the letters she had taken from the wire basket.

The letter she tore open with a hairpin revealed a simple jotter-pad page on which was typed: *Watch out – I remember you.*

Valentina knew that it was from Trish despite the pathetic disguise of having had it posted from Thetford in Norfolk. This was her second childish attempt to frighten Valentina by post.

"Good news?" asked Fydo nonchalantly, ambling through the vestibule in a thin dressing-gown and bare feet.

"It's that confounded nurse. She's still harassing me."

Fydo fumbled with the front door lock and fled from the house. He would never understand either the nurse or Valentina. The sensation of pebbles coated in ground frost against the soles of his feet sent thrills through him and he knew he could cope with that. With the ascetic approach even extreme cold could be mastered.

"You'll catch yer death," said Cahill, ready to wheel the empty barrow back for a refill.

"Have you ever thought that death solves the conflict of life? It proves that our time on earth is just a rehearsal for the great play of destiny."

"Ever seen a churchyard at night, guv?" retorted Cahill.

Fydo vaguely remembered that the Irishman had been a grave-digger.

"Those inscriptions on slabs and stones – they're only there to pretend life isn't over. They're all wiped out by the dark."

Fydo became aware that the chill ground hurt his feet and that he had not yet learned to be indifferent to discomfort.

"I could tell you some stories…" Cahill put the handles down, "… to make your hair curl."

"Cahill," said Fydo, "death is a passing phenomenon. I believe we are all re-incarnated."

"Yeah, I've seen some of those re-incarnated souls. They knocked against the lids of their coffins 'cos they weren't dead."

"That's not what I meant. The soul energy lives eternally, and physical death is just a pause, if you like, on its way to assume another identity."

"They knocked and knocked, and I wasn't to say anything. I see it and I hear it and I say nowt."

"It is your spiritual anguish that conjures up malevolent ghosts in you," said Fydo. "Accept physical existence as a leaf floating effortlessly down a slow river." Fydo tried to help Cahill but then wondered about their conversation.

"I'll tell you a last thing. That Russian spy you've got," started the gardener.

"Vasily Voronov?"

"Yeah, that one. He's weird. He's always snooping around; I caught him in my bedroom. He's the one who threw the stone at Miss Valentina and tampered with 'er tea – one breath of that foul mouth…"

"Cahill. Keep your negative thoughts to yourself."

"I'd call the cops if I was you. I tell you, if you don't I will."

Fydo walked off, busy controlling his resentment of the Irishman's narrowness. Perhaps some men were as ill-begotten as the women in his family.

★

In the block of flats rented by the Soviet Embassy for single employees, Vasily walked up the stairs. If he added up the steps he had mounted since his childhood in the Ukraine, his aunt's stairs in Moscow, to his position here abroad, he could have easily reached the peak of the highest mountain in the Urals. This thought made him laugh out loud.

A door opened and a typist at the embassy peered at him. "It's nine o'clock."

"Is it?" Vasily checked his Soviet-made wristwatch and shrugged his shoulders apologetically.

The typist closed her door sharply. It was nine o'clock, and he should not have laughed in the corridor.

Vasily reached his room, entered and closed the door which did not have a lock.

Valentina had suggested he defect and become a person like her. He took off his shoes. *Was she not merely dragging herself through an aimless childish existence, no doubt retarded by Olga's overpowering personality?* he thought, peeling off his socks to put them into his shoes.

He decided that he wanted nothing emotional to do with Valentina or anyone like her, as he unbuttoned his shirt.

Yet why was it that the discontented worm gnawing in Valentina seemed to gnaw inside him too each time he saw her? It was as if she exposed a lack in his life he had not previously felt.

Vasily pulled off his shirt and folded it neatly for the laundry bag.

The danger did not lie in the subversive manoeuvres of the British Special Services as he had been warned, but in the traps which lay within himself; activated by witnessing in others feelings he recognised as his own.

After taking off his trousers, he aligned the creases and hung them on a hanger.

Were all women in the West like Valentina? Anna was easier to handle. He recognised the process by which she tried to understand communism. She gave him the opportunity to protect her, and thus the first preparation for infiltration was made. Turchin had urged him to make her dependent on him and slowly gain her trust. With time this would inevitably contaminate the others. Yet Anna too had strange streaks in her which he could not fathom.

Now he sat on the bed in his underwear and thought

about his father who must have deliberately protected him from his dangerous genetic tendencies.

He pulled his singlet over his head.

Turchin had told him that his father was an aristocrat. Olga had told him that they owned properties such as Podzhin Hall. It would have been easier for him not to know this; perhaps that was why his father had tried to protect him.

Vasily removed his briefs and was naked.

"Who am I?" he asked the mirror on the wardrobe door. "Am I an aristocrat Kavinsky or am I Voronov, the dedicated Party member?"

CHAPTER
THIRTY-EIGHT

The plane landed at Kennedy Airport. Antonina was back in New York. At the phone kiosk in the arrivals hall she hesitated, coins prepared in her jacket pocket.

If she let Irina know that she was back it would rekindle those emotions between them, the old Russian's needs and Antonina's feelings of guilt and duty towards her helplessness. Worst, strangely enough, was the thought of being offered *Always*.

Sex with a wonderful man had changed things. Antonina was clad in clothes he had bought her. A flower jewel was at her lapel testifying to his respect for her. She felt like a woman with the love of a man in her soul. She felt she had strength.

Decisively she strode to the train station. There were two New York job possibilities for her where a work visa was not needed: the British consulate and the United Nations. Tomorrow she would apply for both. For now she had to take a train into Manhattan and find a simple clean hotel.

★

The UN's personnel department held weekly recruitment exams, so great was the demand for jobs. With twenty-two other applicants Antonina filled in assessment tests. San Francisco job-hunting had taught her about the box-ticking technique and, thanks to the map of the world in her Podzhin Hall bedroom, she felt confident about African states. She put down French as her second language and wrote a short essay on the importance of the United Nations, concluding it with:

> *Despite empty talk, diplomats glowering at each other, and shoe-rapping, it is not up to the Last Judgement to provide peace but to the work of the United Nations.*

She kept her momentum for seven hours. At the end of the day, she was called into an office for a personal interview. By the time she emerged from the tall flat building on the East River, the sky was dark and the flags of all member nations were lowered on their long white poles. She was hired for a three-week trial period during which she was required to attend typing lessons. At the end of it she would get a year's contract and placement in the organisation. Antonina waltzed to the taxi rank. Lucius would be so proud if he knew. Damn it, she could not tell him.

★

After only one week Antonina felt confident with the golf ball typewriter. Even the large character speechwriter wasn't really so difficult to master. Had she been good at it then in the CA Trust Bank in San Francisco, she would never have met Lucius.

The UN reverberated with the twenty-second session of the General Assembly in its sixth week, with its *Decides, Condemns, Calls upon, Reaffirms, Requests, Reiterates* and *Recommends*. More than four thousand people of ninety-six different nations were employed. Hardly a day passed without a political or humanitarian incident demanding UN action, nor a day in which no important person was sighted in the building.

The day after his Majesty Olav V King of Norway visited, and a pregnant Biafran woman lay herself on the floor in protest at the entrance of the building, Antonina got her job placement.

She was escorted into the elevator ascending to the top 38th floor. She stepped out onto a thick marigold-coloured carpet. *The yellow brick road*, she thought. On the wall behind the security man's desk hung a tapestry of white doves on a blue background, signed by Picasso.

Down the corridor she was led into a large and lush office.

"I'm Mariko, your colleague." A young Japanese woman came to greet Antonina. "Our boss Mr Falcone is in the Security Council meeting. This is your desk."

Antonina kept her excitement under control with difficulty; the soft upholstered leather chair swivelled, the file drawers rolled out silently, the white telephone sat on a console, an IBM and a speechwriter stood invitingly on the polished wood surface.

"We're busy. Please catch up on the assembly points and read the provisional agenda for the week to come and the other stuff I put on your desk. We're expecting Eisaku Sato tomorrow."

"Oh."

"Chief of Protocol will brief us later. He's only Prime Minister, not royalty."

"Ah."

"From Japan, you dodo."

Antonina sank into the chair. From the ceiling a camera pointed at her. "Wow," she mouthed and started to read the reports.

A door opened and a short man with a polished face, greying receding hair, emerged. He wore glasses and a sweet smile played on the full lips of his small mouth. There was a thickening on his lower lip. Antonina jumped up. "That's… That's…"

Mariko went over to the man. "Mr Secretary General, may I introduce to you a new assistant, Miss Antonina Brodsky."

The man shook Antonina's hand and smiled into her eyes. "Pleased to have you with us," he said.

"Good grief," Antonina panted.

U Thant left the room, escorted by the guard.

★

At three o'clock they went downstairs to the General Assembly Hall. One of the small anterooms lodged

417

U Thant and his prominent guests, and a second the Executive Office, Antonina's team.

Mr Falcone and Mariko were tense and moved around with efficiency. Already a delegate had objected to an item on the agenda, raising supplementary questions to be typed, roneo'd and distributed amongst the members.

"I've just seen a man in pyjamas going to the loo," Antonina reported in astonishment.

"That's Mahendra Bir Birkram Shah Dev, the King of Nepal, and get us fifty copies of these pages, right now."

The meeting was in session. Behind the famous marble slab sat U Thant, to his left his deputy Chakravarthy Narasimhan and to his right Ralph Bunche.

Mariko and Antonina were seated at a table at the foot of the podium. Above them, in the booths either side of the hall, interpreters worked behind glass windows.

The King of Nepal was led to the speaker's rostrum. "I thank you, Mr President, most sincerely for giving me the opportunity to address this great assembly whose constant search for peace against heavy odds is the principal hope of mankind today. You have striven..." The American Ambassador, Arthur Goldberg, yawned. George Brown sat attentive, and Andrei Gromyko consulted with Soviet diplomats.

"They are all here," whispered Antonina.

The question of the election of non-permanent members of the Security Council came up. "Quick, hand this up to the Secretary General."

Antonina stumbled up the few steps and nearly fell into Mr Bunche's lap. She felt the world focused on her; she could easily shout, "Peace in Vietnam." Instead she gave U Thant the roneo'd pages.

One of the guards, hand at the pistol handle, watched her every move.

"Security is intimidating when one is not used to it," Antonina confided to Mariko.

"You just wait for the visit of LBJ."

"Is he coming? I didn't see that in the agenda."

"After the assassination of Kennedy, do you think we let it be known? Security will be quite something, and so will the work. You need to move from your hotel into a flat within ten minutes' walking distance."

"I'll flat-hunt at the weekend."

"You'll need it by Monday. Don't look at me like that. Go to personnel and tell them to sort it out for you. You're working for U Thant personally. We get what we want and fast. It's a perk."

At five o'clock the meeting was over. Mariko and Antonina went back upstairs. They worked until nine preparing the agenda for the next day. Antonina was told to collate excerpts of the most burning questions raised during the sessions, for U Thant to take home with him. "But he heard them," she objected.

"Sithu Thant often practises meditation during sessions."

Antonina's eyes burnt from tiredness. Her white phone rang. Ralph Bunche wanted her in his office. She walked down the gold road. He dictated several letters to VIPs that had to be immaculately executed.

"When do you need them?"

"Tonight," he said. Antonina swallowed and walked back up the corridor. By half-past eleven she had mustered most of them. Mariko did the rest. Antonina was ready to fall off her chair. "Can I go home?" she asked meekly.

"Soon. First we need to prepare a folder with the incoming night telexes and get the relevant files from archives."

At midnight the bodyguard drove U Thant to his Riverdale residence. The UN building was still lit in most offices.

Antonina collated the telexes. She read,

Pentagon predicts by 1980 in the order of 600-1,200 atomic bombs a week will be manufactured in the world stop Johnson insisting on immediate action on nuclear non-proliferation treaty stop.

The next telex was from Tass.

Communist China called the proposed nuclear weapons treaty a Soviet-American plot against China stop.

Antonina sighed. Like a sleepwalker, she worked. At one o'clock Ralph Bunche decided to change two of his letters. At two o'clock Mariko let her off. "I guess on your first day you can sleep in one of U Thant's office bedrooms."

Past being impressed, Antonina was shown into the sanctum. Glass cabinets displayed elaborate jade carvings in pink, all shades of green and opaque. Antonina marvelled at glittering Manhattan far below. Still dressed, she collapsed onto the bedcover. *How can anyone carve chain links in jade?* She was asleep.

★

She woke and saw a man swaying outside the window. He waved at her. She screamed. The door was flung open and the guard stood in her room, his pistol drawn. Antonina pointed.

He put his gun back into its holster. "That's the window cleaner."

"On the 38th floor?"

"Sure. I've just ordered hot coffee for everyone."

"You mean the others are here?"

"Sure."

Antonina's watch said it was five forty-five. She washed and, feeling crumpled and stale, left her bedroom to join Mariko at work. On the way she stopped. U Thant sat on the carpet, his eyes closed, his legs crossed, lost in meditation. The sun rose over Brooklyn behind him like an apocalyptic halo. Antonina tiptoed past him.

They worked all day without pause. She had to translate a policy statement from the National Liberation Front of South Vietnam. The text was heavy and Le Petit Larousse dictionary did most of the translation. Demonstrating and singing in front of the UN with Ricky had seemed a lot easier.

At the same time she was supposed to write up the excerpts from the morning session.

An anti-draft protester set himself on fire in front of the UN building which caused a short interlude. He was beyond saving, twenty years old and from Flushing in Queens.

She was asked to attend the afternoon session and saw U Thant's faraway look. There was tension among the diplomats and in the recess a simultaneous interpreter was sobbing in the delegates' lounge. "What happened?"

"Nothing. They crack up from time to time." A colleague held out a glass of water to her.

Before the Secretary General left that evening, Antonina brought the excerpts to his office. He smiled his brown-eyed kindness. Antonina sighed from exhaustion. The Secretary General pushed a buzzer on his desk. *Do not disturb*. A red light would have gone on outside the office.

"Take your shoes off," he said. She hesitated. He came round his desk. She kicked them off. "Sit down." She sat on a club seat. He sat opposite her in another. "Concentrate on the bridge of your nose between your eyes; breathe regularly, peacefully." She obeyed. Silence and calm tried to invade her. "Turn the palms of your hands up, like curled leaves floating on a pond."

First, all the impressions swirled around in her head, in her bloodstream. Then slowly, rhythmically with her calm breathing, they were brushed from her, while with every deeper breath a velvety colourless nothing replaced them. Her head felt lighter, her body floated. After a while she opened her eyes and found him smiling mysteriously at her.

"If I had my way in this wicked world." Antonina hummed one of Peter, Paul and Mary's songs.

"Thein Tin, my wife, always keeps a flower near her." Sithu Thant reached for a silver vase designed to hold one flower only. A white rose was in it.

"Flower power," said Antonina.

"Very similar," said U Thant.

She left his office with the rose in the vase. She felt as if she had had a replenishing night's rest. She also allowed herself to remember the man who had introduced her to love.

Night telexes were spluttering out. The American army had lost two dozen men in a jungle skirmish. The Israelis had destroyed eighty per cent of Egypt's oil refining capacity in a three-hour artillery shelling. The Arabs had desecrated a synagogue in Palestine.

CHAPTER
THIRTY-NINE

Anna tried to make sense of the notes she had taken during the lecture but they were too sparse because the teacher of Russian history had spouted data like a robot, interspersed with stale comments. No doubt he had given this lecture in the same way for many years.

Abandoning her task, she went to the window and rubbed her tired eyes. A remedy for her wintry blues could be some fresh air. Perhaps she should go and explore the little wood east of the village.

Buttoned into a tweed jacket, with a knitted hat and gloves, she pushed her cycle out of the vicarage garden, turned into High Street and set off.

Her heart leapt at the sight of Ned carrying a battered petrol can to his truck. He pretended not to have seen her. He opened the driver's door and climbed into the seat. Anna cycled up to him and tittered nervously. Trapped in the vehicle, he eyed her from above.

"The winter-world of England, shelterless and threadbare."

"Is it?" Ned started the motor. She saw his stubby fingers on the key.

"I am off to explore the woods for mental refreshment. Bye!"

"You don't know where to go."

Anna did not tread down on the pedal but waited, her back stooped.

"Ever seen Muntjac deer?"

"No, I haven't. I shall look out for them. Thanks." She started cycling. The truck's diesel engine throbbed as Ned backed out into the road. Anna pedalled down the street. The truck caught up with her and slowed. She hopped from the saddle and ran a few steps in order not to topple over. Ned stopped the rattling and burping truck to lean over the passenger seat. "I'll show you."

"The deer?"

"Yep." The truck started up again. Anna was pleased that her cold-shouldered "bye" had paid off so quickly. There seemed something special about Ned today; perhaps he had had time to think about her. She pedalled off, her heart beating fast. Ned drove down the street and turned right. Anna rode as fast as she could in order not to lose him. The thick jacket was encumbering. At the bottom of the road Ned turned right again and the truck's speed increased; Anna's breath was rasping. Then he turned left, and she was way behind. Sweat drops, despite the cold wind, ran into her eyes and stung acidly. The most important thing was not to lose sight of that vehicle, she thought.

The next turn led into a road which appeared to be private. Anna had never been to these village outskirts before. She concentrated on cycling, her calves burning with the tensing of the muscles. Suddenly before her lay the loading zone of a factory. A forklift truck wheezed by, a load of metal sheets hoisted on its fork. From a corrugated iron shed the high-pitched noise of an aluminium saw screamed.

She skidded to a halt. Out of breath, she brushed sweat from her brows with the sleeve of her jacket and got off her cycle. Ned had parked his truck and was talking to a workman in overalls. There was that instant buddiness about them. Ned pointed at her and struck a disdainful pose, one foot on the inner ring of his front tyre. The three other sides of the factory were fenced in by workshops.

The workman tapped Ned on his shoulder shortly, then walked towards her. She stood defeated, unable to move after her exertion.

"What are you doing here?"

Anna did not know.

"This is private property."

"I didn't know. I'm sorry. I was going to the woods and…" A furtive glance showed Ned watching as if he had staged a buffoonery he would get the credit for.

"Looking for trouble, are you, miss?"

"No, honestly."

"A quickie with one of the lads?"

"No!"

"You've been chasing after Ned. He had to come in here for protection."

Ned by now was slapping his thigh. Two workmen stood close to him, both contaminated by his shameless hilarity.

For a few moments Anna let her mind plunge into the darkness where her trust in Ned had led her; then she turned the bicycle and wheeled it out of the factory complex, her heart as heavy as lead.

"I'll give you some advice, miss. No good chasing them, if they don't fancy you," commented the workman smugly.

"See you, Miss Brodsky," shouted Ned, his tone melodiously mocking.

Leaving the grounds, the sign on the fence read *Sheets, Plate, Rods, Tubes, Corrugated – Cut to Size.* She walked rather than rode, aware that she had made a complete fool of herself.

At the crossroads she dropped her bicycle onto the verge, which not long ago she had passed in an emotional storm. She sat down in the brown prickly grass and put her feet in the leafy gutter. The spear-tipped stalks hurt through her trousers. Life seemed full of selfishness. Treachery waited at every corner. So often she felt shut in by the people around her. They all appeared to be spared the pain of loneliness, which gave them time to hurt others. Not having anything for comfort, her time was taken up thinking about loneliness. She had believed that she had found someone a little like her, misunderstood by others: a poet at heart, a rustic yet with a refined mind.

His cruelty hit her hard.

Anna gazed into the darkness of the drain hole. *I want to experience love: fragile love, love so pure that it would frighten others for they would be excluded. I want a man and a love of my own.*

The dreaded truck appeared on the road. Hastily Anna grabbed the handlebars and pushed off. The thought of being mocked again was unbearable now that she had formulated in her mind what she desired.

The noise of the diesel engine closed up on her. She did not look behind her; she did not look sideways. A horn hooted discordantly right behind. She pulled as far to the left as she could, riding on the grass verge. The engine roared like a hungry tiger. A hasty glance told her that Ned was on her heels. Her front wheel wavered for she had driven over a low-set manhole. She regained control. A few feet further on, the truck bumped her rear mudguard. The impact made her wobble dangerously but she did not fall. Her legs moved up and down and up and down, and she made it to West Street and turned into the shortcut passage between the houses where cars did not fit.

The engine noise was gone and with it the immediate danger. She was relieved by the sudden silence yet her mind perceived the absence as sinister. A dog barked furiously behind a larch-weave fence. She heard his claws scrape the timber. She saw the figure of the vicar walk by the end of the lane. She decided to stay in safety until there was no sight of Ned's truck or the vicar. Tentatively she crept forward in order to peek into Church Lane.

"Hello, hello, hello!"

Anna shrieked shrilly. Ned had jumped over a wooden gate from the garden of the last house. He blocked the passage, filling it with menace. Cornered, Anna stood trembling, passive and abdicating, for she had no way out and had not considered the possibility of Ned leaving his truck in her terror of the vehicle itself.

"Scared, aren't you?"

"Why are you so vindictive?"

"To teach you a lesson."

Not only did he rebuff her friendship but now obviously had decided to punish her for having considered it.

"I have been good to you."

Anna and Ned stood silent, facing each other. Although short, he dominated the narrow passage. She saw the details of the wool loops of his coarse green sweater, the ungainly dirt-grimed hands and the deep weather-lines on his face. She thought she could feel his breath on her although he stood some distance away.

"You've cheated Trish."

"I think you're wrong. We all appreciated Trish's help," she spluttered.

"Oh yeah?"

"Really. Believe me."

"Then how come your mother tore up me sister's rightful possessions?"

"I don't understand you."

"That Viscount Sasha had his lawyer make a contract for a pension, for life, for Trish 'cos he did appreciate the dirty work she had to do."

"How do you know that Sasha did such a thing?"

"'Cos he showed it to Trish, didn't he? But your mother found it and tore it up. For a posh family, of course, it's not proper to give anything to a farmer's daughter."

"There has to be a misunderstanding," said Anna, although she knew instinctively that he told the truth.

"It's a criminal act. Trish is in the right, and your mother will pay for this."

He hiccupped loudly, to Anna's alarm. His strong hand flew flat for her chest and knocked her against a garden fence. "Dirty pack, the lot of you!"

Stunned, Anna remained plastered against the fence. She knew that he would never forgive her.

He started to walk away down the passage. Once his silhouette had disappeared, she too made ready to leave. *They had come so close to making love once in front of that cosy fire in his cottage, and she had nearly lost her virginity, but some dreadful act of her mother had prevented it from happening,* Anna pondered as she emerged into Church Lane to cycle the last stretch home.

With immense relief she saw the familiar chimneys of the vicarage. In front of the pub a gaggle of men stood despite the cold, beer mugs in their hands. One jumped towards her and with a fearless expert grip grabbed her front wheel. Anna fell sideways and caught her leg under the still-spinning back wheel.

"This upper class tart can't even cycle. Shall I call the Rolls, ma'am?"

Anna pulled her leg free; it hurt. The villagers stood around her, hatred wafting from them like a foul smell.

"Been pestering our Ned, have you?" said one, pulling the woollen hat from her head.

"Been cheating Ned and his sis," said another tossing the hat onto the pub's roof with a wide swing of his arm.

430

A third poured his beer over Anna's head. It ran cold down her face and into her collar.

"From now on, we won't let her pass the pub without a bit of fun. You like having fun, don'cha?"

Anna stood rooted in pain and fright.

"This ain't good enough for your class." They pushed her bicycle away from her. "You're better off without it." They propped it on its stand.

Ned appeared in his truck. He parked, grabbed the canister and then poured petrol over the cycle.

"Don't!" shouted Anna.

A lighter was thumb-rubbed. The men stepped back. Her cycle caught fire rapidly. The pub-owner came out. He had one look at the men, one at the burning cycle and one at Anna; then he grinned and went back inside. Anna watched as the tyres melted and the saddle padding burnt vigorously. In the wire basket at the front was her handbag.

She limped away to the safety of the vicarage. A beer mat hit her in the back; another missed and rolled on in front of her. She hobbled as best she could.

The vicarage kitchen was empty. Anna's jacket was sodden with beer. The collar of her blouse underneath clung cold and clammy against her neck. She lifted up the receiver of the telephone near the toaster.

"Mummy?"

"Is that you, Anna?"

Sniffs and sobs answered the question.

"What's the matter?"

"I've been attacked in Brampton. Could I come home please?"

"Have you been raped?"

"I'll tell you later; it all has to do with Trish and Ned, and a legal paper you destroyed." Wild sobs made it impossible for Anna to say more.

"Anna, are you all right?"

"Please."

"I'll be in Brampton in an hour."

"Thank you, Mummy." Anna hung up.

"I never gave you permission to use our phone." The vicar's wife glared at Anna from the door. "Anyway, we need our annex for my sister-in-law."

Anna said nothing.

"You'd better move out today."

"I was going anyway." Anna went to pack her things.

CHAPTER FORTY

"Anyone here?" Fastidiously Valentina stepped over the ribbed ruts of a tractor's wheels embossed into the muddy farmyard. There were many more pitfalls between her and the farmhouse. "Hello?"

A farming tool with a heavy cutting blade stood planted in a mound of manure. From the chicken coop emerged a fluttering of hens and their excited chuckling. Trish appeared at its wire-cage door, an egg in one hand, a rag in the other. Recognising Valentina, Trish yelled, "Ned!"

Valentina ventured a little further and saw that the egg in Trish's hand was coated in dung and feathers. "Trish," Valentina said sombrely while trying to keep a grey dog from her legs with her handbag, "I came to talk to you."

"Ned!" shouted Trish again and there was a ring of desperation to it.

The grey dog sat down momentarily in his need to scratch before taking up sniffing Valentina's legs again.

Trish still stood a safe distance from Valentina. Out of the cowshed flew a pitchfork-load of old straw. In the outside air it steamed as if it was cooking. Trish ran over to the shed's open door, her wellies squelching audibly at each step. A new load of soiled straw flew out of the cowshed. Trish hugged the side of the shed and poked her head inside. "That Valentina Brodsky's here!"

A cow's deep drawn-out moo answered. When Trish stretched her head in again, Valentina used the moment to hit the dog on the head with her bag. He stood motionless, surprised, his tail wagging once more before sinking down.

A short stout man emerged from the shed; his boots were coated in straw glued on with smeared manure. He wore a green sweater and his hair was dark and curly, resembling the fouled straw. Ned pushed his sister aside, strode over the muck towards Valentina.

The grey dog scuttled up to him and nuzzled his jeans before sitting down, peering at Valentina with the same expression as the farmer.

"What do you want?"

"Is there somewhere we can talk?" asked Valentina.

Ned spread his arms.

"Not in this muck."

"What do you want?"

"It's about Anna, and a covenant."

Trish blushed and the egg in her hand started to leak its white through her clenched fingers.

"Yeah, we want to talk about that covenant," said Ned.

"Is there anywhere?" tried Valentina again.

Ned and Trish exchanged glances. The cow mooed.

"You've broken the egg," said Ned to his sister with irritation.

"So?" Trish threw the crushed egg to the ground and flicked her hand several times to get rid of the slime. The dog got up and started licking the egg.

"Me cottage," said Ned and planted the pitchfork.

Brother and sister walked off and Valentina picked her way after them. Every so often the dog accompanying his master turned to eye her.

Valentina was astonished how similar nurse Trish and her brother were from the back. She also wondered what Anna had seen in this primitive farmer bobbing in front of her. To Valentina's relief the cottage garden was without muck; it merely contained rotting weeds.

Ned opened the door of a lean-to conservatory. Through the brickwork of the wall, an opulent fern was growing out of an air-vent. Ned and Trish scraped off their boots on the ledge of the doorstep. They went inside and Valentina followed.

The kitchen was pleasant and there were books. Ned sat down in a spindleback chair while Trish stood, her arms hanging. Uninvited, Valentina sat on the sofa and laughed shortly – a bible lay on the small table.

"What do you want?" repeated the farmer.

When Anna had told Valentina the whole story in the car from Brampton back to Podzhin Hall, she had said that Ned Worship was an articulate poet. If that was a poet, then his pigs could fly, thought Valentina.

"You!" She pointed to Ned. "You hit my daughter, harassed her, and dragged her name into your mud, not to mention her burned bicycle."

He did not answer. The dog curled on the rug in front of the fireplace. His paws had made daisy-shaped prints on the wood-plank floor. Trish looked at her brother as if she did not know what Valentina was talking about. Somewhere a pendulum clock chimed three o'clock.

"And you!" Valentina spun towards Trish, who froze in her posture. "You tried to blackmail me."

Now Ned looked at Trish as if he did not know what Valentina was talking about.

"You're a dirty pack of vermin, the pair of you, and I've got every right to call the police."

"That covenant was in my favour," said Trish.

"No court will agree with you, because you took advantage of an old, senile man, drugged him and possibly even caused his death."

Ned drew in a breath but the siblings remained silent.

"I believe you *sexually* manipulated the late Viscount Brodsky."

"What?" shouted Ned.

Trish dropped her eyes.

"I am right, am I not? You forced an old man into your hands, a helpless sick man. He knew you would kill him, if he didn't do as you said. Blackmail seems to be your second nature, and I wouldn't put great hopes on your first nature either."

"Is this woman telling the truth, Trish?" asked Ned, his dark eyes onyx. Trish stood and said nothing. "Is she?

"The viscount liked me," she said finally.

"Why?" asked Valentina like a bark into the room.

Ned kept his eyes expectantly on his sister.

"I… I had my ways with him," Trish said.

"You did indeed, and those ways are irregular to be polite and criminal to be specific."

"I didn't know that me sis…" started Ned.

"Be quiet!" Valentina was now in command of the situation. "You belong in the same category with what you did to Anna."

He turned sullenly away from her.

"I'll let you both off the hook for now, but if I should ever get a peep or a glimpse of either of you again, then so help me God…" Valentina picked up the bible and smacked it down onto the small table.

The grey dog curled into a tighter ball.

"Is that clear?"

"Yes," said Ned.

"Yes," piped Trish.

"I'll go even further in my generosity – I offer you a present which you don't deserve, but which should make you blush at the slightest pretence of a claim to more Brodsky possessions."

Ned and Trish did not appear to want a present.

"It is in my car." Valentina got up.

Slowly Ned rose. In the back porch, Trish and Ned slid their feet back into their wellies.

All three walked around the cottage to where the Bentley was parked. Valentina reached in to pull out a large parcel. Before she let Ned help her with it, she threatened, "One word, one more gesture, and the police will be on your necks." Then she handed over her present, got into Smelly Ben and drove off towards West Street.

437

Back in the cottage Trish and Ned had not bothered to take off their wellies; they unwrapped the package. It was a painting of a modern kind. In the centre of it was something squiggly with tiny coloured dots.

"What's that?" asked Ned.

"It's very valuable," said Trish, her eyes round with surprise.

"Why?" Ned touched the dry oil-paint with his finger.

"Don't! I tell you, it's valuable. It hung over the fireplace in the music room in Podzhin Hall. It's bound to be worth a lot."

"Oh, we'll sell it then – it's just a smear."

"Never!" shouted Trish. "I want us to live like them too, and have artworks hanging on the walls." With a heave, she lifted Paul's painting and stood it on the mantelpiece behind the clutter of old cups of coffee. The frame was wider than the chimney breast.

"Yuk!" exclaimed Ned, studying the picture.

"You don't understand. This is the most valuable thing you will ever own."

"Is it?" asked Ned, unsure of himself.

CHAPTER FORTY-ONE

Anna was back in Podzhin Hall. She woke early. The bed was warm and her body was intact. Her involvement with Ned was broken, and Brampton behind her. Why had she still felt a certain compassion for Ned when a whole part of her had already left him to admire and dream of Vasily Voronov? Perhaps she had not believed enough that she could dare to love Vasily; she had seen herself only as a mental guide for him, a protector from the family. Now that Ned had decided for her, pushing her out of his life, she could give all of herself to the one she had grown to prefer.

Also she was immensely relieved to be back in Podzhin Hall and had given Grandmother the satisfaction of hearing her admit defeat. Anna smiled, remembering Sasha and his *rebellious peasants*.

She nestled her head into her arm. Now she did not need excuses to be around when a visit from Vasily was announced, did not have to wait for him in the boiler room with a galloping heart. Only time spent with Vasily could re-define her and slowly liberate her shy attraction to him into a relationship and… and perhaps even…

She shuddered with all her limbs in the happy imagination of being touched by Vasily and the bed smelled of lavender-scented linen. "Vasily, my love," she whispered, and outside the dark sky whitened slowly. Soon it would be Christmas again, a better Christmas.

★

In the public library Vasily scanned the section names above the bookshelves. He stopped at *History – Russian*. He read the books' spines. *Russia under the Old Regime: The Romanovs and Their Nobles*. He pulled the book out. His nervous fingers flicked through the index.

Kamenev, Baron; Karpinsky, Prince Gregorii; Kavinsky, Baron Anatole.

Vasily turned to page 125.

Kavinsky, Anatole, Baron, Treasurer to the Romanovs. Born 5 March 1829 in Kishinev; married Anastasia 1849-1884; two sons, Baron Dimitri and Baron Stefan, both killed by bolsheviks in 1917 in St Petersburg.

Turchin had said his father was called Dimitri Kavinsky. Now he read that his alleged father and an uncle, Stefan, were both killed long before he was born. Fury rose in him as he considered the strong possibility that Turchin had just been manipulating him in order to obtain better results on the Brodskys. Vasily had a last flick through the book and found a note at the back:

The data collected in this book are based on scant information obtained from the Soviet Government and testimonies of émigrés. Some data are erroneous. The truth of Ekaterinburg has never satisfactorily been proved, and it is believed that the same applies to some of the aristocrats and their families who may have fled from Russia or shed their heritage by changing their identity. One must remember that, at that time, Russia was in a turmoil of competing philosophies and successive coups.

Vasily closed the book. He still did not know the truth. Somehow it was of vital importance that he find out. He left the library and took the Underground to Knightsbridge in order to buy the Brodskys a Christmas present from Harrods. The library visit had been an unapproved side-trip. He hoped he had not been shadowed.

In Harrods he could hardly believe his eyes. If his father had really been a baron once, he would have shopped in such luxury in Petersburg, or even travelled to Moscow and come home laden with expensive presents. He took in the lavish displays and the overwhelming choice of beautiful and well-made goods. He thought of the choice in GUM Emporium and remembered his Aunt Yelena and her desire for gloves.

He hovered in front of the accessory counter. The glove coating the dummy's hand was a rich plum colour. He dared to touch it and thought of the velvet nose of his father's horse, Siomka.

"They are ladies' gloves," he was informed.

"I want to buy ladies' gloves."

"What size?"

Vasily thought about Yelena's hands lying on the kitchen table in Moscow.

"About my size."

"For a woman, you mean?"

"Well, yes."

The gloves the salesgirl displayed in front of him were of deer leather and thinly lined with silky fur. He stroked them and measured them against his spread hand. He decided on the plum-coloured ones, paid and pushed the crinkling gift-wrapped exclusivity into his coat pocket. Then he checked his watch and was concerned that he had wasted twenty-five minutes in the library and ten at the glove counter. Every minute of his shopping mission had to be accounted for.

Anxiously he gazed around the tempting world of plenty to find quickly a suitable gift. What a shame he had not enough time to go upstairs and revel in other marvels. Walking under a decorated arch from the flower hall into confectionery, his eyes were caught by an inlaid wooden box, its lid ajar. Inside nestled silver-wrapped marrons glacés covered in cellophane with a huge red bow. He bought it.

Back in the Referentura Vasily put the green Harrods bag onto a table to be unwrapped and inspected by the guards. Turchin asked him into the safe speech room.

"I hope I chose something suitably impersonal, yet flashy," said Vasily.

"You did. I have ordered the Vauxhall to be ready for you at one o'clock. Any questions?"

"What do I do if they invite me to celebrate their Christmas with them?"

"Decline politely, but agree to bring back the list Olga is preparing of their lost wealth for what she calls the Kremlin."

"Okay."

"Your progress with Anna is most encouraging. Concentrate on her to find the Ikon. Perhaps Durov will have warmed to you enough to be questioned too. And good luck, Comrade. Christmas is usually an emotional time for them; use it."

★

When Vasily arrived in Podzhin Hall with his offering, he saw Cahill carrying chopped logs for the fireplaces to the back of the house, Njanja hurrying after him with a basket of kindle wood.

Vasily sprinted up the steps and let himself into the dark vestibule, where the stained-glass windows from above the door threw blood-coloured patterns on the marble of the chill house.

Loud arguing inside the music room stopped the moment he entered.

Olga and Valentina stood facing each other, Olga in a mauve chemisier dress, elegant, orderly and confident; Valentina in a riding outfit, her posture aggressive.

"Mr Voronov." Olga turned her intensity away from her daughter. "What a splendid large present. You will spend Christmas with us, I hope. It would make up for the small family we shall have this year."

"Thank you, Countess, but I have a prior engagement."

"The sewage works in Birmingham?" Valentina turned to Olga. "Mother, don't be stupid; they won't let him."

"What a shame. Perhaps at Easter then."

"I must take Rasputin for a spin."

"Make sure you are back by half-past three; I have asked Baroness Aksakova for tea. Mr Voronov, the baroness is dying to talk to you alone."

"Make sure they pay us back first." Valentina spun on her boots and was gone.

Olga cupped her curl. "My daughter mistakes confused subconscious activities for normal thought processes."

Vasily agreed with her but said, "Your painting has gone."

Olga eyed the empty space briefly.

Something pushed him to ask, "Don't you have a *krasny ugol* to worship an ikon?"

She frowned at him quizzically. "Odd that a communist should think of a *beautiful corner* from houses in the old days."

He had the distinct impression that she suspected his ulterior motive. *What would she think if she knew he could be a Kavinsky?*

"By the way," she changed the subject, "Anna has moved back home again. I believe you alone have the power to attract her to Podzhin Hall." Her eyes were on his; then she held out her hand gracefully. "Would you like to take a seat? I have to go and give orders for tea."

He remained alone. It was a crisp December day and a lively fire burned in the fireplace. He contemplated a silver snuffbox but dug both hands into his pockets. Perhaps it was not true; perhaps Dimitri Kavinsky was not his father and had indeed been killed in 1917. But if he were a Kavinsky, then this lifestyle ought rightfully to have been his. He picked up the silver case and clicked it open. It was monogrammed. He yearned to own it: just one such personal perfect artefact to be his, given to him, inscribed with his real initials. Vasily put it back. The desk was unlocked; there might be papers to exorcise his gnawing doubts.

"Vasily! Vasily!"

He spun round and saw Anna in a fur toque standing on the lawn in front of the French windows, waving with one hand and holding a book in the other. Slowly he crossed the carpet and opened the doors.

"Oh, what a surprise to see you here," she chirped happily.

"You knew I was coming."

"Yes, maybe."

He stepped out to her onto the lawn. Her face glowed and her breath emitted milky patterns. Together they strolled away and he left the temptations of the music room behind.

"Anna, remember we are friends now. You must always tell me the truth."

She merely gave him a sideways glance while her hand stroked down his sleeve once, as if to make sure he was there.

Artemis, in perpetual pose of attack, stared blind and

bulbous-eyed into a wintry park where the elms stood bared of leaves.

"For you and me it is not necessary to speak of the truth," she started. "That implies the possibility of lying."

He waited.

"We know anyway, because we *recognise* each other."

At the graves they came to a halt. She pointed. "This old grave is being reclaimed by the earth."

"Whose is it?"

"It belonged to the people who owned Podzhin Hall before us."

Vasily stooped and scraped away the leaves, glued by many rains to the stone slab.

"The writing has faded," said Anna.

"*Nastas*," he made out.

"We reckon it is Anastasia, and look at the year of death."

With frantic scraping, he uncovered the date 1884, chiselled clearly. Nothing more was legible.

The book that morning in the library had stated:

Kavinsky, Anatole, Baron... married Anastasia 1849-1884.

He stood up straight. *MY GRANDMOTHER*, it screamed in him.

Anna did not notice that something so overwhelming had just happened to him. She opened her book, *State and Revolution*, and tried to interest him in the aptness of Lenin's thoughts. "*The substitution of the proletarian for the bourgeois state is impossible without a violent revolution,"* she read. "I've been thinking about…"

The Kavinskys lived here in Podzhin Hall. Did my father ever stand here before his mother's grave?

"Lenin was so methodical in his thought and analysed politics in such a rational, yet inspired way." Her gentle voice stubbornly went on. "Many of his thoughts can easily be adapted to…"

Father had never spoken of his parents. That was not normal and Vasily should have noticed before.

Anna was absorbed in the merits of revolution, while he suffered his own p rivate revolution to which Lenin's wisdom did not extend.

Abruptly, he turned to her. "Did the people who lived here before the Brodskys own anything that is still in the Hall?"

She thought for a moment and he trembled from fear that she would ask him why he wanted to know. "I think so," she said simply.

He took a deep cold breath and exposed himself to further agony. "Did they own the famous Ikon of the Virgin of Kazan?"

Anna avoided eye-contact.

"Did they?" He was shaking now. "Remember, you are going to tell me the truth for friendship's sake."

"I believe so."

Vasily shuddered. Her answer engulfed him. Turchin had mentioned that the Ikon was worth at least one

447

million pounds. *That Ikon should be mine too*, he thought, battling with nausea.

"Where is it?" he managed to ask.

Anna shook her head energetically, unable to answer, and shut her book.

"Why can't you tell me?"

"Because, because I…"

"Yes?"

"I can't"

There was some reason they would not speak about the Ikon. Now he had to find it, not just for the Party, more for himself.

"The Soviet people are always criticised in the West for suppressing information. You make me believe that the same is true of émigrés."

She squirmed. "I wish I could tell you."

"Ah well. Next time. Instead, tell me about Antonina in New York. Do you miss her?"

"She is my identical twin."

"It is endearing to know that you all trust Antonina with the Ikon, I remember now Olga mentioning it. Sorry for having been indelicate earlier."

"Antonina does not have the Ikon with her."

"So, the Ikon is here."

"Please, Vasily."

A horse approached at full gallop across the park, its nostrils steaming. Anna and Vasily dived out of the way. The pounding noise accompanied by the animal's rasping breath passed close to them.

"Antonina and I used to say that our mother never grew up."

Vasily laughed shortly.

"Oh dear, the baroness has arrived," said Anna. A silver Mercedes was parked in front of Podzhin Hall. "We'd better go in for tea."

"You go ahead; I'll make sure your childlike mother is coming too." Vasily walked to the stables, reflecting that he would not give up, until he knew all he had a right to know, *damn it*.

★

"What were you doing milling around the graves?" Valentina glowed from the exercise and the effort of controlling the powerful stallion. The horse pranced in the stable box and Vasily stepped out of the reach of its hooves. She tossed the reins to the groom who tried to calm the animal. He slipped the bridle over its head and Vasily saw the bit lathered in yellow foam.

"Remember, the baroness has arrived for tea. I came to make sure you would appear."

"Bloody tea."

"Your daughter thinks that you are a little too crazy sometimes."

"And I think that she is too young for you, my dear."

She smacked the rump of the horse flat-handed. The stallion tossed its head and snorted. The groom, who was lifting the saddle off the dark-stained back, kept his inquisitive eyes on Vasily.

Unceremoniously, Valentina pulled Vasily out of the stables.

Had his father used these stables?

"Let's elope, you and I – gallop away. You know how to, right?"

"I rode a horse called Siomka in the style you ride, when I was a boy at the farm. It was my father's mare. He trusted her more than Mother and me."

"Divulging some of your past – most enlightening."

He gathered himself and said, "There is a baroness having tea inside the house."

"That old battle-axe. Let's go back the long way."

"Your daughter has a point."

She ignored his words and in an adulatory way gazed at him. "My dearest Vasily, I have come to the conclusion that it is time for you to defect in order to be able to ask me to marry you. Only then can we elope."

There it was again, that treacherous word *defect* to which she had added *marriage*.

"Your daughter was lenient in her judgement."

Heat still emanated from Valentina's body; her eyes were clear and her skin buffed by wind.

"You get us back a large amount of money from the Soviets; I speed up the sale of the Ikon, and off we go."

"Where *is* this Ikon to be sold?"

"Oh, that blasted thing!"

He was alert to every breath and movement of hers.

"It's a year now that we put it up for sale and still nothing. I don't know what Anna did. Olga won't tell me. I called Sotheby's several times. They claim not to know anything about it. *It takes time*, is all Mother says. Our financial situation is shitty, so you see, my solution is not so childish. You make Moscow pay and then you leave them, *Ciao!* I'll get the money, and you to marry me. You will be free and rich, with a wife and interesting daughters. I'm sure we can even wangle it for you to be called *baronet;* now that would make a change for you."

"Quite an impressive fabrication of your mind."

She took his arm. "I need you, Vasily. You are the someone who can make me sparkle and dance. I discovered you, and now I want to hold you. Or do you happen to fancy my daughter instead – Anna, with her boring socialist rubbish? I would have thought you had had enough of that." She gripped his arm. "Are you married back home?"

"No."

"See, there's nothing standing in our way."

"I can think of a few things."

"Oh Vasily, only you can make me calm and normal. Kiss me."

If he really was the Baron Kavinsky, then he should be a man of the world and able to cope with this complicated dangerous woman, but at the moment he was barely master of his quivering legs.

"In here." Valentina stepped from the path and pulled him behind a yew hedge.

"What are you doing?"

"You will get a better idea in a second." Her hot lips kissed him strongly and shortly, inflaming him with her magnetism. A few yards away lay the remains of his grandmother, Anastasia.

"How can we make you grow up?" he defended himself and pulled her back onto the path, thinking with amazement that his subconscious had made him say *we.*

CHAPTER FORTY-TWO

As a trustworthy comrade Vasily acted automatically, doing what was expected of him in every detail of the working day. His body however sprang tricks on him which surely were obvious: his right hand shaking over the document he was given to read; the repeated swallowing of saliva before he spoke. He felt his shirt itch on his back from cheap washing powder.

Walking from one assignment to another in the streets of London, probably observed, he imagined himself wearing the clothes of those who passed, driving the expensive cars in the road. Yet, in his rayon raincoat he still despised the conceited fop flaunting the silk lining of his camelhair coat, or the spoiled brat in his flashy car listening to loud decadent music.

He was living in two skins and neither one fitted him. He needed help and found himself yearning for Anna who was an aristocrat but accepted the Comrade Voronov in him.

★

"Anna," he said, the next time he was alone with her in Podzhin Hall. "Tell me about the family in the old times."

"There was my great-grandfather Mikhail, and my grandfather Ivan, and Sasha's wife Tatyana, but they didn't do anything constructive or contribute to society in any way."

He smiled at her patiently. "When did the Brodskys move to Podzhin Hall?"

Was their conversation not to be about the philosophy of communism? Reluctantly she offered him, "In 1918, after a long train journey from Petersburg."

"What had happened to the people who lived here before?"

"I'm not sure, but nothing very nice, I believe."

"Are there old photographs?"

"Somewhere. Maybe in the attic. Grandfather Ivan had a camera and a collection of hunting pictures, mostly with his right foot posed on poor slain stags."

The door swung open and Valentina came in. "God, I'm bored today. What are you two talking about?"

"Count Ivan's deer-hunting photographs," said Anna quickly and with guilt.

"Heaven help me! Let's play cards!" This was an order.

Once they were installed at the card-table, Valentina stuck a lit Sobranie into a cigarette holder, pushed it to the corner of her mouth and shuffled the packs adroitly while Anna explained the rules of canasta to Vasily. The cards were flicked in fast succession into three piles.

Valentina, sorting the cards in her hand into a fan,

puffed out smoke through the other corner of her mouth.

"Mummy always cheats."

"Talking of cheats, you two aren't bad at it yourselves." She picked up a card from the pack. "You, Vasily, are not just the pretty boy sitting around Podzhin Hall learning to play canasta. You are working for the communist cause. I see a rat in the tall grass when there is one! And you, Anna. Do you think I don't know why you aren't at university today?"

Anna lay down two kings and a joker. "That makes seventy points," she said, ignoring her mother's querulousness.

Vasily picked a card from the pack. "The *sevens* are worth only five points each, is that correct?" he asked and lay down four *sevens*, two *twos* and a joker, and discarded a black *three*.

Valentina picked up a card, glanced at it and threw her hand onto the table.

"She always does that when she's losing."

"Anna, go and do some homework. There must be an essay about collective farming you haven't done yet."

"I…"

"Leave us."

Anna slowly put her cards down and left the drawing room, not without glancing meaningfully back at Vasily.

"Vasily," started Valentina, "do you want to make love to me?"

"I preferred playing canasta."

"Since you are so eager to learn Western ways, you still don't know how aristocratic women behave in bed,

454

do you? There might be more to it than you were told. Come upstairs."

"No, Valentina."

"I'll join the KGB, if that's what you're after." She jumped up, her cigarette nearly grazing his cheek, and grabbed his arm. "If you want to see those old photographs, you'd better come with me."

He knew that she was luring him with a lie but it was a thin tightrope he had to walk. He had to control her destructive games but in a way which would not disrupt his visiting rights in Podzhin Hall.

In her bedroom Valentina whisked at once around him to slide the bolt on the door, then she started to unbutton her blouse. "You drive me insane, Vasily. I don't know whether I hate you or love you, but I want to find out now."

"I agreed to come here to avoid a scene downstairs. My feelings for you are..." he searched for a description, "... brotherly. You are an exciting, lively and beautiful woman. Please, let's not abase ourselves to a shameful act, the outcome of which we both know."

She ignored him and took off her blouse. She wore no brassiere and he noticed with surprise that her breasts were shapely, still firm and round.

Someone knocked on the door. "Vasily, are you in there?"

"Tell her to go away," Valentina hissed.

He felt Anna's presence on the other side of the door.

"Order her!"

455

"I'll be down right away," he said and turned his back on the half-dressed Valentina.

Her reaction was more violent than he had anticipated. She screamed and came for his face with red talon fingernails. He dived sideways, tripped over a stool and scrambled up.

"You filthy tease!" she shouted, her breasts lolling free. "Evil Kremlin manipulator!"

He saved himself from her flailing claws, pulled the bolt and shook her off. She fell to the floor while he escaped onto the landing and slammed the door.

Anna was gone.

That was precisely what sexual practices were about – human degradation. Suddenly he grinned. Had he not dared to go to her bedroom, he would not have been able to defeat Valentina. She was beaten and her fury carried no threat for him – a tempest in a glass. She was just like a temperamental irritating sister.

Feeling years younger and lighter Vasily half-climbed onto the banister, pushed himself to the first step and slid down to the ground floor like a naughty boy who felt very much at home.

He knew Anna had gone to wait for him in the boiler room.

★

It was said in Obodovka, a remote village in the Ukraine, that when the dirty hungry man dragged himself through the village on that cold winter's day, the smell of widow Yugina's *verenniky*, ravioli stuffed with cheese, stung his nostrils. He stopped and promptly forgot where he had come from and where he was heading. As the stranger stood motionless in the snow, sniffing hungrily, Yugina invited him in and served him some of her speciality with sour cream. Having tasted his first spoonful he stopped eating and proposed marriage to her, before taking up the spoon again.

Yugina was seen relaying pails of water into the house. After much serious scrubbing, the handsome Yuri Voronov emerged from under layers of dirt and flea-ridden furs. Then she agreed to be his wife and he asked for another helping of the *verenniky*. That is how Dimitri Kavinsky became Yuri Voronov and lived in Obodovka.

To the dismay of Yugina the marriage was not blessed with a crowd of children, the greatest riches life could offer a woman. However when she had given up hope, seven years into their marriage, a baby boy was born. She wanted to call him Stefan but Yuri, unable to bear the memory of his murdered brother, had insisted on Vasily.

The boy's childhood was spent in the small white-walled cottage under a thatched roof. He played in the summer in the front garden or lay in the wooden pram, watched by neighbours in turns or not watched at all. No brothers or sisters followed him. During the winter he was sent to the crèche. His father helped in the timber-felling and mother worked in the sugar factory in the big neighbouring village. They grew sugar-beet like everyone else and had one cow Vasily called *Moloko* – milk – once he learned to talk. The cow's shed stood at the end of the orchard just beside the small stream where his mother washed the laundry. On the other side of the stream, which could be crossed precariously on planks, three acres of arable land belonged to Yugina.

Moscow lay as far as the moon for them and was as unpopular with the citizens as a clouded evening moon, and so were the rumours brought to the village of Stalin's decision to impose collective farming. No-one ever went to Moscow and, apart from the Soviet officials poking their noses around, no-one ever came from there. There was one exception: Yugina's sister Yelena, who had married a man from Kiev and with him travelled north-east and ended up in the capital.

When Vasily was one year old, things changed in the village; a new age began. The waves of the October Revolution that till now had not had much impact on their lives slowly spread to the Ukraine, and voices from Moscow were heard louder and louder. Meetings of Agricultural Co-operatives were organised with greater frequency. Then came a harsh winter. Yugina hung two layers of sackcloth over the window and Vasily's life was spent in the dark, or shadows at best. He cried a lot because he could not visit *Moloko* or crawl after the chuckling hens.

Spring eventually did come, and the plum and cherry trees were clad in a gauze of white and pink. The small river thawed and the countryside shone the better after the months of snow. However, with spring came also the first mention of the *kolkhoz*. Most peasants opposed the collective and hung on to their land, even those who had little. The idea of creating a farm from Siberia to the Black Sea and from Finland to Alaska, of which each and every one was a part on equal terms, found little enthusiasm amongst them. Some opposed openly and said so loudly after drinking in the inn. Tension grew and two Party members were sent to Obodovka to straighten the village out. There were fights and the richest peasant was taken away, leaving his wife and four children to cope with the farm. Endlessly the birth of a new peasant collective was discussed in whispers under thatched roofs.

In summer the order came from the Uman district headquarters to speed up the collectivisation and within a week to dispossess the most bitter opponents of the *kolkhoz*. The richest peasant was said to have changed his mind in prison and signed a form to join his fifteen acres, twelve cows and all his horses and pigs to the *kolkhoz*. The villagers watched as he was driven back on a tractor. Wordlessly he disappeared into his house to be surrounded by his wife and children. The following night, he hung himself from the crossbeam of his barn, dead but not beaten by Stalin.

Obodovka had to give in. At harvest time all the grain was taken straight to the Party's warehouses, as the peasants who had laboured all year stood watching, their hands hanging, with another winter awaiting them. Instead of being paid for their ploughing, sowing, reaping, threshing, instead of being paid for the sugar-beet carted to the factory, the farmers remained empty-handed. The Soviet district promised them a high place in the list of agricultural contributors to the Workers' Union – a nourishing prospect. The dark Ukrainian eyes shone in anger and hunger.

Obodovka started to cheat. They sowed grain around

their door steps, vegetables in the barns from where their cows had been confiscated. They sowed grain on the edges of woods, and tomatoes in pots in their houses behind windows. In the woods they cut clearings and grew grain there. They pampered the growth, sprayed it with blessed water and neglected the open arable land. Instead of fertilising the young wheat, they cut off the newly forming heads and ate them, leaving the plant to die. Many villages in the Ukraine did the same. The authorities had to amend their plans and it was agreed that not less than two kilograms of grain would be the pay for each work unit. The next year the brigade leaders found ears intact on the corn.

Vasily had grown into a handsome little boy and had started primary school in the village. He was tall for his age. Soft dark hair fell on his high forehead and his hands were smooth and long-fingered. When he participated in a running or jumping competition with his class mates, burly and of peasant-make, he was graceful. He was an attentive pupil, and the teacher lent him books from the common room that he read avidly after school. Yet the others did not bully him for there was a strength in him with which he faced their chafed faces, their runny noses. Instead of mocking him they ignored him.

Yugina was a strict mother and a good cook. Vasily's favourite was home-made yoghurt with sour dark bread. Often she stroked her son's silky hair, shaking her head.

When father Voronov came in from work the day Vasily had received his Pioneer's scarf, the boy sat at the kitchen table doing homework. Without a word, Yuri yanked the red scarf from his son's neck.

"It's an honour to belong to the young communist organisation," Vasily protested.

"It should be worn like this." Father bound the red cloth over Vasily's eyes. Vasily was shaken by his father's reaction and lack of respect.

"Everyone in Class Four got one. I'm a Pioneer now; I promised to obey and contribute to the common cause."

"You are a fool now, like the rest. Who gave it to you?"

"A Party official."

"With glasses and a scar on his chin – the one I saw arrive this morning?"

Vasily nodded.

"Tell me more. Was his name mentioned?"

"No. He frightened me a bit. He gaped at me sort of with hollow eyes, queerly."

"Don't ever wear that in my house," he hissed, pointing to Vasily's red scarf lying on the table. Without a further word he left the house. A little later Vasily and Yugina saw him trotting down the road on the old mare he called *Siomka* after Tolstoy's horse in *Master and Man*. When his dark silhouette had merged with the blue shadows in the raw dusk over the naked ploughed fields, Vasily turned to his mother who kept him hugged to her.

"Vasily, some of that old story of your father forgetting his whereabouts when he smelled my *verenniky* is true. Nobody knows much about him."

"Not even you, Mother?"

"I guess much but I don't know for sure."

CHAPTER
FORTY-THREE

Vasily and Anna were united in conspiracy as they crept up the back stairs to the second landing.

"Valentina has gone out. I saw her. I promise," whispered Anna, but still they tiptoed along the runner carpet past her bedroom.

To the right of the bull's-eye window was a door and the steps up into the attic. The door creaked as Anna opened it and fell shut with a little bang behind them. Vasily put his warm hand on the back of her neck as they mounted the wooden steps together.

The large attic was stuffy. Opaque light was spun with silver threads and her eyes sparkled with excitement. There were no sounds apart from their breathing and the occasional mysterious creaking of the house.

"Watch your head." Anna ducked under the beam. "I haven't been here for ages."

Vasily groped his way over to where flat items were stored upright, one leaning against the other. He tilted some framed pictures to inspect them and a folded card-table fell open. Moths had eaten pathways into the green felt.

Stooping at the loft window, she wiped the dust-blind glass with the elbow of her cardigan. "You can see Oxford from up here." She turned back to Vasily. "You won't find any photographs over there." She crouch-waddled back until she could stand up straight and opened the drawers of a dark *bombé* chest to find them full of pieces of fabric. She pulled the drawer of a small drum-table but it was empty. The drawer of the lamp table was a fake. Lifting the sack cloth to check in some tea-chests, she exclaimed, "Rolls and rolls of worm-eaten wallpaper. Why do we keep those?"

He stepped over a folded rug to check what might have been a picture pushed under the tapestry bench. It turned out to be a drop-leaf for a table.

"I guess the papers and photographs are all kept in the music room, unless..." She bent down to a small leather coaching case and undid the latches. He stood legs astride across the jumble, brushing down his hands. The Ikon was certainly not in the attic.

"I thought so." The case was filled with papers. She carried it to him. He tested his way back and sat down on the only item which seemed dusted, a large chequered travelling trunk. She put the case on his lap. "Check that. There might be photographs."

Eagerly he started to riffle through yellowed and furred letters and papers. Anna continued to roam around and suddenly pulled away a dust sheet to reveal a high-wheeled perambulator.

"It's still here!" she exclaimed, holding the narrow

wooden handle. "Can you believe that Njanja pushed us around the park in this, Antonina at one end and me at the other? We always played footsie, and then kicked each other, and ended up crying." She rocked the pram.

He wrenched his eyes from the papers. Anna's figure at the perambulator in the veiled light stood outlined by a pale glow, and she smiled sweetly. There was something beautiful about her and something sad for she could not possibly remember the time of the pram, and yet what she said had probably happened exactly as she imagined it. Childhood happenings could be known even if never told.

Origins could be proven but only by the known. He tilted a photograph towards the window. "Is there no light up here at all?"

"No." She came to sit with him on the trunk.

"This is the only photograph I've found. Who are the people in that garden?"

She almost snuggled up to him to look.

"That young woman in the huge hat has to be Olga. And the three men at the table are Ivan her husband, Sasha and… I am not sure who that is, holding out a toy horse to that baby, which is almost certainly Valentina. Oh, the peasant girl holding the baby! It's Njanja, would you believe?"

Vasily did not smile. She had to hold herself back from reaching out to touch his hair. It was marvellous to be up in this treasure attic, miles better and more intimate than the boiler room.

She picked a letter from the pile. "Here's a poem

written in Russian to a woman in my family – a love letter!"

"May I read it?"

"No."

He jerked in surprise.

"You have to write your own love letters."

"Oh, Anna. It's a doctor's prescription for cough syrup."

"Too bad." She left his side and went back to the pram. "Will you write me a love letter?" She rocked the pram and it swayed on the little leather straps.

He shut the case with the papers but kept the picture out. Joining her at the pram, he put his hand next to hers on the handle and they rocked it together.

"Can I take the photo downstairs to look at it in the light?"

"You can keep it."

He slipped it into his pocket. "I will write you a letter of endearment," he finally promised and bent his head onto her shoulder, his face against her neck. His mouth travelled up over her chin and found her mouth. She let go of the pram, her hands pushing against his strong shoulders like buffers, and the kiss frightening at first softened as it lingered, melting her face to his. When it was over, she felt a chill brush over her skin, and the thought flashed through her mind that everyone in Oxford could see them up there in the gable window.

She had prayed for this to happen; longed for his affection and physical comfort. With Ned she had done all the battling and with the few male university friends she had known, she had given, she had helped, she had waited, to finally watch them leave with other girls. Ancient history. "Please kiss me again," she begged.

He took her head into his hands, gently inclined it, and kissed her again, not as long and hard but with astonishing familiarity.

CHAPTER
FORTY-FOUR

Antonina had moved to a small flat on East 27th Street, sharing it with a UN translator. Working all hours, Antonina was rarely home and of her flatmate only knew that she never screwed back the toothpaste top and wore knickers with the days of the week embroidered on them. Antonina's physical exercise consisted of walking to and from the UN, mostly in the dark and alongside growing piles of black rubbish bags, as Manhattan was suffering a prolonged garbage strike. *Who would have the strong stomach to clear it away eventually?*

The General Assembly was over and somehow Christmas had come and gone, largely uncelebrated due to the different beliefs in the UN. Antonina had tried to call Podzhin Hall but Western Union was overloaded because of the holiday, and eventually she had given up. The Executive Office staff had organised their traditional Boxing Day boat trip around Manhattan and Antonina put her name down together with that of her flatmate. Slowly the boat motored down the Hudson and passed not far from Governor's Island and Irina, her son Travis, and Ricky to whom she had sent a Christmas card. Refreshments were offered as they circled the Statue of Liberty but Antonina's flatmate suffered from seasickness which spoiled the pleasure for Antonina.

Now it was the last day of the year. Antonina had worked with application and was walking home as freezing snow flurries seemed to sweep her down Third Avenue. New Year's Day 1968 was officially a holiday. Pope Paul VII had declared it a day of peace, and there was a ceasefire in Vietnam.

As a token of celebration she indulged in a large gin and tonic she took upstairs to the roof of the apartment block. Barring international catastrophes she would be free tomorrow. A silver moon was cut into the black sky, the shape of a thumbnail stab. Millions of lit windows lined the canyons and spotlights glittered on the snow-dusted rooftop landscape. She sat on the ventilation extractor. Draping her wool coat tight around her, the collar up to her untidy bundle of hair, she slowly let go of the pressure from her demanding work and thought instead of Podzhin Hall's park under snow: the snowman they had built. She thought of Anna and pulled her coat even closer to her.

In a flat leap a devil-may-care moggie jumped from another rooftop onto hers. Tail up straight like a bottlebrush, the cat buffed along her legs purring.

"Do you know that it is New Year's Eve? I haven't been home for ten months? Do you care about your cat family? Do you care about the atrocious things the Israelis and Palestinians are doing to each other? The killing of small children in Vietnam? No? Lucky you."

She stroked the feline, drained her glass and left the cold.

Down in her flat she poured herself another drink, toasted her family back home, put on pyjamas and slipped into bed where she started to read the newly published *Lolita* by Nabokov.

The doorbell buzzed. She ignored it. It rang again, prolonged. She slipped into her peignoir and went to open the bullet-proof door, leaving the security chain in place.

"Hello, Miss Brodsky."

"Oh, it's you." She recognised the man with the deep, rasping accent who had accosted her in San Francisco, allegedly bringing greetings from home.

"I have something important to tell you," he whispered in a conspiratorial tone.

"Talk. I'm not unlatching the door."

"I represent the Smithsonian Institute in Washington, Byzantine art. Our priority is protecting historical masterpieces, of which the Ikon of Kazan is one."

"My grandmother sold it through Sotheby's."

"I don't think so," he responded, with ominous emphasis. "I am here to help. Your family may be in trouble."

There was a noise in the hallway.

"My roommate is coming home."

The odious man straightened up. He glared at her, his eyes sombre and cross, and then, shoulders hunched, he scurried down the stairs.

Antonina woke late on the first day of 1968. During the night she had taken the decision to speak to the UN head of security to put a stop to the pestering. She stretched voluptuously, planning a drawn-out breakfast, but her flatmate's voice at the door announced that Mr Falcone had just left a message saying she was needed at the UN.

"I can't," uttered Antonina. "I won't."

On the 38th floor the official holiday was no more than wishful thinking. The ceasefire had been broken by the Viet Cong, who took advantage of the truce, attacking American positions and killing a hundred and seventy-six.

"Are our objections going to make the slightest difference?" she remonstrated sitting down at her desk.

"I heard that," said Sithu U Thant. "And the flower on your desk has wilted."

Antonina pulled herself together to work with neutral application.

★

On New Year's Day 1968 the Soviet Embassy in London offered a drinks party to its employees in the reception rooms. A tray was sent up to the cypher clerk.

The ambassador addressed them about the milestones reached by the Soviet Union, giving them an early lead in the space race. He hinted at problems for the unpliant government in Czechoslovakia and emphasised that allies served by weak leaders would have to be taken over by strong masters.

Chilled vodka was served, caviar, and Russian dark bread with herring. The diplomats mingled.

Vasily was sucking the home flavour out of a piece

of bread when the third secretary approached. "In space, we're flying circles around the Americans."

As he left, the scientific attaché blurted out, "There have been failures too, never talked about."

How did he dare criticise, undermine the glow of success? Vasily was appalled and thrilled at the same time. "You'd better stop drinking and watch your mouth."

"Our rocket programme is run by German scientists, you know – Jews."

"Hush," hissed Vasily.

"We have also been helped, they say, by some Russian émigré scientists in the US."

"Really? They work with us?"

Turchin came their way. "*Nazdroviye!*" He lifted his glass. "To extraordinary achievements in the New Year."

"Russian morality can't be trusted: half-saints, half-savages, according to some writer now in Siberia."

Turchin frowned and took the glass from the engineer. "Happy New Year to all of you!" he shouted. "Now, everybody out."

On the way out Vasily muttered to the engineer, "You said too much in there. I am frightened for you."

"I'm only Russian, a drunk Russian. What other Russians are there?"

"You said we're co-operating with émigrés."

"So, now you're going to send me to Siberia?"

"Someone else might. I'm interested in White Russians. Can we talk somewhere?"

"The men's room. I need a piss anyway."

The two men stood squeezed in a cubicle, a toilet bowl between them. Obviously the shedding of alcohol-laced body fluids was clearing the engineer's brain. "What do you want to know? You're a first secretary. I'm technical staff."

"You've come across things that interest me personally."

"Emigré scientists helping to put the first Russian on the moon?"

"Yes, and in your opinion is there a possibility in the future the Soviet Union might accept White Russians as comrades?"

"Brezhnev needs their expertise. He'd suck it from the asshole of a monkey, if the ape were a genius. That's enough. How are we going to explain what we are doing here?"

"You had too much to drink, and I forced you to vomit the excess alcohol."

Cold to the core of his heart, Vasily unlocked the door and left the facilities. *What had come over him? Emigrés, White Russians* had become trigger words that could endanger him.

In the safety of his room he took a knife and poked behind the red fire hydrant. The photograph he had hidden there was gone.

★

In Podzhin Hall on the first of January the groom asked to speak with Countess Olga. She condescended to meet him under the porch, a shawl wrapped around her.

"Out with it, man."

"Rasputin has a chest infection, but Madame Valentina is refusing to take it seriously."

"Rasputin was a Russian peasant endowed with mystical powers and much trusted by Czar Nicolai and his family."

"The horse, Countess…"

"… is an extravagant luxury."

"If he is not treated, I must quit my job."

"Then go."

"The horse, Countess. He is sick and needs care."

"Then you're the right man for it."

"I have actually not been paid for four months now."

"You must get benefit from your dedication to horses."

"Yes, I do."

"I am glad to hear it. Keep benefitting."

★

On the first of January Georgi visited Pavel in the dacha.

In strictest confidence he told his father that their government was preparing to invade Czechoslovakia and that a number of Party members, suitably expert in foreign relations, were to be recalled to Moscow to handle the repercussions.

"Could that include Vasily?" Pavel fretted at once.

"I reckon he'll be short-toured in about three months."

"You have to prevent this at all costs. Promise me. His real targets are the Ikon and the Brodskys."

"I worry about you, Father. What does an artefact

have to do with our national war strategy? Besides, according to Turchin, Vasily's progress is slow and no results have yet been achieved."

"I won't have Vasily come back. Promise me to keep him in London to give him time to do more."

"He also collected two black marks."

"What did he do?"

"He bought some gloves in Harrods without permission, and then, worse, a photograph was found hidden behind the fire extinguisher in his room."

"What's on the picture?"

"Aristocrats in the Crimea, estimated to have been taken in 1916. He must have removed it from the Brodskys, without reporting it to us."

"Can you get it for me?"

"I've seen a copy. Three men, one woman, a servant with a baby, everyone dressed up ridiculously, hats and suits and parasol."

"Go back to town. Get hold of that picture and bring it to me right away. And under no circumstances allow Vasily to be put on the list of those to be recalled early. Son, do you hear me?"

"I obey the Controller. You're losing it, Father. Your pet philosophy is not a priority for today's Communist Party, which is leading the world."

"Well, it should be. It is the most important thing that has ever been attempted."

"Take care, Father." Georgi picked his fur hat from the table.

"Come back. I haven't finished talking yet – come back at once!"

At the door of the dacha, the carer stepped into Georgi's way. "If you anger him that much, he will have a heart attack, and I…"

"… and you don't do Level 4 cardiac care. Get out of my way."

CHAPTER FORTY-FIVE

January was a raw month. An arctic depression over the UK would not shift. Blizzards raged across the country; roads were closed, trains delayed – the worst conditions since 1963. The Brodskys huddled in the music room with the fire burning, their shoulders raised, wrapped in woollies. For two days the hall had felt like an ice box. Anna claimed to have heard a boom in the boiler room and was worried about a gas explosion. Valentina explained, less than patiently, that they were heated by oil. Fydo said that the warmth of a body was sufficient in itself.

A heating man was finally called by Cahill; the enormous underground oil tank was empty. Olga accepted the need for a delivery but was unable to pay the bill. Perhaps in a week or two.

It was only towards the end of the month that timid sunrays made the trees drip with melted snow. Olga, pining for warmth and air to clear her congested chest, strolled towards the wood in her full-length fur coat, her feet in galoshes. Sasha's grave had harmoniously blended with the others as if he had been intended to lie there.

The old lady pressed her hand against her rasping chest to appease the ache of the life which still had to be lived, minute by minute. She felt it all beyond her strength.

Even Antonina, far from their troubles, had alarmed them in her last letter with talk of a Soviet plot. *Was there really someone in the Soviet Government perversely reluctant to let them live in peace in exile, even to the extent of following Antonina through America?*

What about Vasily? Was he a wolf in a lamb's skin? Did the Ikon of the Virgin of Kazan carry a curse for all those who bowed to her, trusting her sweet smile of benevolence? She, Olga, slept underneath the Virgin or rather suffered insomnia beneath her.

Antonina's letter had shaken Olga but she could not let it show, especially not as Vasily had come for his first visit of the year.

Further along, on the border of the woods, she saw him with Anna in her knitted bobble hat. The pair stopped and put their hands simultaneously on a tree trunk. *I must warn Anna about Vasily*, thought Olga, *for she is so easily taken in. Was Valentina right when she insisted that the wooing of the girl was nothing more than a Party duty for Vasily?*

Anna pointed at early snowdrops and he bent to look. *What role is this man playing in Podzhin Hall, and to what end? Just because we are getting used to his presence, a personable man walking around the Hall as if he belongs, it should not be forgotten that he represents the enemy. I must keep my mind on the day in Petersburg when Dimitri was shot and me, in spirit, along with him.*

Vasily and Anna must have moved into the wintry wood. Returning to the hall, Olga saw Aksakova's silver Mercedes in the forecourt. The pleasure of it warmed her. There was still her old friend, someone to talk to without having to explain everything. Olga hastened her steps.

The baroness's chauffeur appeared to have been crying. He was just passing to say that the baroness had died peacefully last night. With care he put an azure-coloured Fabergé egg, lightly wrapped in silk paper, into Olga's joined palms.

"She wanted you to have it," he said with difficulty, got into the car and drove away.

Later that day Olga surprised Durov, not just behind the drapes in the dining room but virtually wrapped into one them. Emerging, holding Sasha's black umbrella, Njanja spluttered with outrage. "Look at zr candlestick."

Olga looked at the sideboard and back to her servant.

"Is zr one, not zr two."

"So where is zr two?"

"Gone. Taken. A thief."

"And you were waiting to hit him with the umbrella?"

Njanja opened the sideboard drawer to demonstrate that the silver napkin rings were also missing. "Not in the house. I search."

"Thank you for telling me, Durov. I will take care of it." Olga took the umbrella and stroked its ivory handle, the gold collar, remembering how often Sasha had sheltered her with him under it. "Please put this umbrella in my wardrobe."

"Silver candlestick more valuable," Durov muttered, leaving with the umbrella.

Mid-February. The Soviet Embassy circulated the news in the left-wing press that a famous White Russian actor had begged to return to Moscow. Turchin had cultivated him. Vasily was under pressure.

He had started fabricating in his reports on his visits to the Brodskys, suggesting a change in their attitude despite the lack of a response to their financial demands. The episode in the toilet with the engineer had left a significant mark on him which he could not explain to himself. Thankfully nobody had been around to report them.

On each visit to Podzhin Hall he discovered a little more about the heritage he now accepted without doubt as his.

★

By March he knew he had made progress with Anna, and sometimes love for him shone in those serious amber eyes of hers. She hardly mentioned her twin these days.

Olga spent most of the time in her bedroom trying unsuccessfully to recover from a nasty influenza. The doctor was concerned about pneumonia.

Rasputin had been driven away, coughing and whinnying, and his hay was burned and the stable disinfected. Two silver napkin rings were found there. Cahill admitted having stolen them and other things to buy medication for the stallion.

While all this went on, Valentina seemed perpetually busy with yoga classes somewhere in Oxford.

★

Orthodox Easter fell in early April. This brought Olga out of her bedroom and Vasily who guided her down the stairs was shocked to discover how much she had aged.

"Don't fuss, Vasily." It sounded like a warning that he should not probe because she was only precariously held together. "We did not have a real Christmas this year," she told them in the music room, "so we will all celebrate Easter the proper way, and that is that."

The next afternoon Njanja put together a *pashka*, an Easter cake of curd cheese, and decorated it with a cross. It tilted to one side but her efforts were suitably appreciated by the family. Anna had coloured eggs by sticking leaves and grass stalks onto the shells, before boiling them in dark onion skin suds. She buffed the shells with cooking oil and the outline of the leaves appeared, white on satin bronze.

CHAPTER FORTY-SIX

The Brodskys' Easter feast was to be held at noon on Easter Sunday, following the church service at midnight in London. It had been arranged that Vasily and Fydo, who was increasingly occupied elsewhere, would join the family at the Russian Orthodox Church of the Dormition.

With an ease which took Vasily by surprise, he had agreed to take part. To Turchin he had argued that it was crucial for him to put in an appearance.

On Saturday night, just past eleven, a yawning Cahill managed to park Smelly Ben in Emperor's Gate off Gloucester Road. Already a large congregation surrounded the arched entrance, on which the brass plaque proclaimed *Russian Orthodox Church in Exile*. Inside, gaunt fasting priests had taken off the black cloth of Lent for the rejoicing of the resurrection.

The congregation filed in – fragile old people, their tremorous hands gripping National Health walking sticks. The majority were women with round faces, grey wiry hair under knotted triangular scarves, their feet in sturdy unflattering footwear. Slowly the church filled with the faithful. The gracious pose of an old aristocrat stood out here and there.

Olga rested on a shooting stick; in an orthodox church there are no pews. Vasily materialised next to her. He turned and gave Anna, standing next to Valentina, a short nod. Valentina had chosen a sporty hat to stand out from the others. Njanja had stayed at the back where she joined a woman much like herself. Fydo was late.

"Fancy seeing you here. Isn't religion taboo in your neck of the woods?"

"We invited him to come, so shut up, Mother," Anna said, surprisingly sharply.

"I just hope Vasily's ambassador can make it too."

"Shush," hissed Olga.

At that moment the double doors were closed, and sepulchral chants from the choir up in the gallery commenced.

The richly decorated interior, the wafting aromatic incense and the semi-tone harmonies wrapped them in mystical enchantment. Hundreds of candles illuminated the polished silver and gold faces of the ikons, smiling kindly or sternly down on the congregation standing shoulder to shoulder. The weeping Christ, nailed to the cross in a side aisle, was bathed in a sea of flickering light, his feet worn by the kisses of worshippers. With the heat of bodies and their enraptured breath the oil lamps in front of the ikons swung gently.

Vasily was overcome by the impact of his surroundings which incited deep-seated melancholy. Not that long ago churches were closed and smashed; priests arrested and sent to the forced labour camps. In his early twenties he himself, on the orders of the man with the scar, had scaled a church roof to cut down the three-barred cross.

When the choir intoned the *Hymn of the Cherubs*, it was difficult to find space to kneel. Anna, resembling a *babushka* with her scarf tight over her head, kept checking him. Olga was one of the ancient exiles who did not kneel because they could not. Vasily sank to his knees, his eyes hypnotically fixed on one of the ikons to prevent the image of Turchin or Miliukov rising before him.

The curtain in front of the middle door of the baroque gilt-framed ikonostasis was pulled aside. The worshippers audibly drew in their breath. The door opened to reveal the bishop with a convex crown on his head. He was in a robe bedecked in a thousand glittering precious stones and inlaid miniatures of gilded saints. The choir intoned a litany. With measured steps he descended to the level of the congregation and made a path through them. Behind him processed three dark long-bearded priests. One carried a tall candle, one a two-armed candlestick, and the third a three-armed candelabra, the candles ribbon-entwined. From their swaying thuribles, puffs of resin clouded the faithful.

Vasily felt intoxicated. No other religion was given to such idolatry, such indulgent emotions, as the traditional church of his country. Was this an insight into the true Russian soul? Could one excise, operate out, such a trait as one would a tumour?

The bishop and priests gathered at the back of the church. The crowd rose. The relentless choir lamented. The bishop sang in baritone from the bible held up to him by a serving boy.

An old woman in a threadbare coat wept beside Vasily. There were none of the potbellied top-hatted rich he had seen in caricatures. This was not so much a religious transport, more an escape back home to Russia, like a drug-induced dream.

Back at the ikonostasis, the bishop sang of Christ's interment and the gallery answered in monotonous and repetitive retort.

Did his father still have to turn his head the other way when passing a desecrated church?

At midnight the clergy processed again with candles to the door and went out, leaving the congregation praying in silence. The priests, who should have circled the outside of the church three times, had to make do in London with going around the green patch of Emperor's Gate in symbolical search for Christ's body in the sepulchre.

Olga coughed dryly, Valentina commented on the hole in the shoes of the man kneeling in front of her, and Anna and Vasily held hands tightly, hidden in the folds of her coat.

The doors opened and the priestly procession returned. Behind them walked a shaven-headed Buddhist monk. His uncovered ears stuck out and his saffron wrap seemed aflame in the aureate light.

"Fydo!" exclaimed Valentina, her voice shrill in the heavy silence. The monk looked up and smiled. Then he threaded himself towards his family.

"You fool," whispered Olga. Fydo appeared beyond caring.

Valentina leaned towards him. "Do you wear anything underneath the robe?"

"Shhh," hissed Anna, pulled cruelly from her mystical experience and physical contact with a lover.

The bishop opened wide the sacred door for all to see a statue of Christ before a medieval ikon. He held his arms up towards the ceiling of the church, proclaiming the miracle of Christ's resurrection. *"Kristos voskressya!* Christ is risen."

The choir burst forth in the melodious descants of *Triumph of Easter.*

"Voistinu voskressya," exclaimed the congregation. "Risen indeed." They rose from their kneeling positions and greeted this miracle as if the most precious gift had been offered to them. Overwhelming relief and joy swamped them after the collective wait in sorrow. Tears flowed freely. *"Voistinu voskressya."* Every worshipper clasped his neighbour, known or unknown, in his arms. Vasily enthused, *"Voistinu voskressya"*, and Anna saw tears flicker in his eyes as he hugged the old woman beside him. Even though Valentina said, "How tacky", she attempted to hug her cousin Fydo, who objected that women were from now on out of his reach. She slapped him instead, which made him smile.

The soprano and alto voices of the choir rose in harmony and immersed the joyful with bright exaltation.

★

Needing to be alone, Vasily left the Brodskys and the church. It was past two o'clock on Easter Sunday morning. He walked up a deserted Gloucester Road towards Kensington Gardens.

Near the Serpentine a mallard stirred sleep-drunk in the grass and nuzzled closer to a female. She acknowledged it by shaking her feathers.

Vasily stumbled along. Why had he never been allowed to learn about other ways? Why did his father not trust him enough to tell him the truth? But if he had, then both of them would have been destroyed somehow.

Vasily sat down on a dew-covered bench.

★

By the time the Brodskys arrived back in Podzhin Hall it was four in the morning. Throughout the drive from London Cahill had whistled to stay awake. At times Njanja had shielded her face with her hands in fright at Smelly Ben's speed, and Olga tried to suppress bouts of coughing.

"I need a drink." Valentina served herself generously with vodka.

Fydo made for the armchair and settled into it, tucking his long hairy legs under him. A begging bowl stood on the floor beside him; it was a large contraption covered in crochet material the same colour as his wrap, and it had a lid, a stand and a shoulder strap. He explained that he would carry it with him wherever he went and beg villagers to donate food. Anna, too emotionally drained from hidden hand-holding with Vasily and Orthodox Easter rituals, simply marvelled at the transformation of her uncle Fydo.

Unsuccessfully Valentina offered vodka around.

Olga, ashen from exhaustion, faced her nephew. "You are disguised as a monk."

"I am a monk – a trainee monk," he retorted proudly. "For you all I am now Phra Dhammakaya."

"All I can say, my dear nephew, is that you appear to be without gender."

"Would you have become a monk had you known how stupid your ears look with a shaven head?" Valentina goaded him.

Anna interfered. "The warm sincere smile in his eyes and his aura of hope make up for his loss of hair."

"Thank you, Anna. Accepting oneself is the first step towards understanding." There was strength emanating from Fydo. Valentina mocked no more. "I am leaving for the community of the Theravada in the temple of Tha Ngam in four days' time," he said calmly, as if telling them he was going to the post office in the village.

Valentina could not leave it at that. "We'll have to have a goodbye bash."

"Buddhist monks leave quietly, without ado. Suddenly they are gone, hopefully leaving some of their teachings behind them."

"Fyodor, are you sure about what you are doing?"

In answer he simply smiled into Olga's eyes and she, after a shaking of head, accepted his decision, and Anna helped her out of the chair.

"Grandmother, it was a wonderful Easter service. It must have been quite special for Vasily in every way. I hope he does not suffer for having taken part."

"Vasily's only reaction can be for him to recognise

what he is made of. There are things you don't choose – he is a Russian. Can you help me upstairs, Anna, dear?"

Valentina, the last to leave the music room, switched out the light.

CHAPTER FORTY-SEVEN

Shortly after Easter, Anna shouted from the vestibule, "A letter from America has arrived."

"You don't have to bellow like an ox." Valentina took the envelope from Anna and with her red nail tore it open. She read while Anna chewed her lower lip. Then she turned the page and read on.

"Bloody hell," is all Valentina said, and with surprising energy ran up the stairs.

"I had a right to know first." Anna's voice trembled slightly.

In the bedroom the sharply closed door woke Olga from a somnolent state.

"It's unbelievable!" Valentina held the letter out to her mother. "Read this letter from Antonina."

In response Olga coughed and reached for the bottle and the spoon on the side table. "You read it," she managed to say.

Valentina sat on the embroidered bergère.

Dear Folks,

I write in a hurry. We're swamped with work at the UN after the assassination of Martin Luther King. Lots of trouble with black people killed in Vietnam. And to the ongoing Middle East crisis is added now the Russian threat on the Czech border.

I've met the President of the United States and he is cute but too short to be effective. I get little sleep but plenty of excitement. This letter I am afraid is to warn you. That guy I wrote to you about approached me at the entrance to the UN, claiming to be Johnathan Snell from the Smithsonian and bringing 'Easter greetings' – all to 'protect me' from danger. He told me some wild story of murder attempts on you, Mum, a shot? And apparently the groom and Cahill are plotting to kill you. He knows absolutely everything about us.

I got him arrested by UN security. The Feds say he is not Snell at all, but some Russian sent here under cover by Moscow. Brezhy is after us. Those Kremlin guys will shrink from nothing. So watch out!

Knowing this now, I can't possibly stay in New York. I've gotta come home and help the family, but I have signed a year's contract and can't leave until October, less my holiday time.

So this is to warn you that something devious, awful, criminal and whatever you can think up, is on the agenda of the Soviets concerned with the Brodskys. You might know why.

Got to rush. Was thinking of you at Easter. Be careful. Much love to all, Your Antonina.

Valentina went up to the bed and gave her mother the letter. "You are going to tell me right now where that bloody Ikon is or I'll wring your neck, coughing fits or not."

Olga pointed to the door where Fydo stood.

"So now you move around like a ghost?"

"A body housing a harmonious mind is weightless. You should persist with your yoga lessons."

"How can I sit still when my life is threatened?"

"Perhaps you ought to come to Thailand. There it will be easier to transcend into harmonious peace."

"Are you leaving or something? You've got a bundle."

"I came to bid goodbye to Olga."

She grabbed the letter from Olga's bedcover to wave it in the air. "This is a warning that I will be murdered because of the Ikon. Cahill and the groom have joined the communists and will come for me. Antonina has been threatened by a Soviet spy and has to come home. Vasily is most probably a traitor, a trained assassin, and I am the target. How can you walk away? I hate you for leaving."

Fydo made a slow movement with his arm.

"Go if you must," Olga said from the bed with resignation.

The monk picked up his bundle. "Adieu," he said softly and left the room.

Valentina span back to her mother. "Now to the Ikon. Where is it?"

"Here, with me, in this room."

"What? Your bed?" Valentina lifted the quilt and then unceremoniously pulled back the sheets and blanket, exposing her mother in her night dress, withered like a shrouded corpse. Valentina attempted to lift up the mattress with her mother on it.

Olga coughed and pointed upwards.

"You're not going to die and go to heaven before…"

"The Ikon is on the canopy roof."

"I don't believe it. All this time. I don't understand. We need the money."

"The Virgin of Kazan is badly broken. Anna on her way to Sotheby's last year…"

Valentina started to push the bergère towards the bed in order to stand on it.

"Please, not now. The doctor should be here any minute."

Valentina carried the seat back to its place. "Are you really that ill?"

A coughing fit answered the question. "Come back to see me later. I have things to tell you."

★

Anna had moved to the forecourt to bid Fydo farewell for he was now walking down the driveway towards the gate, a figure wrapped in orange.

Valentina ran out of the house, yelling, "Fydo, Fydo! Wait."

The figure slowed. She sprinted over the gravel, lost one slipper but ran on in a hobbling fashion.

"Fydo," she panted, "give me the address of your temple. I can't stand it in Podzhin Hall any longer. I'll go mad. Can I come and stay with you?"

492

"The sage is aware of the need of others."

"Got a pen? No of course not." She reached into her pocket and took out her lipstick.

With care, he wrote a long and complicated Thai address on her forearm below her rolled-up sleeve. Then he turned and walked on, while Valentina thoughtfully looked at her arm and resignedly returned to the Hall.

At the rim of the pond Anna stood contemplating and pouting. "That baby toad on the rock has only one hind leg. How can it jump or swim? How can it feed itself?"

"Perhaps someone put in charge of it dropped it and broke the leg off, and now the toad is worthless and we have no money."

Anna quivered in silence.

"Our life here is just too darned for words. Fydo is doing the right thing."

Valentina passed Antonina's letter to Anna. "Read that and weep."

★

In the Soviet Embassy Turchin had asked to see Vasily in the safe speech room. *That is a bad sign*, Vasily sighed to himself.

"There are a few things we have to talk about," Turchin started their meeting. "Tell me first how it went with undermining the Brodskys at Easter. Did they pray to the Ikon? Have you found it? Are we any nearer getting it?"

"There were many ikons but not the Virgin of Kazan."

"So, still no results, and your reprimands increase."

"I know of two: the Harrods gloves and the photograph in my room."

"And… You went to church with them for an Orthodox Easter show which ended half an hour after midnight. Yet you signed back in at half-past three in the morning. Don't tell me you went for a walk and sat on a bench, twiddling your thumbs."

"Well, then I won't."

"Comrade Voronov, you seem to have changed since the start of your posting, so perhaps the news I have for you is just as well. Brezhnev is preparing to invade Czechoslovakia. Those in our service who are experts in foreign policy will be recalled to Moscow to assist with this coup. You have the honour to be nominated."

"When?"

"When? We expect to roll our tanks over the border in October. You will be required to be back in Moscow in about a month."

"A month!"

"Comrade Voronov, are you with me? Frankly, often you seem not to be with us. In confidence, I have been resisting this suggestion of your recall, because Miliukov thought it important you remain and continue with the Brodsky project. After your nightly escapade at Easter, I have changed my mind. This time the Controller's wish has superseded that of Miliukov. You appear put out, Comrade. I am only doing my duty."

Turchin buzzed to have the door of the safe speech room opened.

★

Olga insisted on being left alone with the physician. Njanja had straightened the bow of the bolero over Olga's cleavage with the movements of a concentrated caress before she retreated.

Putting his bag down, the doctor visually assessed the patient's general presentation. After that, he picked up the wrist and neither spoke while he took her pulse.

Shivering, her shoulders drawn up, she tried but failed to suppress another fit of coughing.

"Are you sure you don't want anyone of your family to be here now?"

"Tell me what I am dying of and when, clearly and correctly."

"I've known you for so many years," he started.

She interrupted him. "Don't make this harder for yourself than it need be."

"You are the strongest woman I ever treated and the one with most integrity and elegance."

"Thank you." She heaved to get oxygen to breathe.

"Shivering with high fever is a symptom of your illness. Bacteria have caused lung inflammation, and untreated bronchitis has turned into double pneumonia. The frailness of your age is not helping us now either. Your heartbeat is dangerously fast. Hospital is advisable."

"They have more important things to attend to there."

"It is late but we can try penicillin tablets."

"No tablets. Tell me instead what will happen to me

next. So far, I can hardly breathe at times and feel too weak to leave the bed for any length of time."

"Countess – Olga, take the antibiotics, I beg of you."

"And I beg you to tell me what comes next."

"Pain," he said and dug out a flask from his case. "Morphine."

She eyed the bottle but did not reject it. She undid the satin bow at her neck, as if to help herself get more oxygen. "How long...?"

"To this question..." he took up for her, "... I cannot tell you how much longer you will be with us."

She merely nodded. "The drawer in the dressing table... at the back... the yellow envelope."

He obeyed, his movements slowed by unwillingness.

"Yes, that one. Open it."

He did as told.

"My will. Give it to the lawyer once you pronounce me dead."

"Dearest Olga..." This time he did not correct himself.

"No buts, goodbye."

On the landing outside the bedroom, he found Valentina tracing along the banister with her finger, like a child.

At first he wanted to say something to her, but then did not and descended the stairs.

★

Once the oak door shut behind the doctor, Valentina returned to her mother who seemed to have been exhausted by the physician's visit for she lay spent, her eyes closed.

"Mother?"

With the aid of the bergère near the bed, Valentina managed to take a peek at the Ikon, a dusty familiar Virgin of Kazan smiling up at the ceiling, twilit by the closed drapes. A velveteen pouch containing loose precious stones covered the face of the infant. The relic was seriously damaged.

Laboured breathing started from the pillows, and Valentina suddenly knew with certainty that her mother was dying. She climbed from the chair. Never before had she given a thought to her mother not being alive. *Surely,* she thought, *her mother was invincible; she would come through this.* But the grey face in the hollow of the pillow appeared dead and gone already. Anger and fear rose in Valentina: *Oh to hell with the broken Ikon and with Mother.*

Was there really an option of escape – some place of Fydo's with a wide placid river where the bamboo leaves flit and the sun shines with a difference?

But what about men and what they offered her? Could she exist without attracting them and then punishing them for their lust? Yes, she could. Vasily had put an end to that side of her. A man who preferred her daughter was not even worthy to incite any longer. Or was he just not worthy of her affection?

Valentina loosened her clenched fists because her fingernails dug painfully into her palms and because Olga suddenly sighed in her deep sleep as if expiring.

Valentina fought with herself. For years she had

been incapable of tears. Now she discovered that she had started to weep, as if her body were suffering some physical breakdown. Liquid tears ran hot over her cheeks.

"Mother," she wept abundantly, "I do love you. Don't leave me. I have no-one else to connect with."

★

In the boiler room Anna read Antonina's letter. The jubilant thought that her twin had decided to come home, alas only in four months' time, was shadowed by the words *devious criminal, Soviet agenda*. Anna had met Snell at the Sotheby's drinks party on that fated day, and he was unpleasant sure, pushy as she recalled, but how could the Smithsonian be a cover for criminal activity? And there was no way that Vasily would be involved in stuff like that; he was so well-meaning, shy and soft-hearted. Antonina must have been brainwashed in America. Would she be unrecognisable now, the twins irrevocably separated?

Afflicted by the letter, Anna felt an urge to do something to put right this misunderstanding. If she wrote a letter back explaining how Vasily really was, perhaps even telling her what she felt about him, it would take days to reach her twin.

A better approach was to face Vasily with this questionable Snell and get him to clear it all up. Yes, that is what she had to do for the good of the family. Anna would go to London to the Soviet Embassy and talk to Vasily there in his familiar surroundings.

The note Anna had left in the vestibule read: *Gone to the British Library for reference material for thesis. Will be back for supper.*

Now she was standing in Kensington Palace Gardens in front of the impressive embassy building with a flag hanging limp in a fine windless drizzle. Her journey had been disrupted by maintenance work and closure of the Underground line. In the pushing and shoving, she was parted from her foldable umbrella. Her hair, growing back, had reached an awkward length and was now plastered to her wet head.

A security camera rotated towards her with a little squeak. She had been standing inactive for quite a while, rehearsing her line of: *Good afternoon, I come with greetings from the family Brodsky*, and deciding that it sounded wrong.

A guard appeared behind the glass pane next to the door. She chewed her lower lip. A red bus passed in the road bearing an advertisement for Vaseline.

Vasily. That's why she had come. That was for whom she had come.

Decisively she rang the bell at the metal gate. Nothing happened. She rang again and the intercom system crackled.

"I am here to see Vasily Voronov."

"Do you have an appointment?"

"I don't need one. We are close friends. I am Anna Brodsky."

It buzzed and the gate opened. The guard watched her approach. He let her into the lobby. "Wait here."

A man appeared on the upper landing near Brezhnev's portrait. He stood and looked down at her. The guard talked to a woman at a desk to the side. Some telephoning ensued.

Anna smiled to herself in readiness for Vasily and also not to show fear.

"Impossible." The guard came back.

"Why?"

He seemed surprised by the question.

The woman left her desk. "You need an entry pass. You have to get it from the consular section."

Anna insisted she only needed to see her friend, Mr Voronov, for a moment, but the infuriating woman came up with a long list of obstacles.

Across the upper landing from left to right, two men were walking and talking with papers in their hands. One she recognised as Vasily.

"Vasily!" she shouted up the stairs. "Vasily, it's me!"

The two men disappeared through a door to the right, and from somewhere appeared a uniformed guard with a Kalashnikov rifle on a strap over his shoulder.

"I guess I had better get an entry pass then."

The door was opened for her, and Anna stepped back under the rain which was now more pronounced. As she left the compound and started walking down the road, the security camera pointed at her back.

★

Olga stirred and slowly reached for the bell rope. Only then did she notice Valentina in the room.

"Have you been here a long time, or has the doctor just left?"

At that moment Njanja knocked and came in, carrying a round tray with a cup of tea and Anna's note. "Zr Anna go to library in London."

Valentina, numb from crying, watched Njanja guide a spoonful of medicine from a brown bottle into Mother's mouth, watched Njanja help Olga into a sitting position and from there, leaning heavily on the helping shoulder, she slowly progressed towards the en-suite bathroom. That neither had bothered about slippers was alarming.

The process repeated itself in reverse before Durov left.

"Mother, Anna did not go to the library. Her thesis is written. She went to find Vasily. You must help me stop her seeing him; she will get hurt."

"Anna has strength. She read to me from that thesis."

"Indigestible, no doubt."

"Another facet of Russia. There is passion in Anna." A coughing spasm took over for a while. "Tea," croaked Olga, "please."

Valentina lifted the teacup with care from the tray, feeling the testing eyes of her mother on her face.

"You resemble your father more as you grow older."

Valentina helped tilt the cup to her mother's lips. After that, Olga slid back down in her bed. "The same deep brown eyes as Dimitri."

"My father was Ivan."

Olga turned slowly to face Valentina and focus on her. Some life had returned to her face, even animation in the malachite eyes. "I mean, your real father."

"Ivan was not…" Valentina stared at her mother aghast.

"Your eyes are so much like his. I have never noticed it before so strongly, but then I have never died before."

"Who was my real father?"

"Baron Dimitri Kavinsky."

"Baron Kavinsky, my father? Why didn't you ever tell me?" Valentina's hair cascaded down as she picked out the comb. "I don't believe it. Your morphine is talking rubbish."

"He was a man to be adored, a poet. He wrote many lovely poems. He was also treasurer of the Romanov's jewels. I can just see him looking at me that last time at the dinner in the Winter Palace with his eyes enraged with love. The last time I ever saw him."

"Why…" Valentina was near tears again, "… did you not tell me? Why?"

"Because he was killed that same day together with his brother, Baron Stefan. Shot by the bolsheviks or some other dirty pack. A couple of months before we had to flee from Petersburg on that wretched train you keep dreaming about."

"Did I ever meet him?"

"He adored you. I had to hold him back from showering you with presents. He wanted to buy you a Lipizzaner for your birthday."

"Did he?"

"No. You were only three when we left. He had given you Podzhin Hall in a deed of trust when you were born. He owned property all over Europe."

"That's why the house is in my name. Did Dad – I mean Ivan – know?"

"Ivan was a gentleman."

"But I thought your marriage was solid."

"We respected each other. Don't forget, it was an arranged marriage between the Director of the Imperial Bank, his father, and my father. Excellent arrangements for Russia's financial future, or so we thought then."

"My God, Mother."

"On that horrendous day, Dimitri's servant, Piotr, arrived at our door with the Ikon."

"How did you get the Ikon out?"

"We hid it in a thick padded pillow. Through the journey I lay my head on her. Nobody dared take a pillow away from a suffering mother with a young child – you."

"I am a baroness," said Valentina, and her voice was not her own.

"Dimitri gave me such true happiness."

Valentina jerked her head up, and there was a sudden doomed expression in her drowning dark eyes as she assimilated the truth of her origins. "How about my happiness?"

"You were his pride, my delicious shame; our dark secret."

"There is nothing in all that for me; there never was. My father was taken from me."

Olga turned her arm painfully slowly to try and reach for the spoon but had to desist, overcome by a coughing attack. "The morphine is wearing out. The prayer book in the bedside table," she heaved. "A letter."

To Valentina,

Even as I write these words of sadness, which should be lucid and brimming with glowing young colours, the darkness of my own personality is flowing into my pen. I watch my beautiful child play in innocence, while my mind hears the rumble of the voracious revolution approach with bestial crudity. Weakened by helpless misery, I close the window to summer. Snow has started to fall in silence, bearing witness.

I lift my daughter into my arms to a safety that does not exist. Hugging her, hugging her one millimetre from despair, I can only pray that she will find her blessing in forgetfulness.

DK, autumn 1917.

Valentina looked up from the sheet, and her eyes were swimming in a face distorted with agony.

"That is why I did not tell you. I wanted to protect you from memories." Olga's voice sounded worn.

"Didn't you realise that even then it was too late to forget? I remember deprivation from a father's love, as I remember snow falling." Valentina leaned forward, the letter of her father against her chest, until her forehead touched the brocade of the bedcover. Her shoulders rocked in spasms and the only noise in the world seemed to be her weeping.

Olga's hand, with tired movements, stroked her head gently. "It was not so bad for you. Ivan was good to you. In memory of Dimitri Kavinsky, I made him buy you a stallion for your tenth birthday. You took to riding like a natural. Dimitri was an accomplished horseman. His family came from Moldavia in the Ottoman Empire – your gypsy blood." The old hand kept stroking.

"I see. I see now why Ivan never hugged me, never kissed me. Oh my God! It was unfair not to tell me. Unfair, Mother. Cruel," Valentina sputtered into the cover.

"Was it? I lived off that secret in exile."

"How about me? I would have done better had I known that a father, my father, once loved me."

"You'll live with the truth from now on."

"I am a baroness." She lifted her head out of the covers. "My daughters, Antonina and Anna, are…"

"I wouldn't tell the girls if I were you. They belong to the new generation and have a chance to survive untarnished."

CHAPTER FORTY-EIGHT

It appeared that last night the bell from Olga's bedroom had rung. Njanja, who had been resting in the kitchen, her tress-crowned head in her folded arms on the table, had gone upstairs perhaps for a last errand or summoned to say goodbye.

Come morning, when Valentina discovered that her mother was dead and rumbled downstairs to storm into the kitchen, she could get nothing out of Njanja. Durov just shook her head slowly, continuously, as if she had received a blow to the head and was waiting for the *coup de grâce*. On the kitchen table stood the samovar, unlikely to be polished on a day like this.

"What were Olga's last words?" Valentina wanted to know. "Why did you not call an ambulance, or wake anyone? Did Olga leave a message? Why did she ring?"

Cahill entered the kitchen, cap in hand.

"How dare you appear indoors at a moment like this, you who threw a stone, you who plan to kill me, commie as you now are?"

"Do you hear yourself speak, lady? For the

countess, bless her soul," he crossed himself. "Her time had come; the moon was full, and a large gaggle of black geese flew over the Hall, honking. I've called the undertakers. They will be here around nine o'clock. And just for your information, it was that nurse you hired who threw the stone." Cahill had never said so much all at once.

"I give up. After all, I'm apparently not Valentina Brodsky any more. At least tell me why the samovar is in the kitchen when I need Oolong in the music room?" She attempted to lift it up.

"Zr countess give me."

"Absolutely out of the question."

"Is for zr funeral price. Zr countess ask me to ring telephone number to sell samovar quickly."

★

Alone in his narrow bed Vasily span a web of thoughts. His operational life had been training, believing and obeying – until the Brodskys, and since then it had been weaving, ducking and lying. And then the sweating had started with the Kavinsky blow, which had been accompanied by a comradely clap on the shoulder: *you can see it through.*

But now even that had gone; he was recalled to Moscow. And abruptly it came clear in his mind: a barking voice, a red scarf handed to him, a man eying him across the torrent, a sadist with a sabre scar in the shape of a sickle. That vulgar brute had known Vasily was a Kavinsky and had fucked up his whole life because of it; he had done it out of a deep-seated hatred of the aristocracy.

I have to defect. I want to defect. His father was old; they would not go after him any longer. He had to defect for the honour of his name and title, and Anna was the one who would make this possible. Olga too would help, for she was on his side; Vasily was certain of this. There was no time to lose, not even one day.

★

"Anyone home?" In Podzhin Hall, Vasily padded through the back passage towards the kitchen. Entering, he explained, "The front door was open."

"You!" started Valentina. "You come with me."

In the music room she plunged onto the carpet and crossed her legs, yoga position. He dared sit in Olga's chair.

"Don't worry. Olga is not going to claim it. According to the doctor, she passed away in the early hours."

He jumped up. "You're jesting?"

"You have just missed the funeral home collecting her body for the crematorium. That's what she had arranged for herself."

"How can you say this so callously?"

"Why should I show you how I really feel?" She sat small, lost and even pathetic.

"I am truly sorry to hear that sad news. She was a splendid countess. I will miss her."

"You, you have no right to miss her, and the word *countess* in your mouth sounds like blasphemy. Games are over, you see. I lost my mother and am not a Brodsky. Fydo was right when he said, *Attachment to self involves acute distress.*"

"You must take over from your mother, care for your daughters and make sure Podzhin Hall is kept in the family."

"Not exactly the ground rules of socialism you are preaching. And anyway, what is it to you?"

"A great deal actually, be it only in the honouring of Olga, though there is more to it than that."

"A wavering comrade?"

"Possibly."

"How suitable this news would have been before. Too late. I'm going to Thailand to find a worthwhile belief for myself."

"It is a very long way to go for that."

"Dare mock me. We've both been cheated: you of freedom and me of… everything."

"I don't understand you, Valentina."

"Neither worldly goods, nor sex can provide peace."

He wagged his head.

"And don't you dare pull Anna into any of your louche games. She has no experience with men and thinks she is in love with you. But you know that."

Vasily blushed despite himself.

"I have watched you, Comrade. You have changed – a pity I will miss what will become of you."

"You don't have to go."

"I want to be part of a community of people who don't talk much but who know themselves. I have so much thinking to do, it'll last me for the rest of my days."

509

"In other words, you're giving up? I am disappointed by your lack of stamina."

"Before my mother closed her eyes for ever, she undermined my integrity with a last lashing. I have no choice but to opt out."

"And become a Buddhist monk – or is it a nun? You?"

"And why not me? Why am I supposed to be fickle and wanton? Why shouldn't I give up childish behaviour simply because others have cast the role on me? I now choose for myself for the first time."

"You will be disappointed."

"No more disappointed than I am now. Vasily, you don't understand, no-one can, but I want to understand myself at last."

The words sounded wrong from her mouth but he knew that she meant every one.

"So, I shall lose not only Olga, but you too."

He left her sitting in lotus position, eyes closed, and went into the drawing room where he selected a Sobranie cigarette from the silver case and clicked the gold Dupont lighter, treasuring every move.

This was a beautiful room even though he could not say what made it that. Dimitri, his father, may have sat in this room, perhaps his uncle Stefan as well. Certainly his grandmother Anastasia had. She was still here in a way, outside in her grave.

Vasily paced the room, straightening his spine as he did so. Nonchalantly he put the cigarette between his lips. "It is most unfortunate that we lost our Countess Olga, a wise and grand old lady," he said in Russian to an invisible listener. Vasily let the smoke out of his mouth, only gently exhaling. From the bookshelf he tipped out the back of Fyodor Dostoyevsky.

The way the door to the room was opened told him that it would be Anna.

"Ah!" she cried out when she saw him, then ran towards him, but stopped. "You look so different."

"Everything is going to be different. My deepest condolences."

She raised her shoulders, held them high for a while before letting them drop down. "It had to happen. She was old. I am not going to fall apart because I will miss my grandmother so much. I have *you* now."

"You really think highly of me." He put the Dostoyevsky back.

"More than that. Actually, much more than that. It would be the same if it were two days ago, and Grandmother still alive."

Her confession left an awkward silence.

"You're reading *The Devils*?" she said as a diversion.

"It's a grim prophecy of the Russian Revolution." He had read the blurb at the back.

"I don't want to talk about literature. I am in love with you."

"Then come here." He squashed out his cigarette in an ashtray.

She came towards him as a novice walks to her first communion. He circled his arms around her and crushed her so violently against his chest that he heard her gasp. Her arms came around him and her cheek was warm against his chin.

She had the ability to be a silent refuge for him, and this was the best part of her. He wanted her to stay this for him for ever, give him peace and security, but now kissing her eyes, her temples, her forehead close to the fringe of hair, his body reacted with strong physical longing, a new sensation as if he had a fifth gear he had never used.

"We cannot go back to the boiler room again," she said, as if she had wandered into his mind.

"Neither will we go up to the attic to hide. I think that you have become part of me. I love you too, Anna."

"Say it again. Please. You'll never have to do more than that, and I will already feel blessed."

"Oh Anna, dear generous Anna. I want to say it – shout it. I think we both suddenly grew up. We'll have to make plans for ourselves, but first let us go upstairs to your bedroom."

"But Vasily… How about Mummy, and is this the right time?"

"Your mother is under great strain. She has had a shock and decided to join your Uncle Fyodor to try and find some answers to her problems."

"That's crazy. Mother and Buddhism – I can't think of two things less compatible. And if she goes to Thailand, I'll be left all alone in Podzhin Hall."

"There is me. Anna, would you consider marrying me?"

"Has everyone gone insane today?" She stepped away in mock fright.

"Perhaps everyone has become sane today. Would you consider it? And if you say yes, we'll have to get married straight away, simply and secretly." To ease away her little frown, he added, "I can't wait to have you near me every day."

She smiled a tiny smile and grabbed his hand. "I am frightened."

"So am I, despite my age. By marrying you, not only would I lose my bachelor freedom, but my people would consider it a betrayal of my country. I might have to ask for asylum."

"I'll do anything it takes and will protect you for ever and ever." Anna's voice had risen.

"You even came to see me in the embassy."

"They made it impossible."

"All embassies are heavily protected, especially ours."

"Did you really not see me in the entrance?"

"I was with my superior."

"I made a bad mistake, and you had to pay for my foolishness."

"You won't have to do it again."

"No, you are now here with me."

"Should I take that as a *yes* to my question?"

"Yes," she whispered, with tears in her eyes.

He kissed her on her head. "My dearest girl. This is the happiest day of my life."

In Anna's bedroom he looked around. It was the first time that he had been there, and the furnishing, compared with the other tawdry vulgar displays, was spartan but neat.

He closed the door carefully behind him. When he turned the key she emitted a little squeak, behaving like the virgin she was.

"What are you thinking, Vasily? Look at me. Tell me what you're thinking." Her nervousness showed.

"Darling," he said, "please don't be afraid."

"I am not. In this bed, I have lain many hours thinking of you, dreaming of being with you here." With a shaking hand she stroked over the bedcover and nervously, with small flicking eyes, she watched him sit down on her pine chair and start to take off his shoes, then stop and look at her.

"Anna?"

She swallowed.

"Anna," he said again; it sounded like *Amen*.

With slow steps she went up to him and looked down into his eyes. Her hand reached out and timidly touched his curls. "I must make sure that they are real. I had a dream about you. It was frightening, because we were running and I couldn't keep up, and you became cross, and when you turned your head, your hair blew away. I stood there shaking, while you mocked me, laughing, laughing like Ned Worship. It was ghastly. You see Ned was a friend I had in Brampton; I mean he wasn't my boyfriend or anything like that, but we saw each other…"

The erratic words tumbled from her, and she kept forking through her own hair with her fingers, forgetting about the bow hanging by a strand onto her shoulder. "It's a dream of identity problems, I'm aware of that, but…"

"Have you had any nice dreams about me?"

She pulled the bow off and blushed a little. "We made love."

"Good." He stood up.

Her amber eyes lay open before him and showed him how much she had fantasised over him. Her attempts to become intimate with Ned had been artificial, out of character, born of a desperate hope that she could win acceptance from Valentina. Now here with Vasily everything seemed natural, almost preordained, flowing from her own true personality, unconnected with her mother. She let his look travel right down into her and he started to slide his hands up her chest, over her shoulders and down along her spine until they cupped her buttocks.

Her lips parted. It felt to her as if he had clad her in a gown tailored for love.

"Shall we?" he asked softly.

They undressed and their shadows made bizarre patterns on the wall. When both were naked, Anna looked down.

Again he said "Anna" and moved to stand close before her. He felt that her shyness was struggling against her wish to be a woman for him. He drew her to him and felt her angular shoulder-blades and her small and pointed breasts.

"Show me what to do," she whispered.

He took her hand and guided it down between them. She shot him an amazed look; then he felt her warm hand touching and knew that her sensuality had not been distorted during a long celibacy.

"I love you," he said.

She took her hand back and lay it on her left breast, looking at him demurely. He drew her to the bed and she sighed once deeply, then turned down the bedcover.

Vasily knew that he would not only possess a young woman's body but gain far more: her fragile trust. "I love you," he had said, for he had decided that he did, and he had decided that he was going to be a Kavinsky and a traitor bloody fast, and probably never see Moscow again.

CHAPTER
FORTY-NINE

The phone rang on the desk of Georgi Miliukov. He squinted at it for a moment before answering. The husky voice of the Controller asked him to appear in his office immediately.

"Right away, Comrade Chairman." It had not been a request but an order, and Georgi had detected a certain menace in the hoarse voice. He left his office and locked it. He had to go to another wing of the building and up to the twenty-seventh floor to see the Controller.

As he entered he saw in the mighty man's hand a telex from Turchin of the London embassy, one which had clearly bypassed him. The Controller did not make a move to let him see it, nor did he suggest Georgi take a seat.

Georgi stood and wondered.

"Comrade Voronov has disappointed us." Georgi nodded and felt doom approach. "His task with the Brodskys has not proved fruitful."

Georgi knew better than to defend Vasily or play for time; these were only the opening lines of more unpleasantness to follow.

"Take a seat," ordered the Controller.

Georgi sat down.

"Voronov was seen in the London Orthodox church for exiles at Easter. He kissed ikons and crossed himself, evidently moved and religiously propelled. He was in the company of the Brodsky family and a Buddhist monk."

This sounded unlikely to Georgi. Still he said nothing.

"Voronov has on several occasions used the freedom granted him to indulge in sentimentalities. Our surveillance has recorded him in a library reading about Imperial Russia, in Oxfordshire arguing with Valentina – and kissing Anna."

Shit, thought Georgi. "Anna appears favourable to our cause," he finally offered.

"Do not interrupt me. A room search revealed a family photograph of his aristocratic ancestors that he had hidden behind the fire hydrant. They also found a pair of fur-lined suede gloves in a wrapping from Harrods, no doubt an effort to appear *gentlemanly*."

What did that bloody fool think he was doing? Georgi panicked.

"In the nine months he has been attached to the embassy, he has performed his duties to the bare minimum, and without zeal. And he was incapable of finding the Ikon; we doubt whether he even tried. We can believe that he is a traitor to the Party and the Soviet Government. He has been recalled to Moscow."

Georgi had difficulty assimilating these words.

"You chose Voronov, and I know why. You made an

unforgivable mistake. You are responsible and will have a lot of explaining to do. That's all."

Georgi hung his head.

"Oh, one more thing. You are taken off the case. I shall handle it from now on. A report has gone to the Politburo, including the rather fat file on Voronov's real identity."

Seemingly aged, Georgi rose from his chair, bowed unconvincingly and left the office.

★

That same evening Georgi travelled out to Nikolina Gora. The train recited *it has to be done – it has to be done – it has to be done*, while passing grey apartment towers surrounded by empty lots. Father would not shout tonight; he would weep. Georgi put his forehead against the carriage's smudge-dulled window. Damn his father's fixation. He could not just have left it at murdering the Kavinsky brothers. No, he had to find their servant Piotr and grill him. Piotr's loyalty to his former master had seemed a thing of the past: Dimitri had survived by killing a policeman called Yuri Voronov and stealing his identity. Three years it had then taken Pavel to find him in Obodovka but he didn't just have him executed. "Too lenient," Father had insisted. "A life toiling as a peasant, and his only son turned into a passionate communist – now that's a punishment!"

CHAPTER FIFTY

It was only five o'clock in the morning on the kitchen clock. Valentina, dressed in a pair of cotton trousers and a tunic, waited for the kettle to boil for her Oolong.

In Anna's bedroom Vasily lay awake, one arm heavily and proprietorially draped over the shoulder of the girl who breathed rhythmically in little sighs, each intake of breath causing her lower lip to quiver slightly. Some strands of hair erred over her still features. He would have loved to kiss her pouted mouth; caress the body which had fought so bravely under the impact of a first coitus. He needed Anna's devotion and honest love to protect him from an unknown future, just as his mother had pulled him into their cottage at the slightest sign of trouble in their village.

But it was early, and unfair to wake her and rob her of her needed sleep, so he lay quiet, listening to her breathing. He also heard the noise in the corridor of someone sliding something across the floor. He strained his ears but stayed put. Then he heard a door open downstairs and more noises he could not define. It was too early for Njanja to be up. The more he concentrated, the less he could make of what he heard. The ensuing silence was too intriguing. Gently he removed his arm. Anna snorted shortly. He eased himself off the bed and slipped into his trousers and shirt to go and investigate.

Valentina was in the vestibule holding a carpet-bag and a parcel. Was she sneaking out of the house? He remembered her spending some time on the phone yesterday at teatime but she often did. Was she really going through with this trip to Thailand?

When she saw him coming down the stairs, her look was of such burning intensity that Vasily was momentarily dazzled. Obviously her decision to leave had matured overnight. Demented or enlightened, everything would yield before those daggers.

"Valentina please, I need to talk to you," he said.

She pushed him aside, put her bag down and opened the door.

"Please?"

"Too late."

"It is about Anna and me."

"Don't meddle with Anna." She picked up the bag again, hooked the parcel under her arm and started to descend the steps onto the forecourt where the ornamental pond gurgled. She took a shortcut across the lawn towards the village and, obviously, the first bus to Oxford.

He tried to keep up with her. "I am going to defect," he announced, and a whirring pigeon flew from Artemis's curly hair.

"Do what you like, but don't bother me or my daughter."

"I have decided to marry Anna."

"No, you haven't."

"I would like your consent. Or perhaps your blessing, if you're going to be a nun."

At the border of the wood Valentina put bag and parcel down. "I shall give you some parting advice, Voronov. If you touch Anna, then the wrath of God will descend upon you. We are aristocrats. You're a hired underdog, employed to spy and cheat. Anna will have nothing to do with that."

Anger boiled up in Vasily. She had the nerve to turn her back on all her responsibilities, sneak away without saying goodbye, and still castrate him on her exit.

"We suit each other, Anna and I. We spent the night together."

Before he had time to react Valentina hit his face hard. It sounded like a shot in the quiet of the park.

He noticed that she had removed all her jewellery; then he started to shake from the violent impact. She stood facing him, mad in her brutal naked anger, the carpet bag and package at her feet.

"You can pray for us in your temple," he said. For a moment he saw the realisation of her monstrous decision in her eyes. That untarnished truth made her lash out at him again and again as if he was her conscience.

"I am not gone yet," she panted from the exertion of hitting him. "I'll call your embassy from the airport. I shall tell them of your behaviour, your decision to defect, the entrapment of my daughter to further those ends. I shall tell them that you tried me first. I'll describe your religious fervour at the church, and here," she pointed to the parcel, "is the Ikon which I'm taking with me. No Soviet swine is going to get it."

Later, he thought he had seen a blood-red shutter slowly being pulled over his eyes. The stress of his posting, his true origins, his imminent recall to Moscow, his decision to defect, his confused feelings for Anna: it all exploded in him. He flung himself at Valentina like a wild bear and knocked her to the ground. Their faces were close, breaths mingled and their eyes matched in consuming rage.

"That too, I'll tell them," she laughed nastily into his face.

He hated the chaotic hurt she caused in him and pushed her under him, under his physical dominion.

"Don't drag Anna into your deportation from England," she said, unthreatened by the inferior position she was forced into. "Dying in Siberia must be such fun. As a matter of fact, dying is fun. At least it ends this unbearable madness. Ha!"

Vasily grabbed her hair and bashed her head against the ground to stop her maddening assault.

She clawed the air, aiming at his face to mark him. "You've had it, Vasily, you worthless peasant."

Again he rammed her head down to stop the hysterics but she went on coming at him with her long fingernails, squirming on the ground under him like a wounded beast, strong with madness. Just then she jerked her head up, and her hand flying past his ear left a burning gash. He reached out to grab the nearest stone and held it threateningly over her head, his hand shaking.

"Only a weakling would go for a girl like Anna," she

mocked and attempted to writhe away from under him.

"Shut up!" The stone came down on her head. "You want me, you abhor me; you love life, you hate life. You thrive on excess. Anything and nothing, that's all there is to your unhappy self." He stopped to gasp for air. "I *am* an aristocrat," he nearly wept. "I have always been one of your kind. I have been cheated out of my real status." He took a deep sob-breath. "I am the son of Baron Dimitri Kavinsky."

She did not reply or react to his amazing revelation. She smiled. He noticed blood on his fingertips but not much. Panic swept through him.

A robin hopped towards the bared patch of earth where the stone had left an indent in the soil. Vasily looked at the stone. It was large and had a sharp edge.

"Valentina!"

He moved off her and searched for her wrist. Frantically he felt, but there was nothing alive in her, not even a tiny pulse. He tried her neck. Her body felt leaden.

It was an accident, rang in his ears. *It was an accident, an accident.*

Afterwards he was surprised how rationally he had reacted under the circumstances. He had pulled her body deeper into the wood where there was a dell. He had fetched the carpet-bag and the Ikon and placed them next to her body. He checked again that she was really dead. Her mouth smiled no more; it had fallen open. He had gone to the bonfire heap and pulled the rusty shovel out of the mulch. With it he had shovelled earth as if possessed, shovelling with aching arms until a large enough hole was dug. He remembered thinking ironically that a freshly dug grave lay not far away: the one intended for Olga's ashes. He had dragged the body into the grave he had made and started to push back the soil. Clumps of earth fell into Valentina's open mouth. When her face was covered and haunted him no longer, he had brushed the sweat from his brow. Her feet did not fit so he bent the legs to shorten her. He stuffed the travelling bag against the bent body and started to scoop and paddle earth over the unbearable sight, working at mad speed to efface catastrophe. Then he had stopped and panted. The palms of his hands were red and swollen.

Vasily picked up the parcel with the Ikon and lay it on the buried body. He unwrapped the brown paper and removed the last protective layer from the Virgin's wooden face. He gasped. Despite the damage, the Virgin of Kazan smiled at him softly, with beauty. In her arm sat a baby, pointing a finger at him. The diamond on the forehead was as large as a hazelnut. Her broken corsage was moulded in gold and set with precious stones. On the gold-encrusted frame was the insignia of the Prince of Pozharsky, who had carried the sacred image with him on his crusades in the early fifteenth century. Vasily bent and kissed the relic.

"My love," she said, serious and tender. He looked up and saw Anna through the trees. "You left me sleeping." He had been entirely beside himself for the previous hour.

Anna's face was radiant; she looked just like the Virgin. Her first love-making had transformed her into a woman.

"Anna, don't come here," he begged, calculating that he was probably lost, but she approached. Of Valentina's body nothing showed anymore. He folded the wrapping paper back over the Ikon and started to scrape earth over it.

Anna frowned but said nothing. She had not only acquired womanhood but somehow wisdom.

His face was screwed up in pain.

"Mummy has shown you where the Ikon was, and you are burying it. Why? Vasily, why? You know she will soon find out."

"I got up so early because I heard someone leave the house. It was your mother, departing for Thailand," Vasily stuttered, and his body started to rock.

Anna held onto a tree-trunk. "I don't want to believe this. Tell me it is not true. Are you sure?"

"I saw her go."

Anna came closer and shyly put her hand on his forearm. "It honours you to be so upset about it for me." She bent her forehead towards his chest and he felt her weeping against him. "What shall I do now without her?" she cried. "And Antonina is not here and does not know."

"It will be all right, you'll see. But first we have to get rid of the Ikon. My comrades will never leave us in peace. We have our life together to think of."

"Perhaps it is for the better," she said slowly. "The Ikon has not brought any of us any peace."

"*Mir*," he mumbled crestfallen. "Peace."

★

Counsellor Turchin looked at the policeman with surprise. Both men stood at the portico of Podzhin Hall waiting to be let in. It was not quite eight o'clock in the morning.

"Good morning. May I enquire the purpose of your visit?" asked the inspector.

"I am from the Russian Embassy and hope to find a Vasily Voronov here."

"Interesting. My visit may concern him too."

They shook hands.

"Perhaps I could have a word with you concerning Mr Voronov," suggested the inspector. "My name is Page, Inspector Page from the Oxfordshire Police."

"I am afraid I shall be pushed for time. I came to fetch Mr Voronov."

Page eyed Turchin quizzingly, trying to understand the unspoken in his words. "There have been irregularities surrounding this gentleman. The gardener phoned to say that there have been some unusual things happening here, and suggested that they might be connected with Mr Voronov. I have checked, and we do not appear to have received notification from the Foreign Office of his presence in the Oxford area. Come to that, I do not recall being advised of your visit."

"Many things happen in a house," said Turchin dismissively and knocked at the door a second time.

Inspector Page turned on the portico. "That must be him," he said, pointing.

Turchin turned. He saw Vasily and Anna walking across the lawn, both wrapped in silence.

When Vasily recognised his counsellor, he appeared

to falter, then straightened up. Perhaps it was only noticed by the trained eye of Inspector Page.

Both men stepped down onto the gravel and walked towards the approaching couple.

Page noticed that across Vasily's ear was a bleeding fresh gash, that his trousers were muddy, and that a button was obviously missing from one shirt cuff for it gaped open. His hands were filthy.

The girl had a smiling gaze upon her face, her intent focused on an inward scene. She must have dressed with carelessness for the collar of her black blouse was crumpled and bent inward.

Their appearance did not escape Turchin either. According to his conclusion, the pair were coming from the woods where they had obviously indulged in prohibited fornication. Turchin stayed calm despite his fury and spoke first. "Voronov, your Aunt Yelena has been taken ill. You must go back to Moscow at once."

"Oh no!" exclaimed Anna, waking from her dream.

Vasily found some kind of composure. "Perhaps after helping Miss Brodsky sort out things after the death of her grandmother, I can make the necessary travel arrangements."

"They are made," said Turchin. "You leave at noon today."

"There are some questions I'd like to ask Mr Voronov," intercepted Inspector Page.

"I am sure there are, but there is no time."

Anna looked sideways at Vasily and tried to knot her little finger into his clenched fist. "Can I go with him?" she asked.

"Can you go with him?" Turchin repeated the question while calculating the merits of the request.

"You see, I always wanted to see the Soviet Union, and Vasily promised he would show it to me." Anna tried hard to convey her conviction. "I admire the Soviet people ever so much and…"

Turchin had come to a decision. "You can go to the Soviet Union of course, but it will take a day to get your visa ready. If you send me your passport, I can arrange it and let you know very soon."

"Oh that's good. I need to pack and lock up the house and make sure Njanja is provided for. You see, I am the only Brodsky left here."

"I understand," said Turchin, looking at Anna's hand close to Vasily's.

Vasily said nothing. It appeared to Turchin that he could see every vein on the man's translucent forehead.

In the silence Anna exclaimed, "What a terrible, terrible day! The worst of my life and yet the best."

"Ten minutes with Mr Voronov would give me time for some questions," interrupted Page, irritated by the tragic heaviness spread over those surrounding him.

"Sorry, no." Turchin took Vasily to the car. "Diplomatic immunity forbids it."

Anna anxiously rushed after Vasily. "I'll see you in Moscow then."

"Yes, in Moscow," he answered tonelessly.

"How will I find you?" Anna leaned towards the car in which Vasily had taken a seat.

Turchin answered for him. "You will be met at the airport."

529

The car sped down the drive. Vasily did not turn his head. Anna had her hand raised in a frozen wave.

The inspector was on the steps of the portico, being told by Njanja where he could find Cahill.

Slowly Anna walked back to the park, not without first skirting a fat toad on the ground, pumping and sucking air to and from its vocal sac. *I should have known you would appear today*, she thought. Passing the small grave prepared for Olga's urn with the wooden three-bar cross Cahill had nailed together, she turned her eyes away with pain. At the border of the wood hawthorns were in blossom; numberless white flowers with pink flushes, their stamens quivering in the soft wind like eyelashes. Anna snapped a branch off and carried it into the wood.

At the loose mound of earth where Vasily had buried the Ikon, Anna stooped and lay the blossom over it. She crossed herself in the proper manner, paying respect to the Ikon.

"Please help me," she implored the invisible Virgin, and a shadow tinged with unfamiliar bitterness glanced across her face, wiping out the joy she had experienced the night before in Vasily's arms. Despite her enthusiasm for the Soviet Union, she knew that things between her and Vasily would not be easy over there.

Anna walked away from the Ikon which would never be kissed again.

"Mummy, why did you go to Thailand and leave me here all by myself?" she wailed with the sudden realisation that her mother would be out of reach in a Buddhist community, just as Fyodor had vanished from their lives. What had driven her mother to such an extreme choice? Had it been Grandmother's death or was it that Antonina had been away for so long? Or perhaps it was her fault. More likely Vasily had something to do with it. Anna believed in Vasily with all her heart but to what degree he and her mother had been poisoned by each other she could not understand.

CHAPTER FIFTY-ONE

Anna stepped out of Moscow's International Airport and the inclement spring air smelled unfamiliar. She tried to compare it with something she knew but could not think of anything.

Two men had come to meet her and were leading her now towards a sign saying *Taksi*. Anna was smiling, trying hard to conceal her disappointment that Vasily had not come to fetch her himself. There must have been a good reason and there was no need to panic. The men were presumably Intourist guides sent by Vasily who would expect her to be patient and brave. At one stage he would appear and then be proud of the way she had managed by herself.

"You are going to the Hotel Rossiya, Miss Brodsky," said the younger of the men. "Here is a map of Moscow." He unfolded it and Anna bent to look. The city was built like a cobweb, the Kremlin an angular spider in the middle. His finger ran along an avenue and tapped: "Here, the Metro station and here your hotel."

Certainly the hotel Vasily had chosen for her was well situated near the Victoria Park and Moscow Triumphal

Gate. She was pleased for she would be close to the important buildings, and surely they meant Vasily – for he was an important man here in Moscow. Perhaps she could cycle around and obtain a genuine feel for the city.

Her request was not greeted with enthusiasm.

"It would be unsafe, and we want to protect our foreign guests from risk of accident."

"I shall go by Metro then," she suggested.

"We are sorry, but we must bring you directly to the hotel for registering."

Anna shrugged her shoulders and folded the map. She did not want to be unduly difficult but regretted that she could not savour her first glimpses of the city alone.

"For you," said the young man, and she understood that he meant he had offered her the map.

"Thank you very much," she said and smiled.

They got into a taxi, a guide on either side of her. She was sorry, for their heads blocked her view considerably.

The taxi driver wore an imitation beaver hat and clamped an unlit stump of cigarette between his lips. He did not ask where they wanted to go which was odd, but pulled into the traffic, his face flaccid, his eyes alert.

Anna leant forward. They were driving down Leningradsky, and she saw a park on the left.

They approached a large square with a statue. "Belorussian Place," said one of her guides. He pointed to the statue. "That is Maxim Gorky."

As they waited for the lights to change, she saw gypsy women in colourful long dresses and scarves, selling bunches of spring flowers in front of a Metro station. An old man sat behind a public scale weighing a woman, while her friend watched, holding two shopping bags.

How wintry it still was. She had left Podzhin Hall in bloom, and here road workers with simple wooden planks fixed to broom handles were scraping up the remains of browned snow, like meringue left too long in the oven.

There was a queue in front of a wooden kiosk. The greasy sleeve of an old sheepskin coat appeared and disappeared as newspapers were sold to the customers, each of whom turned away opening the paper at once to read it in the street.

On Sovetskaya Place an old woman pushed a plastic pram around the equestrian statue dominating the oasis of park.

"Yuri Dolgoruky, the founder of Moscow," said the young guide pointing to the man on the horse.

Anna watched the old *babushka* stop and stoop over the pram. Suddenly, she could think of a description of the city in its post-winter mood: odourless, aseptic, petrified. What she had seen so far seemed not to have life but to be embedded in something grey, as fossils lie in stone. Over it all was a stratum of uninspired melancholy.

Surely summer was better, faces smiling and leaves green on the trees in Sovetskaya Place. The *babushka* would remove the bonnet of the baby in the pram so that it could feel the sun.

At a trolley-bus stop Muscovites got off at the back and more on through a front door. *Any one of those could be Vasily*, thought Anna with some excitement. He had probably taken this trolley-bus. She noted its number and decided to ask him when she saw him.

The taxi drove up to the imposing rust-red portico of an immense hotel of at least twenty floors.

They got out of the taxi and Anna felt a moment of embarrassment. "I only have English money," she said.

"You can change it in the Intourist Service Bureau in the lobby."

The young guide walked to the boot of the taxi to remove Anna's suitcase, but the lid appeared to be stuck. The driver, his dead cigarette still in his mouth, got out and gave the boot lid a hefty kick. It snapped open. *There you are, luv*, she thought he would say but he said nothing. She was not in England.

The lobby was as impersonal as an airport check-in hall, with a gallery of tourist shops above. There was no furniture but a carpet with a circled R covered the expanse of floor, where a group of foreign tourists clustered around their guide. Vasily was not waiting for her. Thanks to the help of her guides she was not bothered with many formalities. She signed her name on two forms and handed in her passport with the ten-day visitor's visa and was given a key: Room 1609, one of three thousand two hundred in the hotel.

Her guides made moves to leave her, and she would have liked to ask them so many questions but did not want to take up more of their time. There was only one important question to which she needed an answer. "Will I see Mr Voronov today?"

"Mr Voronov is retained in an important conference.

We'll let you know when he is free. In the meantime, we suggest you do some sightseeing."

Anna tried to hide her disappointment.

"There is nothing to worry about, Miss Brodsky. We'll let you know, and if there is anything more we can do for you, just ask at reception."

"Who shall I ask for?"

They looked at each other shortly. "Mike," said the older one. "Ask for Mike."

"Thank you," she said in a thin voice.

"You are lucky; from your room you can see the Red Square. Oh, and by the way, tomorrow you are scheduled for a city tour with a group. Meet them at nine o'clock in the lobby."

The room was clean and functional. Anna rushed to the window but it gave onto the inner atrium.

She sat on the bed and a feeling of utter helplessness took over. As today, presumably tomorrow, she had to occupy herself with being brave. She had been made love to, had been given love, a love of her own, and this joy now left a void in her where her unhappy self had been for so long. Now she had someone to miss and to prove worthy of. She had made a big step already. "I am in Moscow," she said to herself with incredulity.

These lonely first hours were only the beginning of a long devotion to the man who was willing to give her what she had yearned for. "Vasily," she said into the room, "when can we be together again?"

★

The next morning was taken up with a frenetic itinerary of sightseeing. The group she had joined were of all ages and European nationalities. The female guide took them to Red Square where they visited the Armoury Palace and the parts of the Kremlin open to tourists. There was unfortunately no time left for the Church of the Trinity, because lunch had been arranged in the Zvyozdnoye Nebo Restaurant.

Anna hardly listened to the explanations in good English and missed most of what was explained about the Kremlin wall, on which black granite plates commemorated the revolutionaries killed in 1917. Eagerly she scanned the faces of men passing her.

After lunch, when the tourists were picking up their cameras and bags, she escaped the group and walked back to the hotel. The reception clerk eyed her with suspicion as she slipped into the lift. In her room, she lay on the bed, her head next to the telephone.

Suppose Vasily had called, not knowing Mike had sent her on this tour. She decided to stay next to the phone. A hardy Russian fly kept bouncing into the window, and time ticked slowly past.

The following afternoon a tour of the Tretyakov Gallery of Russian Art was organised, but Anna would not join; it was the gallery she had most wanted to see with Vasily. She spent her time imploring her phone to ring. She prayed and crossed herself but it did not ring. It became imperative that she heard his voice or she would wither and die. In the late afternoon her eyelids drooped, and the hotel room grew dim and then dark.

Evening came and she dared leave her room to eat with her allocated tourist group in the hotel's restaurant but could find little to contribute to the general conversation.

On the third day she was pressured to visit the Historical Museum. She knew she would not be allowed to stay in the hotel again. Listlessly she wandered around the exhibits, stretching from archaeological pre-Muscovite Russia to Soviet Russia's military history. The female tourists became tired so the guide did not take them to the Imperial Russia rooms on the first floor.

The afternoon was free for shopping at GUM department store, a glass-roofed arcade with a fountain, and customers crossed over small bridges on the upper floor. Many were just browsing but those who decided to buy had to queue at the counter for a ticket, then queue at the till to pay, and then queue again to actually receive the item. Vasily was not among them.

Anna walked back to her hotel with the group but declined a drink and went to her room where she sat watching the silent phone.

The next morning it did ring and the much-prayed-for sound rendered her nearly hysterical, but it was only Mike. Anna's voice trembled. *When could she see Vasily?*

"We are sorry, but Mr Voronov has been sent to another part of the country for important negotiations and will not be back for two months."

"Two months!" Anna's composure broke, and she started to cry.

"His superior has left a message to say that your visa will be prolonged if you wish to stay and wait. He also suggested he would take your wishes into consideration, as to how to occupy your time should you decide to wait."

She had come here for Vasily and she would stay until she saw him. Mike promised to come to the hotel at lunchtime and Anna hung up, coiled her body on her bed and cried bitterly from desperate unhappiness, which slowly turned to anger. *Why had Vasily not been given the chance to contact her? They were engaged, for God's sake. Surely no conference or negotiation was that important!* Later she tried to reason herself out of her anger. It was not his fault; she knew it was beyond his control. This country was proving tougher than she had anticipated, or perhaps she proved to be more of a spoilt Westerner than she had thought.

It was clear: if she wanted to see Vasily again she had to kill two months in Russia.

"What would you like to do?" asked Mike at lunchtime.

Anna did not have enough money to stay that long in the hotel.

"I would like to see the country," she said. "Better even, experience farm life."

"There is a collective farm to which we invite foreigners. They can live there for a while and help the community."

"Perfect!" exclaimed Anna with newly found hope. "Yes, I would like to live on a collective farm."

"We shall arrange it. Mr Voronov's superior will make sure you shall find a place there."

"Thank you," said Anna. "Thank you very much." For the first time since her arrival in the Soviet Union Anna smiled genuinely.

CHAPTER FIFTY-TWO

Anna arrived at the Chikova Collective Farm at two o'clock in the afternoon. She knew that she would feel more at home there, occupied by something she wanted to learn about, and the waiting would be easier. It was some consolation to know that Vasily had talked about her to his superior for why otherwise would he have taken so much trouble over her?

Mike, who had driven her in a Volga, gave the collective farm's leader a letter. While he read it, she stood in a large showroom. On the whitewashed walls hung posters depicting farm produce and a graph of output. There was also a picture of Lenin surrounded by a red ribbon tied in a bow at his pointed chin. A long table was covered by a clean cloth and little red flags stood in wooden holders. On the sideboard, painted in rustic motif, were stacked teacups for large groups of visitors.

Anna was not offered tea but was welcomed to Chikova commune by the farm leader. "You will soon know your way about. Your unit foreman will tell you what to do."

While Mike talked to the leader again, Anna left the

room and stood in the sunshine. A boy with a ball under his arm stood, obviously waiting for her.

"Hello," she said in Russian.

He said nothing, pointed and walked towards some long low buildings. She followed him with her suitcase. The sun had elevated her spirits, and a Soviet boy was better and closer to Russia than a surly chambermaid in the hotel.

"What is your name?" she asked as they crossed a loading yard. He rubbed his ball as if to make it shinier and still said nothing. "You do not want to tell me?" The boy shook his head.

He opened a stable door to a tiny room and she understood that it would be hers. When she turned, the boy was gone. She hung up her dresses and skirts on the nails planted in the wood of the door and changed into trousers.

When she went out again, the boy was bouncing his ball a little further away, reciting a ditty she thought sounded like: *Pioneer wherever cheer, the Komsomol comes after*.

Anna ran her hand shortly through his unruly hair and he ducked away. She went to report to the comrade unit leader for work.

★

Three weeks after Anna had arrived at Chikova, she was sitting on an upturned crate scraping earth from beet together with other women, only one of whom was a foreigner – a student from Cuba. The foreman came and called her to reception, because someone important had asked to see her. Her heart leapt with joy. *Finally!*

She brushed her hands on the apron and tried to control her nervousness.

In the reception room she saw her reflection in Lenin's picture glass; she looked dishevelled and unkempt. She tore the apron from her waist and brushed back her hair, licked her finger and drew it along her eyebrows.

Outside the gate a chauffeur-driven limousine was parked. Mike hailed her towards him. She was asked to get into the back of the car. Vasily was not in the limousine. This time she could not see anything, for the car's windows were discreetly covered by grey curtains. The chauffeur drove at fast speed. Anna asked her companions either side of her where they were going but neither seemed in a conversational mood. *They are bringing me to Vasily*. She hugged this thought to her.

After a swift forty-minute drive, the chauffeur slowed and stopped. They got out and she found herself in a birch wood. This time she had no problems recognising the perfume in the air – so that was Russian air as well! It was pleasing.

A dacha stood in a clearing in the woods. It was large and sported a glass verandah leading down onto a well-kept lawn between silver trunks.

Walking with the silent men, she was led into the dacha and motioned to take a seat on a carved bench. She still did not know where she was or why. From behind a closed door came animated voices but they spoke in fast Russian she did not understand.

Eventually the door was opened and Vasily appeared. She sprang up. "My love, thank God!"

Her lover had altered almost beyond recognition and wore a neglected blue jacket and a pair of crumpled trousers. Behind him appeared a burly man in uniform.

"Vasily?" She walked up to him but Mike stepped quickly in her way. Anna tried to read Vasily's face to understand the meaning of it all but his eyes gazed right through her.

"Let me talk with him. Give us some time. We are promised to each other," she pleaded.

The uniformed man ignored her and pushed Vasily through the front door. *That was a policeman*, she thought, and her heart beat lumpily while she felt sweat in the palms of her hands. She glanced at Mike and his comrade. Were they policemen too – secret policemen? Something had gone terribly wrong.

Now it was her turn to be led into the room which resembled a hunting lodge. On the wall a bear's head was mounted on wood and over a large fireplace were deerhorns. An old man sat in a wheelchair, spearing her with his small eyes in a big hairless fleshy head. A scar in the shape of a half-moon disfigured his chin, salted-and-peppered by the white and grey shadows of stubble. A middle-aged man with wavy hair and similar small snake eyes had his back against the glass door to the verandah. From somewhere a cat miaowed.

Anna's whole body now felt limp with dread. The abandonment of Vasily had deprived her of all strength. The menace-laden atmosphere in the room made her shiver.

"Anna Brodsky-Kavinsky," the old man said. He rocked his head cackling, and she thought of a gangster chief from films. "You have come to the Soviet Union to be with Vasily Voronov."

She did not dare say anything. *Oh Vasily! What has this man done to you for you to leave me?*

"Cat got your tongue?"

Oh my darling, come back and help me endure this.

"It will be tricky for you to spend time with Voronov. Our comrade rushed away in a hurry, because he is due to leave for Vorkuta. You don't know where that is, do you? It's the region of our coal mines."

"Why… why would he want to go there?"

"Because I asked him to."

This old gangster was for real, thought Anna and started to feel a threat she had never known before. "Will he be back?" she asked and did not recognise her own voice.

"I know he had promised to show you round Moscow. It's not going to happen. He will remain in Vorkuta."

"In the coal mines?"

"Why don't you have a seat?" he invited her, pointing to a leather armchair made of the hide of some murdered animal.

Rigid, Anna remained standing. She glanced at Mike and his mate. They were blocking the door.

"There must be a mistake. I only came for a few days to visit."

"Did you now?"

"I also think you have me mixed up with someone

544

else. I am a close friend of Mr Voronov, and my name is just Brodsky, not Kavinsky."

"Of course, you care for Vasily, for he is your half-uncle."

"I don't understand." Anna felt heat crawl over her.

"I shall explain. I think you'd better sit down. You see, there is no hurry, neither for me nor for you, to go anywhere."

She collapsed on the armchair.

"Since you have shown so much understanding for the Soviet cause, I personally made it possible for you to get here so quickly and easily. I also made it possible for you to live in a collective farm according to your wishes. I am only too happy to help make you welcome."

The younger man near the window coughed into his hand.

"But I want to go home."

"Did you not say to Vasily that you would protect him for ever and wished to share your life with him?"

Anna felt like passing out but caught herself in time. *Vasily had betrayed her.*

"We are hospitable. We will give you the chance to experience the same life he has led, and to get to know our peasant communes from first-hand experience. Would you like that? You are invited to stay on a collective farm, perhaps not the one you're in now. Surely it would be a most rewarding challenge to work with your hands for food and lodging."

"You have no right to keep me here. The British Embassy will take care of me. They'll look for me."

"Did Mike not ask you to write to the embassy expressing your wish to experience farm life?"

Yes, she had written to the embassy saying just that, and they would not be concerned about her prolonged visa. Anna felt like screaming but she did not.

"Would you care to listen to what Georgi is going to play us?"

The younger man switched on a tape recorder: *I mean, I understand you and your people in Russia. Individualisation in the personal sphere is reactionary – petit-bourgeois absurdity. I care for you as much as for socialism. You can trust me; in fact, I think I would do anything for communism. It is a good thing to give the workers and peasants more rights. I am a Leytenanta Shmidta Russian, myself.* It was her voice, although the words had been edited.

"I personally could not have expressed it better. Perhaps not exactly music to the ears of those at the British Embassy."

Vasily had secretly taped her words!

"You see, we are only trying to help you," added Georgi.

"I shall inform my sister at the United Nations." Anna fought a losing battle.

"Why not your mother in Thailand?"

"My mother will be back shortly," she said and her brain worked relentlessly: … *he did not love me, he betrayed me, he used me because he did not love me…*

"We shall tell you more about your mother later. You deserve to know the truth. Vasily was co-operative and frank in the end. But we still don't know where the Ikon is after all that – isn't that vexing?"

546

"Please let me go home."

"You have not shown any interest in my statement that Vasily is your half-uncle, have you?"

"I think I have heard enough atrocious lies."

The old man turned to Georgi. "She's got some claws. Perhaps we'll leave it for now, don't you agree, son? We'll get her here again."

"That would keep it interesting, Father."

"In the meantime, Anna, you will have time to remember where the Ikon is, and perhaps other things might pop into your head. We strongly suggest you write to your sister about how happy you are going to be in the commune, but not yet. You need to learn to thresh first, and we want Antonina to get back to England."

Anna was more shellshocked than despairing. She sat quite still for a few minutes with her eyes closed and her arms clamped against her. Then she looked at the sadist dry-eyed. "Will I ever see Vasily again?"

"I doubt it. The climate in Siberia is particularly unfavourable to those who buy fur-lined gloves in Harrods."

"Who are you?"

"I am a dear friend of your grandfather, Dimitri Kavinsky. Unfortunately he died yesterday in the Ukraine. He enjoyed farming. I am sure you will too."

Anna stared at the ugly old man with cold abhorrence. She would have preferred to be beaten or even shot instead of this crucifixion.

"I know nothing about a Kavinsky."

"You look tired, Anna. Mike will drive you to the

new farm. I shall call for you again, and then I will tell you more about all sorts of interesting things."

Anna was led from the room by the man called Georgi who smelled of stale cigarettes.

CHAPTER
FIFTY-THREE

Four months later

A biplane soaring in the autumn sky described vast loops over Lambourn Downs. Outside the village of Hatley, in the road at the entrance to a south-facing Georgian hall, a black car roof shone. A figure dabbed with a dot of red appeared, coming out of the car and passing through the pillar posts and their wide-open iron gates that looked like guards with drawn swords. Gradually the figure, carrying a case, proceeded on the light gravel belt towards the Hall, a large property standing chaste and self-contained. From above, two chimneys led directly into the vulnerable heart of the house.

The figure, a woman, half-turned as if hesitating before moving again on surer foot towards a dried-up oval fountain in the centre of the forecourt – a halo to the house. She stood undecided again but then crossed the vivid white dash of the steps to disappear from sight under the portico.

In the park surrounding the property patches of lawn were encased by autumnal shrubs in the colours of Braque. To the south-east the painter had daubed the canvas with a statue from which four paths radiated out over the green lawn. Further still from the house lay the tiled roof of the stables, shining with a mulberry gloss. To the north-east stretched smooth parkland carefully landscaped, ending in a confusion of gold and rust where deftly applied brush strokes indicated a little wood at the boundary of the property. Just beyond, an ugly scar showed where works to enlarge the road were in progress.

A thin wisp of cloud passed, erasing the image as if someone had wiped a cotton cloth over wet paint. The biplane puttered away.

No-one answered the knock. The oak door was not locked. As it swung into the vestibule, she heard the faint tinkle of the chandelier. As men do in respect, she pulled the red beret from her head.

"Hello," she spoke out, not shouting – as if the house would be offended by any intrusive noise.

She had received a letter from Anna about the death of Olga and Valentina's intention to join Fydo in Thailand, insinuating that this was just one of their mother's whims. Since then, Antonina had been immersed in work and counting the weeks till her return.

Despite the telegram she had sent with the details of her arrival, nobody had picked her up from the airport, and the phone in Podzhin Hall seemed to be out of order. She had had to pay for a taxi.

"Anna? Mother?"

Antonina opened the door to the music room. Lemon-tinted late September light filtered in, drawing patterns on the carpet. The samovar was gone and the roll-top desk closed. The gramophone was still in its place with the row of slate records and there was Mother's tambourine. Above the mantelpiece the outline of the Virgin of Kazan still showed. Nothing had replaced her.

It was mostly in this room that they had lived, secluded and suffocatingly close, spared the necessity of working for a living. Their Russian ways, aliens in Oxfordshire, and the wound of having lost the country they had believed to be omnipotent, forced them to depend on each other. In this stifling proximity there had been not enough affection or sympathy; each had striven to survive by drawing strength from the next. Her time in America allowed her to see this clearly. It hurt.

A gust of wind swirled down the chimney and stirred old ashes in the fireplace. Antonina shuddered. Things had gone bad for those she had left behind. It felt as if she had returned too late. Her mother must have gone to Thailand after all, so there was only Anna left. But why had she not been at the airport?

Pensively Antonina walked past her suitcase, still standing forlorn in the vestibule, towards the back-quarters. In the kitchen, Aladdin's cave, she noticed the flagstone floor had been swept and the pine table scrubbed. The cooking holes on the Aga were covered by their blue ceramic lids. Apart from a two-plate portable Calor gas stove and a used mug on the draining board, the kitchen appeared dormant. Copper pans turned gold-vermilion hung neatly on their nails in descending order of size. Just as she decided to go and look for Cahill, the back door opened.

Njanja stood shrunken and brittle in the square of light. Durov's white plaits pinned to her head were thin, and with deep-sunken eyes she peered into the penumbra of her kitchen. Suddenly she came alive as if touched by an electric spark.

"Miss Antonina! Heaven be blessed!" She crossed herself hastily.

Antonina swallowed hard. "Njanja!" Then she clasped the tiny ancient Russian in her arms and realised, feeling the frail bones against her, that Njanja would only stay alive if she made her. Antonina broke loose. "I desperately need a pot of hot tea."

"Oh, Miss Antonina, zr Njanja is still zr Njanja at Podzhin Hall and you…" she looked at Antonina, "… so beautiful, so like zr countess."

Antonina laughed, relieved at her nanny's revival.

Njanja reached for the matches and lit a candle. She started to take the tea things from the cupboard. "Ah, no zr light, no zr cooker, and the Hall so dirty." The cup clattered on its saucer in her hand.

"We'll straighten all that out, don't you worry. Where is Mother?"

"She go to Thailand."

"My sister?"

Abruptly Durov stopped making tea and stared at Antonina. "You are zr countess now." She put the crockery back.

"What are you doing? Where is Anna?"

"Zr silver, zr Worcester for zr countess. You are zr countess." She walked out of the kitchen; Antonina followed her. In the dining room, by a trick of the mind and in the dimness, she saw them all sitting around the table, the picture of an upper-class family in full regalia. The vision faded. Antonina's finger, drawing along the cherrywood table top, left a dark line in the pale dust.

Durov piled chinaware onto a silver tray from the sideboard.

"Let *me* carry the tray. And *you* tell me where I can find my twin."

In silence they re-crossed the vestibule.

"Please," said Antonina putting the tray down and waited. "Durov!"

With a hanging head Njanja said slowly. "Zr Miss Anna, she go to Moscow with bolshevik."

"That Soviet diplomat? Why? Njanja, why?"

"Love."

"Oh, my God!" Antonina sank onto the bench. "So the two of us are alone in the house."

Njanja nodded.

"Cahill?" Some hope was in Antonina's voice.

"He still work in garden. No pay, but has room and food. Not much food."

"I am so sorry I did not come home earlier."

"You now here. Is good."

★

Night came early. Having the choice of the rambling Hall, Antonina decided to sleep in her grandmother's bedroom. She unpacked a few things and hung the beautiful clothes Lucius had bought her on a hanger, and laid the Cartier brooch on Grandmother's dressing

553

table, before putting on her three sweaters, one over the other. A candle flickered on the bedside table. The tea in the skin-thin porcelain cup had gone cold. Before retiring she had carefully locked up the house, her new responsibility chilling her as much as the house itself. Tomorrow she would settle in properly, get her head together and face the papers in the roll-top desk.

Near the bed hung the bell-rope, trembling slightly in the draught filtering from the untight window. The only item belonging to Olga which had not been stored away was the oxidised silver hand-mirror on the bedside table. The intricately engraved monogram read OEB for Olga Ekaterina Brodsky. It weighed heavy in her hand. Slowly she turned it. Filling its frame was the face of a twenty-four-year-old woman. Was it that of Anna as well? As she stared, the pupils in the centre of the eyes contracted, ceramic cloudy patterns flared from the pupils to the darker rims, dark eyelashes curved up. Crinkly lines had begun to appear on the lips of the shapely mouth and there was a tentative furrow in the otherwise smooth forehead. Antonina shook her head and her chestnut hair tumbled forward. *We are attractive but not beautiful – not stunning like our mother or grandmother. Good night, Anna, my other self. I have neglected you for so long, wherever you are.* She lay the mirror on the bedcover and blew out the candle. Exhausted and jetlagged, she opened up the bed and crawled between ice-cold sheets.

★

Her dream turned turbulent and suffocating. Antonina thrashed and fought against entombment and was woken by her writhing. Her hair was plastered to her moist temples and sweat bathed her body. The room in which she lay was dark except for a tinge of faint blue light from the lace curtains. She tried to calm herself. Nothing – there was nothing unusual to be frightened of. She listened. Through the thumping of her heart, faint throaty singing reached her from downstairs. Every fibre in her was alert. The tune slowed, the voice turning deep and hollow as if the gramophone were winding down.

Ochi Chernye! They were playing the record in the music room to which they had danced on Olga's eightieth birthday. Goose pimples crawled from the bottom of her spine and moved upwards, coating her back and nape and chilling her scalp. She sat bolt upright in the bed. The canopy was like the coffin lid of her dream. The music stopped.

With trembling fingers she reached for the matches but realised that she had left them in the kitchen. Suddenly out of the bedcover appeared the face of her grandmother. It glared at her with those striking eyes. *Grandmother had died in this bed*. No, the hand-mirror! It was her own face in the mirror she had dropped on the covers.

Anna, come back to me. I am now here to help. What have you done? And with whom? Antonina remained huddled in the bed, yearning for morning to come.

CHAPTER FIFTY-FOUR

In the morning she faced the first day of her new life back in England. One day her mother would be back from Thailand, bored with it, and Anna would return from Russia because her visa would run out. It was even possible that Fydo might return to a civilian's life. In the meantime Antonina was going to do her best to keep Podzhin Hall afloat.

First she opened the French windows to air the music room. Reassuringly, no slate record of *Ochi Chernye* was on the turntable. It was another sunny autumn day and the songs of birds were pleasing. She sat in front of the roll-top desk. Njanja came in with a tray bringing her a cup of tea, alas no biscuits.

On top of stacks of papers lay the engagement diary. On 17 April: *Cremation at 3.00 pm, call vicar, specify blessings only* was written in Anna's small writing. There were multiple entries for visits by Vasily Voronov and for 10 May was *Aeroflot 7.30am. Call taxi.*

At the bottom of that Thursday the pen had noted *Goodbye.* Antonina fought back tears because that had been written for her eyes.

She gave her attention to the papers. There was a wad of Imperial Russian bonds. One for one million roubles had a large hole burnt in it. They obviously had not been honoured by the Soviet Government. Next was a pile of bills and an even larger pile of final demands. There were some receipts; silver had been sold in Oxford including the samovar.

She flicked through the remaining documents looking for the sale of the Ikon, but found nothing.

The Brodskys had run out of oil, electricity, and money back in July. She opened a still-sealed letter from the family lawyer; his fees were two years outstanding. She refrained from opening more letters. This was disastrous. She would have to sell the Hall.

A squeaking came from the park. She bent out of her chair to peek outside and saw Cahill pushing a wheelbarrow. Light-footed she sprinted across the grass towards him and noticed that evergreens had climbed up on Artemis and were tickling her armpits. When she caught up with Cahill, she noticed Uncle Sasha's pearl-handled revolver pushed into the gardener's belt, and small potatoes in the wheelbarrow.

"So you're back." Cahill put the barrow down. "I grew these, planted a vegetable garden. We can't just eat air."

"And what's the pistol for?"

"Rabbits and rats. Now that you're back, do something to help."

"I will, I will. Just tell me, do you know what happened to Anna?"

He picked up the wheelbarrow. "A letter came for Durov. Miss Anna is visiting a farm in Russia."

"Durov can't read."

"It was in Russian."

"And that's it? Visiting a farm for more than two months now?"

"Stupid girl, making cow eyes at that devious spy."

"Who are you talking about?"

"Your sister and Vasily Voronov."

"Manners, Cahill."

"Manners don't pay."

She noticed how gaunt he was and realised that she had to take him the way he had become. "Nothing from my mother?"

"Buddhist monks aren't allowed to write letters."

Antonina walked towards the graves. In America she had lost touch with the problems back home. A first step would be to transfer her savings from the UN salary into a bank account in Hatley; it would be a drop in a vast ocean of debts. And after that she would contact an estate agent and put Podzhin Hall on the market.

She walked further to the wood and encountered a yellow digger where part of the park wall had been taken down. Two workmen in yellow hats were moving in its vicinity.

"What's going on here? You've broken down our wall."

One yellow hat came her way. "The road is being widened. You will have received the order from the council. We'll put the wall back, but further in."

That was a blow, she thought. It wouldn't look good for potential purchasers of the Hall.

"How much are you eating into our property?"

"Oh, about three yards."

"Could you put up a temporary fence to tidy it up?"

"Sure, madam. You are?"

She hesitated. "Countess Brodsky, just returned from America."

He touched his hard hat, and she returned to the house.

★

Antonina found Smelly Ben out of action languishing in the stables, and therefore set out on foot to Hatley and the bank.

The bank manager allowed her a free call to Savills in London because the telephone was disconnected in Podzhin Hall. The estate agent who took the call could not entirely conceal his delight at being given the Hall to sell and proposed to drive down that very afternoon to have a look at the property.

Back home she did not even attempt to dust or hoover, hoping the neglected state would be perceived as endearingly dated. On the windowsill the summer flies were dying.

Although dismayed by her decision to sell the Brodskys' home, she thought grimly that someone had to do something radical and that someone had to be her.

In the kitchen Njanja boiled potatoes in a pan on the little stove.

"Which hand?" Antonina asked her, concealing her hands behind her back.

"Butter for zr potatoes?"

"You have to say right or left. Never mind. There."
Antonina held out a box of Cadbury chocolates.

"No chocolates. *Nyet*. No want chocolates. *Nyet*."

Antonina calmed her down. "I have also bought
basic food." She brought in two carrier bags and started
to unload sugar, flour, butter, milk, meat, fruit and
vegetables.

Durov touched some of the things as if to make sure
they were real, still heaving from the upset of money
wasted on luxuries. "What is this?"

"Cornflakes. Americans eat it with milk in the
morning."

"Hmm." She put the food away, as a furtive rodent
would hide its survival rations.

Savills did not dilly-dally. Earlier than arranged,
Antonina answered the knock on the door to find a man
in a grey suit displaying a practised *trust-me* smile. *Charlie
Brown's Snoopy does that sometimes*, she thought. In the
forecourt was parked an aubergine-coloured Mercedes.

The estate agent looked around what he called the
entertainment rooms, taking notes, and she followed at
a distance watching his reactions. Those reactions meant
money at the end of the day.

He liked the chandelier. *Murano*, he guessed right.

"Does it go into the sale?"

*It personifies Podzhin Hall. It has clinked over the heads
of many Brodskys.* She did not say this to him. All she
said was *yes* and experienced a wave of upset despite
having so carefully prepared herself. Why should
she alone suffer the consequences of the family's
destitution? Anger rose in her like bile as she was

forced to invite the salesman up the familiar staircase while he inspected nooks and crannies and tested one squeaky tread. She raged only briefly against fate before despair took over. All their money was gone and so were the people who had mismanaged it, leaving it to her either to walk away or to fix it. She was also still jetlagged and yearned for a hamburger with fries and a strawberry milkshake.

After the bedroom inspections on both floors the agent wanted to see the serving quarters.

In the boiler room he knocked his signet-ring against the boiler. "Empty," he said. "Does it work?" He scribbled on his note pad. The need to re-wire and upgrade the whole heating system would be reflected in the price.

"The boiler beast works perfectly well if there is heating oil in the tank, as do the electrics if we pay the bills, and they re-connect us," she defended herself.

"I see," he said, a little confused. "Beast?"

The kitchen threw him. "Quite unusual," he could not help muttering. Antonina thought that each pottery head and cow-creamer face was eyeing the man hostilely. *Did he notice it?* A rattling behind the larder door made him even more uncomfortable. Antonina opened the door to reveal Njanja cowering inside.

He stretched his neck forward in utter surprise.

"She will not be included in the sale."

Antonina accompanied him back to the vestibule, accepting that he was only doing his job. She asked him outright what he thought the exceptional Hall would go for.

He picked up *exceptional,* and wiped over his brow with a handkerchief.

"Seven hundred and fifty thousand pounds is a realistic figure."

"Good. I'll hold you to it. No less than that. Should you not find a buyer in a short time, I will invite Knight Frank & Rutley to come and have a look."

Once he had driven off, Antonina returned to Njanja. Instead of being in an uproar, Durov was concentrated on making *Always* because Antonina had bought honey. Her childhood with *Always,* Irina and her *Always*, and now back to the *Always.*

Sitting at the kitchen table, chin in hand watching Njanja's earrings dangle, Antonina's mind processed the steps to take once the Hall was sold and the money in the bank. First, bills would have to be honoured and the lawyer asked to work for them again. Second, a small property had to be purchased with a spare room for Njanja. The remaining money had to stay in the bank for Mother, Anna and Fydo, and she would have to find a well-paid job.

"Countess Brodsky?" A male voice sounded at the tradesman's entrance.

Antonina recognised the yellow-hat man from the road enlargement project.

"What can I do for you?"

"Eh, Miss, Countess, er…" He pulled the hard hat from his head and held it against his chest.

"What do you want?"

"We've found a body while digging."

"A body?"

"The dead body of a woman, buried on your land." He looked down at his muddy boots. "I've sent someone to get the police but thought perhaps you should come and see."

Silently she followed the man to the wood. All work had stopped and workers stood staring at her. At that moment a police car with a blue flashing light came to a stop, and two men emerged plus a woman in white overalls. They officiously took over and moved the workmen back.

"We only saw a hand first."

Antonina followed the policemen, incomprehension like an anaesthetic shielding her from reality. She peered between them at a shallow grave in which lay the body of a woman, her face alabaster and pitted, her hair knotted and stiff, but nevertheless – her mother.

Antonina turned away. Her head was spinning and her body in freefall. She stooped and retched. Someone patted her back, another supported her arm. The siren of a second police car wailed.

"We found this on top of her."

Antonina dared to glance again at what was held out to her and recognised the Ikon in wrapping paper.

A policeman approached. "Miss Antonina Brodsky, I believe? You all right? I'm Inspector Page. Pleased to meet you."

She nodded, feeling unreal.

"Do you recognise this body, Miss Brodsky?"

"It is my mother." The inspector caught her in her swoon and held on tight.

★

Antonina sat at the vanity table and began to compose a letter to Anna. Downstairs she heard the front door open and close; voices slowly died away. Finally Podzhin Hall was left to itself and she dared to think aloud.

Whoever killed Mother buried the Ikon with her so the Ikon is the clue to the killing, she reasoned. There had been nothing but trouble with it. She remembered Snell in San Francisco, Snell in New York – the Ikon, always the Ikon. The fact that the killer, most probably a Russian agent, left the Ikon behind meant that it was worthless. Surely Anna knew more. Despite her tiredness, Antonina continued writing the letter.

★

The next morning, before her coffee had cooled enough to be drunk, the inspector was already back to inform her that Valentina had died from several blows to the head, and that the work of the forensic laboratory was hampered by the unfavourable condition of the body. The inquest was scheduled to take place in four days. He also insisted that Antonina tell him of any news she received from Russia as soon as possible.

In Hatley villagers stared at her when she went to the post office and the grocer's. The grocer's wife disappeared behind the bead curtain the moment Antonina entered the shop. Her credit facilities were stopped as of that day.

★

The day of the burial was overcast and uninspiring. It rained continually, shrouding the scene in grey. Antonina and Njanja stood at the small grave as the little pot of ashes was lowered into the drenched clay. Njanja crossed herself while Antonina held the umbrella; then they switched. The vicar read the text for funerals in his prayer-book. No-one had come from the village.

Antonina had wanted to destroy the ill-omened Ikon by cremating it with her mother but the funeral director had told her that the stones would not disintegrate despite the extreme heat. Olga had refused to sell it, no matter what the consequences, so Antonina would not do so either. She decided to donate the Virgin of Kazan to the Russian Orthodox Church in London.

With the last of her savings she had bought chrysanthemums, cut their stems short and arranged them in Mother's tambourine. She laid it on the grave.

CHAPTER FIFTY-FIVE

Over the last three months, Savills had brought a string of potential customers to look at Podzhin Hall. They poked their noses into drawers and marched through the rooms as if the Hall were already theirs. Later Antonina learned that most of them had no serious intention of purchasing but had come to imagine themselves living somewhere so grand. One of the viewing parties was Arabs in full flowing gear. Antonina shied away from the black yashmaks of the harem. She roamed around like a homeless cat, keeping mostly to the servants' quarters.

Njanja disappeared in the kitchen each time car wheels crunched on the gravel outside. Otherwise, she played stone-deaf.

Together they ate their meals in the kitchen.

Antonina had decided to auction the furniture and *objets d'art*, and this disrupted any pretence of a home life even more for now the estate agents let the valuers in and vice versa. Pieces of furniture were moved around that had not been touched for generations. She pinned a note saying PRIVATE to Olga's bedroom door. Inside, she had rescued the photo albums, records and her personal belongings.

It was Christmas Eve and freezing cold in the house. Njanja lit the oven with wood felled by the workmen enlarging the road, and they kept the door open as a source of heat.

As a present Antonina had chosen Njanja one of the silver snuffboxes from the dining-room table where the silver trinkets had been laid out for valuation. In her skirt pocket she carried her own present: a letter, the precious letter she had received from the Soviet Union. It had been delivered the previous day. The envelope displayed many dirty thumb-marks, and if the address had been written by Anna then she must have been trembling.

On Christmas Day Njanja and Antonina erected a young pine tree. Its decorations were Meissen figurines strung up by their neck. No-one disturbed them; Antonina had locked the gates to the park. Cahill, despite loving the macabre, graves and such, had been horrified at the discovery of Valentina's body. He had left to spend Christmas with family in Ireland. He would not be back.

By late afternoon a turkey breast roll sizzled in the oven, emitting old-fashioned smells. Njanja laid the kitchen table with Worcester porcelain. Antonina played the record of liturgical chants from the Russian Cathedral in Paris, and they left the door open a crack to hear it. They pulled crackers, wore paper-hats, and Njanja won a plastic crocodile. Antonina's joke read: *What do reindeer hang on the Christmas tree? – Hornaments!* Slowly they ate their feast and knew that enough would be left over to sustain them during the following days.

Antonina decapitated a champagne bottle, and they toasted each other. When Njanja cleared the meal away, Antonina settled to read her twin's letter.

My dear sister,

I am incredibly lucky, for your letter was forwarded to the farm I am staying in now. Also, I was given paper and pen to answer you, and a well-meaning official promised to make sure it was sent.

You must wonder why months have gone by and I have not come home. Once I was in the Soviet Union, I felt so much at home here that I asked them to prolong my visa.

Today is St Nicholas Day and soon you will celebrate the commemoration day of your belief. A good opportunity for me to write. Please excuse the scrawl, but my hands are a little sore.

Imagine my luck, for I have been invited to live on a collective farm, amongst labourers. This is where I work now. I shall not give you the address for I might be moved to another. Just think of me, working alongside brothers and sisters. I have learned some more Russian, but my vocabulary is still limited and mainly about crops and farm machinery: the most important things, actually. I wear blue denims and a scarf like the others. They gave me a new name; it sounds melodious.

The Soviet Union is a well-organised country. Next year, we plan to increase our output in wheat by fifteen percent using the same workforce. If we achieve this quota, we will get a star to pin to the stable door: a great honour. I contribute as much as I can.

Vasily Voronov unfortunately has left my part of Russia.

Back in the Soviet Union, he saw things in their right light again and turned his interest to coal-mining. I do not have his address for he will be moving around too. Before he went up north, we had one brief encounter at the official's residence. Since then, I have been asked back three times and offered sherry, and spent an interesting time learning important things you ought to know about Vasily, that will answer the questions in your letter.

Our mother was sadly killed by misadventure. She had blackmailed Vasily into being disloyal to his country. She had undermined him and forced him to profess to wrong Western capitalistic values. Under provocation, Vasily defended himself and hit her with a stone, the morning she was to leave for Thailand. You see, I do not know what exactly went on between them, but I knew enough to understand that there had been enormous tension.

I arrived in the wood where it happened shortly afterwards and found Vasily in the process of burying the Ikon, which I believed he had found and removed from the Hall. In fact, it was Mother who had decided to sneak away with the Virgin out of greed. I did not know of course that Mother had been buried already by Vasily, but I saw that he was deeply upset. You do not know, but I think the world of him and more. Had he been exposed for stealing the Ikon, his life would have been destroyed. I helped him bury it, because I agreed with him that this religious idol was at the root of so many problems for the family. Anyway, that day was all very mad and unreal.

The Soviet official has confirmed that the Ikon is definitely the genuine Virgin of Kazan. Now that you have found her, you must sell her to Mr Snell via Sotheby's, and you will be able to keep Podzhin Hall and live comfortably.

The official has told me something else quite astonishing. Mummy's father was not Ivan Brodsky, but a Baron Dimitri Kavinsky who was Olga's lover back in Leningrad when it was still under the Czar. That baron escaped the punishment of the Revolution and changed into a peasant, a bit like me. He married and had a son, ten years after Valentina. That son is Vasily and therefore Mummy's half-brother. Apparently, it was when Vasily heard this that he decided to go to Siberia. The official, forever helpful, organised his immediate departure. I shall never see Vasily again, which is just as well as he is our half-uncle. I think I am coming to terms with my old life, so full of madness and wrong concepts. Remember, I always had a penchant for the country life.

On the kolkhoz now, all is covered in thick white silence. In the morning, every fence post wears a white beret. The same feathery ice tufts are on the beams of our dormitory, and I have to give my clothes a good spanking before I can put them on.

Everyone is kind to me and helpful. The comrade foreman, a woman, rubs a mixture of axle grease and pig's manure on my hands, and the calluses go down in forty-eight hours. I had a good friend who taught me how to carry thirty-kilogram sacks on the back without my legs buckling. You should see how strong I am now! Unfortunately he became disturbed and climbed the fence one night, and now he is gone.

The food is good and abundant. Mostly, we prefer what Fydo used to like before he left. There is also black bread and potatoes. We get tea in the afternoon, very English. So much time spent out in the healthy fresh air makes me sleep better than I ever managed before.

On the first of October we did not work. We received vodka and cigarettes. We hung up bright red banners, and a strong gust tore one away and wrapped it around the crown of one of the three tall birch trees, irretrievably out of reach and forever reminding us of the heroes' day.

All around there is so much loveliness, in the woods, the fields, as the seasons change, and colours and moods alter. One last interesting thing I want to write to you about is the abundance of toads in all the ponds and rivers. Like those from the fountain in front of home, they clamber out and hop about everywhere. Here, however, they are not squashed, for there is very sparse traffic.

My bed is right under a window. On full-moon nights, despite my tiredness, I lift the sacks from the opening and gaze up at the sky. How amazing that the same electric unblinking moon shines down on you!

I hug you with all my strength and wish you were here with me.

Your twin, Anna.

Antonina smelled the letter, looked through it against the light and carefully checked the inside of the envelope; then she put it back into her pocket.

"How is zr Anna?"

"Njanja, my sister is fine, just fine and happy."

Antonina went up to the bedroom. After reading the letter again, she opened the window and gazed into the scudding evening clouds which occasionally let the moon reveal itself, a sharp defined disc bathing her in electric light. Then she returned to her bed and sobbed her heart out.

CHAPTER FIFTY-SIX

It was the second day in the new year, 1969. Snow had fallen. The park of Podzhin Hall was hidden under an ermine mantle.

Savills had received an offer from an institution planning a health farm and another from a developer, but both were under the asking price. When an American finance house offered the full amount, Antonina signed the contract. The family lawyer, back working for her, was handling the sale.

She stood at the French windows, a glass of dark wine in her hand, and watched Inspector Page in a macintosh, the collar raised, trudge up the snowy path. She would have preferred the first visitor of the year to be someone else.

She received him in the music room, the only habitable corner of the house offering heat. A fire blazed and stacks of robust logs were carelessly piled up around the grate.

The inspector puffed from cold and toasted his hands in the heat of the crackling flames. "You left a message at the station saying you have received an answer from your sister."

Antonina pulled the envelope from her skirt pocket and wordlessly handed it to him.

"Would you like some wine, inspector?"

"Too early in the day for me."

"It's warming." Antonina poured herself a new glass while he looked quizzically at the bottle in her hand: Mouton de Rothschild 1917. He frowned.

"You see, I want to drink as many bottles of Grandfather's wine cellar as I can, and I don't have much time to do it."

The inspector lifted an eyebrow, said "interesting" out of habit, and took a seat to read Anna's letter, while Antonina sipped the precious wine absent-mindedly, prowling around the room, stroking furniture.

When he had finished, he rested the pages on his knees and moved forward in the armchair.

"As I suspected, Vasily Voronov killed Valentina Brodsky."

"Yes, he did."

"From what your sister writes, he met his punishment over there and is serving more than an English sentence. Voronov is unfortunately outside our jurisdiction, and we have no choice but to close the case."

"How about my sister? Is she an accomplice to the crime?"

He looked at her. "Your sister says she did not know, and I believe her because I was there when Voronov and she came back from the woods. She was flushed with love, not crime. Now she is far away and writes that she likes it where she is."

Antonina refilled her glass. "And you believe her?"

"What do you mean?"

"The toads are a hidden message to tell me that she is sentenced for life in the Soviet Union."

The inspector gave Antonina a glance but found her face turned towards the wall.

Noiselessly, he saw himself out.

She drained the glass and watched him make his way back down the drive towards his car, his head bent. He had taken the letter with him but she had noted in her heart the three tall birch trees, one with the First of October banner wrapped in its crown – the only way ever to identify where her twin really was.

★

In the afternoon the auctioneers were packing up the antiques. The house was being dismantled. A man walked into the music room without bothering to knock.

"Would you please do something about your servant?" he demanded. "She keeps sneaking in to steal back ornaments. We found her in the kitchen hiding them in her clothes. She said that bolsheviks were swine."

Antonina smiled sadly. "She is old and confuses this with the Russian Revolution."

She mounted the stairs to the bedroom where she sat on the four-poster bed, cornered like an animal.

I must not cave in with self-pity because Anna is doomed, and we will be parted forever, she thought. *My life has to go on somehow.*

And she sat powerless in this bedroom where silk and

tapestry, rosewood and dark mahogany blended together in peaceful harmony. Soon she would be forced out of this last corner of safety to confront reality. The estate in which every room, even the park, was branded by the past, and each object was a relic of the family, would be lost. Would she walk through life reminding those around her that she was a Brodsky exiled from Podzhin Hall, which with time she would decorate with a golden hue, as Olga had garnished her lost Russia?

On impulse Antonina rushed to the wardrobe and pulled out Olga's hydrangea taffeta dress. Hastily she undressed and stepped into the camphor-smelling gown. Straining to reach the hooks down the back, she adjusted the whalebone corsage and brushed out the folds of the ample skirt. At the vanity table mirror she pinned her hair up into a chignon and dusted her exposed cleavage with a powder puff. Opening the middle drawer, she lifted the pearl choker from its satin-coated box and lay the cold snake around her neck.

In measured steps she majestically swept across the room, feeling and hearing the material swish around her.

"My dear count," she said aloud in a haughty voice, cupping her fringe. "My great-grandfather was a grand duke, and long shall our illustrious name live. Get the troika ready!"

A firm knock on the door interrupted her escapist charade.

"Enter," she said grandly, draping herself on the vanity table stool, turning her head away from the intruder.

"Excuse me, madam. May I… Gee whizz!"

She twisted on her stool. "Lucius," she whispered.

The noise of furniture being pulled across the floor below evoked a rehearsal for a play.

"Christ," he repeated his utter surprise. "And you are disguised again. The last time, wasn't it Doris Day with a bathplug chain and later, beautifully, a hotel dressing gown?" He came closer to her. In a stone-coloured twill jacket over blue shirt and a cravat, he had retained his raffish air.

"Lucius, are you real and in this room with me, or am I hallucinating? I did knock back a few glasses of wine."

"Stone-sober in my case; I have to be the one who is hallucinating. From a typist who could not type to a countess in full regalia." He made her a deep bow.

"The CA Trust Bank in Frisco. That seems so long ago now. Since then I have worked for a year at the UN."

"And missed me?" He tilted his head and smiled his wide American smile.

She crinkled into standing position and felt his dry warm hand on her powdered shoulder and remembered it caressing her. His laughter lines were a smidgen more etched; his pond-green eyes shone young. In the mop of his lustrous mahogany hair were a few white threads. "I did think back to the Sheraton Palace, and the picture on the wall…"

"… of Charles in his armour on a horse who watched us on the bed and probably fell off the mare."

She dropped her head back and laughed and laughed, dangerously close to hysteria. When she recovered, she said, "You bought Podzhin Hall?"

"I bought Podzhin Hall."

"Can you explain to me why you did that without trying to get in touch with me?"

"I didn't know it was yours. You see, a lot has happened to me."

"That is not an excuse. More happened to me, trust me."

"After you left, I felt inspired and encouraged and persisted, with more technical guidance and engineering help, and designed a viable sports car."

"A lot of forks must have been sliding across dinner tables."

"Precisely." He emphasised the word with excitement. "I have been hired by MG Motors to run their sports car division worldwide."

"In Abingdon. I remember telling you that our house was nearby."

"I need a home nearby."

"For you and your wife?"

"Yes, for me – and hopefully my wife."

"For God's sake, could you not have chosen another one? You must have remembered Podzhin Hall – I told you about it."

"To be truthful, I did not remember that name. What I remembered was the feel you left with me after you had gone back to New York and out of my life. Oxfordshire and an old family home: yes, I did look for that – because of you! There are a surprising number of impressive properties around for sale. Coincidence made me put in an offer for this one."

"Fate," she said. "Not coincidence."

"And an excellent thing Fate is, because here I am seeing you and touching you again."

"Fate has not been kind to me. You will be living here with your wife, and I will have to rent a two-bedroom flat in Oxford."

"With that cumbersome skirt, you will need three at least."

"Don't you mock me," she began, and then, "You're not married, are you?"

"No, I am not."

She gave herself away with a significant sigh of relief.

"Would you please get out of that costume so that I can get closer to you?"

His straightforward speaking reminded her of her short Californian hippie time, a careless existence awaiting a new adventure each day. Since then, that sensation of life-lust had become suppressed by hard UN work and by the painful needs of her family, crowding space and time, caging her. Only the tiniest spark of positive personality had remained to lead her along.

"Flower power," she said, still recovering from the impact of his appearance, and those two words seemed to clash with everything surrounding her.

"Peace, man," he responded holding up two fingers, which fitted even less into Podzhin Hall.

Laughing and weeping at the same time, she pulled from the drawer of the dresser the Cartier brooch. "I never could say thank you for this precious gift. I wore it for special days at the UN."

"And missed me?" He smiled his wide American smile, so devastatingly handsome.

"How about you. Did you miss *me*?"

"During the four hundred thirty days and…" he checked his wrist watch, "… seventeen hours, not a bit."

Lucius went downstairs so that she could change back into Antonina. On the blouse she pinned the Cartier flower brooch, and her hair was unrestrained.

Downstairs, the rumbling and shouting had died out. In the music room he stood near the fireplace and smoked a cigarette. She closed the door behind her.

"Why is there no painting over the fireplace?"

"Of all things to ask, you *had* to ask that very question?"

"I tell you what – let's send a telex to my brother Vance and ask him to make the Sheraton a tempting offer for Charles on his horse. Then he can bring the picture over here, and I can show him that designing sports cars is a paying job."

"I love you," she mouthed for only herself to hear, and then in all seriousness, "Lucius, there is a lot to be said in a short time. You have signed a contract to buy this house and must want to get on with it."

"Some things between us have already been said, and done. Extremely well done, as I recall."

"I am in no way prepared for this emotional involvement. I have only just returned here and am overwhelmed by the impact of what has happened. Selling our family home with all it contains is shocking. My sister and I have been both stifled and protected in this house. When I have to leave, walk away without turning back, there will be no skin on me; a sigh of wind will be able to wound me."

He stubbed out the cigarette in Valentina's ashtray. "Okay." He brushed past her to the door. His voice echoed in the vestibule. She saw the auctioneer meeting up with him. They talked; the auctioneer called over a man with a clipboard. More intense negotiations, and then Lucius returned to her.

"I've cancelled the auction. I told them I will take the contents as they are."

"Everything?"

He came up close to her. Overwhelmed by him, she closed her eyes. He kissed the tip of her nose. "Everything."

EPILOGUE

October 1982

Three children played in the park on a sunny autumn Sunday. Many trees in the wood had been felled by a recent storm, and Artemis had lost her head. The mordant noise of a chainsaw bit the air as the gardener chopped the felled trunks into logs.

"She looks stupid without a head," said the eldest boy.

"Maybe Daddy can glue her head back," said his brother, Ivan.

"You can't do that with an old statue."

"Ever heard of super glue?"

"Heard of super stupid?" The boys chased each other around the statue. The girl had picked Michaelmas daisies and wound them into wreaths with dried grass.

"Look at our sissy sister playing with flowers."

"I am not sissy. I'm making presents for the graves."

"Who cares about rotten old graves?"

"I do, and they aren't rotten. They are our old Russian aunts and grandfathers and things."

"I'm an American," said Mikhail proudly.

The girl started to distribute her flower-offerings on the graves. Mikhail sat on one of the slabs, kicking his feet.

"Mikhail, don't sit on that grave."

"Great-grandmother is dead. She won't mind."

"It's wrong. We must care and pray for our old relatives."

"Rubbish! Dad is American, and so am I."

Ivan defended his brother. "The Americans play real football. The boring old Russians don't."

"You both can't help being half-Russian," said the girl with superiority.

"I'll help it," said Ivan and imitated a quarterback's throw.

"That's it – Mum is calling." Mikhail jumped from the grave.

In front of Podzhin Hall was the Range Rover so their father was back from the airport.

The children chased each other across the lawn.

In the vestibule their mother stopped them and made them wipe their feet.

"Children, Dad is back with a very special visitor. It's my twin sister, your Aunt Anna," she explained and, her face already red from crying, she cried anew.

The children filed into the music room.

In the armchair near the fireplace sat a woman who looked like their mother but old, for she had white hair and wrinkled hands. Dad was busy opening a bottle of champagne.

The girl advanced towards the chair and laid her last bunch of flowers on the woman's lap.

"For you," she said.

The aunt put her arms around the child, who felt the body holding her rock in sobs. When she freed the child from her embrace, the aunt said, "Olga, you are a very pretty girl."

"You are my aunt from Russia," said Olga.

The aunt nodded.

"How is it in Russia? I am so interested. I want to come and visit you."

"I live in a nice small house of my own and have some land. I also own a pig, some chickens and a dog," she said.

"Do you speak Russian?"

"Yes, I do."

"Say something in Russian to me."

"*Blagadarya bogu na etot dyen.*"

"What does it mean?"

"It means, God be blessed for this day."

"What's the name of your dog?"

"He hasn't got a name."

"How do you call him then?"

"You know, I've never thought of it; he just comes."

"My brothers are both silly. They want to be Americans because of football."

"Mikhail and Ivan, go and say hello to your Aunt Anna," ordered their mother.

Embarrassed, they advanced slowly and offered their dirty hands before retreating to a safe distance again.

"Come, I'll show you our park," suggested Olga, tugging at Aunt Anna's sleeve.

"I know the park. I once was a little girl playing in it, like you."

"Oh, I forgot," said Olga, finding it difficult to believe that the white-haired woman had been a little girl here once.

"Let's toast to Anna's return," said Lucius and distributed the champagne amongst the adults. "It is thanks to a rising new Soviet leader, a Ukrainian-Russian peasant, that we are able to send her money, and that she has her little house and can come and visit us."

"And maybe even plan to come and live here again." Antonina wiped her eyes.

"But this is our house."

"Children, your Aunt Anna owns half of Podzhin Hall."

"Maybe when I am old," Anna said, and Olga stroked over the back of her hand as if she was caressing a pet.

"As things stand, I hope to buy a cow next spring,"

"Wow!" Olga's eyes were round. "Do you know how to look after it?"

"There is this widow farmer who is helpful to me."

"In every way?" Antonina offered her twin an appealing look.

"You!" Anna bantered, which did not conceal how pleased she felt.

Lucius lifted his glass again. "May Gorbachev achieve promotion from the Politburo to lead Russia in a new revolution, and may the word *comrades* apply to everyone, East and West, so that we have a chance to learn to respect each other."

Antonina started to sniffle. The two boys kicked each other in the shins; they could think of no better way of hiding their embarrassment.

Acknowledgements

I thank my father's family for our time together in their manor house. It was only later in life that I came to appreciate what lay behind their eccentricity: alien and insular amid people who conform to other norms.

Every time I brush my hair 100 times I think of my stunningly beautiful grandmother. The taste of vodka brings with it a yellow salon and the gathered family. Gregorian chant weakens me to tears, and the song 'Dark Eyes' summons my passion-eyed aunt twirling around the room. The ring of a silver dome lifted off a serving plate reminds me of our Russian nanny. Some White Russians have framed their imperial bonds as mementos – my memories have made me write this novel, and I immensely enjoyed doing so.

With gratitude to Geoffrey who helped me achieve it, and to Samantha and Pascale for their support and feedback. With fond memories of U Thant's kindness, including the rose vase he offered me which I still use. Many thanks to the Fishers on Governor's Island, to the Perrys in Mystic, to Father Maurice, and to all the generous and hospitable Americans I met on my travels. With a big hug for my kind-hearted sister Eva who shared my childhood. And a respectful bow to our old friend Pete: thank you for letting us watch you become a Buddhist Abbot.